THE ORGANIZATION-part one
All By My Lonely
by
Black Coffee

THE ORGANIZATION- PART ONE, ALL BY MY LONELY

Published by True's Relate Publishing
THE ORGANIZATION-PART ONE, All By My Lonely
Library of Congress Control Number: TXu 1-794-675

REGISTERED TRADEMARK-MARCA REGISTRADA
ISBN:0-9844701-2-3
Printed in the United States of America
Set by True's Relate publishing, LLC
Cover design by Gregory Spencer of Misvision Graphics
info@misvisiongraphics.com
Logo design by JayRocOne of JayRocOne designs [age 15]

Requests for information on ordering, scheduling the author
for signings and appearances,
address to Black Coffee's websites;
www.blackdollone.com
www.truesrelatepublishing.com
Amazon.com/Author's page: http://www.amazon.com/-/e/B008S1WOZ2
Fan Page on Facebook:
https://www.facebook.com/TimeWillRevealFanPage
THE ORGANIZATION group:
https://www.facebook.com/groups/TheOrganizationByBlackCoffee/
THE TIME WILL REVEAL group:
https://www.facebook.com/groups/BlackCoffeeCrewNation/
Twitter:
http://www.twitter.com/AuthorBlkCoffee

Manuscript Preparation: Black Coffee
True's Relate publishing company
P.O. Box 2911
Gulfport, Ms. 39505
blackdollone@att.net

II
THE ORGANIZATION-PART ONE, ALL BY MY LONELY BY BLACK COFFEE

PUBLISHER'S NOTES

III

[Quote]
Rules of the profession
"Only the five A's;
Accuracy, Acuteness, Ability and Absolute Anonymity."

IV

FOR: Baby Doll

FORWARD

ALL BY MY LONELY

"I DIDN'T NEED PEOPLE COMING AT ME WITH THAT, *'HE'S THE REASON YOU DON'T HAVE A CONSCIENCE'*, BULLSHIT!'
IF YOU FEEL I DON'T HAVE A CONSCIENCE, THAT MEANS ONE, OF TWO THINGS. EITHER YOUR NAME IS ALREADY ON MY LIST. OR IT'S MOST LIKELY *GOING* TO BE. MY SUGGESTION TO YOU, WOULD BE TO SPEND YOUR TIME AND ENERGY TRYING TO CHANGE YOUR FATE. SO I DON'T HAVE TOO.
GOD IS THE LEAD I FOLLOW. NOBODY'S GONNA RUN ME. ANY DIRT I DO OR HAVE DONE. I DID IT........., *ALL BY MY LONELY!*"
-BABY GIRL

FORWARD 2

"It's a living Derrick," Baby Girl says, "It's a good living at that. And I'm good at it. Besides, you've benefited from it, as well."

"You're good at a lot of things, Lovely," he says, "A lot of *different* things. This shit is going to get out of hand, woman."

"Out of *hand*?" she asks in surprise, "This is what I was born to do. I don't get out of hand. I get things, *in hand*."

V

It's December 2006. Two weeks before Christmas. Baby girl is a highly paid professional. The best of the best, at what she does. She's a pro who camouflages her real job through her husband's career. Her man is a superstar in the Hip Hop industry and she's head of his security. He's always followed by paparazzi whenever they're outdoors. She's been able to keep her *main* job a secret, thus far. He first found out about her profession in 2004 He's been insisting she stop doing it, every since he found out. Lovely knows her 1 and only love is correct. She has to leave the murder-for-hire business soon and for good. Or it could cost her the most important things in her life. She reflects back to the beginning of her life with Morales Enterprises to see how they got to this point.

THE ORGANIZATION-PART ONE
ALL BY MY LONELY

TABLE OF CONTENTS

THE INTRODUCTION

TABLE OF CONTENTS--7
BACK IN THE DAY---8
THE DON--23
MEETING THE FAMILY---------------------------------44
THE BOY FOR LIFE---------------------------------------58

THE STORY

CHAPTER ONE   TIS THE SEASON------------------76
CHAPTER TWO   DADDY'S WORK------------------87
CHAPTER THREE   GETTING IT IN------------------105
CHAPTER FOUR   TAKIN' HITS---------------------121
CHAPTER FIVE   THE ORGANIZATION 101----139
CHAPTER SIX   THE OTHER LIVES-------------152
CHAPTER SEVEN   USE WHAT YOU GOT---------165
CHAPTER EIGHT   DOWN TO RIDE----------------189
CHAPTER NINE   "GOOD GIRL GONE BAD" --206
CHAPTER TEN   BAD WEEK FOR POLITICS-221
CHAPTER ELEVEN   DON'T START NONE--------244
CHAPTER TWELVE   ROCK STAR VIBES-----------257
CHAPTER THIRTEEN SHOW TIME-------------------273
CHAPTER FOURTEEN A FAMILY THING-------------290
CHAPTER FIFTEEN   STALKED UPON WORK-----310
CHAPTER SIXTEEN   OLD "MARKS"----------------318
CHAPTER SEVENTEEN ..AND NEW SHOES----------331
CHAPTER EIGHTEEN   THE KILLING FLOOR------348

<u>INTRODUCTION</u>
Back In The Day

Growing up Black *and* in the south, most say has no advantages. But that's not how Baby Girl saw it, at all. She was born; Lovely Walker and nicknamed, *Baby Girl*. In her opinion, growing up black in *America* had disadvantages. *Period*. She's *heard* that being poor and black is like double jeopardy. If that's the case. Then the saying that money is the ultimate equalizer, must be the truth. Because, even though Lovely is black, plus born and raised in America. She is very wealthy. As in, *filthy* rich. She has no memory of ever waiting in a line, in her entire life. She learned that nothing breaks through all of those discrimination barriers, like good old fashion, American, *in God we trust*, cash money. She remembers, many times, when whites visited their estate looking for help from *her black parents*. But she grew up learning that when her step-dad was a kid, those same people wouldn't allow him to sit next to them on a bus. Nor in a diner. She was told about these situations, many days and nights, by the man of the manor, *Mr. Donnie Morales*. Donnie couldn't even attend their schools but as a wealthy grown man, they would come to him for support of their benefits or politics. Stepfather Donnie Morales or *The Don,* had been able to escape a lot of the oppression in southern America because of his family's wealth. His great grandfathers money got him schooled overseas, with the *proper* Englishmen, so he was better educated than those in America. Who would've sought to hold those who looked like him, to a minimum. Those same folks who wanted favors, when Baby Girl was a child. Were the same ones, who's parents would hold a brown paper bag next to the skin of Don Morales and try to deny his certain, *inalienable* rights. That denial was based on whether or not he passed that brown bag test or not. But The Don had money. So he would get what others, who looked like him, couldn't get. In her lifetime, Baby Girl would learn that the right amount of money could buy a *Malcolm X* type the loyalty and security from the KKK. If he would've trusted it. Or even a David Duke type, with the right cash, would have the pleasure of being the leading man in a relationship with a woman like *Lena Horne.* Whom most males, of that day, fantasized about already. Though money was always plentiful, it never ruled over Baby Girl. She was a different breed than the females in age bracket. She was blessed to have grown up rich, in worldly things. But more importantly, she was rich in black pride and black history. She was raised to be humble. She was taught how to survive off the land, if necessary. She knew how to milk cows and goats. And how to pick up eggs from their chicken coops. Before she was Kindergarten age, she could kill a chicken with her bare hands. And with a small knife, she could take the life of a pig or a cow. She knew how to make butter from scratch and how to start a garden, to grow her own food. She was a beautiful black country girl. With maximum intelligence and a nanny's patience.

Her mother married into Black Panther Pride and old money. Money that often landed them in *The Fortune 500.* The Morales' had the type of money that afforded them the ability to give Baby Girl the best things the world had to offer. From education to mannerism. Like her step-daddy Don, Lovely was educated in foreign schools during her tender years, which gave her a huge advantage over the kids who couldn't afford to study abroad. Later in her life, those kids would make her aware of the disadvantages she'd never known anything about. She was studying and living abroad at the age when most kids

9

started elementary school and that's when she learned her independence. She would learn freedom and loyalty too. She would also learn to recognize a con artist, as well as pure corruption, at a very early age. The 1 thing she loathed more than bigotry, was a good-for-nothing pan handler who's only plan for success was to plot on someone else's good fortune. Having to survive in a foreign country, by herself, at the age of 6, taught her self awareness, a lot of fearlessness and much confidence. But the 1 lesson she learned with ease, even before going to boarding school, was how to handle her *weapons*. She learned to love guns at the same age and time that she'd learned to read books.

Baby Girl was the only child born to her mother, Wanda Wilkes, in October of 1982. Her government name is Lovely Walker. She was born in Atlanta Georgia and raised primarily in New Orleans Louisiana. Her biological father's name is Roger *"Big Dog"* Walker. He was a hired gun and the best of the best, when it came to active killers. But the man who would raise her and teach her the things which enabled her to flourish in life, was Donnie Morales aka *"The Don."* He was Big Dog's boss.

In the beginning, Wanda loved Big Dog, dearly. But he had no desire to be marriage nor father material. He was what was called, *a rolling stone.* He fathered 9 children, throughout the country, with 5 different women. Lovely was child number 7 and the only girl child born to him. Big Dog belonged to *The Brotherhood,* out of New Orleans. The Brotherhood's main job was disposing of ne'er-do-wells for, *The Organization.* Big Dog's prime occupation had him traveling all over the United States and in foreign countries too. If he'd made any babies abroad, he'd never copped to them. Nor did Donnie Morales have any knowledge of them.

10

Big Dog and Wanda met while he was on a business trip near the *S.W.A.T. S.,* in Atlanta. It was the business which involved, as Big Dog described it, *"Taking out the trash."* Wanda was an RN at *Grady hospital.* She met him 1 very late evening, in February of 1978. Him and his partner, Teddy *"TJ"* Jones Sr, had come into the emergency room for treatment. Teddy had taken a bullet on the job and needed to be patched up. Wanda was the head nurse on duty, that late evening. That's how they'd come to meet. They hit it off, instantly. Big Dog was a ladies man and a smooth talker too. So smooth, in fact, that he visited Wanda in Atlanta, many times after that 1st meeting. And he never gave her 1 hint that he was living with 2 other women, in 2 other states. Not knowing that bit of information, Wanda became his 3rd roommate, in as many states. She allowed their relationship to become sexual by July of 1978. They dated for a total of 5 years, which took Wanda on a roller coaster ride of emotions, month after month. Though Big Dog never really committed to her, he'd insisted that she be faithful to him and she was. That's how Wanda was raised to believe that a lady behaved. Faithful to 1 man and only 1 man in her life, at a time. And even though she knew very little about Big Dog's life or what his employment was. She stayed loyal to him and waited for him, for those 5 years. All the while, his real employment remained a mystery. She figured it had to be something like a soldier or a policeman. Because Big Dog and his partner TJ, always carried guns. Plus their 1st meeting happened because TJ had been shot. But Big Dog was far from a policeman and even farther from the legal side of the law. Wanda had heard him and Teddy talk about their boss and their brotherhood, from time to time. *The brotherhood* was run by the Morales family, out of New Orleans. It was called the brotherhood

11

because all of the members were male. That was the requirement. The Morales family had been strong politically, in Louisiana, for years. For decades, they'd been even stronger commercially, throughout the world. But what wasn't publicized, was that the Morales family was larger than life, in the underworld.

Wanda had traveled to New Orleans, many times, over the course of her and Big Dogs 5 year relationship. Or lack there of. But the trip she took to the *big easy* during Christmas of 1982, after Lovely was born, would turn out to be life changing for her, her baby girl Lovely and *Morales Enterprises*.

Wanda gave birth to Lovely in October of 1982. Big Dog was present for the delivery and he signed her birth certificate. He promised he would take care of their little girl, financially. Which he did. But he wasn't there, for much else. He also said he would take care of Lovely's first Christmas but Wanda would have to bring her to New Orleans, for that to be possible. Still believing and trying to give Big Dog the benefit of the doubt. Wanda hopped on a Greyhound bus, with her 2 month old baby girl and headed to New Orleans, Louisiana.

When they arrived at the bus station, Big Dog wasn't there to meet them. Wanda was in a strange city with an infant child at Christmas time, with very little money. All she had was Big Dog's pager number. She would always use it whenever she needed to get in touch with him and he would respond, eventually. She was at the bus station with just enough money to get back home, if she had too. But she didn't panic. She was feeling angry enough to do, just that. But her desire to give her baby girl a Christmas fit for a princess, as Big Dog had described it, convinced her to stay and make the call. It was a phone call which would ultimately change the lives and the fate

12

of her and her baby daughter, little Lovely.

"How could he not be here?"

Wanda thought, out loud, that day in the bus station.

"He knows how much I hate the city."

She paged the beeper, same as she had done, any time she wanted to hear from Big Dog. In less than 1 minute, the pay phone rang. This wasn't like Big Dog to respond, so soon. But she answered it with much anticipation. There was a strange, yet soothing man's voice, on the other end.

"Hello?" Wanda said.

"Hello," was the reply.

Wanda said, "I need to speak with Roger, please."

"He's not available," the man's voice said.

The man didn't expect that Wanda was in New Orleans and he said as much. That's when she panicked a little. But the soothing voice, on the other end of the phone, comforted her right away. The man's voice had the same signature drawl that Big Dog's had. But she could hear in his tone and voice that he was more refined. More cultured. He put her at ease, instantly. She told the stranger, her story and how she came to be sitting at the bus station, 2 weeks before Christmas. The unidentified man, then insisted she wait right there and he would send a ride for her. Her and Lovely waited in a portable TV chair, watching local news.

Within a half hour, a super stretched limousine pulled up in front of the bus station. The driver jumped out and ran inside. He was holding a sign which read: *"Wanda Wilkes and Lovely"*. Wanda stood up and approached the driver. She said, "I'm Wanda Wilkes."

"Yes ma'am. Do you have any bags?" the driver asked in that similar signature New Orleans drawl that she loved, so much about Big Dog.

13

The driver introduced himself as Charles. Wanda then, pointed to her and Lovely's bags. Charles grabbed them and led her to the Limousine which he had double parked, in front of the bus station. She followed him. He opened the trunk and shoved her and Lovely's bags in. He opened the back door and ushered Wanda inside. Wanda got in and was pleasantly surprised to see a brand new baby car seat, already in place, for Lovely. Charles strapped Lovely in, ran around and got into the drivers seat and proceeded to leave the bus station.

"Are you taking us to Roger?" Wanda asked.

"I'm taking you to Morales Manor, ma'am," Charles told her, "Those are my instructions."

Wanda sat quietly for the rest of the ride and assumed Big Dog had told the driver where he'd be. Though she didn't favor New Orleans, she did love the scenery, the culture, the food and the people. She wasn't a fan of city life, at all. She lived in Cobb county because it wasn't as busy as Atlanta's, *Fulton* and *DeKalb* counties. She only worked within the city limits. But New Orleans had a different feel. The citizens on the streets seemed to walk in rhythm, to a beat that played in their heads. *Lee Circle* and the street car rails gave the city that old timed French feel. While the high rise buildings, 1-way streets and the many spaghetti junctions, assured any visitor that they were in a metropolitan area. *Canal Street,* with it's many stores, street vendors and shops, was merely window dressing for the loved and infamous *French Quarter,* located within the blocks, just above it. Wanda had been to *Bourbon Street* with Big Dog, so she was familiar with the area. She rode in luxury as Charles crossed the Mississippi river bridge and onto the West Bank. He seemed to have driven straight out of the urban area of the city and right into what looked like, country bayou swamp lands. The trees that lined the roads was filled with the

14

grayest moss, she'd ever seen. He took many turns and covered much more highway, before the road seemed to have run out. Then he turned down a long narrow winding road. Nervously, Wanda clutched Lovely close to her, as Charles slowly crept up to a large wrought iron gate. It had the large initial "D" in the left gate and an "M" in the right gate. Charles spoke something through the voice box, at the huge entrance and the large gates opened, allowing them to pass. Wanda sat even closer to the luxury car seat, which held her only true valuable and most prized possession. Her Lovely. She was amazed at the lay of the land, beyond the gates. It looked like a small city. There was many houses, of all sizes. Then the limo stopped in front of a very large *"Designing Women"* styled mansion, where a butler stood on the circular drive beneath a canopy, waiting to open the back door. There was maids, cooks, several security guards and more staff, standing uniformed and at attention, on the stairs which led to the doubled front doors. Those doors stood more than 10 feet high. And each single door was more then 8 feet in width. Charles pulled the limousine under the canopy which protected them from the morning dew and swamp fog, which hung in the air like pesky old ghost. The butler opened the door and helped Wanda out of the car. He unfastened Lovely's seat and took her out. Then he cradled her to his chest like a priceless heirloom, before handing her to Wanda. Charles got out and retrieved their bags from the trunk. The butler escorted Wanda and Lovely up the 10 huge ceramic steps, which looked like the entrance to the Smithsonian Museum of Natural History. As they passed through the house staff, who waited on the landing, they were greeted by name. They passed through the large double doors and entered the foyer of this huge estate.

Wanda was impressed with the home, from the very

15

beginning. In the large foyer, there was vaulted ceilings which were more then 30 feet high. Just to the right side, sat an old fashioned baby carriage. There was a woman standing next to it, who introduced herself as Maggie, assistant to the nanny. Wanda was thinking this had to be a palace like Queen Elizabeth's, if even the nanny has an assistant. Maggie told her to lay her sleeping baby in the carriage and she did. Then the butler, who's name was Alfred, told Wanda to come with him. He would push Lovely while showing them through the estate, to their suite.

"We're going to be staying here?" Wanda asked with surprise in her voice.

"Yes ma'am," Alfred answered, "You will be the guest of Mister Donnie Morales, during your stay in Nu Awlins."
Alfred was a very jubilant guy and he seemed to have extra spunk when he said the bosses name. It was then that Wanda realized she was in the home of Big Dog's boss, *The Don*! But what she didn't know, is that she was standing in a home that would be hers, in the near future. She was still nervous but very happy to be out of the bus station. She knew she was in a place where Big Dog was sure to come-a-calling. That was his employer's house. Surely, he would know how to find her.

Alfred strolled Lovely, in the beautiful antique carriage, around the huge parenthesis shaped staircase which faced the front foyer. A humongous crystal chandelier hung overhead which gave the front entrance that antebellum feel. It had to have weighed more than a ton. The long hallway, on the left side of the huge stairs that led to the suite which would be home to Wanda and Lovely, for the next 3 weeks, boasted many exquisite rooms and artifacts. Each room looked as if it was designed to represent a different world culture. While still, all that was there to behold, was just elegantly decorated. One

16

of the rooms reminded her of the living room in her late-great aunts house, which she was never allowed to enter as a child.

When they reached the suite where Wanda and Lovely would sleep, Alfred said,

"This will be you and miss Lovely's quarters, ma'am."
Wanda was wide-eyed as she entered the area which had plaques on each door that read; *Lovely's Suite*. It looked like a picture straight out of *Better Homes and Gardens*. It was decorated in antique heirlooms. The large bed was made up with an elegant handmade spread and had all of the matching accessories. The windows, the furniture and the bedding was simply, picture perfect. One large set of windows, doubled as an entrance into a lovely patio and garden area. The view of the landscape and the bayou which encircled the back of the estate, would render anyone breathless. Wanda knew it was more than a large enough space to accommodate her and Lovely. But Alfred ushered her through the suite and showed her to the bathroom, which was larger than the 2nd floor of her Condo.

"This is so beautiful," Wanda said, "This is a beautiful home. We'll be just fine in here."

"Ma'am, the baby has her own room, just through here," Alfred said.
He led them to a second bedroom adjoined to Wanda's room, on the other side of the large bathroom. It was a nursery fit for a princess. It was decorated and stocked with everything a new mother needed, to care for an infant baby girl. Including a nanny, who stood just inside of the door.

"Hello ma'am," the nanny said, "I'm Cherry. I'm the head nanny and I'll be assisting you with Lovely, while you're here. Anything she needs. I'll get it for you."
Wanda thanked Cherry with a smile, as she took in the

ambiance of the suite. She couldn't help but wonder how the servants already knew her and her daughter's names.

"I didn't even ask you, *your* name," Wanda said to the butler because she didn't hear him when he'd said it.

"I'm Alfred, ma'am," he said, "And the driver, his name is Charles. He'll take you anywhere you desire to go. Cherry will assist you while you're inside the manor. Enjoy your stay at Morales Manor."

And with that, Alfred left her and Lovely, with Cherry.

"Well let's get you two settled in, then," Cherry said with that drawl that Wanda was finding very familiar, by now. Cherry removed Lovely from the carriage and placed her in a beautiful hand carved, antique bassinet. The nursery also had an antique crib plus a Queen sized princess, poster bed.

"This room has everything," Wanda said.

"Yes ma'am. This room was decorated *specifically* for little Lovely," Cherry told her, "She has everything she'll need. Even after she grows up."

"*Grows up?*" Wanda asked in surprise.

"Well, yes ma'am," Cherry said, "Mister Donnie plans for Lovely and yourself to spend a lot of time here. This suite had been set up, just for her. Hopefully, you'll accept Mister Donnie's gracious invitation to live with us."

Wanda was puzzled. Her mind started to work negatively, at first. She wondered if Big Dog's boss had plans of trying to take custody of her only child, as a means of helping Roger escape child support.

Why else would she have her very own suite in his home?

Even the name plate on the 2nd set of doors read: *Little Miss Lovely Walker's suite.* She had never met Mr. Donnie Morales and already he'd made space in his home, for her baby. She

18

didn't see her name on anything, in this entire suite. Still, Wanda couldn't help but notice that Mr. Morales had done more in preparation for them, in a half day, then Big Dog had done in over 4 years. She had no plans on living at the manor, permanently. Nor was she letting her daughter come here without her. She wasn't exactly sure why Lovely had a whole suite dedicated to her. Big Dog had never discussed his boss, in detail. But someone was going to have to give her some answers. And very soon.

"We were only planning to stay through Christmas, Cherry," Wanda told her.

"Ah, yes ma'am," Cherry said as she attended to her duties of putting away Lovely things. "I assume you'd like to have a bath and get comfortable, ma'am? You can go on and do that. I'll take good care of Lovely until you're finished. I've put everything in the bathroom, for your bath."

Wanda was a little skeptical about losing sight of Lovely. She was also taken away by all of the servants and everybody calling her, "ma'am". She was only 38 years old and older folks was calling her "ma'am." Still, she couldn't help but wonder how Mr. Morales knew so much about her and Lovely. Yet, she had never met him. And she wondered what his *real* plans were, for her daughter. He had a entire suite in his home decorated and named, just for Lovely, for Christ sake. And Wanda wouldn't know his face, if he'd walked right past her.

"Where is Roger?" Wanda asked Cherry.

"Ma'am, your bath is ready," Cherry said, as if she was ignoring the question about Big Dog's whereabouts.

"Yes Cherry. Thank you," Wanda said as she leaned over the bassinet and kissed Lovely.

Then she decided she should go on and enjoy the bath and not be so paranoid. If Mr. Donnie had wanted to kidnap Lovely.

19

He could've easily done it, long before they got here. With all of those roads, bridges and streets they'd passed. Charles could've forced her from that Limousine, along the way and she never would've found them. Nor her way back to the bus station. She goes on into the bathroom.

Cherry had set out everything Wanda needed for a relaxing bath. A beautiful queen robe was provided. As well as a laced *Christian Dior* lingerie set, in her size, with the tags still attached. There was a book titled; *Time To Learn part 1* by *Black Coffee* and a bottle of exquisite *Moet* champagne, chilled to perfection. Nanny Cherry had also set out strawberries in a beautiful sterling silver dish. There was scented candles burning too. The scent of vanilla filled the suite. After seeing the *Moet*, the lingerie and the vanilla candles, Wanda wondered just how much did this Mr. Donnie Morales know about her. So far, he had gotten everything right. Right down to her underwear size and her favorite scent of candles.

"Roger must've told him everything," she said to herself, as she undressed and submerged her body in the huge antique tub.

"There are jets in the tub, if you desire a Jacuzzi bath," Cherry said, through the closed door. *"Enjoy your bath, ma'am."*

"Please, Cherry. Call me Wanda," she insisted.

"Yes ma'am. Excuse me. Miss Wanda," Cherry said with a giggle. *"I'll leave you to your privacy."*

"Thank you so much, miss Cherry," Wanda said with a smile, "Everything in here is wonderful. So much more and a lot better, than I'm use too, at home."

After finishing her bath, Wanda went to Lovely's side and was happy to see that she was still there. Cherry was still there too. She was rocking Lovely, in the huge rocking chair, in the far corner of the nursery where she'd read her a book while Wanda had her bath.

"How was your bath, Miss Wanda?" Cherry asked.

"It was wonderful, Cherry. Thank you, so much," Wanda answered. "I'll take Lovely, now."

Cherry handed the beautiful baby girl to her mother.

"I'll go assist the cooks with today's menu, if you don't need me, right now," Cherry said.

"Yes Cherry. We'll be fine," Wanda said, "But I do have one question."

"Yes, Miss Wanda?"

"How did you know me and my daughter's names. And how does mister Morales know all of these things about us?" she asked.

"Oh, Miss Wanda," she said with a smile, "Mister Donnie knows many things. He insists on knowing about the lives and families of all of his employees. He's a very caring and giving man."

"So will Roger find me here?" Wanda asked.

"I'm sure he will," Cherry answered, "Mister Donnie has invited all of his employees to dinner, this evening."

"Thanks, Cherry," she said, "You've been wonderful."

"Why Miss Wanda. You say that like you're leaving, already," Cherry said with a slight chuckle. "You and Lovely enjoy your quiet parlor time. I'll only be a page away," she said and handed Wanda a 2-way radio. Then she said, "If there's nothing you need with me, right now. I'll be back for you, at dinnertime. Just call me, if you need me."

With that, Cherry smiled. Then she turned and exited the suite, closing the nursery doors behind her.

"Well, Miss Lovely. I don't know where we are. But so

21

far, each and every person here, knows us. And they're bending over backwards to make us feel at home," Wanda said to her cooing daughter. "And you will get to see your daddy, tonight."

Wanda and Lovely spend 2 hours in the suite, alone. Lovely took a nap while Wanda relaxed, redid her nails and enjoyed *Black Coffee's* book.

<u>THE DON</u>

Big Dog showed up for dinner, tonight. He played with Lovely, for only a few minutes, before retiring to the parlor with Wanda. Cherry took Lovely for a stroll in her new carriage, around the grounds, while Big Dog and Wanda talked. Though he's known throughout the organization and around the world, as Big Dog. Wanda always called him, Roger. She liked that better than addressing him by some nickname.

"Roger, is this where you live?" Wanda asked.

"No. I only come here when I'm called," he answered, "And not before."

"Then why did mister Donnie have us to come stay here? And why did he answer your pager?" she asked.

"The pager is a perk of the job," he said, "It's the one I use for personal contact. But I had a job to do. Whenever I'm working, I can't have a pager with me. No personal items are allowed on the job. And boss having you to stay here, may mean he's sweet on you. I know he's been wanting to meet Lovely, every since he heard she was being born. He's been planning for her to come to his mansion and you too."

"So mister Donnie keeps your personal pager when you work?" Wanda asked, thinking he was just telling another one of his famous lies to mislead her.

She wasn't buying any of what he was saying and she didn't even bother to elaborate on that, *'maybe he's sweet on you'* part. It didn't even seem right too.

"Yes Wanda. He does," Big Dog said, shocking her, *"All* personal items have to be left behind. That's the number one rule. And that's the Don's way of assuring that we're focused on the job. The turnover rate is a hundred percent, when there's no outside interruptions or interferences. And we don't carry any identifying materials on us, either. Nor do we tend to any personal business while on the job. None of that. Not until the job's complete, reported and booked."

"I'm sure you're going to tell me that," she said with doubt in her voice.

"I'm only telling you the way it is," he said with a straight face. "You can ask him, if you think I'm making it up. He may tell you."

"I see," Wanda said, "Well, I'm not going to do that. But I do wanna know if you told him about us."

"That's apart of the job, Wanda," he said, "The Don insist on knowing everything about the folks who work for him. But he was *particularly* interested in you and then, Lovely too, after she was born."

"Why do you keep saying that?" she asked, "Why would you even tell me that another man is sweet on me and wants *your* daughter? It's like you don't care about me, at all." He didn't answer. Which left her feeling, rather uneasy. She knew he was always very secretive about the particulars of his job. And that conversation was more open than he'd ever been. She didn't want to make him shut down and not talk, at all. So Wanda decided to stop with the questions, at that time. After all, she had come to New Orleans to meet Big Dog. And though her day had been spent with a lot complete strangers, Big Dog was finally with her and she had missed him, terribly.

"I had my six week check up, before I came," she said and smiled. "And this *is* my suite. Well, not mine. Actually, it's our daughter's suite. It even has her name on everything. But I was invited to stay in it too."

"Uh huh," was all Big Dog said as he moved closer to her, while she sat on the day bed.

"So what is it you plan to do, in *your* suite?" he asked.

Big Dog was a dark skinned, very tall and thin man, with strong facial features. He had the darkest eyes she'd ever seen on a man. He had long hair, which he kept in cornrows. Or sometimes, he wore a big Afro. Though that was more of a 70's style. Big Dog never really followed any trends. He did what he was comfortable with. Even in his everyday life. He was a very vibrant man and very sexual. Usually, when Wanda would try to have a conversation with him. He would shoo away her talk, by kissing her. He hadn't done that, so far. Which she found more strange, than him being so talkative.

She finally said, "You haven't even kissed me, Roger."

He kissed her, immediately. It really felt like he'd missed her. His kiss felt like he hadn't been close to a woman since he'd last been with her, the night before Lovely was born. But after knowing him for over 4 years, Wanda knew that was unlikely. He kissed her but it wasn't the usual Big Dog aggression. He was holding back and she wondered why. Their next mild kiss was interrupted by a knock at the door.

"Yes?" Wanda asked.

"That's the boss," Big Dog said and he moved away from her, then he got up and went to open the door.

Wanda was nervous in anticipation, as she waited to see what this Mr. Donnie Morales looked like.

Big Dog opened the door and in came a tall fair skinned, athletically built man with wavy hair and light brown eyes. In one word. He was *striking*!

"Hello, Miss Wanda. I'm Donnie Morales," he said, in an even more pleasant tone. "I am very pleased to *finally* meet you. And to have you and miss Lovely as guests, in my home."

"Thank you, sir," she managed, "We really appreciate all of the hospitality."

25

"Call me, Don," the boss said, with a handsome smile, as he seemed to be checking her out.

He added, "And it's my pleasure. I've been waiting for the opportunity to meet......," he looked around and said in an asking tone, "*Lovely?*"

He looked around as if he was looking for her baby girl.

"Oh yes. She's here too," Wanda answered, "Nanny Cherry has her in the gardens. I have a radio. Would you like me to have her to bring her back in, to meet you?"

"Not a problem. I can get her, faster," he said as he pulled a radio from his pocket which looked a lot more advanced, than the ones her and the staff have.

He called out to Cherry. Within minutes, she came strolling back into the garden entrance doors, with Lovely. Mr. Don picked Lovely up from the carriage and kissed both of her cheeks. He excused Cherry from the suite. Then he cuddled Lovely to his chest, like she was his own, while he smiled and said, "She's a princess, miss Wanda. And she should be treated and raised like one."

Next, he turned and looked at Big Dog. His face held a very impatient look.

He said, "You have work to do. You got your package, right?"

"Yes, Don. I've got it, right here," Big Dog answered as he patted his chest pocket.

"Well, you should be on your way, then" the Don said smugly.

"Yes sir. I was just about to get a move on," Big Dog answered before turning to Wanda and saying, "Duty calls."

He gave her a light peck on the cheek. He kissed Lovely, while she was still cuddled to Don's chest. The Don's look was even more impatient. Big Dog exited the suite without another word and left Wanda and Lovely, alone with, The Don.

Wanda didn't understand why the boss would insist that Big Dog leave, without spending any quality time with her or his daughter. But she didn't feel it would be a good thing to voice it, at the time. She felt a bit nervous, being alone in that suite with a strange man. But Don started an engaging conversation with her, which was in such a friendly manner that it put her at ease, instantly. Don had a way with words and a very soothing voice to deliver them with. This was the same voice that had comforted her, when she'd called from the bus station. He was a very pleasant man and Wanda couldn't help but notice that he wasn't wearing a wedding ring. She also noticed that he seemed, awfully taken by her. He was mildly flirting with her, when he said,

"You know, I told Roger he lost out on a good thing, when you decided to visit. He should've treated you like the queen, you are. And this one here," he paused as he looked down at Lovely, who he was still cuddling. He brushed her cheek and continued, "This one here, he should've smashed the earth to make her comfortable. I surely plan too."

He was chuckling, as Wanda's eyes stretched in disbelief.

"If I didn't know any better. I'd say you were flirting with me," she said suddenly.

Then immediately, she wished she could've taken it back. But his next comment, left her *really* stunned.

He said, "Well, I hope you don't mind that I am. You're a beautiful woman, Wanda. I said that, the first time I saw you."

"I'm sorry. I don't remember *ever* meeting you," she said, "And I would've remembered you."

"Well, we didn't actually get to meet, face to face," he said, "I flew to Atlanta to handle the medical bills, for TJ, the night when Big Dog first met you. I didn't introduce myself. You were very busy, tending to your patients and all. I just

27

looked in on TJ. Then went back down and signed for the bill at the check-in desk. Afterwards, I went back to my hotel suite."

"Oh. I didn't know. I mean. I never saw you," she managed.

Then, Don went all the way in and started to reveal how he'd come to see and fall for her, nearly 5 years ago.

"I told Big Dog, I wanted you, for myself," he said suddenly, "I even asked him to get your phone number, for me, when you got a break. I definitely would've done it myself. I had urgent business to get back to the hotel, to take of. Or I would've waited until you got that break. I left him, with simple instructions. But obviously, he did all of the talking for himself."

He kissed Lovely's cheek again and continued, "I still haven't forgiven him, for that. I told him I was jealous that he got with you and I still am. I'm not for that, at all."

He smiled. Wanda didn't respond. She didn't know what to say.

"I don't wanna make you uneasy. But I'm the main reason Big Dog doesn't have much time to visit with you, anymore," he revealed. "Me, *personally*. I didn't want it to work out. And after this princess was made. I knew I had to make a move. Because I wasn't willing to allow him to do better than me. Even if he'd wanted too."

She blushed as Don continued to make his move.

"Hopefully, you'll give me the opportunity to treat you like the queen, you are," he said bluntly. "This little princess has already stolen my heart."

They shared a laugh. Still, Wanda didn't dare respond. She was in awe and he was still talking.

"Well, I won't stay. I just wanted to come down and formally,

28

introduce myself," he said as he handed Lovely to her. He brushed Wanda's cheek with his thumb. She froze where she stood. As he started for the door, he said, "I wished I'd done this, that night, in seventy eight," he said, "Because that would be my daughter, you're holding, right now. Instead of Big Dog's. He should've been putting in overtime with you. And not *assing* out of his responsibilities as a man and father. I let him know that, every time I see him too."

Wanda blushed openly. Before he left the suite, Don turned and said, "You know, contrary to the name Roger wears. I'm the Big Dog, around these parts and parts beyond."

He closed the double doors, leaving Wanda speechless. She scrambled around the suite and got together, all of her clothes. Not to leave though. Not at all. She wanted to make sure she put the best outfits out, to wear, in succession, while she was in the Don's presence. She had butterflies in her stomach and felt like a school girl, at that moment. No man had ever looked at her, the way the Don had. Nor had one ever spoken to her with such conviction. Not even *Roger*. She couldn't help but be giddy about the man of the house being attracted to her. He was gorgeous, fine and wealthy. And he was, *The DON!*

Christmas at Morales manor was a huge event. There was the decorating of the estate and the grounds. Which all of the employees and their families took part in. There was many huge Christmas trees, all over the estate. One in the center of the doubled driveways which led up the mansion. One in the main foyer of the mansion. The Christmas dinner, in the grand dining room, included all the employees of Morales Enterprises. Plus their families and the entire Morales family. The grand dining room held 450 people and the small dining

29

room, which was where the kids ate, held another 200 people. There wasn't an empty seat, in either dining room.

Don had 4 sons, who attended with their mother, the Don's ex-wife. His 4 offspring were grown and had families of their own. None of them were friendly, either. Wanda knew, from watching them, that she didn't ever want Lovely to be stuffy and uppity toward anyone. She would talk to Don about that later. And he would tell her that they took on that form from their mother's side of the family. He's been divorced for 20 years and his sons were still minors, when they split. His only influence in their lives, was being their sole source of financial support. But his ex hadn't been diplomatic, at all. Not when it came to honoring their joint custody agreement. And with his many businesses, he was out of the home and the country, a lot more, when their sons were young. The divorce had been bitter and his ex-wife still harbors negatives views of their nuptials and him. That had caused conflict at every meeting, for the 1st decade after their divorce. He had also told Wanda, he had never wanted to marry again. Not until he laid eyes on her.

Don bought Lovely everything he thought she might need, wear and use, between Christmas day and the next time she would come to visit him. Him and Wanda got closer during her 1st visit to Morales Manor. She didn't see Big Dog anymore, during that entire stay. Nor did he try to call her. But after meeting and hearing the Don's side of the story. She knew why. She secretly wished Don had stepped to her, that night she'd met Big Dog. She was already taken by Don and his intrigue. Don was a very powerful man. Wanda caught on to that, immediately. Everyone that came around seemed to be owing to him and did extra, to please him. And they all called him, "The Don." Yet, he was the humblest of all of them. She knew that was unusual for the filthy rich. They would usually look down their noses at you, before speaking. If they had even spoke, at all. She observed how all races were at his beck and call. Even Caucasians. That was something, all together different, for her to witness. In 1982, race relations was still touch and go. But around the Don, they all but worshipped him. This made him even more attractive because it was more then obvious that he was, *the man*.

The Don gave both, Wanda and Lovely, a Christmas fit for royalty. Wanda had received more, at that one Christmas, than she'd received in all the other thirty eight Christmases of her life. The Don had given Lovely stocks in his company that were worth more then 7 figures. Not to mention, they each got a growing wardrobe, every toy and gadget that was popular. And even some that wasn't even on the market, yet. He also offered Wanda the services of his youngest nanny Maggie, as an extension of his home and assurance that he could keep up with Wanda and Lovely. Until they returned to his manor again.

On the 2nd day of the New Year 1983, much to the dismay of Donnie Morales, Wanda and Lovely returned to Atlanta by air. He wanted them to stay, indefinitely. But Wanda said she had to get back to her job. The Don had asked her to stay at his estate, retire and never work again. She didn't see being able to do that, right away. She needed to think about it and decide how to handle her lack of a relationship with Big Dog, before delving into another situation with anyone else. It was a fact that Big Dog hadn't been attentive in the past. And whether that was due to the interference of The Don or not. Wanda had *been* feeling that it was time to excuse him from her life, for a long time. If they hadn't had a daughter, she would've done it, already. Him not

31

showing up or calling, wasn't going to suffice, any longer. Even before she met the Don, she was contemplating it. That trip to New Orleans and how Big Dog reacted, was what she was going to base her final decision on. He failed miserably. After all, Big Dog was Lovely's father. And it bears mentioning that, not only did he not try to visit Wanda again. But he didn't return to visit Lovely again, either. There was no excuse going to be good enough to explain that. Surely, The Don didn't stop him from seeing his *own* daughter. Wanda had put up with his lack of attention to her. But when it came to her precious Lovely, he wasn't getting a pass.

Once she was back in Atlanta, her and Don Morales talked, every day. The Don insisted she stay in touch with him and keep him informed on how Lovely was progressing. In his heart, Lovely was already his child and Wanda was already his woman. He'd wanted to demand that they stay at the manor, forever. But that wasn't his style. Still, it would only be a matter of time before they did. The Don wanted Wanda and Lovely as his own family and the Don usually got what he wanted.

In the meantime, he expressed to Big Dog that he wanted him out of Wanda's life, for good. Lovely's life too, for now. Just until she was older and could be introduced to him. The Don had told Big Dog that he wanted to adopt Lovely. And even though Don knew that Big Dog was looking to shirk on his duties. It was still a shock to Don when Big Dog agreed without even thinking about it twice. After all, he hadn't been doing his duty as a man or a father, before then. Big Dog didn't dare argue with Donnie Morales. He saw it as a way to get off the hook for child support, anyway. Big Dog ended all contact with Wanda, immediately. And for the first time,

32

Wanda didn't try to find him. She continued talking to Don, every single night. Eventually, he started visiting them, 3 or 4 times a month. He felt he had gotten a 2nd opportunity to be with Wanda and he wasn't going to waste anytime letting her know that she was the only woman he had eyes for. She had never been wooed like that. She was swept off of her feet, in no time. Every week, something arrived for her and Lovely. Lovely's gifts were always age and season appropriate. Or it was a new account, of some sort. Wanda's gifts were always something tasteful, elegant and usually, very expensive.

By the time Lovely was 2 years old, Big Dog was completely out of the picture, as far as being intimate with Wanda was concerned. The Don knew Big Dog, well. He had confessed to Don, back when he first found out Wanda was pregnant, that he wasn't ready to settle down with any, 1 women. During the last 2 years, Don had made it obvious to Wanda that he wanted her and Lovely in his life, for the long haul.

"I can be the husband you deserve and the father *that* sweet little princess needs," he'd said, 1 night over the phone. "Big Dog was never going to settle down. It's not even in his nature."

Wanda had managed to except this truth, shortly after her and Lovely's initial visit to Morales manor. So by the time Lovely was 2 years old, she was completely over Big Dog and moving on. Her and Lovely visited Morales manor, many times. Even if it was just for a weekend. The Don had been to Atlanta, many times, to visit them also. Wanda and Don had become quite close and had become a couple, officially. Wanda's later visits to the manor, found the staff calling her the "*Misses*" of the manor and she shared the masters quarters with Don. The master quarters is the size of a small mansion, by itself. It's located to the right side of the parenthesis shaped stairs. The *entire* right side. Lovely's 4 room suite was now, all hers. She had her nursery, bedroom, bathroom and a study area. Which doubled as a sitting room while she was still a toddler.

Don and Wanda had gotten engaged before Lovely's 3rd birthday. And by Lovely's 4th Christmas, Don and Wanda were married. Don moved them from Atlanta to Louisiana, immediately after. He allowed Lovely to keep Big Dog's last name but he formally adopted her, by January 1986. The suite which was already designed for her, was then renovated and brought up-to-date. Wanda became the official woman of the manor. She redecorated the masters quarters to her liking, once they were married. That was at the Don's request.

"I have so many plans for Lovely," Don said to Wanda, 1 night as they was preparing for bed. "I want her to have the best education money can buy."

"Donnie you are a wonderful man," Wanda said, "I'm so glad you chose me as your wife. You've taken me and Lovely into your life and made *our* lives more wonderful, than I could've ever imagined. More wonderful than I'd ever dreamed of."

"Wanda, baby," he said, "I believe we were meant to be together. I saw myself with a woman like you, before I ever laid eyes on you."

That made her smile.

He said, "I know that sounds a little strange but it's true. I dreamed about you that same night that I first saw you. I called Big Dog back and insisted that he not forget to get your phone number. He said you'd already left for the evening."

"Well now we know that wasn't true. Don't we?"

"I reminded him the next time he set out for Atlanta. He

34

told me you was already sweet on him," Don said, "I wasn't pleased with that news. But I decided not to interfere."

"I wish you would've," she said suddenly, "Aside from Lovely. He hasn't done anything to enhance my life. He wasn't doing anything to enhance hers, either. That made it a strained situation, all the more."

"If I'd known he wasn't going to be good to you, then," he said, "I certainly would have. As *soon* as I found out he wasn't being an honest man. I started running interference." He laughed at his own statement. Then he said, "I was just set on having you for myself."

"Well you have me now, Donnie. And I love you for it," Wanda said, "And Lovely loves you too. You're the only father she knows. I won't change that unless you want too."

"I plan to keep it the way it is, until she's older," he said, "Then we can tell her about him. She has other siblings too. But she's the only girl and she's still the baby, so far." Wanda didn't even know Big Dog had other children, until that revelation. She immediately agreed with the Don that what he suggested, was the best way.

****

Morales Manor was equipped with all the luxuries. Swimming pools, tennis courts, basketball courts, softball and baseball fields and a park, with pavilions for cookouts. The manor had everything. It sat on a plush and very impressive, 1275 acres. Lovely was riding horses and swimming by age 3. The Don was a master at marksmanship. He trained Lovely to shoot targets by 4 years of age. She was such a great shot that Don started entering her in marksmanship competitions by age 5. She won every contest for her age group. She even won championships when she competed against shooters, up to twice her age. One of her biggest rivals, at age 6, was Mark Genolli. He was 10 years old. Them being rivals was fitting because their families were rivals too. Rivals in the cleaning and disposal market, that is.

The Morales was the top family in the killer-for-hire business. The Genolli's were number two. The Genolli's were also known to have mob ties, which many feared and they were known best, for that. Lovely and Mark would remain shooting rivals, for life. He was sweet on her from the beginning. But she never liked him. She could beat him at everything, which made him less attractive to her. She was being raised to never surrender, never conform and to select a man who was a challenge for her.

After the November 1988 marksmanship competition, which she won, her and Mark wouldn't see each other for 20 years. By then, everyone would know and expect them to be rivals. By then, she would also be the only one who wouldn't be afraid to take him on. Most feared the Genolli's, back then. But not, the Don. And in the future, neither would his *Baby Girl*. The Don trained Lovely to shoot, for 1 reason and 1 reason only. So she could inherit *The Brotherhood* and make it coed. She was the only human he was going to trust to have ownership of his establishments and the brotherhood was the centerpiece. She was already going to inherit the manor and Morales Enterprise. But the Don wanted her to run *the brotherhood*. Because with her marksmanship dominance, she would certainly be perfect as the leader of; *The Organization*. The only way to be eligible to lead it, in Don's eyes, was to be the best shooter in the world. He knew Lovely was *well* on her way to being, just that.

"You got that eye, like your daddy, Baby Girl," The

36

Don would always say to her. "You will rule this game until you decide you don't want to rule it anymore. No one else will ever change that. Only you. You've got your daddy's eye and you'll set marks on the world."

He was speaking about himself. He nicknamed her, Baby Girl. That name would stick with her throughout her entire life. Even long after Big Dog, The Don and Wanda were gone.

Lovely was becoming better known as Baby Girl, when she reached school age. She turned 6 years old in October 1988. That following January, instead of staying in 1st grade in Louisiana, Don and Wanda sent her to boarding school in Great Britain.

"She's going to learn independence, at a young age, Wanda," Don had said, "She's so intelligent. She's going to shine at that school."

"I know she will. But it's still so hard and she's so young, Donnie," Wanda had said.

"Do you trust this decision, Wanda?" he had asked.

"Yes, honey," she answered, "I want the best for Lovely. Of course, I do."

In January 1989, Don, Wanda and Lovely flew to the United Kingdom to enroll Lovely in the best boarding school in the world. Moving to a foreign country brought new challenges, for Lovely. She was use to the dialect of the people in New Orleans. But in England, they spoke with very thick tongues and accents too. Only they sounded like they was speaking faster and skipping words. Most of their speech sounded as if they was asking a question. More than making a statement. She had to get use to it and she did, after only a few weeks.

By her 6th month, she was 1 of the most popular girls at

37

Tristan Academy. The students at Tristan ranged in age from 5 to 18 years old. She learned to speak just like the Brits, with an accent which fooled everyone. Even the naturals. She learned British manners, terse, curt's when necessary and their mannerisms, as well. Tea time was at 4pm, prompt. She learned that their holidays and events were slightly different than those in the United States. But she had to get use to it and celebrate with the rest of the country. She did that and learned to love it. She especially loved when the older girls would add a spot of Vodka to her tea. Being in boarding school didn't only bring challenges. It brought out her boss lady behavior too. Curtness was something she learned to wield at her discretion. Her and her dorm mates were very rowdy. For instance, they would sneak out of their dormitories to go get liquor. She met a lot of friends in her 1st year at Tristan. The Den mothers were very strict but not as strict as the nuns. Most of the British girls rebelled but Lovely did not. At least, not to the knowledge of the superiors. It was discovered early that Lovely was a brilliant leader, a planner and an organizer. She would come up with plans for the other girls to carry out. Whether good or bad. Whenever she would have a disagreement with a British girl or any other foreign girl, she would find a way for them to compromise.

"If we learn to compromise now," she said, in late 1989 after she had turned 7 years old, "Then when we're the leaders of our countries, we will respect each other's opinions. My daddy told me I am going to be a very powerful young woman, one day. You'd better try to stay my friend. I think that would be best. Don't you?"

That worked every time. The other girls knew Lovely wasn't afraid of anything or anyone. After all, she was already thousands of miles away from home, on her own and not even in double digits, age wise. Her best friend at Tristan went by the name; Andrea Schröer. She'd come from Germany in 1990. Everyone called her Schneeflocke. That meant Snowflake, in German. Lovely called her Snow or Snow baby. Snow called her, Baby Girl. They were as thick as thieves, from day one.

Once in 1991, another girl in the dorm was plotting to beat up Snowflake. Her name was Agnes Borland. She was already 15, six years older than Snow and Lovely, who had both turned 9, by then. Agnes was spreading the word, all over the academy, that she would bust Snow up. The other students were instigating it, like crazy. So Lovely told Snow not to worry about it. She had a plan that would stop Agnes from bullying her, for good. It was a tactic she'd used on another girl when she first arrived, in 1989. The girl was Charlotte Perry. Charlotte was 13 and Lovely was only 6, at the time. Charlotte tried to intimidate Lovely and she made fun of her New Orleans, southern drawl. Lovely warned her not to make fun of her and she gave her good reason not too.

"Because I don't like it and I'll get you for that," Lovely had said but Charlotte persisted.

Lovely got her and she got her good. But then, Lovely had to go to classes and sleep in a section of the dorm called Solitary hall. A section where you was the only person on the whole hall, with 2 nuns and a Den mother. The 1st discipline incidents were logged, if expulsion wasn't required. But they didn't get reported to the girl's families, until the parents were present.

Lovely gained all the respect needed for beating up a 13 year old, when she was only six. Lovely was big for her age. But still, Charlotte was more than twice her age. They were the same height and to Lovely, that put matters in a whole new light.

39

So when her best friend Snow, was stressing a threat from Agnes, Lovely told her how to put it to rest. She told Snow to take the D batteries out of her big radio and put them in her fanny pack. The next time they saw Agnes, Snow was to step to her and ask her about the rumors she was spreading. Lovely told Snow that if Agnes denied it. Then that meant she was afraid and just talking shit. But if she admitted it, then she told Snow to take off her fanny pack and start wailing on her. Not even giving her a chance to blink.

A week later, Snow got her chance to confront Agnes. Once Agnes admitted she'd been telling the yard she was going to kick Snow's ass. Snow did what Lovely suggested. She busted Agnes face up, pretty badly. Snow got reprimanded and was nearly expelled. Until the others told the Den mothers and nuns that Agnes had been picking on Andrea, for more than a year. Snow ended up receiving suspension which amounted to her being in solitary rooming, for 1 full week. She had to have classes alone with just 1 Den mother. That wasn't fun at all. Snow was happy to get back to her dorm and her best friend Lovely, the next week. A report was sent to Don and Wanda.

When Lovely visited home, that year, she wasn't punished at all. The Don thought it was cool that she was resourceful and knew how to plan and strategize. That's what he'd raised her to do. Take care of herself and her family. He bought her a diamond bracelet as a reward. He bought another one for her take back to Andrea for the 1992 school year, as well. Wanda didn't like him rewarding her for fighting. Or for teaching someone else to harm another person. But she didn't make to much of a fuss about it. She knew the Don's word was going to be the final one.

In 1992, for *Saint George's day*, Lovely got drunk for

the 1st time, at only 10 years old. The Don was unhappy about that incident and he demanded she be punished. She was and it resulted in what was ultimately, time out. Wanda was pleased he'd ordered punishment for her and she rewarded him with a full day in their master suite. Just the 2 of them.

Drinking wasn't frowned upon in the UK. Not even for minors, apparently. Her and Snow joked that they must be in Russia, where the Vodka flowed freely. Lovely did learn a lesson on how to handle her liquor, though. She never got drunk again. Though she did consume alcohol, often while living in the dorms.

She was also able to continue her marksmanship while in the UK. She competed and won competitions there, as well.

Don and Wanda visited about 2 times a year. They took her home for Christmas, every year. Except 1992. Don wanted Lovely to go a full year, with no break. Because the next year was going to be her last.

Lovely was the organizer and the chief of the girls in her dorm. And the Den mothers *and nuns* knew it. Ultimately, she was promoted to dormitory assistant or DA, at age 10. That opened up a whole new can of opportunities for Lovely. Her duties consisted of keeping order in her abode, submitting plans for down time and along with the other DA's, assisting the Den mothers with schedules and activities for all the students.

Lovely's 1st week brought on new challenges and new situations. Lovely had more of an inside track on how things were run. Which gave her more vision into how to surpass or to get around the rules. She had more access. Like the keys to the exit doors, passwords and codes for the alarms, security guards, outside of the dorms and all the way out to the border gates.

41

"Now this is power," she said to herself as she sat at her post, one late evening.

There were always room chimes going off, simulating that someone was opening a door. It was her duty to investigate why the door had been opened. Going to the bathroom was the most common cause or excuse used, for when a door was opened. She had used that excuse herself, from time to time. When in fact, she was sneaking to another girls room to get in on the free alcohol and weed that had been brought in. A lot of the girls knew Lovely was all business, so they had to find a way to penetrate her. Because that would give them a way to bend the rules their way. Lovely was willing to hear their demands. Many of them wanted to sneak boys in so they could have sex. Lovely knew this was doable but she had demands of her own. She used that as leverage to earn money. If they wanted her to look the other way, then they had to pay her and pay her, big time. Which they did. Then some of them took it even farther. They wanted to sneak to the boys side of the academy. Again, Lovely would unlock the hall door, disable the pass alarm and cover for them. That paid, even bigger. She shared all of her extra earnings with Snow Baby. They made plans to go into business together, 1 day and use the money to get it started. Neither girl had any idea of when that business would open or where it would be. But they knew it would be a type of business that delegated others to do something. And at the same time, it would be built around what a person could do and not how they looked. They looked forward to the days their dorm mates wanted to be their promiscuous selves. Because the pay was good. But sneaking off to be with a boy was something Lovely would never do, herself. She wouldn't allow Snow to do it either. She was happy when she learned that Snow never wanted to go with the

42

other girls, anyway. Her and Snow had similar morals and wanted to save themselves for the man they would ultimately marry. That was just 1 of the many similarities they shared. They were both blown away by the fact that they were so similar. Yet they were from communities that was continents apart, with different foods languages, laws, economies and skin tones.

"Our skin doesn't determine who we are, Baby Girl," Snow had said to her, "I love you like my sister. Because of who you are. Not for how you look."

"Excellent," was Lovely's response, "We should rule the world and teach everybody that. And we're going to start with the United States. That is one place where skin tone means *everything*. We'll get our business set up and running. And then, we can find that special boy to be our husbands. But mine has to be perfect. He won't be allowed to hurt me, at all. Because if he does, my daddy will kill him."

They laughed hard. Although, neither of them knew just how true that statement was.

The Don had been very specific with Lovely, about boys. He told her, she was only allowed to get involved with a boy, when she was prepared to be with that boy, for the rest of her life.

"I will only meet *one* boy," Don had said to her, "And if he doesn't meet my standards. I'll have him removed from your life. Then and only then, will you be allowed to bring another boy to meet me. So be sure you understand me. And pick a guy you really want to be with. For life. Just not before you're a teenager. And if you learn to love him. That's good. But if he hurts you. I'm gonna kill him. You will learn to think the same way."

43

MEETING THE FAMILY

Lovely would spend 4 school sessions in the United Kingdom. She came home for Christmas break, the first 3 of the 4 years. By Christmas season 1993, she'd finished her formative education at Tristan Academy. Don and Wanda attended her graduation, where she finished at the top of her class. She headed back to Louisiana, for the rest of her schooling. She was 11 years old when she returned home.

"Lovely. Now you're ready to go back to Louisiana and attend school," Wanda said, "You've got a great head start, baby girl."

Though she wasn't considered fluent in either language. Lovely had learned to speak French, Spanish and German, pretty well. She'd met and befriended a lot of girls and boys, at the Academy. When she graduated and left for home, she had to leave all of her friends behind. That was another difficult feat in young Lovely's life. She'd only had 1 friend, her age, prior to Tristan. That friend was the head cook's niece. Her name; *Epiphany*. Before Lovely left Tristan, her and Snow held onto each other for more than 15 minutes. On that day, they were both leaving the airport, headed back to their separate countries. They promised they would see each other again. Yet, neither of them had a clue of how that would happen. Not then, they didn't.

After returning to America, Don and Wanda decided it was time for Lovely to meet and know her birth father and her siblings too. She had seen Big Dog on many occasions. Before Tristan and during her breaks too. Because he still worked for her daddy, Don Morales. But she hadn't been told that he was her biological father. This Christmas, not only would she meet him as her real father. But she would also meet 3 of her brothers. Immediately, she didn't care for having another father. Still, she accepted him but only as another of her many uncles. Which is how she referred to all the men who worked in the Don's employment. Even though her reception to Big Dog had been lukewarm, she was anticipating meeting her siblings, a lot. She'd grown up, an only child. With only Epiphany to play with, during holidays and the summer. She remembered wishing she had a sibling who could've gone with her to Great Britain, 4 years ago. So she wouldn't have had to go, *All By Her Lonely.*

The 1st sibling she met was the oldest of Big Dog's offspring. His name; Roger Walker Jr. Big Dog had made 2 more sons since Wanda had Lovely. Lovely was no longer the baby but she was still the only girl. Roger Jr was 21 years old, 10 years older than Lovely, at the time him and Lovely met. He was indeed Big Dog's oldest child, by Big Dog's own words. He and Lovely were the only offspring of Big Dog's who was given Big Dog's last name. Roger Jr was the spitting image of Big Dog too.
Lovely met the 2 boys who were born after her, as well. Danny Baker was nine. Two years younger than her. He had his stepfathers last name. Then there was Bruce Barnes, who was 4 years old. He was 7 years younger than Lovely. Bruce is Big Dog's youngest child, as far as everyone knew. Bruce was the baby and had his mother's last name. Wanda found out about Danny and Bruce, immediately after they were born. Unlike the way she'd found out about Roger Jr and Big Dog's others 5 sons, in Philadelphia. Don Morales had told her about all of Lovely's siblings. He kept her up on the current events of Big Dog's love life. Just so she would know, without a doubt,

45

she'd made the right decision to stop seeing him and moving on.

Roger Jr lived in New Orleans. Danny lived in Mississippi and Bruce was born in Denver but lived with his mother in Atlanta. During this holiday season, while she was meeting the 3 brothers in the south, Lovely was also told she had 5 other brothers who was born between her and Roger Jr. Those 5 and their mother live in Philadelphia, under the last name of, Wells. It was also said that if Big Dog would've ever married either of his children's mother, the woman in Philly would've been the one. That statement came from the Don, himself.

Roger Jr was better known to everyone, as Six Nine. He was very tall and thin and could pass for Big Dog, 30 years ago. He smiles as he picks Lovely up.

"Everybody calls me, six nine," he said to her, "I want you to call me that too. Okay?"

"Okay," she said as she giggled.

She was immediately taken by her big brother. He was protective of her, instantly. She had grown up thinking she was an only child. But after coming back from Tristan, she found out she had 8 brothers. Those 8 brothers have other siblings. Some of them have their own kids, plus many cousins, play brothers and sisters and more. She had a huge family, instantly. That discovery made her ecstatic. She was begging to follow Six Nine home, that day. She looked forward to meeting and visiting with each and every one of her brothers. Six Nine was taken by her too and he wanted to grant her, *every* wish.

"If it's okay with your mama and daddy," Six Nine said, "I'll come and pick you up, sometime. I can take you out to my mama's house, in the third ward. Then you can meet my other brother's and sisters. We live in the wards."

"What is the wards?" Lovely asked and her English accent was very prevalent. She asked, "Are they my brothers and sisters too?"

"Ward is a name used to separate sections of the city," Six Nine told her, "They're gonna call you their sister too. But they have a different daddy then me and you. My sisters and brothers. They all have other sisters and brothers by their real dads. Just like me and you. Plus me and my brother named Kid, have some best friends who we do music with. We all act like brothers. You will be a little sister to all of us."

"I'd like that," she said, still smiling. "What kind of music do you do? Is it like *Tupac*?"

"Yes," he answered her and chuckled, "We do Rap music."

Then Danny cut in, giggling. He said, "She talks funny."

"Don't make fun of me," Lovely told Danny. "I'll get you for that."

Everyone laughed. They thought it was so cute the way she snapped at him. Lovely didn't laugh because she was sincere.

Lovely went to visit Six Nine's family before Christmas break was over. Six Nine and his brother Brad, who's nickname was Kid, lived next door to his mother in a shotgun styled, duplex home. Those houses was the norm, in what was labeled as the inner city part of the wards. Six Nine and Kid have 8 other half siblings. All girls. Six Nine wasn't the oldest of his mother kids. He had 4 sisters who were older than him. He had 4, that were younger but all of them were older than Lovely. His 4 older sisters had their own homes and the 4 younger sisters stayed with their mother. Brad, his only brother by his mother, was 19 and better known as Kid. He shared the duplex house with Six Nine. There were others boys

47

who lived there, with them. Six Nine and Kid call them their brothers, even though they wasn't blood related.

Marcus or Mark D was 19 and best friends with Kid and Six Nine. He was also the DJ for their music label.

Terry or Soldier, as he was called, was 17 and a rapper. He already had a CD on the streets which was in heavy rotation. He was the most popular of all of them, with a personality made of gold. He had the interest of many girls, music labels and music representatives.

Craig was 14 years old. They called him, Baby Boy. He was a rapper, as well. He had 2 street CD's out and just as many girls, as Soldier. But Baby Boy lives with Six Nine and Kid, all the time. Not just part-time, like the other non-blood brothers.

Another of the rappers was named William. He was 13 years old and his nickname was G-Dog. Lovely thought he was cute. But when she told him that, he told her,
"Thanks. I'm your big brother, so that's why I'm cute. Because you're pretty too."

The youngest rapper was named Greg Lee. He was better known as, Lil Geezy. He was 2 weeks older than Lovely. He was happy to not be the youngest of all of the children, finally. Lovely was happy she was no longer an only child. And she was even happier to know, she had so many brothers.

There was lots of other guys who hung around with her brothers. More then 50 of them. But according to Kid and Baby Boy, the others guys wasn't anyone she needed to know or remember. They weren't the ones who would be around her, for the remainder of her life. Only Six Nine, Kid, Mark D and Soldier, Baby Boy, G-Dog and Lil Geezy were the ones she had to see, know and respect, as her brothers. Along with Danny and Bruce.

They welcomed her into their family, with open arms, instantly. They even started acting like her body guards and protectors, from day one. She liked that, a lot.

"You're the only little girl, around here," Soldier said, "We're gonna look out for you and we're gonna have to teach you the ropes. For when you hang around here. And how to survive too. You're gonna need to know the code, for out here in the hood!"

"*Hood*? Why do you call it the hood?" she asked, "I thought it was the ward. That's what six nine told me."

"The wards. The hood. Same thing. You *hurd* me?" Soldier had said, "Because we get thangs poppin', out *chere*, *bay bee guile* [baby girl]. Day in and day out!"

"What does, get thangs poppin', mean?" she asked.

"It means, we shoot at any niggaz that come on our set, trying to *ack* bad," Soldier told her.

"I know how to shoot, too," she said with excitement in her voice and all the boys laughed.

"She talks *funny,* man," Lil Geezy said and he laughed.

"Don't make fun of me, Geezy," she said, "I don't like that. I'll get you, for that."

They all laughed again. Again, Lovely didn't laugh because she was sincere.

"We're gonna teach you the hood slang," Baby Boy said, "We gonna get you straight, out *chere*. You *hurd*?"

"Okay," she said.

She liked that. But the part she liked the best, was that they liked to shoot guns.

"We gotta get you a street name," G-Dog said, "Miss Lovely, sounds like a good name."

"Miss Lovely ain't original, man," Baby Boy said, "She's gonna need a gangsta' name."

49

"How about, *Baby Girl?*" Soldier asked.

"I like that name. That's what my daddy calls me," Lovely said.

"Then, Baby Girl it is, then," Soldier said and all of the others agreed. "We ain't gonna change shit. *Not one fucking thing,* that the Don put down. You *hurd* me?"

And from that day on, Lovely would be known and called, Baby Girl, by everyone.

All of her brothers, which now included all of the males on Six Nine's record label, had a lot of respect for her daddy, the Don. They told her, he was the man and he had all of the connections for all types of business.

"Even the music business," Kid said with a glossed over look in his eyes.

When Kid spoke on the Don, she noticed a special gleam in his eyes. They told her she was lucky to be his daughter. But she already knew that.

She had spent much of the Christmas break with her big brother and his family. And she'd gotten to know, all of the boys well. She'd picked up on some of their street slang, already. The brothers had introduced her to all of their friends, *in the hood.* They had warned them not to mess with her, in the wrong way.

"She's family," Six Nine told them, "And that's Don Morales' daughter. You *hurd* me?"

And just like that, she was made in the 3rd ward section of New Orleans.

The 3rd Ward was 1 of the roughest sections in the city. She soon learned that her brother and his crew was at the top of the list, of the most feared and most respected, in the Magnolia projects, Valence street and the surrounding areas. It was cool to her that her brothers feared her daddy, Don.

50

Because everyone around their way, feared them. Lovely would be known as Baby Girl, better than she would be known my her government name of Lovely, from that point on.

Lovely went back to her marksmanship competitions. And the 1st person she was pitted against, was Mark Genolli, of course. He was still in the game, from years before. She met a newcomer to the scene, from an old family name which Don Morales was familiar with. Emilio Pantango was in the competitions now. He was Mark Genolli's age, which was 4 years, Baby Girl's senior.

"It took him this long to turn pro?" Baby Girl asked her father Don, as she prepared her weapons for competition. Don said, "He's not even a pro, compared to you, baby girl." That was all the encouragement she needed.

She took that competition and every other 1 she entered. Just as she had always done. By this time, she was being recruited heavily by the military and even some terrorist organizations. They wanted her to be their mercenary. But that was never the Morales' style. Regardless of the fact that she was only 11 years old, Baby Girl's name was on the wire as the shooter to hire. She was going to represent the Morales family, one day. They were proud Americans and proud to *be* Americans. No one from the organization would ever join any group or organization, which was anti-American. Or anti *anyone* with Morals. The most hilarious invite she'd received, had come over her daddy's computer. It was an invitation to be a marksman for the white knights of the ku klux klan. The Don laughed hard, when that one came across his desktop. Reason one. The obvious. And reason two. The klan couldn't have done any research on her. But if they had and still wanted her. Then they must've had plans on taking her out. Don knew

51

it would've been the other way around, though. He had even considered getting their information and having a package done. Just so she could wipe them out, 1 by 1. But Don thought better of it. They weren't mercenaries and they only took out anyone who was commissioned to be hit. And those who were trying to do them or a family member, personal harm. He explained to Baby Girl what the invite was about and why she couldn't take it. He had to do that, without giving away any trade secrets. She couldn't know about *The Organization*. Not until he was ready to bring her into it, fully.

"Just like I taught you," Don had said, "The way you stuck up for Snow, at the academy. Is the same way I want you to be, in life. Take care of your family, first. Always trust *your own* instincts, only. They will never lead you wrong."
She took his words to heart and kept them there, for use in the future.

Christmas and New Year's passed and it was time to get her settled into the New Orleans public school system. The day Wanda and Don went in to enroll her, they were pleased to learn that she wouldn't be going into the 6th grade, like most 11 year olds. Instead, she was advanced enough to be placed in 9th grade. Though Wanda thought she should continue in private schools. Don suggested she go on and enter into public schools, at that point.

"I want her to be well rounded," he'd said, "This is a test of her humility. I want her to feel at home, around any class of people. I want her to treat every person, the same. Unless they give her reason to treat them, otherwise. And Wanda, she's intelligent enough to know the difference. She will never follow anything or anyone, if it's not what she's about. At the same time, she needs to have patience with those

who are less fortunate than her. The less fortunate will appreciate her efforts towards them. Much more than a wealthy one would. Also, I set it up with Joyce, *Six Nine's mother*, for her to go to school in their district. With Craig [Baby Boy], William [G-Dog] and Greg Lee [Lil Geezy]."
Wanda didn't hesitant to agree with Don. She knew he'd done his homework. She knew he wouldn't send their daughter anywhere, where she wouldn't be looked after carefully. Don had workers everywhere. Including in the New Orleans Police Department and the school system, as well.

Baby Girl enrolled in school and attended 9th grade at *George Washington Carver* high school, with Baby Boy. Baby Boy barely went to school. Though, he would hang around it. But he started showing up regularly, after Baby Girl was enrolled. That way, he could look after her. He was a hustler, just like Six Nine and the other brothers. Baby Boy would sell drugs during school and thought nothing of it. He was very popular for his rapping abilities and he had a lot of comrades. He had a lot of girls too. Those girls instantly clicked up with Baby Girl and forbade anyone to look at her wrong. That was the order Baby Boy had given them.
William or G-Dog was in the 8th grade. Greg Lee or Lil Geezy, was in the 6th grade. Their middle school was on the same grounds, right next to the high school. So Baby Girl would see G-Dog and Lil Geezy, during lunch period. She would see Baby Boy anytime she was out of class. Because he was always on the yard. He rarely attended his classes. She had no idea how he was able to do that and get away with it either.

By the end of the fall semester, Baby Girl was on course to be promoted to 10th grade. She only had to take 2 classes

53

during the spring semester of her freshman school year. That gave her free time to horn her skills, in the basketball gym.

In the fall of 1994, she was a full fledged sophomore and she hadn't even turned 12 years old. She never looked back. She tried out and made the basketball team, that year. She also met and befriended a girl named, Marjorie Petal. Marjorie, who's nickname was MJ, was on the basketball team with her. MJ liked Soldier. MJ was already 15 years old. She took Baby Girl under her wing, just as the other girls had done, who liked her brothers from the wards.

"I know Soldier ," MJ had said, "I'm crazy about that boy. But he won't act right. He's always fucking around wit some other bitch. But he claims he loves me."

MJ and Baby Girl would practice after school, each day. Soldier would pick them up and bring them to the 3rd ward, to hang out. MJ and Soldier was having sex with each other. They would leave Baby Girl alone, only long enough to sneak in a goodie, in Soldiers room. Baby Girl really liked that Soldier and her new best friend was close. But she also knew Soldier had lots of girls. As a matter of fact, all of her brothers did. She got to see that firsthand, when she celebrated her 12th birthday, in the 3rd ward.

Her brothers had thrown her a big block party or a DJ, as they called it. Everyone, who was anyone to her brothers, showed up to celebrate. It was at *that* party that Six Nine learned of a new dilemma with 1 of his ex-girlfriends.

His ex-girlfriend Sherry, showed up at his mothers home with an infant boy. The baby she'd named Jordan, was almost 2 months old. Sherry was claiming Six Nine as his father. Six Nine already had a son with another woman named

54

Sandra. And Sandra was in attendance, at the DJ. Sandra wasn't pleased that Sherry had showed up, either. Her and Six Nine had a 3 year old son. Sandra was adamant about Sherry not being there and she wanted her to leave. As it so happened, Sherry hadn't come to the party to stay. She only wanted to drop Jordan off. She said she would be back to get him, the following morning. No one believed she would be back. Still, Sherry left Jordan in Joyce's house. She left him with no diapers, no formula or anything.

Baby Girl went inside and picked up Jordan. She barely put him down, for the rest of evening. She took a liking to Jordan, instantly. He was so cute.

"Looks like you're gonna be just like Big Dog," Baby Girl said to Six Nine. "With all of these sons, for different women. That's the same way our real father was."
Six Nine just smiled but he offered no comment. Baby Girl wondered if he had anymore kids, out there.

Six Nine knew Sherry was in no condition to be a fit mother. Because she had been experimenting with cocaine. One of the reasons her and Six Nine didn't stay together, was because Sherry had developed a crack addiction. But Baby Girl would learn later, that Sherry blamed Six Nine for her addiction. Six Nine denied it. But it was most likely true.

Six Nine always had crack around because he dealt it to the streets and he had never barred her from using it. Sherry started off just sampling his powder supply. But by the time she gave birth to Jordan. She had a full blown addiction to crack cocaine.

For that reason, Miss Joyce told Six Nine, it would be better if they kept Jordan. Because Sherry was in no shape to be a real mother to him, anyway. Six Nine didn't agree, initially. But his mother Joyce insisted. So Six Nine decided

Jordan could stay on with them. But he would have to stay on his mother's side of the duplex.

The following day, when Don and Wanda came to pick up Baby Girl, she didn't want to leave without Jordan behind. So, Joyce and Six Nine said it would be okay if he went out to the manor, for awhile. Jordan left with them and spent the entire day. That 1 day, turned into 3 days. Wanda, Don and all of the staff at Morales manor, fell in love with little Jordan too. Baby Girl asked her parents if they could keep him, forever. She told them Six Nine didn't want him and neither did Sherry. The Don knew that was very possible, so he didn't waste anytime. He wanted to give Jordan some security and the possibility of a good life. He contacted Six Nine and his mother Joyce, about the allegations from Baby Girl. They all but confirmed every word she'd said. Wanda was heart broken to know that such a beautiful baby boy, like Jordan, had no real home. Her and Don wanted to keep him, as well.

The next week, was when Six Nine, Ms Joyce, Don and Wanda talked about the possibility of a legal adoption. Six Nine agreed to do his part, to make it happen. He knew his biological son would have a wholesome lifestyle with Don and Wanda Morales. Baby Girl was proof of that.

It took nearly 2 years and a lot of paperwork. But in 1996 and by Jordan's 2nd birthday, Don and Wanda had legally adopted him. A wing of the manor was renovated for him. They'd left him with the Walker name, just as they had done when the Don adopted Baby Girl.

"Now, I have a little brother at home with me," Baby Girl had said.

She was overjoyed. She didn't get to see Danny and Bruce, as often as she saw Six Nine, because they lived out of state. So to have another sibling in the house with her, was a dream come true. Growing up alone and being off on her own, for much of her young life, Baby Girl had always dreamed about having a large family. Her family was getting larger, every year. She still hadn't had the opportunity to meet her other 5 brothers, from Philadelphia. But she was going too. If it took the last breath she had. No one had any information on them, other than Big Dog, And he wasn't willing to cooperate, at that time. It was just something about having his past and his real lifestyle exposed to his only daughter, that he couldn't agree with.

Meanwhile, Baby Girl thought of Jordan as her own child. She took him everywhere she went. Especially to the 3rd ward, so he could see his real daddy.

September and the fall of 1996, marked the start of Baby Girl's senior year of high school. She turned 14, the next month and she was already nearly done with high school. She was also being recruited by top colleges for her basketball abilities. She'd set records at *George W. Carver*. They'd won 2 state titles in the 2 years since she'd joined the team. She was a starter and a shooting guard, with an automatic jump shot. She was already 6 feet tall by her 14th birthday and she was just getting her menstrual period. Something all of the other girls, at the high school level, had been experiencing for a few years. She was a local celebrity and a big name in basketball. Her brothers shared that same celebrity, for their music label. Baby Girl was very popular in the state of Louisiana. But she was yet to see a boy who captured her attention. That would happen, sooner than later.

Musically, Six Nine and the guys had gotten bigger in the city of New Orleans in the years since Baby Girl had first

57

met them. They had put out several CD's, over the last 2 and a half years, that they sold, primarily from the trunks of their cars. But they had more CD's to come. They'd also started to do concerts. Not only in New Orleans. But in other cities, in the state of Louisiana and the surrounding states, as well. They traveled a lot, which kept Baby Boy, G-Dog and Lil Geezy out of school, a pretty good bit. Baby Girl would travel with them to Texas, Tennessee, Mississippi, Alabama and Florida, when they went to do shows. But Wanda and Don wasn't going to allow her to miss school, in order to go. There was going to be no change in that order. Six Nine and her brothers decided to schedule some out of town shows, on the weekend. Shows they could leave New Orleans for, on Friday. And return by Sunday evening. That worked out perfect for Baby Girl. And Don had even started to send 2 or 3 men from, The Brotherhood, to act as security for them. But mainly, for Baby Girl.

THE BOY FOR LIFE

It was during an October show in Texas, 2 days after Baby Girl's 14th birthday. Her brothers brought a young local rapper backstage, who'd made a name for himself, in the Houston area. His name; Derrick Blake. He went by the stage name; *MC Young D*! He was 15 years old and to Baby Girl, he was gorgeous. She liked him from the first time she laid eyes on him. He was smitten with her, as well. They talked backstage during the entire time her brothers were performing. By shows end, she was convinced she'd met the boy she wanted to get to know better. The boy she would introduce to her daddy, *the Don*.

After the show, Six Nine and Kid invited MC Young D to become a member of their label, *The 3rd Ward Soldiers*. He accepted their invitation with gratitude. And by the time they wrapped up the Texas tour and was ready to head back to New Orleans, he'd left school to travel back with them.

In the next 2 weeks, Young D and Baby Girl became closer. So close in fact, he'd asked her to be his girlfriend. She darned a huge smile and said yes. This was something she was very unfamiliar with. But she knew what had to be done, if Young D was going to be allowed into her life. He had to be approved, first. She told him he would have to meet her mother and father, first and get their word. But she certainly wanted him as her boyfriend. He told her he was ready to meet her parents, whenever she wanted him too. She liked that answer, a lot.

Six Nine and Kid objected to their relationship, in the beginning. Both of them was still, very protective of her. They had never even let any boy get close enough to her, to talk about any of the boyfriend/girlfriend types of conversations. But Baby Girl was determined to see Young D. She liked him and he liked her too. So instead of forbidding them to see each other, Six Nine decided to have a talk with MC Young D. Whom they all called, Young D or D, for short. Six Nine told Young D if he was just playing around with Baby Girl, just to get some quick sex, then don't even mess around or go near his little sister. He told Young D that Baby Girl was better than that. And that game, was going to cost him his life.

"She's the only sister I have, that's close to me and she's got a lot going for herself," Six Nine told him. "So if you want to see her, *seriously*, then you're gonna have to be with her and her only. And you will have to treat her right. Her daddy is the man around these parts and parts beyond. And if you hurt her, he'll have your head taken off."

Young D said he understood and his intentions with Big Girl was honorable. Six Nine insisted he meet Wanda and Don before he could give his approval. Young D told him he'd been waiting on Baby Girl to invite him over so he could meet and talk to them. But she was yet to do so. Six Nine told him, he would get Baby Girl on that, right away.

On the possibility of Young D and Baby Girl being a couple, Kid was a totally different story. He wasn't anywhere as open to accepting Young D, as Six Nine was. No matter who approved of it. Six Nine felt sure Kid would come around, if Young D was able to get Don and Wanda to give them their blessings. So he took Young D to the manor, himself and he finally met Baby Girl's parents.

Initially, Wanda and Don was against the relationship because of Baby Girl's age. But Young D was persistent.

"I'm only fifteen, myself," Young D said, "I've never met a girl, like Lovely. She's so smart and she's independent

60

too. She's beautiful. She knows how to talk to me and make me feel like I'm special. I've never had that happen before. I've never liked a girl, the way that I like her. I'm not playing around with her. I can't think of nothing else but her. Her name describes her, perfectly. Inside and out."

Don told Young D he would need to meet and speak with the members of his family before he could even consider it, any farther. Young D gave him his mother's phone number, right then. Don dialed the number and handed Wanda the phone.

Wanda ended up laughing and talking with his mother, Annie Holmes, for hours. His mother gave her the full description of her son and how important he was in her life. After talking with his mother, his aunt and his grandmother, Wanda's feelings changed, instantly. She went back into the parlor and joined Don and Young D.

"Your mother sounds like a beautiful sister," Wanda said to Young D. "And she loves you, dearly. They all do. I didn't know you was already trying to be the man of her house, though. You're only *fifteen*."

"Yes ma'am. I know. But my mother is partially disabled, so she can't *really* work," he said, "She do the best she can. But it's never enough. She didn't want me to do street stuff to make money. So I'm gonna be a rapper. Everything I've made from my shows, so far, I give it to her."

"That's very honorable," Wanda said and Don agreed. Wanda thought he was very charming. She could see why her daughter liked him and wanted to introduce him to her and Don.

Young D was very charismatic. He was a responsible lad and very handsome too. He had a magnetic smile and a pair of very dreamy eyes. He was a proud country boy, who was the apple of his mother's eye.

The Don had done a background check on Young D. The 1 thing on Young D's wrap sheet was a few priors for assault against an adult male, a few years back. That adult male was his mother's ex. He had been abusive to Young D's mother and he had caused her partial disability. Young D was very little when the abuse started and had suffered some of it, himself. But when he grew older and stronger, he took his step dad on. Young D started to whoop his ass, whenever he disrespected his mother. He wouldn't just beat him up. He would stomp him out, convincingly. Then he would drag him out of his mother's house and leave him on the sidewalk, for dead. Young D was only 10 years old when his step dad sent his mother to the hospital, with a ruptured disc in her back. He was still 10 years old, when he whooped his step dad, for the first time too. Before Young D showed him that he could beat him. His step dad had beat on his mother, at least once a month. So after realizing he could whoop his step dad, Young D started beating him, at least once a month. Until he decided he would move and leave his mother alone. After that, Young D got the nickname; Young Death. It was shortened to Young D and the name stuck. When he started to rap at age 12, he kept the name everyone was familiar with and used Young D, as his stage name.

Both Wanda and Don was impressed with Young D, for protecting his mother. Through his connections, the Don found out everything about him. He knew his government name was Derrick Blake and from whence, he had come. He'd checked it all out. Young D told him he was going to rap with Six Nine and his crew. But Don asked him for his rap name, that 1st day and Young D was hesitant about telling him. But the Don was persistent too. Young D found the courage and told him. He stood in a submissive manner and said,

"My rap name is Young Death but I go by Young D."
Don Morales kept a serious face, as he leaned in towards D and said, "Well, Young Death. Meet Old Death."
Don's face was chiseled stone, for a solid minute. Wanda, Young D and Baby Girl were all quiet. Until Don burst out laughing. That was the first relief Baby Girl felt since Young D had arrived.

After meeting her parents, Young D was determined to grow on them. He planned on not being a stranger. Each time Baby Girl's brothers went out to Morales Manor to pick her up, Young D went with them. And he would talk with Don and Wanda, each time. Until they were both convinced, he would do right by their daughter. Don gave him advice, one time and one time only.
"Take care of my princess. She is my life. If you hurt her. I will kill you. *Period.*"
Young D said he understood and he would not hurt Baby Girl. He told Don, he saw Baby Girl as the kind of girl he could spend the rest of his life with. And that he wanted to become a famous rapper, so he would be rich enough to give her anything she wanted. Don told him, *he* had already done that. All he would need to do was to make her happy and keep her an honest woman. Again, Young D said he understood. With that, Don and Wanda gave them their blessings. Baby Girl was happy that her parents had accepted the first boy she liked.
From then on, Baby Girl and Young D were inseparable. Baby Girl would go to the studio with him, whenever she could. Wherever she went, she brought Jordan along. The 3 of them acted like they were a little family. Young D was invited to the Manor for Thanksgiving, that year. Along with the rest of the 3rd ward soldiers, of course. But the day

before Thanksgiving, was a huge day in Baby Girl and Young D's relationship. At Soldiers house, the Wednesday before Thanksgiving, Baby Girl gave Young D her virginity. He was experienced but she wasn't. He'd been sexually active for almost 3 years.

Their sexual encounter made Thanksgiving day, very tense for Baby Girl. But not for Young D. No one knew about the Wednesday encounter, except Soldier and Baby Boy. Young D was closer with them, than he was with the rest of *The 3rd Ward Soldiers*. The 3 of them hung together, a lot. He had confided in them about what him and Baby Girl wanted to do, before it happened. And Soldier had allowed them use his room, for the encounter. It was the same room Soldier would use every evening after school, with MJ. Or some other girl.

After Baby Girl became sexually active, her senior year was a blur. Between her marksmanship competitions, her basketball games and the 3rd Ward Soldiers shows, she was going somewhere all of the time. Plus she was destined to get a division 1 scholarship for basketball. She had a boyfriend, a boastful basketball career and she was #1 in the country, with a bullet. *Literally*. She was growing up and coming into her own, very fast. But Don couldn't allow her to graduate high school without them, first having that serious talk about the family business. The Don decided to have that conversation before she finished high school. He felt *that* was the appropriate time to do so.

He brought her into his office in March of 1997. Just before her spring break started. He showed her the run of the place and explained each and every business he owned or owned stock in. Whether his involvement was major or minor. He told her about *The Brotherhood*. For the 1st time, she really understood what her real father Big Dog's, relationship was to

64

her daddy. And why he hadn't been fully able to settle down with her mother or any of his other women. Later, she would call and forgive Big Dog for what she'd thought was him wanting to dog out her mother. Don also told her, he would only trust 3 people to run and know the intricate and intimate details of his business. He told her that 2 of them was already in the room, with him. She looked around. There was no one in the office but him and her.

She smiled and said, "Okay, daddy. I'll make you proud."

"I already am, Baby Girl," he said, "And I have been for fourteen and a half years. I trust you to do my bidding. If something was to happen to me. You would be expected to keep my businesses rolling, smoothly. Just like I do."

With just that 1 statement, Don had put the weight of his entire empire's future on her 14 year old shoulders. Don had already learned that he had a terminal illness and he wouldn't live much longer. Baby Girl was hell bent on showing him that she could do it. Next, he told her about *The Organization* and what he intended for her to be *in it.*

"Baby Girl, this is what I've trained you for," he said, "It's a family tradition. Me, my sons, Big Dog and TJ, are getting to old to carry out assignments."

He said, with that powerful laugh he had, "But TJ's son has been trained and you *will* see him. But only when the time is right. Trust me, Baby Girl. You will know when the time is right."

He wanted her to be the professional of the Morales family, if anything should ever happen to him. He told her, emphatically. "Never allow Gus Davis into my office. And if he does have to enter it, per a plan you're working on. Never let him have access to my computer, any of my pass codes or my bank accounts."

He told her, Gus Davis' only job was to arrange packages. Then, he gave her a key. He told her it was a master key. It would open anything associated with his office, starting with the door. From there, she could find anything else she needed, for any job or any business of his. He showed her the computer, she could find all of the assignments for the family on. It was 1 which had the securest network in the world. Only top government officials, CIA and the top levels of the FBI, could access it.

"Want they put us in jail?" she asked him.

"Baby Girl, they're *ultimately* responsible for all of the work that comes into this computer," he said, "And we're like a military soldier. We never question *why*. We just follow the orders. Understand?"

"Yes sir," she said.

"If it's in here," he said, pointing to the computer, "then it's secure. And no one is to access it but you and whomever you train, to work for the family."

Baby Girl knew her daddy had faith in her and he saw her as a responsible person. Because he was turning over the estate to her, if something were to happen to him. Everything he owned, would become hers and Jordan's. Not his older children. Not his grandchildren. Not Wanda. But her and her adopted brother, only. She stuck her chest out, instantly. She had the trust and respect of, *The Don*. Not many grown folks could boast of that and she still had nearly 7 years to go, before she would be legally grown. She was proud that her daddy expected her to do the same job he did. That was an honor. For in everybody else's eyes, that she knew and even many whom she hadn't met yet, her daddy Don was *the man*!

During the weeks of meetings with her daddy, Baby

Girl would also learn each and everything she would need to know to maintain Morales Enterprises. She learned and understood that there was 1 person whom her daddy wasn't exactly trusting of. That man was Gus Davis. He lived on the property and had no real family. He did odd jobs for the Don but not of the *execution style*. The closest Gus got to *hitting*, was researching possible marks and arranging the packages, for the hits. Don never offered her an explanation as to why Gus wasn't trustworthy. And she had learned, never to ask. Just to trust his word. Which she did.

Next, Don made Baby Girl aware of their rival families. The Pantango's and the Genolli's. He told her that, for the last 25 years, the Morales family has been the top family called upon by the government, for target disposal. Which meant, they got the biggest contracts. That was something, any other family in the business would envy and want to change. He told her, they would always be civil and social to her. But never trust them and never allow them to yield her work.

"The Pantango's and the Genolli's will never be our friends, Baby Girl," Don said to her. "Never accept an offer from *either* family."

That statement set in her mind and would become fermented. She knew she would never forget it. Because she knew it was a matter of her life or death, if she didn't heed what her daddy said. Satisfied that she had obtained all of the information she needed to stay alive and on top of the game. The Don told her, she was done with her indoor training and she was dismissed.

What she didn't know, was there was something overtaking The Don, that he'd failed to tell her about. He never told her of his ailment because he didn't want her to worry nor panic. But his illness was the reason he had the talk with her, at that time. Instead of waiting and doing it, on her 18th birthday. It was due to the diagnosis he'd gotten, 2 weeks prior. Which only gave him 4 years or less, to live. Don didn't even expect to live until she turned eighteen but he didn't tell her that part. Because The Don never wanted or accepted sympathy from anyone. No one else would know of it. Nobody but Don and his physician and that was the way he wanted it. It was an ailment which had passed on through his family, genetically. Don expected to be stricken with it during his lifetime. The same illness had retired all his forefathers to the grave. That is a fact he hadn't shared with Wanda, even prior to marrying her. But knowing he would contract it was the reason he made sure he gave Baby Girl everything she needed, to be successful in life. She was a natural at being independent. He figured that was all a part of God's plan, from the beginning. He also figured that was why God had sent Wanda to him, in his dreams, more than 18 years ago. The Don was ready to turn over the reigns of his empire to his youngest daughter. He wanted her to begin by the time she was 16 years old. Two whole years before anyone else had been allowed to take hits. Not even him or his sons. Not anyone who's worked in this business, started before 18 years old. But Baby Girl was the best of the best and Don knew he could get her in. He submitted her name as she left his office, that last evening.

With the 3rd Ward Soldiers label picking up regional appeal and them having 2 songs on the radio, which were in heavy rotation. Major labels started to take interest in them.

By May of 1997, Baby Girl was preparing to graduate from high school at age 14 and at the top of her class. At the same time, the 3rd Ward Soldiers inked a major distribution deal with Unity Records corporation for 225 million dollars. The Don had gotten lawyers for them, before their Unity meeting. The contracts were to both of the parties liking and the union was formed. Thus, the 3rd Ward Soldiers music label became yet another business under the Morales Enterprise umbrella. Six Nine was very happy with the arrangement. But Kid, not so much. He liked the idea of them having major distribution. Just not with Morales Enterprises having a 3rd of the profits. However, he agreed to the deal because he wasn't willing to pass on $75 million dollars. He figured he could work something out later, with the Don and buy him out. The Don told him that would always be an option. But they would have to buy him out, in full. That would cost, the $175 million he'd put up to secure the deal. Plus whatever the forecast shares showed for the next 5 years, from the day the option was implemented. There would be interest and recovery charges, as well. Kid wasn't crazy about that part but he wasn't going to test Don and take a chance on losing it all. Two days after Baby Girl's graduation, the contracts were signed and 3rd Ward Soldiers were completely legitimate.

Baby Girl and her best friend girl MJ, had both signed scholarships with LSU for the 1997-1998 school year. By then, everyone in Baby Girl's family was doing well, for themselves.
Baby Girl's freshman year of college was uneventful. Don wanted her to have a year to get accustomed to school and being away from home, again. Before he put her to work. She did excellent in her classes and on the hardwood too. But it was during her sophomore year in college, 1999-2000, when she started to use her marksmanship skills to make income.

Don had Big Dog to commission Baby Girl for a few jobs, he'd set up in early 1999. Those jobs would carry on through 2001. Even after both of her fathers were deceased.

69

Don set up Big Dog, as her agent, so he'd know that she was indeed ready and able to do the work.

The first 7 contracts for Baby Girl was set and arranged through her real father, Big Dog. That went on, right under everyone else's nose. Even Wanda and Young D. After her early successes, there was a huge change in her family structure. Which meant her packages would have to start coming directly from Gus Davis. He would keep her very busy. While all the time, she knew she had to watch Gus with an extra steady eye. Because her daddy Don had told her, Gus could not be trusted.

Over the next 2 years, Baby Girl suffered 3 traumatic loses in her life and she was left without any living parents. That hardship would also leave her feeling totally independent, of anyone.

In late 1999, Big Dog would succumb to a heart attack and die.

Then, in January of 2000, because his deal with the 3rd Ward Soldiers had never panned out, Young D had gone back to Houston. Him nor Baby Girl could understand why he was never given a chance to release a CD. Nor was he featured on any of the hit records with the major label, Unity Records. Her and Young D were baffled by that move.

But before they could even get closure on it, later in January of 2001, Don Morales passed away from Kidney failure. Simply because he refused to do dialysis. Don Morales was a proud man. He wasn't going to allow himself to be seen as a crimple. He would never accept being a victim. And being sympathized by others, was something his pride wouldn't allow.

The next lose and probably the most severe blow to

Baby Girl's conscious, was when sweet Wanda died in August 2001, from a massive stroke. It was 3 months after Baby Girl graduated College, at 18 years of age. Those 3 deaths hardened Baby Girl's heart. It also made it easier for her to take out marks, without conscious. She felt like she was all alone, in the world. And though she still had Jordan, her brothers, Young D and her staff at the manor, things just wasn't the same. She was left to raise Jordan, who turned 7, 2 weeks after Wanda died. Baby Girl was prepared to raise Lil Jordan, with the help of Young D, his family, the manor staff and all of her brothers.

Young D was very much in her life and he still brought money for Jordan. Though Baby Girl had inherited more than enough to take care of everything they would ever need. Young D would serve several short stints in jail. Both in New Orleans and in Houston during the same 3 years that Baby Girl was losing her 3 parents. Young D would also survive being shot, before ultimately catching his big break into the music business. Thus bringing some relief to the stress Baby Girl was feeling, from him being in the street game. He and Baby Girl remained a couple, though his relationship with Kid soured badly during those same years.

Baby Girl inherited Morales Enterprises, Morales Manor and all of it's staff, as well as *The Organization*, in early 2002. Then, her and Young D were legally married, at the manor, in mid July of 2002. Just months before she turned 20 years old. She still didn't like that Young D never got a deal with her and brothers label. She felt as though Kid didn't like him because of his relationship with her. She was *partially* correct. Even after they'd gotten married, Kid still resented Young D. He seemed to resent their relationship more, after

71

they were married. Baby Girl felt it was why Young D's welcome to the label, which Kid shared with Six Nine and now her, had never come through. She saw it as her fault that Young D never got to rap on any of their records. Young D, Soldier, G-Dog, Lil Geezy and Baby Boy remained like brothers, with Six Nine as the oldest brother. But Kid never warmed up to Young D. And he swore he didn't sign Young D to their label for other reasons. But he was never able to share what those reasons were.

The fall out between Kid and Young D hardened Baby Girl, even more. Her relationship with Kid became strained, over the years. She had taken it in stride, after she had finished college. She wanted to rekindle her family, so badly, that she had even gone to work in the 3rd Ward Soldiers offices. She worked as a label publisher, to see if she could smooth things out for Young D. Still, she continued to take contracts. Just to keep her skills polished and sharp. She had several encounters with the Morales family's arch enemies, along the way. All of which, she came out of victorious.

The Morales' competition came from the 2 families her daddy Don had warned her about, primarily. The Genolli family and the Pantango family. Her and Mark Genolli were the best in the marksmanship competitions, in her pre-teen years. She'd beat him in each and every event. She was the best, of the best. Period! But after she was fully in charge of *The Organization* and *The Brotherhood*, she also learned what their family's were all fighting over. It was to have sole control of the entire shipping industry, worldwide.

Donnie Morales was against the drug trade. His family had come into prominence during what was known, back in the day, as Prohibition. Until 1960 or so, *The Morales Organization* maintained total control of the shipping trade.

72

With very little adverse action from any other corporations or families. But when the drug trade became a big money business, the Morales family found itself in the middle of a war. A Drug War.

Drugs were being imported into the United States in huge quantities which the government knew about and for the most part, *harbored*. Urban sections of metropolitan cities were being targeted with those drugs. To maintain a stronghold on all the docks, the Morales' had to dabble in the drug trade. Just to give a sense of security to their loyal comrades in other countries. That kept their trade of other products, moving freely without disruption. But it was never something the Morales' were particularly fond of. Nor did they plan to stay apart of.

However, Baby Girl didn't care what made a mark, *a mark*. Whether they were short on a drug load or a shipping payment. Or whether a rookie organization was trying to make a major move on her families territory. Each time she executed a contract, she was doing her *daddy's work*. That's what the Don always told her, when she would asked him what he did for a living.

"Daddy's Work." he would say.

She made lots of contacts in the music business while working at the 3rd Ward offices. But she could feel the family and the brotherly vibe, falling down around her. Kid was the major reason. Soldier, Baby Boy and G-Dog had all left the label and struck out on their own, by the end of 2002. Baby Girl remained there but she knew she wouldn't last much longer. She missed her man. She missed her brothers too. And most of all, she realized that any of them coming around

73

the offices, just wasn't going to happen. The tension between Kid and everyone else was so thick, it could be cut with a knife. Still, Kid didn't compromise. Not 1 bit. He wasn't even willing to try and work things out.

By the end of Jordan's 4th grade school year, in 2004, Baby Girl left the 3rd Ward offices, for good. She moved to her property in Mississippi, where she could see her husband at her leisure. Of course, she brought Jordan with her. She moved to Mississippi because she wasn't ready to live in the manor, without her parents. She hadn't even tried to find the strength to sleep there, since Wanda's sudden death.

By June 2004, both Danny and Bruce moved to Mississippi to live with her too. Young D had made it big in Hip-Hop, by then. He wanted her to come out on the road with him. She decided to take him up on his offer. It wasn't until they were celebrating their 2nd year anniversary in 2004. That her *real* job was discovered. It was discovered by, none other then her husband, Derrick "MC Young D" Blake, himself.

In the beginning, he thought it was fly. He liked being married to a hit woman. But in 2005, she gave birth to their 1st child. A baby boy they named Derrick Blake Jr. It was then that Young D's feelings about her occupation changed. He no longer wanted her to take hits. Because he didn't want their child growing up without his mother. Same as he had done, for much of his younger days.

Later in 2005, the catastrophe known to the world as; *Hurricane Katrina,* would severely damage Morales Manor. Katrina damaged many of the staff's homes, on and off of the property and also, several of the Morales Enterprise businesses. The manor had to be totally renovated. Baby Girl

74

set the wheels in motion to have it repaired and restored. During renovations, her and Young D lived mostly in 1 of their Houston homes. Danny, who was legally grown by then, still lived in the Mississippi home with Bruce, who was in 10th grade. Jordan, who was a 6th grader, lived in Mississippi with Danny and Bruce.

Baby Girl had inherited the Atlanta and Mississippi properties, from Wanda. But the home in Mississippi needed repairs after Katrina, as well. It would take a year to finish the Mississippi home and 2 and a half years to finish, Morales Manor. Young D would still encounter run-ins with the law. Though he was making legal money in music. And Kid was still trying to run interference with their relationship. Kid never stopped insisting that they shouldn't be together.

When Young D turned 26, in 2007, he and Baby Girl had another son, who was born on Young D's, 26th birthday. They named him Donovan Prince Blake, after *The Don*. That was when Young D became more insistent that she stop taking murder-for-hire contracts. So far, she hasn't stopped.

"Being in the loop is gonna pay off, one day, Derrick," Baby Girl had said to Young D.

But no matter what her excuse was. He still insisted she find a way out. She calls him Derrick. He calls her Lovely.

Check out the tale, as we move into the present day.

----THE STORY----

CHAPTER ONE
TIS THE SEASON [2006]

"It's a living, Derrick," Baby Girl says, "It's a good living at that. And I'm very good at it. Besides, you've benefited from it, as well."

"You're good at a lot of things, Lovely," he says, "A lot of, *different* things. This shit is gonna get out of hand, *woman*."

"Out of *hand*?" she asks in surprise, "This is what I was born to do. I don't get out of hand. I get things, *in* hand."

It's 2006. Two weeks before Christmas. Baby girl is a highly paid professional and the best-of-the-best, at what she does. She camouflages her real job through Young D's career. He's a superstar in the Hip Hop industry now. She's the head of his security. Young D is always followed by paparazzi, whenever they're outdoors. She's been able to keep her main job a secret, thus far. Young D first found out about her profession, in 2004. He's been insisting she stop doing it, every since. Baby Girl knows her, one and only love is worried for her safety. But she can't leave the murder-for-hire business. It's her life's work.

Some decay has surfaced and she has to locate the problem. Then get rid of it, before her mind can ever be settled. She also needs to help her husband understand that this isn't a job she can just leave or relocate from. The only way to retire, is to die or eliminate all who pose a threat. She knows her occupation could cost her the most important things in her life. Her son, her family, her husband's success and their future. So her plans are to work, expeditiously to find that decaying cancer. Then relieve the world of it.

Young D has a heavy tour schedule to resume. Baby Girl is not only on his security detail. But she's his publicist, also. She's devoted most of her time to their son, their marriage, their homes, his career and hers, as well. She is also an avid writer of novels, songs, poetry and interviews. She's penned notable songs for other artist, in the music industry. And she has also worked on the straight to video movie, done by The 3rd Ward Soldiers label, prior to the fall out. Baby Girl has made a name for herself in the entertainment industry. But only as a writer. Young D wants her to pursue her own music identity, as an artist. She's against it, for the simple fact that she doesn't and never has liked, *media attention.*

"That could be suicide, for me," she says, "You know what I mean, Derrick?"

They're at *The Peabody,* in Memphis. Young D has a show tonight with Memphis' own, *Three Six Mafia.* He's their guest artist.

"How much time do we have, before I gotta go to the venue?" he asks, "Cause I don't wanna spend it all, talking about this same shit," he says as he agrees with her on the occupational suicide part and further pushes his point. "You need to quit the family business, Lovely. Don't I take good care of you?"

"You're wonderful, Derrick," she answers, "It's not about how much we have or don't have. I do what I do because only I can, right now."

"*Lovely,* you professionally waste muafuckaz. Then you come home and care for our son, like nothings happened," he adds with sarcasm. "And you come at me hard, if I even buck on a nigga. But you do it to people, you don't even *know.* Even now, while you're pregnant."

"That's the best way," she answers in her usual calm. "So would you feel better if I only killed people I know?" She giggles and moves closer to him. She starts to rub on his

77

shoulders, seductively. She doesn't want to talk about her work, anymore.

"I'd feel better if you only killed people, who mean to do harm to our son or us," Young D says. "I worry every *time* you're out of my sight and I can't reach you, Lovely. I don't know if you're dead or alive. That's not easy to handle, baby. I'd feel a lot better, if you only did things to protect *our* family."

"Then feel good, Derrick," she says with a smile. "Because that's exactly what I do. I protect my family. My *entire* family."

She covers his lips with a wet kiss, to prevent him for speaking anymore. He quickly reciprocates. And just like that, the arguing stops. They're so highly sexual, that there is now way *any* kind of disagreement could curb either of their appetite, for the other.

"By the way. We've got four hours before show time," she says, finally answering his question.

"I'm gonna need all four of *'em,* to get some understanding around here," he says with a sexy smile. "Time to get my preshow on."

He removes her clothes quickly and lifts her up onto the hotel vanity top. They engage in a passionate kiss, as he undoes his belt and jeans. He lets his jeans drop to his ankles, revealing the silk boxers underneath. He kicks his feet free from his jeans and pulls his penis over the top of his boxers.

"I need to taste that," she says as she slides down off the counter and goes down to her knees.

She takes him into her mouth, gently. He moans with pleasure. She knows what he likes. She works that magic she has on him and it doesn't take long before he's ready to burst. She's spent 10 years learning how to please him. And judging by his

78

reactions to this head job, he's getting. She's learned her duties well.

"Oh, Lovely!!!" he yells from the sensation, he's feeling. He's about to climax and she wants it. He gives her his huge load, as he leans against the wall for balance. She holds onto his dick and sucks up every drop, he releases. But she's not done with him, just yet.

"I got to get this shit back to, *hard as a brick*, Derrick," she says, very seductively.

He reaches down for her and pulls her to her feet.

"I've gotta lay you down," he says in a demanding voice. "I want everything you've got to offer."

He takes her to the king-sized bed and lays her across it. He joins her. Quickly spinning her torso around to where her, already moist pussy, is directly in front of his face. His dick is within inches of her mouth. She indulges again. While he starts to lick and suck on her pearl tongue.

"Oh *God* yes!" she screams out.

They're on a mission of pleasure. From 69 to rodeo style. Seesaw to doggy style. Then back to missionary. They have a very intense way of fucking off 2 hours, literally. Then it's time for a quick nap, for an hour.

When they awake from their nap, they have a light meal. Then they call Houston to check on their son, at Young D's, mother's home.

After an hour or so, of being entertained by Derrick Jr's antics, they get ready for the show.

Baby Girl inherited Morales Manor and it's full staff, in New Orleans, after her mother died. She'd also secured the properties Wanda left to her in Atlanta and Mississippi, for her and Young D. Her and Young D also have 5 homes, in his hometown of Houston. Young D has a studio and Baby Girl has an office, in each of their homes. The 5 Houston homes are all situated on 1 property. Baby Girl and Young D live in one. His mother, sister, half brother and grandparents, live in the largest one. The other 3 homes are for guest and his labelmates. Baby Girl has a business office in their Houston home. That's where they live, primarily, nowadays. But she has to travel to Mississippi or New Orleans, when she has a package to receive. It has to be this way because of the job she does.

The packages of material for her marks, still come from Gus Davis in New Orleans. Gus remained at his regular position in *The Organization,* when Don Morales past away. It's always better and most professional to have your mark materials hand delivered, to avoid a leak into the wrong hands. When Baby Girl is not in New Orleans. Gus has to insist she get to within a few hours drive. This is so her mark package can be brought to her, person to person. So anytime Baby Girl travels to New Orleans or Mississippi. Young D gets anxious. He always feel like she's going to pick up material for a new mark. Most of the time, he's right. It bugs him because he knows her life is in danger, at the same time. He just wants to be the one to protect his woman.

She travels to New Orleans, a week before Christmas. She tells Young D, that her and Cherry are going to do some Christmas shopping for him and Derrick Jr, so they *can't* come. He doesn't totally believe her, because he knows that isn't the only reason she's going.

"Well, I'm gonna check on the manor too, Derrick," she says sarcastically. "It's not finished. But the staff is back in it,

80

around the clock, nowadays. That means it's livable again," she jokes.

"Lovely. I love you and be careful," he says and seals it with a kiss. He adds, "Make it back home, *to* my son and *with* my son. *Okay?*"

He stresses that she be careful. For his namesake's sake and for their 2nd son, which she's 6 months pregnant with. She promises she will, before kissing him again. Then she kisses their son goodbye too. Afterwards, she hops aboard her airport shuttle which is waiting on their driveway.

}Morales Manar-6 Days before Christmas, 2006{

"The Pantango's and the Genolli's will never be our friends, baby girl. Never accept an offer from either family," The Don had said.

Baby Girl is driving up to the Manor again and she can almost hear her daddy's echo. The manor's staff promised her they would make sure the manor kept the smell of vanilla scented candles, which was her mother's favorite. They have done, just that. Except for the bedding, in the master suite and a few minor changes for Baby Girl and Young D, Morales Manor will stay, pretty much the same as it had been, all of her life.

Cherry the nanny, Maggie the assistant nanny, Alfred the butler and Charles the chauffeur, plus Addie Mae the head cook and the maids, Jennie and Mable are all still on staff. And they all still live in the homes, provided for them and their families, by Don Morales. Right there on the same grounds, for convenience. The property around the Manor is always buzzing, nowadays. Baby Girl and Wanda had encouraged the staff to become entrepreneurs, since they was very good at their individual crafts. The Don had left healthy settlements for all of them, which made it possible for them to branch out and start their own businesses too. When they launched those businesses, they opened them right there on the manor property.

Morales manor grounds looks much like a farmer's market, by day, with all of the traffic which frequents the many small businesses located at the front of the property. While the manor itself, sits off to itself, quiet and tranquil.

Cherry, Jennie and Mable run a daycare center, on the grounds. Addie Mae and her staff have a catering business which is doing very well too. They serve breakfast, lunch and dinners, each day, from their home-style restaurant. It was renovated from public kitchens, on the grounds. The Don left Charles the fleet of cars from the estate. He started a limousine service. Alfred does what he does best. He teaches etiquette and holds classes, 3 times a week, at 1 of the centers on the grounds.

Alfred is also the longest employed, of all the staff. He was the closest to Donnie Morales, out of all his employees. The staff is always happy to see Baby Girl, when she arrives. As usual, they're waiting for her, just outside the main door. She always remembered them doing this, when she returned from school abroad or LSU. That was their protocol. They always remind her of the first time she came there. And that they had done the same thing for her very first visit, back in 1982. She had to kiss and hugs each and every 1 of them, before going into the manor. The same way she'd done, when she was growing up.

She's walking around the entire manor. She's checking to see that everything was done as she had instructed.

"It's looking real good around here," she says with a

smile. "Katrina did her share of damage. But I'm so glad the original structure is still in tact. And that y'all was able to save everything. Y'all have done a great job, getting the house back operational. Thank you, so much."

They all tell her, she is most welcome, before going back to their duties. Cherry brings her bags to the master suite to unpack them. She makes light conversation, while Baby Girl changes clothes.

Then Baby Girl says, "I'm gonna work in daddy's office, for a while. Then we can go shopping. We have to be sure and buy lots of things, for all of my guys. That way, Derrick will know that I *did* shop."

She giggles as she heads toward the door, to Don's office. She unlocks the door and heads in, as Cherry is still talking.

"We sure will get some shopping in," Cherry yells, "But misses baby girl. That would be *your* office, nowadays."

Cherry adds and giggles back.

"Oh *yeah*! Right," Baby Girl says as she smiles, "Well, I'll be in here, for a bit."

She returns the giggle. She'll never get use to the fact that the manor is all hers, now. She's also feeling happy to have the staff around. For this will be her first overnight stay here, since Wanda passed away. She unlocks the office, goes in. She closes and locks the door behind her.

"So what's the business?" she says to herself, while turning on the desk lamp and then the computer.

She gazes around at the office walls and sees the memoirs of her days growing up here. There are pictures of her on visits home from the UK. There are pictures of her, with all of her brothers that she's met, so far. One of her with Big Dog, on the day she learned he was her biological father. There's 1 on the desk of her, Wanda, Don and Jordan. It was their 1st family portrait. There's also 1 she'd added to the office. It's her, Young D and Lil Derrick's, first family portrait. She'd put in the office, when her and Young D brought their son to Morale's manor, for the first time, to meet the entire staff. Addie Mae and Cherry was in Houston for his birth. They will also be there for the birth of the son, she's carrying now. Don kept pictures, trophy's and ribbons from various competitions she had competed in, from basketball and softball to track and field and marksmanship. All of her events are pictured here. The marksman pictures, in particular, catches her eye today. In each photo, she is 1st place. In second place, is always, "Mark Genolli," she says aloud as she rolls her eyes.

Mark use to have a serious crush on her during her preteen days. But she never liked him. She felt like he only liked her because she beat him at everything they competed for. The 2 of them are in direct competition, still to this day. She's always mindful of her main adversaries. The Pantango's and the Genolli's. That's etched in her memory. Her and Mark Genolli use to compete at many marksmanship events, all over the world. And he has *never* beat her. He hasn't and Baby Girl has plans of keeping it that way. She rarely lost and never lost to anyone, within 5 years of her own age. Simply put. She was a natural, who was born to hit targets. Just like the Don and Big Dog.

She sits behind the desk, looking at her computer as she waits for Gus Davis to call. It's only a few minutes later, when the office line rings.

"Morales manor. May I help you?" she says, answering the desk phone.

It's Gus Davis. He has the contract ready for her. She looks over the details on her computer. This is the way the Don it set up, so he could insure that Gus was handling the marks demise, correctly. Gus knows nothing of this computer program.

"I'm putting the package together now," Gus says, "You'll receive it, in the morning."

"Okay," she says and they hang up.

She surveys her office again. Still not believing she's even allowed to be in here, by herself. This is where the Don had conducted business. She'd only come in here 5 times, when it was his. Today, she's going to work on some of her writings while she has some quiet time. She's missing her son and her husband, already. Young D must've been missing her too. Because ironically, he calls her, within the moment. She talks to him on her cell phone, while she works.

"You must be missing me, like I'm missing you," she says to him.

He's called to say he's coming in from Houston, to be with her in New Orleans, at Morales Manor.

"I'm meeting Soldier and Baby Boy there too," he says.

"*Here*? When? *Today*?" she questions, "What time?"

"They'll get there around four or five, pm" he says, "We're doing a show in the crescent, tonight."

Soldier and Baby Boy had left the 3rd Ward label and acquired their own music labels. Which kept their music moving, successfully. Young D is very close to doing the same thing. He already has the label name, the logo and the artist. Immediately after the first of the year, he'll seal his independent deal, with Unity Records, most likely. Every chance him, Soldier and Baby Boy get, they do shows together. They're all very active on the Hip Hop scene, nowadays. The 3 of them are still very much like brothers and leaving the 3rd Ward label, seemed to have only made them closer.

"I'll be there before they get there though," Young D says, "I'll be there by three o'clock."

"Okay, Derrick," she says, "I'll see you this afternoon!" They hang up.

Baby Girl locates Cherry and they leave to go do some Christmas shopping. She's going to buy special lingerie for tonight. Her and Young D had shared a lot of intimate moments, at the manor, over the years. Most of them undercover from Wanda and Don. Or so they thought. This will be the 1st time they've been back at the manor together, for the night, since Wanda died. Baby Girl had lived with Six Nine after Wanda passed away because she didn't have the strength to stay at the manor alone. Her and Young D got married at the manor but haven't consummated their marriage, *in the Manor*, as of yet. Young D will be arriving today. Because he feels she's still not ready to be at the manor, alone. He'd contacted Soldier and had him to book a show for them and Baby Boy. So the 3 of them could be there with Baby Girl.

Soldier and Baby Boy are still protectors to Baby Girl too. That's a job they'd taken on when she was 11 years old and fresh out of boarding school. Those feelings will never change for them. Young D has the main job of making sure she's comfortable and protected. He's her husband, head of household, her lover and her best friend. There was no way he was going to allow her to come back to the manor, for a night and not be there with her. Not for the first time, since losing her mother.

CHAPTER TWO
DADDY'S WORK

The *House of Blues* show is filled to capacity, with standing room only. Soldier, Baby Boy and Young D pull it off, without any problems. Well, not any *major problems,* at least. Baby Boy had to get up in 1 of the promoters faces in order to get paid in full, before going on stage. Soldier had to have his backstage ladies heavily screened, before they could be allowed in. Because 1 of his ex's is still angry. She'd put the word out that she wants to cut him,

"From his nuts to his neck, for marrying another bitch!"

Other than that, the show was a breeze. Young D didn't experience any problems with pay or women. Baby Girl had secured his money before leaving the manor. As for the groupies, Baby Girl lets them feign and flock. For she knows her man is only thinking of her. And he's leaving *with her,* as well.

She has a great time at *The House of Blues*. She feels the same way she use to feel, 10 years ago, when all of her brothers did shows together. She sits in the main VIP, tonight. Just like she likes it. Six Nine, G-Dog, Mark D and Lil Geezy are there to show their support for Soldier, Baby Boy and Young D. And though he was invited, Kid never showed up.

After the show is done, they all talk briefly in the celebrity lobby, as they wait for valet, so they can load into their vehicles. Baby Girl was raised to spend money inward, first and foremost. Before letting someone else profit from Morales Enterprises. In keeping with what she was raised with, she'd hired Charles' fleet of limousines to get them to and from the House of Blues.

Before they can even load up, Baby Girl does what

comes natural to her. She inspects all of the vehicles in their fleet. Then, they pile in and pull off.

Baby Girl still doesn't relax. She keeps her eyes on all the vehicles in the fleet, while they're rolling, as well. From experience, she knows other hit men try to use high profile events to snuff out the competition. Or to remove a target. She has a new package coming within 24 hours. Which makes her *vulnerable*. Someone just might try to catch her off guard. She has to be on point, at all times.

The entourage is going back to the manor for the after party. Only family and their closest friends are allowed to come. They're in a fleet of black trucks. From Hummers, Lexus, Infiniti, Cadillac's and Benz's. To Chevrolets, Fords and Nissans. They parade in style to Canal street and get access to interstate 10.

They hop on the interstate, cross the muddy Mississippi River bridge and go on over to the West Bank. Baby Girl, Young D and DeJuan, D's best friend, are in the H2, with Charles doing the driving. Baby Girl had taken the passenger seat as she's done, since she was a little girl. Everybody else chose to be chauffeured. The entire time Charles is driving, Baby Girl's eyes are glued to the side view mirror. That was the reason her daddy Don taught her to get, *"a seat with a view."* She's watching for anything out of the ordinary. She knows if there's a hit coming. It's going to be on her, before anyone else in their entourage.

When they was leaving the event, she noticed they'd picked up a tail. With all the street shooters in the 3 entourages combined, Baby Girl is the only 1 who notices they're being followed. And she wants to end this before they get any closer to Morales manor. She has Charles to stop at a local supermarket for food and liquor.

While her and the guys are preparing to head into *Swegmann's* grocery store and load up on afterparty staples, she notices the tail pull in and park, at the far end of the parking lot. She doesn't alert anyone because she knows what this is about. While the guys are wilding out, she steals away to herself and calls Gus.

"Did you send my package early?" she asks.

"No. In the morning. Like I told you," he replies.

"Thanks" she says and hangs up.

She rejoins her group of rambunctious fellows and continues to carry on their conversation, as if nothing has changed.

"We need to get some food to take it with us too," she says, "I didn't have time to get groceries yet. And the staff won't be cooking for us. Not at this hour. I'm not even going to bother Miss Addie Mae."

Before going into the store, Baby Girl hops back into the H2 and grabs her *Get to Work* bag. It's the 1 which houses and holds her *Ruger 9mm select with the lynx silencer*.

"Let's get it done," she says as they start toward the door of the store.

Young D looks at her, suspiciously. He knows that bag. He also knows there's a threat, near. He reaches back into the Hummer, grabs his pistol and tucks it into his waistband. Baby Girl notices him, immediately.

She grabs his arm and whispers in his ear.

"Leave it behind," she says, "You won't need it, Derrick. I've already got the drop. So please baby. Don't get yourself in trouble. I'm legal with mine and you're not. Plus, the alarms won't pick up mine. But they *will* get yours."

The rest of the pack of guys are voicing their opinions about who's going to do the shopping and not wanting it to be them. They aren't thrilled about even having to be in the grocery

89

shop parking lot. But they are hungry. Plus they know they'll all have the munchies, later. Still, Soldier wants to make his case for avoiding the trip inside the supermarket, all together.

"We'll wait out here for you, while you shop," Soldier offers with a chuckle.

He's still standing near the cars, watching out to see if his crazy ex-bitch has trailed them from the *House of Blues*. She'd threatened to slash his tires. He's being driven tonight but he knows, from experience, that it never mattered if the tires were on his car or not. She would damage any vehicle that assisted him in avoiding her.

Young D is more concerned about his wife. Just him knowing that a threat is near. And that his wife is going to have to show her stuff soon or be killed. He steps in and offers a quick solution. He has to provide some aid in keeping Baby Girl's mission a secret.

"Nah. Here it is," Young D says, "Me, Juan and Baby Boy will go in and shop wit Lovely. Soldier, y'all can head on to the manor and get shit started."

"That's a bet!" Soldier yells.

He didn't want to hang around the parking lot, any longer, anyway. So he gets the rest of the entourage back into the vehicles. They load up and head on to the manor with a few of their groupies, in the trucks with them.

Young D, Baby Boy, DeJuan and Baby Girl prepare to shop. The tail is still across the parking lot, watching Baby Girl, as Soldier and all but 2 vehicles leave. Baby Girl can see him from her peripheral vision. He's lighting a cigarette.

"Dying wish, ha?" she mumbles, "Hope you had a meal too."

The tail sits and waits. It appears he wants to wait for them to go into the store, before he gets out. He's not even aware that

90

he's already been spotted by Baby Girl. Nor that he's just become *a mark*. He smokes his cigarette as he prepares to follow the 4 of them into the store. Baby Girl still pretends not to notice him, as he gets out. She takes a cart from the outside, front of the store. She checks for alarms on the automatic doors, before passing through them.
No. Alarms are on it. Good. No alarms on.

She goes into execution mode. She counts the camera's and checks them for positioning. She slows down so the guys can pass through the doors, while the front camera is sweeping the parking lot. That way, none of them are on camera entering the store. From experience, she knows the front and rear camera's record times. But that's not a usual occurrence for camera's on the inside of supermarkets. Still, she's mindful that none of them are on the camera's, at the same time. She's always aware of video and security measures.

They walk in, semi separate. Which, for a motion censored camera that disrupts the sequence. The mark has made up ground. It's apparent to her that the mark doesn't know camera system operations. Because he's closer behind them now. The front camera catches him entering the store. But not them.
A fucking rookie.

Baby Girl and the guys pick up produce, hot links and a cheese tray or two. Plus they grab some beer and liquor too. As Baby Boy goes to get chips, salsa and dip, Baby Girl looks at the aerial mirrors. She notices the mark is on every aisle they're on. More specifically. Every aisle that *she's* on.
Do this bitch know who he's dealing with? Apparently not!

91

She feels disrespected, as she chuckles to herself. Then, so that everyone on the aisle can hear her, including the mark. She says,

"Derrick, I think I'm going to find the bathroom, baby. I really have to go. *Bad*. That passion fruit mixed drink that I had at the club, made my stomach hurt, something bad."

Young D, Baby Boy and DeJuan laugh. Baby Boy and DeJuan are thinking she has the bubble guts and will be in the bathroom, for awhile. That's exactly what she wants them to think and the *mark* too.

"You want me to watch the door?" Young D asks with a smile.

"No," she says, "Keep picking up what we need, please. So it won't take us too long to meet up with Soldier, at the manor. I don't want Miss Addie Mae getting up, thinking she has to cook, at this time of the morning."

She leaves for the bathroom, as the guys continue to shop. The mark takes the bait and veers off to find out which lane is directly in front of the bathrooms. While he has to familiarize himself with the store, Baby Girl doesn't. She's been here 100's of times with the staff and her mother, for groceries. And with her friends too. Getting late night liquor and cigars to roll weed in, during their party days.

As soon as she leaves the aisle and away from the guys, she dashes toward the bathroom. Knowing the *mark* has to find out where the bathrooms are located first.

She enters the hallway which leads to the bathrooms. She checks for camera's positioning. There's only 1 camera. Just outside the hall. In the mirrors, she can see the mark advancing toward the area. He's not even seasoned enough to check the mirrors, like she has done. It simply pisses her off more, to know that some asshole has been so disrespectful of her talents. That they sent a green ass toy soldier, to fuck with the best of the best.

I guess I'll have to kill babies too, at some point. May as well be tonight.

The term *babies*, in the assassin business, is a word used to described those without experience. Those who don't know the ins and outs, the shortcuts or those 400 level tactics which often times are the difference between hitting the mark or being the mark.

She proceeds to the back. Soon, she is out of the *soon-to-be*, dead man's sight. She runs into the ladies room quickly. She turns the faucets on high, leaves a wedge in the door so it doesn't close completely. Then she darts back out. She ducks into the broom closet, across from the ladies room entrance and prepares her weapon. With the faucets running hard, it gives her advance knowledge of when the mark opens the bathroom door. The running water will send an echo that will bounce off the hallway walls, when the door is opened fully. She'll know he's in there. Just in case she can't risk peeking out of the closet.

Quietly, she screws the lynx into place. She doesn't need her scope for this one. She pushes her clip in slowly, to avoid a loud click. Once it's in place, she cocks it. She can hear the footsteps of the mark. He's in the hallway. He can hear the water running in the ladies room. He thinks she's in there.

"Yes," he whispers, "Go on, you spoiled little rich ass bitch and wash your hands. You'll never get them clean enough."

What did he call me? For a baby, he's an arrogant son-of-a-bitch. That's for sure.

She peeps out at him, from the closet. He has a smug look on his face. She can tell by that look on his narrow ass face, that he thinks he's got her hemmed up. Somebody failed this soon-to-be corpse, by not telling him of the caliber *markswoman* he had been sent to kill. For he is way to unskilled to even be in her training class. If she was to ever give one. He's totally green.

He draws his weapon. Again, in plain camera view. Then he darts through the bathroom door. The camera shifts away from the hallway. That's when she exit's the broom closet quickly, with her weapon raised.

Once the mark is in the bathroom, he aims toward the sinks where the water's running. She's not there. He bends down to check the stalls for feet. He sees none. He slowly starts to look under each one, thinking she may be crouched on the toilet seat.

Before he makes it to the 3rd stall, Baby Girl slides into the bathroom and catches him off guard. He turns around, surprised to see her just entering and already drawn. She doesn't waste time with casual last words or witty 1-liners. With no questions and no response, she puts a peanut sized hole in the middle of his forehead. She watches for the abstract art, his brain fragments paint against the wall and the 3rd stall. Quickly, she advances toward him and gets control of his weapon before his whole body can collapse to the floor. She has to search him to see, from which family he was sent.

"Genolli's dude," she says, "I knew you had to be a baby. You got the jewels that random Genolli's get. I should've asked you if these jewels was a gift. But I killed you, too fast."

She knows the markings, the detail, the M.O., the clothing and the jewels, of all the families in the business. Every family has a signature.

The Morales Organization's signature is a Black Panther and the Mighty Black fist.

"You fucked with the wrong family, rookie," she whispers with a smile.

She disassembles his weapon and puts it in her bag. She can always add it to her collection. But even if she doesn't keep it. She doesn't want some kid to stumble upon a weapon while trying to use the bathroom. As far as the blood and the dead body. Well, that's another story. If she had the means too, she would dispose of the body too. But in a public supermarket, with alarms on the back doors and camera's covering 75% of the place, she can't risk removing him at all. Still, with gloves on, she pulls his body into the last stall and pulls his pants down. She smiles as she notices he isn't gifted in the pants area, either.

"I would be mad too," she says as she spots his cocktail weenie. She sits him on the toilet, with what's left of his head and face, leaning on the wall. She clears the bathroom of all traces of her. The blood on the stall, the wall and the floor, she leaves there. She leaves the water on and plugs the sinks. The overflow will wash all the blood that's on the floor, down the drains, if it runs long enough. But surely before long, someone in the all night supermarket will do a bathroom check, to clean up.

I just hope they got a strong heart.

She exit's to the hallway, checks the camera's position. She waits until it rotates away from her, before she emerges into the back aisle. She grabs 3 large bottles of *Pace Picante sauce,* then runs to catch up with her family. She's just in time too, as Young D was about to head down from the diary section to see if she was alright.

"Did y'all get everything you want cooked?" she asks.

"Yea," Baby Boy says, "We're ready to check out."

"How about you?" Young D asks, "Did you clean good?"

Baby Boy laughs. Baby Girl smiles at her husband. Knowing he knows what's just happened.

"Always, baby," she says and smiles.

She knows, he knew what that bathroom break was all about. Whereas, the other 2 guys didn't.

Young D has learned how to read the signs. He didn't see the tail when they picked it up. But when she grabbed her *Get To Work* aka "Get to the money" shoulder bag, he knew shit was officially, in play. He also knows that his wife is a professional.

"Yes, I cleaned good, baby. And I didn't get none on me, either."

Baby Girl says that just to make the others laugh harder.

"You'd better not," Young D replies as he gives her a sweet kiss.

Baby Boy is making jokes about her getting shit stains on her clothes. DeJuan giggles slightly. They don't have a clue as to what Young D and Baby Girl are speaking on. One day, they might.

But for tonight, they checkout at the cashier, then head back to the 2 vehicles. Charles and the other chauffer had left them running, with the heat on. It's a cold December night, in *"The Big Easy."* The 4 of them load up in 1 of the Hummers, while the 2nd one, follows them. They head to the manor to cook, drink, smoke and enjoy each others company for a few hours.

Baby Boy still makes shit stain jokes, all the way down the highway. He can't get over himself. His jokes are very funny. For what he thinks actually happened. But the reason Young D and Baby Girl are laughing, is because they know the joke is on him. Baby Girl isn't sure why DeJuan *isn't* laughing. Maybe he thinks she'd think it disrespectful, to her. But she will find out later, that isn't the reason he keeps a straight face. That isn't the reason, at all.

Once at the manor, Baby Girl thanks them all for coming to share this 1st night back in the manor, with her.

The food is cooked and they eat in 1 of the 2, smaller dining rooms. Then they retire to the smoking parlor, for more liquor and smokes and a lot more family fun and laughs.

"Before I get a buzz. I have to say thanks to my big brothers, Soldier and Baby Boy for coming to look out on me. On my first overnight stay, back at the manor," Baby Girl says, "And to my husband. Who's always, right on time. Thanks, baby daddy, for having my back. *Always.*"

They laugh at the *"baby daddy"* comment before Young D says, "That's husband, to you."

"We're family, baby girl," Soldier says, "That's how we do it."

"For sho, baby girl. That's how we've always done it," Baby Boy adds, as they all have their fill of all that's offered. Soldier adds, "And ain't shit gonna change."

The after party has gone well. Now it's time for bed. Young D pulls Baby Girl up by the hand, pulling her to her feet.

"It's time to lay it down, my lady," he says with a devilish grin.

She follows him around the right side of the parenthesis shaped staircase. The side, their master section is on. They

97

enter the hallway, leading to the master section of the house. Which is 3 stories high. Finally, after passing through their master sitting room, the mini kitchen, the parlor and lounging area, they reach the stairs and elevator which leads to their spacious bedroom. He picks her up and carries her onto the elevator. He pushes the button for the 2nd floor. The master section of the manor is like a 3 story house, all by itself. With a huge bedroom suite that covers the entire 2nd floor. Along with the master bathroom, with his and her *everything*. The 3rd floor is another sitting area with a heated Jacuzzi, a Sauna and a small exercise room. Plus a huge balcony that wraps around the entire section, with outside stairs that lead to their bedroom balcony and their 1st floor balcony.

On the 2nd floor, in their bedroom, Young D lays his wife down gently on the bed.

"It's been a long day, Derrick," Baby Girl says.
He agrees with her. They undress and climb under the covers. He can't wait to talk about her job. He's fascinated by it. Though he loathes it, at the same time. He has a love/hate relationship with her profession.

"You did the muafucka that was in the grocery store. Didn't you?" he asks, as he cuddles her close to him.

"Yes."

"He was coming to kill you?" he asks for clarification.

"Yes."

"Then that part, I get," he says, "But why would he be after you now? Is there another mark y'all competing for?"
Young D definitely has a love/hate relationship with his wife's profession and Baby Girl never lies to him about it. She's schooled him on the ins and outs of her profession, as best she could. Without breaking any of the codes.

He knows her life is always at risk, in general. But in

her profession, the only way to become a mark, is:
1. *Have a price tag put on you.*
Which means someone pays money to a professional, to have you killed. In this case, the potential mark is notified by the family they work for, that money has been placed on their head.
2. *Have the package on a new mark which pays a lot of money.*
All the pros, worth their salt, want the top hits. They will eliminate the competition to insure that they are the 1 who gets to the mark and collects the reward. This is always an option to look into. For each time a pro receives a new mark. They can become a target, themselves.
3. *Become labeled as a tyrant or rollover, a snitch. Or a disloyal person.*
One who cannot be trusted. One who knows, no loyalty. Not even loyal to his or her own organization.
Young D knows what could make his wife a potential target. He lays there holding her, as he mentally eliminates the options he knows aren't in question.
Baby Girl is loyal to the Morales family crest and business. So option 3 is out. Now he's questioning whether someone has put a price on her head and he asks as much.
    "No," she replies, "I haven't received any notification of a hit on me. *Remember.* I told you that my family, most likely Gus, would notify me of a hit on me."
Then option 1 is out too.
    "Baby, do you have a job in play?"
    "I can't answer that, Derrick," she says, "You know that. And I do follow *all* codes and guidelines."
    "I can guess which option it is, baby," he says, "So you don't have to answer. But I see, asking you to stop, wasn't an option either. Ha?" he asks.

"Derrick, it's not that cut and dry," she explains, "If I just walk away from the organization when they need me. Then I could be seen as a tyrant. It's not gonna stop pro's nor the other families from trying to hit me. It will make them try to hit me, for sure. You know I'm daddy Don's, only *real* heir. The only one who can keep the Morales name in the top ranks. And in rankings with the Genolli's and Pantango's. If I just walk away. My family gets taken over," she says, "I can't do that to my family's honor. That includes all of you guys too. Plus our son and the one, on the way. We will be targets, *forever*. Even if they get me. That won't stop them. They'll take my heirs too."

"What are you doing to our sons?" he interjects.

"Derrick, that's not fair," she says.

"Fuck if it *ain't* fair," he says, "What's not fair, is my son could be motherless, *any* fuckin day. Or the one you're carrying could be dead now, if you hadn't got the jump on that fool at the store. What am I suppose to tell Lil Derrick, if that happens?"

"It won't happen," she says, "You don't have to tell him anything."

"Lovely, when is it ever gonna be the right time for you to stop cleaning?"

"When the USA docks are completely legitimate," she says, "When the drug trade stops. When the other family's stop seeking control of my family's empire."

"When, baby? Just tell me, *when?*" he asks desperately. He knows Baby Girl had been trained for this since she was 4 years old. The Don trained her. But Young D figured at that time, The Don was just simply teaching her another skill. And he had never said to her, "*I want you to be a hit woman.*" He thought he'd just trained her to be the best shooter. What

100

he doesn't get, is *the Don* trained her. *The Don did.* No one else can boast of that. Not even her biological father could've said that. None of the men who work or have worked for the Morales', can claim that. With the respect that everyone in the pro game has for the Morales name. They know Baby Girl *can't* quit. On principles, alone.

Young D is a fan of loyalty and he loves honor. He has always been torn over his wife's job. But at the same time, he understands her loyalty. He just wants to know when she'll stop. He just wants her to be okay. He just never wants to be without her. Or to live without her.

"So when can you stop, *per* the family crest and all that?" he asks.

"When I can be replaced with someone equal to my ability," she says.

"Damn. *Never.*" he states, as he lets out a deep sigh.
Suddenly, she straddles him in the bed and says,
"Derrick, I don't want this to be a problem for us. I never wanted that. That's why I kept the job on the low. It's why I never told you about it, in the first place."

"But people kept ending up *mysteriously* dead, in the places where we just happen to be," he says, "And the police started questioning my staff, at every other turn. And I still didn't get it. Not until I found the Jesus piece of my enemy, in your private stash. Back in two thousand and four."

"He was trying to find someone who did contracts," she says, "So he could have you hit. I told you that."
Information of a new hit or someone searching for a pro, gets delivered to each active family, eventually. The pro hits usually come through the Central Intelligence Agency aka The CIA. But for someone just trying to get someone killed. For instance, like Young D, wouldn't have that kind of priority. That would

101

be word of mouth. And it's usually carried out or through, by some crooked police officer. The word gets to the professionals eventually, if it's out there long enough. But these aren't the types of hits the professional families commission. That's small time. Young D's enemy had no status in the pro game. Thus, him and his request was small time. He was talking to gang members about wanting to put some change on Young D. He had been offering to pay $10k to have him killed. No one had stepped up to take the hit. The information eventually made it's way to another source, who reports to the families.

When the information reached the Morales' family, still no one had accepted the hit. Gus saw it and recognized Young D. He notified Baby Girl. She set up a meeting with the purchaser and gave him a bargain price of 7 grand, knowing he would bite and show up. He showed up for the meeting. She killed him, quietly. Then she took his money, his drugs and his jewels. She made it look like a street hit. Afterwards, she went back to her Morales manor office and killed the hit search on her husband, from his enemy. Which can be done at any time, from the computer in the Don's office. Anytime a pro with that software wants to dead a hit request. They can. The thing is, if they do kill the request. It will eventually be traced back to the computer, they'd done it on. If it's done without cause or permission by the purchaser, then the eraser can and will become a target.

But as far as the hit on Young D was concerned. There hasn't been and most likely, won't be anymore said about it. Because it was from street beefs in the music industry. And because Young D isn't in the murder-for-hire business, like Baby Girl is. Young D's situations are more about bluffing and/or boasting, then they are professional. Baby Girl still takes the bluffers out, regardless. For there is no way to tell if they have accessed a professional family or not.

"But you don't keep momentos from other marks," he says, "You take the weapons from pro's. So why did you keep a memento from him?"

"Because that one was personal," she says, "He wanted you killed. Not because of business, per say. But just because you had all the action, in Houston. That's dumb shit. Plus the bread was low. How are you gonna put a measly ten kay on my love?" she asks as she giggles, "Someone could've been desperate and took the offer. He was shopping a hit on the man that I love. The only man I fuck. He had to go."

"You came to New Orleans for a hit," he says.

He isn't asking but telling her.

"….And to shop for you and man. And to check on the progress of the renovations to the manor," she says, finishing his sentence.

"The dude, tonight. He was trying to snuff you out to keep you off a new mark," he says, "Is that right?"

"Yes, that's right."

"Who's the mark?" he asks, knowing full well she will never disclose that information.

Not even to him and not before a hit. He will have to wait until the mark is carried out. This is only 1 of the few times, Young D has known about a hit, before she actually did it.

"Derrick, you know I can't do that," she says as she laughs. "Not even when I know who it is. Which I don't yet."

"When do you find out?" he tries.

"I can't reveal that either, love," she says, "Why don't you just fuck me now. That would be the best way to get a rise out of me."

They both laugh. He has 1 more question.

"Do you think you'll ever retire?" he asks.

103

"When I'm dead or exposed or replaced," she says, "And I will have to train my replacement. Before the family will feel comfortable with letting me go."

"Train me," he suggests.

She smiles before saying, "Derrick, you're too emotional for the profession. You have to be *very* disciplined. Very much in control of your emotions."

"You're in control of yours. Except when I'm fuckin you," he boasts, "You let go, then."

"Hell yea, I do. I'll admit that," she says, "But that's because those are real emotions. I can't control those. A mark doesn't make me emotional. Because it's the job. And usually, they're strangers. Even the guy who wanted you killed."

"But he was personal, so you just kept something from him?" he asks.

"Yes."

"Have you ever done that before?" he asks.

"No."

"I'm ready to see some emotions from you," he says, pulling her down to him for a long kiss.

"Bring it out of me then, Derrick," she purrs, "Only you can do that."

And he does exactly that.

CHAPTER THREE
<u>GETTING IT IN</u>

Young D wakes up 6 hours later. He finds that Baby Girl is gone and she left a note for him, on her pillow. She'd also left his meal in their mini kitchen, for when he wakes up. The staff is already abuzz, around the manor. The note she left is telling him she has talked to their son in Houston and he needs to do the same. Because his junior is being a bit much for his grandmother to handle, without either of them there. It is now, 5 days before Christmas. She also reminds him to go shopping. In that part of her note, she writes; ....,
Of course, you have to get all of my gifts, Derrick. [I'm smiling]
☺ *So go to Lakeside Mall and don't be shy.* ☺
I love you, Lovely.

He smiles when he finishes reading the note. Then he gets out of bed and goes into their bathroom for his daily.
Looking at Baby Girl's vanity, he notices all of her personal items are still there. Her monogrammed watch, her wedding rings, her class ring, wallet, purse and cell phones. Her identification cards, credit cards and driver's license are still in her wallet. She has fakes for all of the above, obviously.
"She's on a job," he says to himself.
She always leaves her personal items behind. Just in case she gets caught up or killed. There would be nothing to positively ID her with. Nothing that would lead back to her family.
It wasn't until after she started the profession that she was able to understand why her real father, Big Dog, was so hard for her mother to get in touch with, back in the days.
But as it turns out, Young D isn't as understanding about it. As a matter of fact, he's worried to death.

If she was to get kidnapped from the house. I wouldn't even know it. If she was having an affair. I wouldn't no shit, either.

He's thinking all of this, to himself. Being her husband and her natural protector, this is what worries him the most. The chance that she could be laying dead somewhere. Or barely living and him not even knowing where to start the search.
I love you, Lovely. Just be careful, baby. Please.

Cherry warms his breakfast in the microwave and he eats. He's hearing sounds from voices in the house, which alerts him that the rest of the guest are starting to rise too.

It's 11am when he joins the others in the smoking parlor. They start back up from where they'd left off, over 6 hours ago. Their energy is slowly but surely rising, as they get their 1st high of the day and get wired up.
"We still gotta get gifts for our Lil *shorties*," Baby Boy says, "We may as well hit the stores. We don't have to be nowhere until tomorrow night."
They inquire about Baby Girl. Young D tells them, she's already out shopping for him and their son. Soon after their buzz kicks in, they all leave to go shopping and visiting family.

****

Baby Girl pulls onto the top floor of the parking garage, next to where the *Grand Casino* in Gulfport Mississippi, once stood. She parks her Caddy truck against the rail which faces north. It's noon. She has 1 hour, before her mark is to be near the premises. She looks over her itinerary, once more. Her target will be dining at Percale's restaurant. It's just across

across Highway 90, to the north of the hurricane Katrina battered casino property. The mark is scheduled to be there at 1pm, for lunch.

Baby Girl has a whole jacket on a mark, which is called a package. It contains pertinent information which assists her in making the hit go smoothly. For instance, what the mark did to become *a mark* and how he lived before becoming, *that mark*. The package she receives, gives her the information she needs to set up, get to and retire the mark. The more she knows about the mark before he or she is in play. The better it is for her to carry out her task. She'd received his package early. She reviewed it on the drive over. In just that amount of time, she's prepared. Behind the cover of her tinted windows, she prepares her weapon. She has timed the property security which still patrols the garage.

"Two vehicles, every fifteen minutes. Just like clockwork, they pass on the top floor," she observes aloud. "That's totally lacking and really, it's fucking *unacceptable*. If someone was being attacked up here. Or needed their help, immediately. They would perish. Fifteen minutes is a lifetime, in my business."

It's 12:35pm. Her mark is due to arrive at the property, across the street, in 25 minutes. Security has just past through again. In another 15 minutes, at 12:50, they'll be back through. From then, she'll have 10 minutes until her mark arrives at 1pm. And a 5 minute window, before security returns, at 1:05pm. *That's four and a half minutes longer than I'll need.*

At 12:50, security passes. As soon as they're out of her site, she runs down the stairs to the next level. She lets them pass her there. Then she leaves a detour sign for garage traffic. So no other cars will come to the top floor. She whips back up to the top floor and grabs her equipment from the truck. She doesn't even allow herself to think of how much faster she could move, if she wasn't almost 7-months pregnant. She positions her stand near the rail. Then slides her high powered rifle onto it and attaches her scope.

At 1pm, on the dot, her mark arrives. He gets out of his chauffeured limo, flanked by 2 women. She can see him through her binoculars. Now she searches for him, in her scope. She has him in her sights. In a split second, she fires. She sees him fall. She moves quickly. She grabs her equipment and loads it back into her truck. Then she jumps in, starts her engine and heads down toward the exit. When she reaches her detour sign, there are no vehicles approaching. She jumps out, grabs it and stashes it on her backseat. She drives on until she's out of the garage. Now, she has to be sure the mark is permanently down. So she turns left onto Highway 90. This allows her to pass right in front of Percale's, inconspicuously and before the show goes live, with police and EMS. She can see her mark laying prone. On his face. On the ground. The women who accompanied him, are frantic. Baby Girl leaves the scene, immediately as she tunes in her police scanner. That's where she'll have to listen for confirmation of her marks demise. If a mark isn't killed on the 1st attempt. That usually blows the hit. Because the mark usually hires bodyguards, security and surveillance. Depending on how prominent the mark is. And they are usually, very prominent. Baby Girl has never failed on a mark and she has no plans on that ever happening.

She takes a right onto Jeff Davis Boulevard, in Long Beach, Mississippi. She notices that there is still *very* visible damage from Hurricane Katrina, on the Mississippi Gulf Coast too. They were hit harder by wind and surge, then New

Orleans had been. New Orleans damages came, primarily from flood waters. Which was a result of the levees not holding up. Some say the levees were deliberately blown up. Baby Girl tends to support the latter. If there is ever a name released of someone who ordered that blow up, she would push to make it public. Then fund any group who demanded that person be charged, In the meantime, she would be shopping for that person's package. She'd love to get that package. No matter how many of them, there are. And she knows she would get the hits for the main culprits. The ones from government. *Local, state and federal.* Baby Girl often talks to herself while driving alone. Today is no different.

"They ain't doing shit to bring all those citizens back home. Hell, they got new plans circulating the city, for a whole new look. I hope the bitches responsible for the catastrophe, *after Katrina,* become marks. I would love to get some justice for my comrades and people who are still suffering. Still evacuated. And still homeless. *Kanye West* and *David Banner* was right. Bush and his GOP administration don't give a fuck about it's black citizens. And dare I add, they never have. The evacuees were called *fucking* refugees, for 3 *days*, for God sake. *Juvenile* was right too. City government don't give a fuck, either. They don't want the citizens of certain wards to ever come back. I would take any hit. From the city, on up to the top of this fucked up feeding frenzy, in Washington DC. I don't give a fuck about them either. The feeling is mutual. All of that shit needs to be exposed."

She reaches Interstate 10, merges west and heads back to New Orleans. She passes the Diamondhead exit and pops in a *Juvenile* CD to ride too. As *400 Degreez* plays *Intro*, she reminisces about her life back in 1998, when this CD was at the top of the charts.

First and foremost, she still had all of her parents. It was the summer before her sophomore year of college and before she became a *professional cleaner*. She was just Don Morale's only daughter and the heir to a multi-billion dollar empire. Which had been in existence for 60 years. With the top disposal organization, for the last 30 of those 60 years. She was the heir to a billion dollar estate, complete with a staff who had businesses for which she would inherit a piece of, as well. She was set for life, already. And most of her friends wondered why she had even bothered to go to college. That was those friends who didn't have a clue of how to keep money. Even if they had managed to be lucky enough to make some. To her, back then, the manor was just a nice place to bring her brothers and friends from the wards. For free swimming, food, relaxation and a piece of the good life. Those were the trouble free days. The days before she had to be responsible for someone, other than herself. Now she's a wife, a mother and a big sister too. Her own mother had passed on, after both of her fathers died. She doesn't have any grandparents left either. Only step relatives, which really amounts to her having to be self sufficient. Because the price of her leaning on them, is just too high. They always wanted something in return. Something worth far more than whatever it was she had gone to them for or about. *Notorious B.I.G.* said it best when he said, *Mo Money, Mo Problems*. Listening to the song *Ha*, she sings along as she does a lot more thinking.
That's you ridin in that bad ass Benz, ha?.....................,
That's you that can't keep a ole lady, cause you keep fuckin her friends, ha?

Life was so much simpler then. The worst tragedies she had known by 1998, was the deaths of *Eazy E, Tupac and Biggie.*

110

"Those was the good ole days," she says to herself. "They still call me, Baby Girl. But I'm a woman now, with all the responsibilities that come with it."

By the time the remix of *Ha* featuring *Jay-Z* is playing, she has reached the city limits of New Orleans. She drives over the river to the west bank and back to the manor. She drives back to the staff section of the estate, to see Gus about her issue. Then she heads back up to the main house.

She knew her husband would still be there. But she's happy to see her brothers Soldier and Baby Boy have hung around too.

"Hey, baby girl!" Soldier yells as she walks into the parlor. "Where the hell have you been, all day?"

"I went to see six nine," she lies. Knowing they haven't seen nor spoken with them. Because none of them have been on speaking terms since the label split up, years back.

The guys have shopping bags strewn all over the place. As they scramble to hide certain items and bags, she giggles and says, "Oh y'all hiding your bags from me. I'm gonna have a merry Christmas. Aren't I?"

"Don't you always?" Young D says as he's reentering the parlor.

She kisses him with passion, then he says,

"Your son said you need to come home. He wants you."

"I know he does," she says, "He told me to come home, this morning. That's where I'm heading, from here. What about you?"

"I gotta head back too," he says, "The tour is still going on. We need to get back to the tour bus."

"Yes, we got Dallas, in two days and Wichita Falls, two

111

days before Christmas," she says, giving him the update on his itinerary. "We can fly back to Houston for Christmas Eve and Christmas day, after that."

"Cool," Young D says as he follows her up the stairs. This time and to their master suite, so he can witness her take. They go into their bedroom. She opens her Black *Louis Vuitton Carry all Innsbruck* bag, which she'd actually just gotten filled when she settled up with Gus Davis. Inside of the bag, there is $250,000. Young D is taken back when he opens the bag and sees nothing but 100 dollar bills, in 25 neat stacks of ten thousand dollars per bundle.

"Damn! Who the fuck did you hit? Bin Laden?" he asks and they both laugh.

"Some potential casino owner," she says, "Somebody didn't want him to bid on those properties."

"What properties?" he asks.

"What's left of the casino properties, in Mississippi," she says.

"You went to the *Sip*?" he asks, in shock.

"Yes," she answers calmly, with a smile.

He smiles and shakes his head, as he places her wedding rings back on her finger. He plops down on the bed, then lies back.

"What?" she asks, as she can sense there is another question coming.

"I take it you got him, ha?" he asks.

"Yes. My police scanner confirmed him dead at the scene," she answers, "So I went right on to Gus, for my cheese. Before coming here."

She picks up the Louis bag and dumps the crisp stacks of money, all over him as he lays on the bed.

She says, "I'll make it rain for Christmas, Derrick."

He smiles.

Then she says, "And I need to get emotional before we leave the manor."

"Let me help you wit that," he offers.

He grabs her hair, first thing and pulls her into him. Kissing her very aggressively, as he adds,

"I was so worried about you, baby."

He sucks hard on her neck, as he whispers, "I always drive myself crazy. Wondering if you made it out, okay."

"I'm okay, Derrick," she whispers back, before she comments on his present actions. She says,

"Oh, baby. This feels so good to me. You know how to bring me back home, just right."

He takes 1 of her nipples into his mouth and suckles it, like he's starving. She kisses his face and forehead. Anywhere else on him that she can get her lips on. He's overheated and ready. His hands seem to be covering every inch of her body, simultaneously. He can't wait any longer. They strip, quickly. He enters her, immediately. She gives off a long moan and says,

"Oh, baby! I need you. I need to feel you."

He goes to work, instantly. Suddenly, the bed isn't daring enough for him. He pulls her to the edge of the bed, so he can put 1 of his feet on the floor. With this new leverage, he's able to go deeper, faster and harder and with more consistency. He's fucking her with everything he has, as she squeals,

"Oh Derrick! Oh baby! Fuck me, baby!"

"Ah, it's so good, Lovely," he whispers, "I need you too, baby."

He churns and pumps his ass harder and faster, still. She's sliding off of the bed. Her momentum takes them down to the floor. But that doesn't stop anything. He rolls over on his back. Pulling her up, on top of him.

"Ride your cowboy, Lovely," he orders.

113

She obliges him, as she takes him into her, slowly. She's moaning as his hard dick invades her and fills her to capacity.

"Oh, baby," she moans, "Damn. I'm horny, Derrick."

"I ain't mad at that, Lovely."

He pushes up into her, in rhythmic strokes, which drives her wild. He's caressing her breast with 1 hand. While massaging her throbbing clitoris with the other. There are sounds coming from her, that are a major turn on for him. She feels a tingle in her lower spine. He wants her to wet his dick and he tells her as much. He works her pussy, the way he needs too.

Within minutes, she cums loud and long. It feels as if the room is rumbling. There's an earthquake taking place, right on top of him. With the measurements of a perfect 10, on the Richter scale. He slides her back toward the bed and leans her against it, face down. He enters her from behind. He rams his dick, back inside of her. He's feeling as though he could get his nut, any second now. But he doesn't want to cum. Not right away. He wants her to have, at least 2 orgasms, before he gets his. He wants her to be able to relax. She always sleeps good, after he fucks her well. She needs to rest for the upcoming birth of their 2nd son, which she's carrying beautifully, right now. He loves the extra heat her pussy has, when she's carrying his seeds too. It makes sex even more intense. As if they needed anymore intensity. He starts to moan and gasp while fucking her, doggy style.

"Lovely, girl this pussy is good, baby," he oozes.

He's very near an explosive orgasm but he doesn't want to cum. He doesn't want to be done yet. He pulls out, rolls her over and opens her pussy with his fingers. He puts his face in it. Sticking his tongue as far into her hot moist box, as he can get it. She screams, as waves of that previous earthquake sends aftershocks through her body. Which causes her to jerk and gyrate. As if she's suffering from some sort of seizure. She grabs his head and holds on, as his tongue plays a symphony of tag with her rock hard clitoris. She's wetting his lips and mouth with a brand new orgasm, within seconds. While he conducts her orchestra of ecstatic moans with his stiff tongue, which is sure to bring on even more wetness.

"I'm loving it, Derrick," she moans.

"I'm loving it too baby," he whispers, "I can't get enough of you."

He licks her until she slows her gyrations to a slow churn. Then he brings her face to his crotch. Though she was already heading that way. She knows the rest. She stimulates the tip and the head of his dick, as he moans and lays his head back. She can feel his dick vibrating in her mouth. His climax is on deck. She takes his dick into her mouth and sucks it down her throat, as far as she can, without having a gag reflex. He's trembling so bad, he has to lean against the bed. He's moaning and holding her head with both hands, as he guides his dick in and out of her mouth. He can't hold it, anymore. He grips her head hard. She can hear his breathing pattern change. He's still trying to prolong his climax but it just isn't going to work. She's sucking him and talking shit to him, at the same time. She's asking for his sweet nut and he lets her have it. She keeps it all and swallows him like she'd learned to do, back in college. He's done. He falls back on the bed, pulling her with him.

"Let's get a nap before time for us to leave," he says, breathlessly.

"Perfect," she moans, as she cuddles up close to him.

They fall asleep, sweaty and satisfied. The $250,000 is still scattered on the bed and floor, around them.

Houston, Texas

It's Christmas eve. Young D and Baby Girl are at their Houston home, with their son Derrick Jr. Her 3 younger brothers; Danny, Bruce and Jordan are in Houston from Mississippi, for the holiday season. Young D's mother, Annie, has just shown up to pick up her grandson and Jordan. They're going to spend the night at her home. Annie's home is at the front of this large Houston property. Danny and Bruce are hanging out with Young D's labelmates. While Young D and Baby Girl wrap gifts for everyone and assemble toys for Jordan and Derrick Jr.

"What time are y'all bringing Santa Claus over?" Annie asks, with a laugh.

"Before sunlight," Young D says.

"If you make it home by then," his mother Annie adds.

"I'm chillin' tonight, mama," Young D replies, "You know the holidays are for family, right?"
He laughs at himself while Baby Girl rolls her eyes at him. Young D *has been* unfaithful, a time or 2, during their 10 year relationship. And even during their 4 and a half years of marriage. He has many females claiming him. Especially since the fame from his Hip-Hop career kicked in. It seems as if the outside women come in flocks. But Baby Girl takes it all in stride. She's never been insecure about any relationship. And certainly not her relationship with Young D. However, she has had to fight a few times. But Young D always seems to control his *"bitches and ho's"*, so they're not in Baby Girl's path. After his *"holidays are for family"* comment, Annie gives him the hand to talk too, as they walk her outside and up the walkway, to the largest home on Young D and Baby Girl's, 55 acre estate.

There are 5 family homes on this land now. With 2 having been completed, 2 months ago. 1 house is massive. He built that 1 for his mother, his sister, his stepbrother and his grandparents. It has 9 bedrooms and 5 full baths. Plus 3 half baths, a huge waterfall fountain, out front, a swimming pool, hot tub, basketball and tennis courts.

The 2nd home is for him, Baby Girl and their family. It has 6 bedrooms and 3 full baths. Plus 2 half baths. It's situated 100 yards behind his mother's home, the main house. It almost reminds Baby Girl of the servants quarters at Morales manor. Or a pool house at a large estate. It's a huge home, in itself. But when you compare it to Annie's home, it's smaller in stature.

The other 3 homes are regular sized family homes with 4 bedrooms, 3 baths and a half bath, in each. In the 3 homes is where his labelmates stay. They're also used for when they have out-of-town guest, which they have, quiet often.

Baby Girl and Young D put Derrick Jr to bed, at Annie's house and kiss him goodnight. Annie says Jordan can stay up until 10p.m.

"Okay. We'll be back over here with all of the gifts and all of their stuff, in about three hours," Baby Girl says to Annie, as her and Young D make their way out the door.

"Make that five hours," Young D says as he chuckles. "I've gotta have some daddy time too."

Annie laughs as she pushes him out the door behind Baby Girl and says, "I don't know anybody in this world that have sex as much as y'all do."

"Maybe we should enter Guinness," Young D jokes.

Baby Girl says so long to his mother and pulls him along the concrete path with her.

"It's not too chilly tonight, either," she says.

"It don't seem like it's Christmas eve," he adds, "Except for all the decorations and the money I spent."

They return to their home and begin the task of wrapping presents and putting together toys, before the house phone rings. Young D grabs the phone.

"Yeah. What up?" he answers.

It's Six Nine and Kid, calling to wish Baby Girl and the boys a Merry Christmas. Kid is on the other end.

"Let me speak to my baby sister," Kid says, in a disrespectful tone.

"Not until you speak to me first, nigga," Young D says, "You called *my* house."

In a very dry tone, Kid says "What up and Merry Christmas. Now can I speak to Baby Girl?"

Young D passes the cordless to his wife and says, "That nigga still haven't accepted us, after eleven *motherfuckin'* years."

Baby Girl can hear, in her husbands voice, that he's pissed. That angers her, as well.

"Hello?" she says.

"Hey, Baby Girl," Kid says, "You ready for Christmas?"

"As ready as we're gonna be," she says, "Are y'all ready?"

"Yea. We're good, ma," he says, "We got some things for all the boys. Here go Six Nine. We need to know where to bring them too."

He gives Six Nine the phone before she can say anything else.

"Hey, Lil Lovely!" Six Nine says with excitement.

He's in a great mood. He sounds totally opposite of what Kid had sounded like. But he always does.

"Hi, biggest brother. How are you doing?"

"I'm good," he says, "It's mad quiet around the house, since you and my baby son moved out. I'm about to get paranoid."

She laughs loud as she remembers the hundreds of times, her brother had demanded she turn down the stereo or the surround sound. She lived with him for the next 3 years, after Wanda died.

"Six Nine, you don't ever call him your son. Until you're trying to make me feel guilty for not bringing him to see you," she says with a laugh and switches him to speakerphone.

"Well, I haven't seen him since last Christmas," he says.

"Why not? He's been in Gulfport, going to school," she says, "I tell you that, every time we talk."

She backs him into a proverbial corner. He has no response. Other than a chuckle. Six Nine doesn't have beef with Young D. Only Kid does. But in Kid's presence, Six Nine acts rather weird. It's obvious he has a hard time choosing between his siblings. He wishes his label was still 1 big happy family. But that will never happen again and they all know that.

"We need to get these toys and gifts, to you," Six Nine finally says. *"Can you meet us, somewhere?"*

Young Dee can hear the conversation. He chimes in.

"Bring it to the house," Young D interjects, "You drove all the way to Houston. Come on over."

Six Nine accepts instantly but for Kid, it takes a bit more jousting. He finally says he'll come with Six Nine. But that was only to get them off the phone and into the car.

"We'll come and meet y'all on Lil York. Right off the expressway," Young D says, "And y'all can trail us back."

Young D and Baby Girl lock up their house, immediately. They take Young D's, 2007 Avalanche and meet Six Nine and Kid on Lil York, as planned. But when they arrive, they find out the plans have changed and Six Nine and Kid won't be trailing them to their home, after all. Baby Girl figures she'll try to change that decision. They load all of the gifts and toys onto the back of the Avalanche and tie them down.

Then Baby Girl asks, "Are y'all gonna come to our house?"

"Nah. We gotta get back to New Orleans," Six Nine says, "We gotta play Santa Claus, in the morning too."

She knows Kid had gotten to Six Nine while her and Young D was driving to meet them.

She hugs them both and says, "Well next year. Why don't we all do Christmas at the Manor. Or here, at the main house?"

No one responds, right away. Young D and Kid glare at each other. Neither of them speak a word to the other, during the entire meeting. That breaks Baby Girl's heart to see that they still feud because her and Young D are together.

"We'll have to see about that, Lil sis," Six Nine offers. Him and Kid load into their Escalade and head for the interstate. While Baby Girl and Young D return to their north Houston estate, with all the toys and gifts in the Avalanche.

In the Escalade, on the way back to New Orleans, Kid is not in a pleasant mood.

"That nigga fuckin over Baby Girl, like it's a sport," he expresses to Six Nine during their ride.

"She loves him, Kid," Six Nine says, "They have a whole decade invested. Neither one of them wanna walk away from that. They got a pretty good life, going for them. Give it a chance."

"Fuck that shit!" is Kid's response. "She still don't know what that nigga doing, right under her *fuckin* nose."

"Baby Girl is only innocent to us, Kid," he says, "She knows more than you give her credit for."

Kid turns his head and looks out the window. He's not in the mood for positive conversation about Baby Girl and Young D's relationship. He's never accepted it and he never will.

CHAPTER FOUR
TAKIN' HITS!

"Do you think Lil Man will like this truck?" Baby Girl asks.
Her and Young D are back at the house, after meeting her brothers and getting the presents from the boys.
"Yea. Anything he can get in and move or drive. He's wit it," Young D says as they chuckle.
"He already has a Benz, to drive around in, from last Christmas," she recounts, "Now he's getting a Hummer H Two, to go with it."
"We're gonna have to get him a double garage to handle all of his whips," Young D jokes, "Our new baby boy got a lot of presents in here too."
"Yes, Derrick. We got him a gang of stuff, already," she agrees, "We don't have anything left to buy, before he's born."
"Oh but his daddy will think of something," he says as they gather the things to take to his mothers house, for later this morning.
In just a few hours, their son and Jordan will be buzzing around the huge family Christmas tree, in Annie's living room, tearing open presents.

Christmas day is wonderful. Derrick Jr clowns with his toys. But there's 1 in particular, that he doesn't care for, a whole lot. It's the toy pony. It's 1 he can ride but there's still a problem. The pony doesn't move around. He can only rock, back and forth on it and he wants it to move.
"I not like dis boney," 2 year-old Derrick Jr exclaims, "Boney is a big dummy."
Young D cracks up laughing at his son. Which makes his son

laugh too. Annie steps in and promises Derrick Jr, she'll rectify the situation.

"We'll get rid of that dummy boney, if my baby don't want it here," she says as she giggles with him.

"Nana's not gonna let no *dummy* boney stay at *her* house." Derrick Jr smiles, handsomely. He's satisfied that his dilemma is a top priority. Baby Girl is agitated with her son, just a little.

"He's being ungrateful, y'all," she says, "He should be happy, just like any other kid would be. To have all of this stuff for Christmas. But he wants a real pony. A *real pony*. He has real horses. There are lots of horses at the manor. Pponies too. He just thinks he's suppose to have them here, as well. I don't want y'all to curtail to Lil Man 's, *every* wish. He owns horses and ponies. He'll ride them when we're in New Orleans. But this property isn't going to be wild kingdom. He'll have to wait until he goes to New Orleans, to ride a *real* pony."

They all laugh at her wild kingdom comment. She doesn't laugh. She just looks at her husband because she knows he's going to go all out, trying to get his 1st born and namesake, a real pony, here in Houston. He senses his wife's disdain and looks at her, as if she's being underhanded.

"He's gotta have it though, baby," Young D says with sad eyes and a slight grin.

Derrick Jr is displaying the saddest eyes ever too, while his father pleads his case for him.

"He has four ponies at the manor, already," Baby Girl says, "This case is closed."

She's over it. Young D isn't helping matters any, as he eggs on his son's demands. With the same sad eyes his junior is displaying, he says, "Maybe he's gonna be a cowboy."

Again, they all laugh. She can't help but chuckle at his comment.

****

At the Manor, early Monday morning, Alfred and Addie Mae conduct the weekly staff meeting, as usual. Before they start their routines. They not only go over the weekly plans for the grounds and meals. But they also go over the agenda for the spring bazaar which is held at Morales Manor, every year. While Addie and Alfred are passing out the itineraries, Gus breaks the silence with 1 of his many complaints. Something he's always been known to do.

"I've been working for this manor for nearly thirty five years," Gus says, "And still, I feel like a damn errand boy. I need to be able to have access to the main office. To insure that I'm doing my job, the best that I can do it. Especially since Don's been gone. I should be running my section of this enterprise."

"Lovely is in charge," Alfred says, "She'll handle things, the way she sees fit. If you have a problem with any part of your job. From salary to more work or less work. Take it up with her."

"She's not here enough, to run things," Gus tries.

"Everything is running just as smooth as it was, ten years ago," Addie Mae says, "Just hush up, Gus. You ole fool. You always come up with these complaints that never go *anywhere*."

The staff giggles as Gus Davis continues,

"She's somewhere, pregnant anyway. She's got six or seven other places to live in and manage. I don't think she's gonna be able to run it all. Not and be a mother and wife too."

"She's doing a hell of a job, with all of them," Cherry adds with a smile. "Master Don taught her, very well."

"And she's as smart as a whip," Charles adds.

123

Seeing that everyone's against him, as usual. Gus wisely backs off.

"I'll have her to give you a meeting, if you would like me too," Alfred tells Gus.

"Hell *no*. I don't want no meeting," Gus says, "What I want is to feel like I'm worth something, around here. Instead, y'all keep me down the way, in a darn dungeon."

"Gus, that's the place you picked out," Addie Mae says as she chuckles. "We all have the same accommodations. And mine is just fine. Plenty of room for my grandbabies to run around in."

Gus decides to be quiet for the rest of the meeting. He knows Baby Girl is the one who will have to upgrade him. If it's ever going to happen. But she's on maternity leave, preparing to have her and Young D's, 2nd son. Addie Mae and Cherry are flying to Houston to be with her. Meanwhile, Gus pouts throughout the meeting while *none* of the staff pay him any mind. In the senior staffs opinion, he's lucky to still have a job at the manor and he should shut up and be grateful.

****

On March 22, 2007, Young D turns 26 years old and welcomes his 2nd born son, Don Prince, into the world.

"You know why we keep having boys, right baby?" he whispers to Baby Girl as she drifts into a much needed sleep. "Because your pussy is so good. Women make boys. Remember that."

She smiles slightly and drifts off to sleep. She's very groggy from the Demerol she was given, during labor and delivery.

Young D walks out into the lobby where the remainder of their family and friends are waiting on news of the new boys

124

arrival. DeJuan is standing guard and only allowing those they know, to get near the family waiting area.

"It's another boy, family!" Young D screams as he hugs Soldier, Baby Boy and the rest of the family.

Annie goes in to check on Baby Girl and the baby. Young D's sister Angela, goes in with her. Baby Girl is sound asleep. They sit down in her room and hold Don Prince while Baby Girl sleeps.

"My brother makes some beautiful babies," Angela says, smiling at her new nephew. "He's got the fattest jaws."

"They named him Donovan Prince Morales-Blake. After Don Morales," Annie tells her, "This here is, *The Don.*" They share a smile before talking with the nurse, on duty. She tells them that young Donovan is perfectly healthy and Baby Girl is doing just fine. That's good news to all.

Addie Mae and Cherry are still here. They had accompanied them, in labor and delivery. Just like they'd done with Derrick Jr. They knew Baby Girl would want them there. Since Wanda is no longer living. Addie Mae is her Godmother. She had Christened Baby Girl when she was 2 years-old. Right after Don and Wanda got married. Cherry is the Godmother to Derrick Jr. They will both be Godmother to Don Prince. Cherry is going to tell Baby Girl about Gus' behavior at the Spring bazaar meeting. But she'll do it after she's rested and recovering.

Derrick Jr gets to hold his brother and he's not willing to give him back. Not until his father takes him.

"That my baby, daddy?" he asks, in his 2 year-old broken language.

"This is your brother, Lil Man ," Young D says, "This is *my* baby. Just like you're my baby."

His pint sized namesake, whom everybody chooses to call Lil

man, doesn't like that answer. He bucks against his father, for the next 5 minutes, trying to make him give him his little brother back. It doesn't happen and soon, Lil Man tires himself out and takes a nap in his mothers room.

March has been a busy month for Young D and it's not over yet. Not only does he welcome a new son into the world. He also drops his 1st *SoundScan* cd, opens his own clothing store called *Houston's Finest* and a new restaurant called *H-Town Cuisine*. His label finds a home with *Atlantis Records,* instead of *Unity*. His label letterhead reads; *H-Town/Atlantis Records*. His mother Annie is put in charge of the label. His younger sister Angela manages the clothing store, along with his step-brother Corleone Blake and his grandparents run the restaurant. Young D signed many acts to his label, this year. He has his homeboys from Houston, which includes his best friend DeJuan, who has been with him since they were in 3rd grade. He signed *Gat em* and *High Top,* as well. The 3 of them along with Young D are collectively known as, *The Kilo Clique*. He signs *Big Daddy,* out of Miami. A veteran rapper who's been in the game, for years. *Big Daddy* had done time in jail and needed a hook up so he could get back on the scene and on his feet. Young D always listened to and liked his music. So when he heard Big Daddy was looking for a music home, he sought him out and signed him, on the spot.

His other acquisition is a group from California called; *The PA or The People's Army*. They're veterans, as well. They're most notable for working with some of the most influential, most loved and most significant rappers in Hip-Hop History. Young D's label is expected to do very big things, in a hurry.

They celebrate Derrick Jr or Lil Man's, as he's called, 2nd birthday in April. His nickname is Lil Man, just as his daddy's had been, when he was a toddler. To celebrate his 2nd year on earth, Lil Man has a birthday party fit for a prince. With all of the extras, including *real* pony rides. He is *ecstatic*.

Today, Baby Girl and Young D pay homage to *Big Proof* of the Group *D-12* from Detroit. Young D calls the members of the group to show that he's thinking of them, on this the 1-year anniversary of Big Proof's death. He was killed on Lil Man's 1st birthday. After Lil Man's party last year, Young D and Baby Girl flew to Detroit to be with the group.

Not willing to stop with the royal treatment he's shown to his Jr, Young D puts together a surprise trip for the 4 leading ladies in his life. His wife Baby Girl, his mother Annie, his sister Angela and his grandmother Pat, are the 4 women he's been working tirelessly for. He had to accomplish this surprise without alerting either of them. Which was quite the task, because Baby Girl is *very* sharp. With help from the staff at the manor, he's managed to pull it off. He's going to present it to them on Mother's day. He'll have an extra surprise for his wife too. Surprising Baby Girl, proves hard to do because of her profession. But he's determined to make it work, just once.

It's mid-May. Mother's Day is wonderful around the Blake estate. Baby Girl, Annie, Pat and Angela are treated to the time of their lives. Each of them receive a 5 day/4 night stay, in St. Tropez. With no kids and no men. Just the 4 of them, being wined, dined and pampered for the entire 5 days. Of course, Young D ignores his own *no men* rule. After he'd added it to the trip description. He then charters a flight in for the last 2 of the 4 nights and shares Baby Girl's cabana. His excuse is that he has already gone 6 weeks without sex,

127

following the birth of their youngest son, Don Prince.

"I had to stay out of my pussy for six weeks," he whispers to her, after finishing an energetic session of sex.

"I got a lot of time to make up for."

"Derrick, you know good and well we didn't wait six weeks," she says as she laughs.

"Almost," he tries, as he chuckles.

"No way. We made it for three and a half weeks," she says, "Not even four."

"But that's six, for me," he says as he laughs.

She can see his point and agrees, as they laugh more. They enjoy the final 2 days in St. Tropez, with the other 3 ladies in his life.

They head back to Houston, on day 5 and start the preparations for their Annual Memorial day Bar-B-Q at the Blake estate. This years event will be 1 of the biggest, to-date. For more than just the food, folks and fun. But there's a cloud which has hung over Baby Girl and Young D's marriage for more than a half decade. This cookout will bring things into a perspective view, like never before.

****

It's Memorial Day weekend and the entire clan are ready for this huge Annual Bar-B-Q. This is a long standing tradition in Young D's family. It has been since, before him and Baby Girl got together. But this year, Baby Girl's quirks about 1 of the guest are intensified. She has had these uneasy feelings for the last 6 years of their relationship. It will finally come to a head, in 2007.

Back in 2001, 6 years ago, a female named Kierra Ramsay had shown up at the BBQ, claiming Baby Girl's soon-

128

to-be husband, as her man. Baby Girl had a huge problem with that claim, back then. She had confronted Kierra about it and Kierra had reiterated her claim. Baby Girl wiped up the grounds with her, that year. Still, Kierra returns, event after event. And for *some* reason, Young D's family seems to welcome and tolerate her. Baby Girl hates that part. Young D ignores Kierra, for the most part. But Baby Girl can tell there's friction between them. She wants to know why. She has asks Young D, many times and the answer is always the same. He always says, "She don't mean anything to me. We had a fling, once."

"So all of a sudden, she's like family?" Baby Girl would say.

"No, baby. She's not family," he would respond, "She's cool with my sister and my mama."
Baby Girl never liked that answer either. But she took it in stride. She resolved that she would have a sit down with Annie and Angela, to try and come to some kind of understanding as to exactly what Kierra meant to this family. She hadn't done the sit down, thus far. But that's only because she wants to observe their actions, this year. She never wanted to ruin the event for everyone, by causing a scene. So she'd kept her emotions in tact, since the fight in 2001. Baby Girl is determined to make this an enjoyable event, for all involved, again this year.

As the event gets underway, security has to secure, then direct an entourage of trucks into the property. To Baby Girl's surprise, she see the SUV's which are arriving, are from New Orleans. She expects Soldier, Baby Boy, G-Dog and their families to come. They always attend their events, in Houston. But the trucks that are coming in right now, are filled with Six Nine, Kid and Geezy, along with their families and friends.

Baby Girl is super excited.

"Oh my God!" Baby Girl screams as she runs to them, "I'm so happy y'all came. Why didn't y'all tell me, you was coming?"

"D invited us, right after Christmas," Six Nine says, "And we got a new nephew to see."

"Yea. We're gonna come see family, baby girl," Kid adds, "You gotta know that."

"How are you doing, baby girl?" Geezy chimes in.

"I'm good. Are y'all good?" she asks, still smiling big as they all answer, affirmative.

"I'm good but you still talk funny," Geezy teases.

"Alright," she says as she giggles, "I'll *still* get you for that too."

Geezy has always teased her with that comment. Every since the 1st day they met. She's learned to just laugh at it, lately. They all unload and she shows them to the inside of the main house, where they can freshen up.

Kierra arrives at the same time as her brothers do. Kid seems to know this girl, a little *too well* for Baby Girl's comfort. She's following him toward the house. Until DeJuan steps to her and shows her which direction she's welcomed in. Baby Girl watches her.

Who the fuck is this bitch, to my family?

She doesn't say anything. She observes Kierra, her buddies and Kid, all day, from a distance.

The event is *pretty much* drama free. Lil Man is a clown, much like his father and he looks exactly like him.

Young D is a dark skinned, tall, medium built man with smooth skin. He has the darkest eyes, Baby Girl has ever seen on a man. He has long hair which he keeps in braids, most of

130

the time. He's a very vibrant and sexual man. Much like she was told her real father and the Don had been. Only Baby Girl always adds Young D's credentials, in a matter-of-fact tone, to get the point across, *thoroughly*.

"Derrick isn't leaving his family. Nor is he starting any other ones," she always says.

"He's married to me. The only mother of his only children. And he has provided on his own, *four* of the eight homes that we own."

She's exactly right. Young D bought 4 homes on his own. The 5th one they built together. The other 3 homes, she inherited. Baby Girl can't help but notice the similarities between Derrick's features and those her real father had.

"I guess I'm attracted to the same thing my mama liked, in the beginning," she says to Young D.

"And the end too, for you," he says as they both chuckle. "But you see, that's why she gave us her blessings. She knew you was gonna see me, regardless. She thought I was handsome too," he says with a boyish grin.

Their son sees his father clowning and joins in, instantly.

"I guess he stuntin like his daddy," Geezy says as they all laugh.

~Get buck wit me, watch me do the damn thang, get buck wit me, watch me do the damn thang. ~

Suddenly, Baby Girl's phone rings. It's the Gus Davis contact ring tone, which plays the hit single, *Get Buck* from Nashville rapper; *Young Buck*. She remembers all of the stuff she's been told about how Gus talked trash about her and her handling of the Manor estate matters. But she isn't going to alert him, that she knows. She's just going to observe his behavior from here

On. The same way she's doing with Kid and Kierra. She answers her cell phone, playfully.

"Hi, family," she says while smiling.

"Hello, Lovely Girl. Happy Memorial day," Gus says, "And happy belated mother's day."

He sounds like he's in a very festive mood.

"Thanks. Same to you," she says "You should've come over here."

"I'm in route now, actually," he reveals, "I'm calling for directions."

She tells him to stop at the next exit. Her and Young D will come meet him and guide him in. He does.

They go meet him and he trails them back to their Houston estate. Young D is curious. He knows Gus is her agent. He wonders why he's in Houston. And he asks as much.

"Who's on the list now?" Young D asks his wife.

"You know, *awwwwwwwwready*, that I can't tell you that," she says and they both laugh.

They pull back into their estate, park and go back to the festivities. But Young D is still curious. He watches Gus, throughout the cookout. Baby Girl does too. Gus is spending a lot of time, talking with Kid. Then he moves away from him and closer to Baby Girl and Young D's house. Kierra is still seated next to Kid, where she's been, all day.

But later, when Kid does move from his seat next to her, Gus moves too. They both walk away from the other party guest and even closer to their home. Baby Girl notices them go inside of her house, when they think no one is paying attention to them. Neither of them have asks her or Young D, to go inside. She knows they both know the rules. Gus can't even come up to the manor without announcing it, first. Yet, him and Kid have just walked into her and Young D's house and

132

closed the door. And Kid's arrogant ass doesn't even speak to Young D before doing so. Nor when he's around him.

"The nerve," Baby Girl says to herself.

She eases around to the side of her house, slides in through the garage door and enters through the kitchen. She wants to know what they're up too. She gets a good visual on them and stays put, to see exactly what they're sneaking around for. She witnesses Kid receive a package, like the ones Gus does for her. *What the hell?*

She continues to observe. She has to be sure of what she's seeing, before she steps to them. If it's a mark, and she can't think of anything else that's packaged that way, then she wonders who the mark is and why is he giving it to Kid, in the first place. She has to halt this process, so she rings Gus' cell phone as she makes her way back outside of the door.

"Hi, Lovely Girl," he answers, "What can I do for you?"

"I need to speak with you, right now," she says, "Can you meet me at my house. The second biggest one, in the back?"

"Coincidentally, that's where I am now," he reveals.

"*What?*" she asks acting surprised, "How are you in my house and I don't know it? Does Derrick know you're there?"

"No. Kid brought me in," he says, "We didn't think it would be a problem."

"Does Derrick know Kid is in our home?" she asks, "Because he hardly speaks to my man. The nerve of him to be inviting anyone into our home. But when we invite him, he doesn't even show up."

"Well, he's here now," Gus says.

"Uh huh. Well the both of you need stay there," she

133

says, "I'm on my way down to the house and I'll need to clear the air, with both of you."

As she heads around to the front of her house, she's still wondering why is Kid getting a package and who the hell is the mark. She walks onto her porch and reaches to open the storm door, while being conscious of staying calm. At the same time, she's opening the storm doom, Kid is opening her front door and leaving out.

"Hey, Lil sis," he says jubilantly. "My nephews are looking fine, Baby Girl."

"Thanks Kid," she says, "We're doing our best to be good parents."

Kid kisses her cheek and rejoins the cookout. She goes on in to meet Gus, in the Parlor. Knowing she'll deal with Kid, momentarily.

"What's on your mind?" Gus asks.

"Why are you in my home and why are you meeting with Kid?" she asks, "And giving him a package?"

"You're pretty good," is all Gus can say.

"I'm the best. Answer the damn question, please."

Gus smiles with pleasure. He knows how observant her trained eye is. He acts glad that she hasn't lost any of her touch.

"He needs the work. I have the marks," he states, "Business is business."

"He needs the *work*?" she asks, confused.

"Yes."

"What work?" she asks, "*My* work?"

"Yes."

"How the-" she rethinks her words, "He cleans?"

"Yes."

"For the Org?"

"Yes."

"Since when?" she asks impatiently.

"Recently."

"He cleans and he's been hired?" she asks, knowing damn well she's the only who can do that.

"Yes. He's still fairly new," Gus says, "But yes, he does."

"Since when, I asked you?" she asks again, "And who gave the okay for him to work for Morales?"

"About a year now," Gus reveals, "He came to me and wanted to get on. He did two jobs, with your real daddy. Only then, he didn't know it was contract hits. He just thought it was someone who owed Big Dog."

"Who gave him the okay?" she asks again.

"Well,.."

"Don didn't and I didn't," she says, "So by creed and on honor, he shouldn't even be in a discussion about my business."

"I wanted to get someone else in here to help you out," he tries.

"You don't have the authority, Gus," she says.

"I just thought-"

"Apparently not," she cuts in, "He isn't a pro and he wasn't hired by me. He isn't even suppose to know what the hell is going on. And you up in here, putting marks in his hands?"

Gus stutters for words to use. He isn't having any luck and he can't speak fast enough to get a word in, before she comes back at him.

"Why is he getting the marks and not me?" she asks, as she pretends she's going to let Gus feel like he can assign work without her okay.

"You've got two packages, I have to give you," Gus

135

admits, "I know you're a new mother. I just didn't want to load you down, by having you have to run out of the house for whole weeks, at a time."

"I'll manage," she says, dryly. "This is *my* thing. No one else's."

"I sense you're unhappy with my decision," he says.

"Gee! *You think?*" she releases, "You come to my home and give my jobs to someone else. And that's *not* suppose to bother me, *any?*"

She's pissed. She is the best pro her family has. She's done up to 5 marks in as many days, with no traces. What the fuck is this load of bullshit, Gus is dumping on her? And right here in her *own* home.

"I can reassign it, if you'd like me too," he offers quickly.

"I'm telling you too," she spits, "And I will remain the *only* pro, *in play*, as far as my immediate family goes. Until *I* give you further notice. Don't do this again. Or you will be looking for a job. Kid's experience is in *street* violence and gang banging. There's no room for that kind of shitty work, in this game. He never got a contract *directly* from the Don. That should have settled it all with you. But I see that's not the case."

She orders him to call Kid back up to her house. He does.

Within minutes, Kid is standing in front of her and Gus.

"She wants to keep all of her assignments, Kid," Gus says, "She's the primary. She can make that call."

"I'm the *only*. Not just the primary," she corrects him, "I'm the only pro, for Morales."

"How the fuck can she tell you who can make money in this shit?" Kid asks angrily.

136

"She's the boss, Kid," Gus says, "That's the way Don Morales saw fit. We have to respect his order."
Kid reluctantly gives the package back, still unopened.
"Good. You didn't open it," she says taking it from him. "Because then, I would have to kill you. You shouldn't even have had the package in the presence of other people, Kid. That's not professional. Remember, bro, I love you, dearly. But this is not a line of work for you."
She locks eyes with him and says,
"You're an emotional trigger. There is no room for that in this business. You should train with me, first. Then I'll see about getting you some work."
"Baby Girl," Kid says, "I've *been* doing this shit. Even before you was. Soldier, Baby Boy and G-Dog. They use too hit muthafuckaz. For me and for your real pops. I got Lil shooters out there, now. Doing this dirt on the daily, Baby Girl. You heard of any of them falling?"
This info tells her, she needs to be more hands-on with Gus.
"From this day forward. No work comes out that I'm not aware of," she tells Gus, "Or you can find another job."
"None has, until today, Lovely Girl," he says, "The work they've been doing, was only to show me that they was building a resume'."
"I'll have to approve those resumes'," she says to Gus, while still looking directly into Kid's eyes. "If they prove to be applicable. Then and only then, I can see about getting them placement. One other thing. Don't *ever* call me Lovely. Call me, Baby Girl. The only person living, who calls me by my real name, is my husband. Do you understand?"
"Yes. Okay," Gus says.
With that, the discussion is closed. Rather Kid wants it to be or not. She's the H.M.I.C. or the *Head Muthafucka In Charge* of

the Morales Family. She lets Gus know that he had best act like he knows that. Baby Girl now knows what the bitching by Gus Davis, at the Spring Bazaar meeting, was leading into. This little display of muscle was for him to see, if he could edge her out of her authority.

I wish a Muthafucka would make me bust they're fucking head!

CHAPTER FIVE
THE ORGANIZATION 101

Gus and Kid go back to the cookout. Baby Girl takes her 3 assignments and puts them into her safe, in her and Young D's bedroom.

Soldier, Baby Boy and G-Dog arrive with their families and get settled. They all have a great time as the cookout moves on into the early evening hours. Everyone has eaten, at least twice. There are several games going on, at the same time. On the card tables, basketball courts and tennis courts. Baby Girl and Young D are playing basketball. They're on the same, 3-on-3 team, along with DeJuan. The 3 of them usually beat every other team. Soldier and his wife Debra, usually takes command of the spades table. While Baby Boy and High Top dominate the domino's tables which are referred to as; *Bones*. When it comes to Bid Whiz, mama Annie is the master. They have rented space walks, snowball vendors and pony rides, for all the kids. They always have enjoyable things for all their guest, of all ages. The pony rides is what has Lil Man wanting a real pony, so badly.

"This one is *my* boney," Lil Man says.
He's been in the saddle of the only black pony in the bunch, for over an hour. He refuses to let any other kid ride it.

"You want me to tell your daddy to get you this one?" Lil Corleone coaxes his younger cousin.

"Yes I do." Lil Man says with a goofy smile.
Lil Corleone, who's 12 like Jordan, runs to tell Young D and Baby Girl about their oldest son's request. Young D says he'll have it, for sure. Because he's a good kid and he deserves it.

"He has more than any two year old can ever play with, right now," Baby Girl says as she wipes her face with a towel after their 4th basketball victory, in a row.

"He's getting one," Young D says, "Case closed."

He looks at Baby Girl and smiles, real goofy.

"We may as well get a ranch, out here in Texas too, then," Baby Girl says, being condescending.

"It ain't no thang," Young D says, "Let's do it."

She rolls her eyes at him, as they break from the basketball games. It's almost sunset. The laborers are ready to set the concert stages up, on the courts, for the live entertainment portion of the barbeque.

Of course, all the artists in attendance are going to do a little something, as they always do. But the special guest, this year, are Port Arthur's own; *UGK* or *Under Ground Kings!* Two of Young D and Baby Girl's favorite rappers, *Bun B* and *Pimp C,* along with the *Trill Family,* which consist of *Lil Boosie, Weebie, Big Head* and *Foxx* are the special music guest. The guest who need to shower and change clothes are going to use 2 of the 3 guest homes.

Baby Girl and Young D go the their home to shower and change too. She picks out their gear and lays it on their changing tables. Young D is wearing some pieces from his own clothing line. The *Derrick Blake* casual collection. He's wearing an oversized white t-shirt with his name trimmed in rainbow rhinestones, on the front along, with his labels logo. It has H-town Records on the back. For bottoms, he's wearing his own denim *acid 5 deep pocket* jean shorts. They hang on him perfectly, Baby Girl thinks. The classic Reeboks in white and multi, made specifically for him and approved by the company, is his footwear. He's also in talks with Reebok about a joint venture which could find them producing a line of shoes for his label. Young D is dressed and applying his 1-of-a-kind jewelry. He looks sharp.

Baby Girl is wearing her *Satin Overall Jumpsuit* with the Capri cut legs. Underneath it, she wears her *Fashion Lab Skull Castle* printed tube top. She's had it altered to mid drift length and Young D instantly takes notice. She's wearing soft extra white socks with *Pastry's Sprinkle Cake Runner* shoes designed by *Angela and Vanessa Simmons*. They are the daughter's of *Reverend Run of RunDmc*. Baby Girl has already laid out their attire, for later too. Young D has a Polo in multi colors, from his own clothing line and it matches his wife's fit, to a tee. For bottom's, he's wearing his full length acid denim jeans with 7 pockets. The 6th pocket on the jeans is called the stash pocket. The 7th one is the Gat pocket. Of course, their both extra deep. He'll sport a fresh pair of *Timberlands* to complete his ensemble. On stand by for her, Baby Girl has her *Lot29 Roll Up Capri's* with a *Harajuku Lovers Reversible Circus* Hoodie and her *Jimmy Choo multi sling backs,* with the 2-inch heel. She's almost the same height as Young D, so she doesn't want to overdo it with heels. She'll change into this outfit for the after-hours portion of the outdoor event. Young D may or may not change. It depends on how much fun he's having, at the time. She sports her jewels too. Her wedding set is always the flashiest of her jewelry and she insist that it be. Anything bigger on her fingers would be gaudy and she doesn't do gaudy, at all. Her engagement ring is huge. It's a 10-karat solitaire surrounded by 12 smaller diamonds. Her wedding band has 12 diamonds too. The set values at 6 figures. She's the heir to Morales enterprises. Of course, Young D went all out on her rings.

"She's the Don's daughter," he had said, "She always had the best."

He wasn't going to allow that to change, now that she's married to him.

Baby Girl's best girlfriend since high school, Marjorie Petal-Ray or MJ, and her husband Tony Ray of the *Dallas Cowboys,* arrive just in time for the concert. Baby Girl and MJ catch up on times while they apply makeup and touch up their hair. Tony gets up with Young D and the guys and finds a Hennessey bottle. He's already the center of attention when Baby Girl and MJ make it back outdoors. It's show time.

Baby Boy, Soldier, Young D, Lil Geezy and G-Dog, along with their crews, all turn it out as opening acts. The Trill family do their thing too. When UGK takes the stage, everyone has their buzz on and they groove until, way past midnight. UGK doesn't deny any of the crowds request. From *The Southern Way* to *Underground Kings,* they give the people their proper UGK fix before they finally let up.

Baby Girl goes to get dressed for the after party and Young D follows her. She's still singing,
"One day you're here, baby...... Then you're gone...... One day you're here baby........."

"You can play that ringtone for your marks," Young D suggests to her, as they laugh.

"Oh but really. That's not funny, Derrick," she says, "I have that tone *awwwwwwwwready.*"

"You already play it, don't you?" he asks.

"Yes. Sometimes. After I'm done," she says and giggles. They split their sides laughing. When they finish dressing, they return to their guest.

Baby Girl checks with all the security and body guards. Everyone is still in place and their areas are still at maximum secure. She'd set them to chores, immediately after hanging up with Gus, this afternoon. She knew she would be in play, very soon. Her and Young D rejoin their guest, at the after party.

"Riding Dirty is still my favorite UGK joint," MJ says

in a loud voice so she can be heard over the music, "We use to play that shit out, in the wards. I *still* do. Do y'all remember that?"
Everyone agrees and cosigns her.
"I got a pocket full O' stonez-z-z-z," Tony sings.
Even Kid seems to have loosened up and started to enjoy himself, since UGK performed. He and Six Nine are staying in Houston until tomorrow. They're staying with girlfriends or friend girls, of theirs. Baby Girl doesn't dare question them about whom it is because she isn't sure if she wants to know. They probably wouldn't tell her, anyway. Because she knows their significant others and they're like family. She's upset with them for not bringing their longtime girlfriends or wives, with them.
Kid's reply is, "We don't take sand to the beach."
Meaning, they don't pack pussy on the road. They just get new pussy, wherever they happen to be. Baby Girl reiterates the fact that she doesn't need to know.
"T-M-I," she sings, as she frowns.
Soon, she excuses herself from the party. While her guest are enjoying themselves, Baby Girl slips away to Annie's house. She has 2 sons and younger brothers to check on, before she can totally feel free. Danny's not present. He's 22 years old now. He's working and going to college, in Atlanta. He couldn't make it for this holiday, due to his job. He had called earlier to say hello to everyone. Bruce is outside with Gat Em and the other teens. After she puts the babies down and tucks in Jordan and Lil Corleone, she heads to her home and to the bedroom safe. She has to familiarize herself with her new jobs.
"Let's see who has gotten their death dates," she says to herself, as she pulls the paperwork out of the 1st package and smiles.

Mark #1 is in nearby, Galveston Texas. Mark #2 is in Lafayette Louisiana. Mark #3 is in New York city.

"Gus was trying to get Kid fresh in H-town, I guess. Not even, *niccah!*" she says, as she laughs to herself. She continues with a giggle and adds, "I run this shit and this city too."
She sips from her merlot as she surveys her packages.

The Galveston hit is on a long time Longshoreman union president named, Dennis Montgomery. Dennis has been the president of the Local Southeast Chapter of the ILA since 1964. He's retiring soon. He has always been known for being very vocal against organized crime, drugs and how they relate to the shorelines of America. He's gone on record saying he will bring these organizations down.
How has he managed to stay alive, all of these years?

Reading his jacket, she can see that Montgomery was always a thorn in her daddy Don's side. But they managed to stay out of each others hair. To make a long story short, Dennis never refused any of Don's offers.

"Ugh. Oh yea," she mumbles to herself, "He took payoffs from daddy, so he's not a strict one for the rules, at all. He's a hypocrite."
She despises phony people. Even if he wasn't phony. She would find something wrong with him. Because he's a mark. She's programmed to disassociate herself from them and to discredit them, in anyway possible. For Dennis, she doesn't have to reach far. He's a contradictor, at it's finest. In the last 6 years or so, he's gotten fresh and more vocal. Bold, even. He's been throwing his weight around and bucking the system which had put him in power.
Lovely *"Baby Girl"* Walker-Blake continues to talk aloud, "Nobody's paying him, anymore. So he's turning snitch, ha?

144

That's what the fuck, this is. You're retiring, alright. You damn right, you are. To the grave. You hypocritical, son of bitch. I have to teach him about playing with my big daddy Don. How the fuck is Kid gonna do that? He's as green as the gecko from *Geico*."

She laughs to herself, then says, "This is my shit, brother."

It's 2am, Tuesday morning. This mark expires in 22 hours.

"Midnight tonight," she says aloud.

He's been in play for 2 hours and so has she.

The Lafayette hit is Chadwick Donaldson. A hypocrite too. She's very familiar with his *crackheaded* ass. He's worse than Montgomery, in her opinion. He's the likely candidate and successor for union president, with many of the same views that Dennis Montgomery has already.

"Cleaning up the docks of Organized Crime," she says, with doubt in her tone. Then she says, "*How* Chad? When all of the *known* drug importing and exporting, isn't even on your list of things to clean up? It is with Montgomery."

She has a huge clue as to why Chadwick is okay with the drug trading. Hitting him is what is known in the business as collateral. Taking out the next in line or a future *potential problem*, before it becomes a problem. It leaves their associates numb and it usually discourages any cowards from running for the office and expressing the same views. In other words, it sends a strong message that someone isn't willing to have things any other way. The most likely purchaser of this hit is a drug kingpin. Or the DEA, playing Sheppard to their flock of sheep. But Baby Girl is too familiar with this #2 target.

She attended LSU with his only daughter, Chadrella Donaldson. Chadrella was a self-proclaimed debutante. Really, she was just an uppity ass negro, who had come from a money family. But she had no real charm or friends. Only the kind

145

money affords. She was known around campus for paying students to hang out with her. Baby Girl had convinced MJ not to bust her face up. But to get money from her, instead. It was when Chadrella had once tried to date, Tony Ray. He was MJ's fiancée, then. Chadrella had no real friends. She was daddy's little science project. Or that's how Baby Girl saw her.
"A test tube baby," she says as she laughs.
She laughs again and amuses herself while she studies her packages, thoroughly. She knows Chadrella's history and how she came to be born. Chadrella's parents were told they could not conceive a child. Through the use of fertility drugs, they got a daughter and then a son. Baby Girl remembers Chadwick's secret too. He's a groupie for the *Golden Triangle* manufacturers. She knows his bad habits, well.

It was 1 night after an LSU football victory, in the fall of 1998. She had just turned 16 and was in her junior year of college. So was Chadrella but Chadrella was nearly 20, same as MJ was. Chadrella had asked Baby Girl and MJ to attend a party with her and she would pay for all of their expenses. This was to keep both girls from whooping her ass, about Tony Ray. It was also suppose to gain her some brownie points with the newly, world famous 3rd Ward Soldiers artist, who would be in town to perform, after the next week's game.
Only because my brothers were famous.

Baby Girl had gone to Chadrella's dorm to meet her. But she had already left on an errand. Her father was in her room alone. He was cooking something on a spoon. He freaked out when Baby Girl barged through the door.
"Don't you ever knock!?!" he had screamed.
She remembers him panicking because she had just busted him, about to shoot himself to oblivion, with heroin. After

146

realizing she had caught him. He settled down and thought of a bribe. She was all for a bribe, as long as it was his money going into her pockets. Quickly, Chadwick tried to clean up his indiscretion with her.

"Are you the young lady my Chatty is going to the party with?" he had asked her.

"Yes, sir," she answered, as she was raised to always be polite to her elders.

"Do you have a driver's license?" he asked her.

"I do," she had said.

Then he gave her the keys to his 2000 Mercedes 600 series. At that time, the only way to get that car was to special order it. She remembers because her brother Kid had just ordered one. Baby Girl took the keys and waited for Chadrella in the lobby, as Chadwick had instructed. He'd told her, whatever they needed for that night, Chadrella had his permission to put it on his unlimited *Rush Card*. He had given it to her, earlier.

"I may as well get Derrick something too." she remembers saying, as she laughs. "Hitting his ass is going to be *too* damn easy."

She already has a plan of execution, for him. This hit goes into play on Wednesday, at 6am. It's called a play, 24 hours before it expires. He's in play as soon as mark 1 is done. Chad will expire by 6am, Thursday Morning.

"And he never got rehabilitated," she says as she glares at his package. "How is a junky gonna run and win another office? Only in America. It's time to show his union, just what they was about to elect."

The NYC hit is not so much connected to the ILA, like the first two. But it is related to the docks and the drug trade. The marks name is Tito Lopez. A druglord out of the boogie down Bronx, who runs 12 gangs or crews, of longshoreman

throughout the east coast ports. In fact, he's a kingpin who's name has come up on the Drug Enforcement Administrations hot sheets. His lifestyle has become too flamboyant and too flashy. He's a self proclaimed baller with GQ looks, boys club money, exotic women, fancy cars and coke parties. You name it. He's doing it and doing it, big. He had been warned by several agents to tone it down. He hasn't and now, it's too late. He's on tap, primarily because of his big pimpin' life style. A major doesn't do it like that, in the drug business. Only minors and street hustlers, do that. That's the first thing minors do, is go out and buy a flashy car and some flashy ass jewels.
Dumb shit!

Tito is a major player and the DEA is about to shake him down. They'll get him because he's sloppy. And just like any other pussy ass bitch, he'll roll over or turn rat. Because he won't be willing to do the federal time for racketeering, that he's going to get. It happens all the time, to major dealers. They tend to want to snitch on their bosses when they get shook down. If he talks, several well known organizations will be jeopardized. The Don's can't afford to let him live, to be arrested. Let alone, go to trial. His name had hit the sheets, last week. Which means the DEA will run their investigation from 6 months to a year. Just to build a case on him, that will stick. In the meantime, crooked agents will try and get him gone, lost, out of touch or reached. Just to protect their cash cows.
"I won't need *nearly* that long," she says aloud.
Tito's mark is set for Friday at 9pm. He'll expire Saturday night. But Baby Girl will do him in, be out of Manhattan and back to her children, before her oldest son's favorite cartoon plays, on Saturday morning.
I'll be back in time to make the cereal, for me and Lil Man .

She puts her packages back into the safe and secures them. Then she rejoins the after party.

"Hey, baby. Where have you been?" Young D asks as he's obviously having his share of party flavors.

He's buzzing, big time. He has that sexy twinkle in his eyes too. She straddles and faces him. Then puts her arms up on his shoulders and pulls his face toward hers.

"I had to put the babies to bed and check on the house," she answers him with a kiss on the lips.

"I need to go walk my dog, baby," Young D says to her, "This pill kickin in."

Everyone who hears his last comment, starts to laugh. Baby Girl smiles at him. Assuring him that she's willing.

"That's what you call it, Young D?" Bun B asks, as he laughs, "Walking the dog?"

"Hell yea, bro," Young D says as he laughs.

Kid and most of her New Orleans brothers have left. They've gone to go stay with whomever they're staying with, here in Houston. Gus is back in New Orleans. Baby Girl received his text while she was going over her assignments. Kierra and her crew had left, just before Kid. At one point during the day, Baby Girl had missed Young D and Kierra. But she wouldn't allow her mind to play tricks on her.

"It was a coincidence," she had told herself.

Soldier, Baby Boy and G-Dog are going to stay here, at the estate, with their families. They always do, as do Young D's crew. They're all at home, whenever they're at each others spots.

"Y'all hold it down," Young D says, "It's me and my wife's bedtime."

Young D and Baby Girl say goodnight to all of their guest. MJ and Tony have already retired to their room, at Young D and Baby Girl's house. The rest will fall in at 1 of the homes, when they're done partying. Young D takes Baby Girl's hand and they walk to their house.

"What's poppin with the murder-for-hire business?" Young D asks.

He nearly stumbles from intoxication, after entering the house. He walks on into their bedroom, holding her from behind. He's planting traces of kisses down the back of her neck.

"Sshhh. Not so loud. MJ doesn't know what I do," she whispers, "You know that."

"Yea, I know. I didn't think I was talking that loud, baby," he whispers.

"Maybe it wasn't you. Maybe it was your dog," she says as she laughs.

"Oh, he damn sho barking and ready to talk to your sexy ass," he says as he's removing her clothing and cementing on each spot he bares.

She's removing his, at the same time. She kisses him with fervor and says, "Mmmmm and I'm so anxious to hear what he's got to say to me too."

He has her completely nude, within a minute. He moves to the bed and lays down on his back.

"Come here, Lovely," he says.

He always says her name, so sexy, in her opinion. And the only opinion that counts. She obeys her husband, as he has her to straddle him. Then he puts his arms between her legs and pulls her towards his chest. Then to his chin. He lifts her and cups her ass cheeks, in either hand and lifts her knees up off of the bed. He pulls her pussy down to his face.

"Oh my God, Derrick," she moans, "You was really

ready to put it on me. Wasn't you?"

He mumbles something affirmative, with his tongue never leaving the insides of her pussy. The vibration sends a shock wave through her body. They both moan again. He does his duty. Working her clitoris, like the master he's become. She reaches her first climax and returns the oral favor. He's extra loud, this morning.

"You loving this, Derrick?" she whispers before taking him to the back of her throat.

He can't speak. She's flicking her tongue, from his balls to that little line which divides his sack from his asshole. He loves it. She turns on the speed and he sighs aloud. He frowns in intense pleasure. She's back to the dick now and she shows her familiarity with the art of pleasing it. He comes hard and loud. He isn't done, by a long shot. His penis is as hard as brick, still. She sits on it.

"You on one, ha Derrick?" she whispers as she rides him.

"Mmm hmm," he moans the affirmative.

He's rolling on an *ecstasy* pill. He's in this, for the long haul. She's only hoping she'll have enough energy left to kill a man, in a few hours. For now, this man is killing her softly with his dog and she's loving it. She loves the way he walks it out. She lives for it and him too. He's so fucking pleasing and definitely, damn good.

CHAPTER SIX
THE OTHER LIFE

"YOUNG D'S "OTHER LIFE" ON TUESDAY MORNING"

Anyone would think, having a hired killer as a wife, would be a sure fire deterrent for any man not to cheat. But not Young D. Even though this fling started long before he knew about Baby Girl's *taking hits* profession. He hasn't stopped it since knowing about it. For reasons that he thinks are good. But what woman would be willing to risk death to sleep with a husband, if she knew what his wife was capable of? No one! Bit Baby Girl's job is a very well kept secret. On the other hand, her power is no secret, at all. What woman is fucking Baby Girl's husband?
Kierra Ramsey, the usual suspect!

Either Young D doesn't have good damn sense, no will to live or this Kierra has something of biblical magnitude proportion hanging over his head. This lingering guest and hanger on, at all of the Blake's functions which had gotten Baby Girl's attention 6 years ago. Has access to the jewels in Baby Girl's household. The head of household's jewels, at that. Kierra doesn't know about Lovely's profession. If she did, surely she'd find another object for her affection, besides Derrick Blake aka Young D. But she doesn't know. So she's been plotting since last nights event, on how she could get another round with, *"The D"*.

Kierra's on the phone with her girlfriends, early this morning. Making plans for when Young D's wife goes out of town again. Through Annie, she finds out when Baby Girl will be gone. Then she goes through hell and high water to monopolize the time Young D has away from his wife. His mother Annie isn't in on Kierra's plot. But she does have a reason for telling Kierra when Baby Girl is away. It's not for her to hook up with her son. Not at all. Kierra is aware that Baby Girl take trips often, without Young D. And he does likewise. Kierra has even tried to be the replacement wife for Young D, when Baby Girl is unavailable. And though he has assured her that she could never be that. He's still living a double life, just like his wife. Only his 2nd life involves cheating. Not killing. Not yet. His double life is 1 with a secret, he feels will surely cost him his relationship with Baby Girl. And if she knew what this secret was, it could cost him his very life too. So then, why would he do it?

There's no doubt in his mind that he loves Baby Girl. More than himself. But it's something about this whore Kierra, that he's been unable to shake. At the same time, Kid is aware of this same something and that something is what assures Kid, that Young D doesn't now nor has he ever deserved to be in his kid sister's life.

That something wasn't taking place from the beginning of Young D and Baby Girl's relationship. It came much later. So that's not the reason Kid doesn't like them together. Perhaps he wanted them parted, so bad that he created this something, to split them. That remains to be seen. But nonetheless, there is still something and that something has a name. That something's name is, Danica Ramsey. Kierra and Young D's, 4 ½ year old daughter born just 12 weeks after Young D and Baby Girl said, "I do."

Danica was born in October of 2002. Young D was raised to do what's morally correct. That is Annie's only reason for telling Kierra when Baby Girl is away. So she can bring Danica by to see them, without giving up her and Young D's secret. It would be all the same to Annie if he would just

153

tell Baby Girl and get it over with. That way, Kierra wouldn't have any hold on her son. Young D hasn't told Baby Girl, yet. And Kierra has pulled back from bringing the little girl over. Now, she demands that he come to her place to see Danica. This is so she can continue to throw herself on him. After he told Annie, Annie insisted from that day on, that he tell his wife and end this nightmare. Every since that day, he's said he would. But so far, he hasn't done it. Annie feels it's because he's afraid she won't accept it. Young D knows that's not it. He never wants to tell Baby Girl. Initially, he had hopes that he would prove not to be the father. Through the paternity test which was done, after the little girl was born. Young D knew of Kierra's pregnancy, the entire time. Because, not only did she tell him but Kid did too. Still, Kierra is a whore and she's very loose with men. She had many men in her life and bed, at that time and she still does, today. Kid being 1 of them. Kierra was known to leave with the highest bidder, back then. She still does now. She's a material girl. But unlike Madonna, she doesn't earn hers through moral nor legal talents.

For one, she strips at 1 of Houston's gentlemen clubs called, *The Anatomy*. It isn't a secret that many of the girls trick with the customers. But Kierra is definitely the top prostitute of the establishment. She even gets 1st dibs on the new customers because she has a long tenure. She had and still has, many men. But Young D had become her regular, back then. Because she knew he was on his way to the limelight.

They had met in 2000, when Young D returned to Houston, from New Orleans, with no music deal to speak of. He had gone back to the street hustle, nearly fulltime. But he still stuck to his love of music. He kept recording and grinding for a deal. He also had a few whore's on the stroll, selling their bodies and bringing him the cash. Cash he used to buy many things. Including things for his girlfriend, who eventually became his wife, Baby Girl. Some of his whore's went to strip clubs to get work. Some ended up in, *The Anatomy*. This is how Young D or Derrick, got introduced to Kierra, from the start. She stripped there and wanted to whore for him, like the girls she worked with and he allowed her too. Though he was no longer with the 3rd Ward Soldiers label, he was still in touch with Baby Girl. She was his lady still, no matter what happened or didn't happen with the music or any other phase of their lives. Baby Girl was in the spring semester of her junior year, at LSU. But she didn't have as much time to spend with him, as she'd had in the past. He felt neglected by her, all of a sudden. She would explain to him that she was a junior and had much more class work to do. But he didn't buy that. At one time, he even thought she was being unfaithful. But he had no proof. Unbeknownst to Young D, at the time, that was when she first started the killer-for-hire craft, which made her private life schedule, very unpredictable. Young D had even traveled to LSU, one evening to surprise her. Only to arrive and find out from MJ, that she had gone out of town. MJ wasn't sure where Baby Girl had gone. Nor when she would return, which made it seem even more suspicious. So on this same trip, Young D went on into New Orleans to talk with Wanda and Don. He talked to them about what seemed to him like Baby Girl's lack of enthusiasm about their relationship. He didn't know what else to do. He loved her, dearly. But he was a vibrant young man, at the same time. And he had his needs. Wanda assured him that her daughter was just overwhelmed by the increased challenges of college, as she neared graduation. Wanda didn't have a clue that her only child was killing people. Neither did Young D. Not at that time. But the Don expounded on it a bit more, as only he could.

"She's going through some courses of learning how to take over the family business, Young D," Don had said, with a blank expression. "She's still the same Baby Girl. She just has more responsibilities now."

Young D expressed to Wanda and Don, his desire to marry Baby Girl after she finished college. He asked them for her hand in marriage, during that same meeting. Don had told him he had to,

"Take care of Baby Girl like a man does for his woman. She's a princess, raised with morals and manners," he had said.

Before him and Wanda gave Young D their blessings, which they did give him, Don told him that he would work on getting solo label deals for him and the other brothers, who had left Kid and Six Nine's Label.

"Because you're going to need a way to give my Baby Girl this good life that she's use too," Don had said.

After that conversation, Young D told everyone about his intentions to get married. He told everyone except Baby Girl. Because he wanted to formally propose to her. Everyone else agreed with their relationship. Just as they had done, back at Young D's 1st Thanksgiving dinner with them. Only Kid still didn't accept the relationship since the beginning and he certainly wasn't agreeing that Baby Girl should marry him. Young D knew Kid didn't like him with Baby Girl and figured, him being with her is the main reason he was never featured on any of the songs or CD's the 3rd Ward label pressed. It was weird to Young D for Kid to have this big of a hang up over him loving his baby sister. He felt like Kid secretly wanted her, for himself. Since she wasn't his, *blood* sister. The beginning of the end, was when Kid spotted Young D with Kierra, in The Anatomy. It was one night in the spring of 2000. This was before Don Morales had passed away. Young D didn't even try to play if off. He knew it didn't matter, as far as him and Kid's friendship was concerned. That was just another reason for Kid to say he shouldn't have his little sister. But what Young D didn't know, at that time, was that Kid was also 1 of Kierra's regulars. And he still is today. Young D still doesn't know about them. He never found out about Kid. But he knew of many other men, Kierra was sleeping with. Had he known about Kid and Kierra, he'd probably be a little closer to figuring out this twisted puzzle, known as his life.

When Kierra first announced she was pregnant, in March of 2002 and that Young D was the father, he shunned her, completely. He didn't believe she knew, without a doubt, who had fathered her unborn child. Kierra persisted with her accusations of him as the father. She wanted someone else from his family to know about the baby. Figuring he would never tell them. And when she heard that he went to New Orleans to marry Baby Girl, in July of 2002, she sent a letter to his mother Annie. She told Annie the whole scenario. That's when Annie became aware of the pregnancy.

Once Annie returned to Houston, from the private wedding ceremony and read the letter. She relayed it's content information to Young D. That was when he told her, his side of the story. She suggested he was right to follow his heart. He loved Baby Girl, so he should have married her. But Annie had also told him to tell Baby Girl about the child, which was on the way, at that time. She told him to take a paternity test when the child was born. Young D had indeed married his love, Baby Girl. But he has never told her about the child. He took a paternity test, when Danica was 3 weeks old. The test was positive. Still, he didn't believe it, then. He still doesn't believe it now. He thinks there was something underhanded done, to get a positive test. He just can't prove it. Not yet. In the meantime, he has the fear that if he tells Baby Girl about Danica, she'll leave him, for sure. Or she'll kill him. So he hasn't said a word and he swore everyone else to secrecy.

His mother Annie, his sister Angela, his step brother Corleone and all of his homeboys, know about Danica and Kierra. Everyone knows about them. Except for Baby Girl. On her side of the family, Soldier and Baby Boy know about them and they don't want Young D to tell Baby Girl, at all. Kid knows about Danica but Young D isn't aware that he knows about her or this part of him and Kierra's relationship. Young D really values Soldier and Baby Boy's opinion. Because they are the closest people to Baby Girl, from her family. And they had advised him not to tell her, back when he first found out. They still feel the same way, today. Back in the day, they were adamant that he should not tell Baby Girl. Back then, they had plans of getting rid of Kierra but that hasn't happened yet. They still insist he don't divulge this secret to their baby sister.

"That will break her heart, cousin," Soldier had said.

"Let that one ride, player," Baby Boy had advised. Young D took their advise to heart and decided not to tell his wife. But he vowed that he would stop seeing Kierra. He tries to avoid her. But that proves harder to do, then just saying no. Even though, he doesn't have any emotional ties or connections to her. They *supposedly* have a child together. Annie had raised him to be responsible. He takes his responsibilities, in stride. He takes care of his child, by providing total support for Kierra. Something she was looking for, *any man* to do from the beginning. Danica became her own little personal financial plan, since Young D was willing to pay for her silence. As long as he agrees to keep her with enough cash to pay all of her bills and to keep her ass in *Gucci* and *Prada*. Then she won't alert Baby Girl about the child they conceived 2 years after the chance meeting, that took place while Baby Girl was in Baton Rouge getting college educated.

Young D had slept in late this morning. He'd gotten pretty fucked up, at the event last night, with UGK and their gang of celebrity friends. He wakes up to a note on his wife's pillow. He knows for certain, she's on a job. He's loaded still, as he tosses and turns in bed. Following an awesome fuck session, after leaving their friends outside, they had fallen to sleep, instantly. Baby Girl had awakened him around 8am, with some provocative head and a quick fuck, before she had to get up and run *some errands.*

After his wife is gone, he's awakened again by the phone ringing. It's his mother, this time. He knows his sons are still at her house. She never calls for him to come get them, when Baby Girl isn't home. Because she knows he isn't the best sitter for them. He figures her call is about the 1 person that he least wants to think about, this morning. Or any other morning. *Kierra Ramsey.* He finally picks up the line.

"Good morning, son," Annie says.

"Is it, mama?" he asks.

"Well, maybe it's not *totally* good," Annie says, "But Danica is wanting to see you, this week. I was thinking you could go get her tomorrow, when Baby Girl leaves and just bring her out here."

"I don't know if I wanna risk that," he says. Even though his entire family knows about the little girl. He doesn't want to take the chance that someone else may see him arrive, with her. Or that his oldest son Lil Man , who is as smart as a whip, may remember her and then make mention of her when his mother gets back home.

"I know it's a risk. But it's worse for you to go out there and be seen at her apartment," Annie says.

"Mama, I'm sick of this shit," he says, "I really am. Why don't you call Kierra back and tell her to go to hell. Then I can just file for custody and Danica can live with us."

Annie laughs but she knows how frustrated her son is with the whole situation.

"Before we can do that, son. We will have to tell Baby Girl and -"

"That's a risk, I know I'm not willing to take," he says, "She'll kill me."

His mother doesn't know about Baby Girl's profession, so she thinks he's exaggerating. What Annie does know, is that Baby Girl is an heiress to a fortune, with more money than she can count in her lifetime. So if she wanted to dismantle Young D's future, she could do it without getting out of bed. Annie feels like that's what's bothering her son. Not only him feeling that Baby Girl would divorce him. But Annie doesn't know of Baby Girl's skills. She knows she has businesses to run. So she figures that's what keeps her on the road, a lot. Besides, that's what Baby Girl usually tells her is the reason she has to leave. Young D, since learning of his wife's skills, usually plays along. He would say something like, he didn't want to go on those trips with her, for the boring business meetings. So Annie had bought Baby Girl's explanation, accepted it and never had a reason to question it. Baby Girl started telling Annie about the trips in advance. Once she became a mother. Because she needs her to watch her and Young D's sons, while she's gone.

"Derrick, I believe she loves you enough, that she would handle this better than you think," Annie tries, "You will have to tell her why you never mentioned it and how Kierra has been holding this over your head."

"She won't forgive me. She'll kill me," he says again.

"She'll be mad, at first. I'm sure," his mother says,

"But what's going to really make her the most angry, is all of the shit that has been going on since the first lie started."
She's trying to make him understand that if he tells Baby Girl about the pressure Kierra is putting on him, to sleep with her, to keep this secret. Then the pressure will go away because that will stop the secret, all together. Young D says he'll think it over, some more. But he has always said that and never came to the conclusion that he should tell his wife.

"Derrick, it's been five years of thinking it over," Annie says, "I want this shit to end too. And I want it to end, with Baby Girl still in that house with you. You have to trust her to believe in you. Just like you believed in her, from day one. When it came to her brother Kid, not liking y'all together. She didn't let him stop anything. Not a *damn* thing. Because she really loved you and she still does. That has to count for everything, son. Lovely is a brilliant woman and she loves you, with all of her heart. You've got to give her a chance at the truth. You may even surprise yourself. That little girl is sweet, true enough. But she looks nothing like our family. Tell your wife, son. And end this. With the people she knows and have at her disposal. She can help you get to the real truth, in no time. And she'll definitely end this whole charade with Kierra and her bullshit demands. I am here for the both of you. Give your wife a chance."

"She'll end both of our lives," Young D insists.

"What kind of life is it, when you're at Kierra's beck and call, every other week?" Annie asks.

"I know you're right, mama," he says, "I have to tell her and soon. I just don't wanna lose her."

"I don't think you will, son," Annie says.
Young D takes it all in, again. Then he asks his mother if she's still willing to help him tell Baby Girl.

161

She says she is and she looks forward to it.

"Lovely is like my daughter," she says, "I met her when you two were still children. I adore her and I know she loves you, with everything she has. A mother knows that, automatically. I want her to be with you and you with her. And right now son, with this secret, you are not with her, one hundred percent. You may think she doesn't know it. But I'll bet you she does. She may not know the particulars. But she knows something isn't right about Kierra. The same things that she has said to you, she has said to me and Angela too."

He asks his mother if Baby Girl has ask her anything about Kierra, lately. Annie tells him she asks her again, yesterday. During the cookout.

"She wanted to know why is she always coming around," she says, "And she said, she acts like she's family but none of us ever really talk about her. Nor is she invited to family days. So she wanted to know why is she coming to our parties and acting like she's a hostess."

"Damn," he says, "She said that? She didn't say nothing to me."

"Well, she did to me and Angela," she says, "It's time to end this. Before it's too late. I don't even want Kierra to know when Lovely is away. Not now that I know what she's doing with it. But for that little girls sake. If she is my granddaughter. I just don't want her to suffer."

"I'll fix it, mama," he says.

"You had better fix it, quick. Because Kierra has already tried to call me, today," Annie says, "I didn't answer it. I just waited until it stopped ringing. Then picked up and called you."

"I'll take care of it," he says again, "I'm coming to get man. But let Don stay until Lovely gets back."

His mother says okay and they hang up.

Meanwhile, across town, Kierra is up to her usual tricks. Trying to horn in on Young D's free time. She has already called and left Annie a voice mail. Saying that Young D needs to see Danica, soon. She's planning to call her back and when she does answer the phone, Kierra plans to find out exactly when he can see their little girl. Then she can demand that he come over and see her. And make sure that they can have some private time too. Kierra still plots on how to get with Young D, during Baby Girl's next trip.

"I know she got to have some damn trip to go on, soon," Kierra says to her girlfriends, on 3-way, "She's usually going somewhere, every week. But I think D's been bullshitting with my time. I don't even know why his wife is hanging around here, *this* long. She needs to go on a business trip. I need that dick. *Shit!*"
Her and her girlfriends laugh.

"Key, you got other dick that you can get, girl," her friend Trina says, "But you just want your baby daddy. And that nigga don't even claim your ass. He aint even checking for you, boo boo."
She giggles because Trina knows Kierra isn't only wanting to fuck Young D. She wants him, for herself. Now that he's a millionaire. She wants to be his woman, on record. Young D had long told her, that was never going to happen. She even argues the fact that him and Baby Girl never admit their relationship, in public.
But Young D tells her, *"That's just media shit."*
Kierra has threatened, many times, to divulge his secret. Then he gives her a little of his attention and that shuts her up. Because she knows if she did tell, that would end her whole

163

game. For now, as long as she has Danica as a hold over him. He'll be in her clutches, forever. That is, unless he comes clean and tells his wife. Each time Kierra threatens to tell Baby Girl, he warns her that would cut off her ties to him, as well.

"If you tell Lovely and she leaves me. I'm not gonna fuck with you," he had told her, *"And all I would have to do then, is pay child support for Danica. Not all of your fucking bills. So think about that. If you ever fuck up my shit. You'll be fucking up your own shit too."*

He knows she doesn't want to do that, so she settles into her position as the other woman. One of many other women, in Young D's life, since his celebrity went up. He's got 100's of groupies and so called "ride or die" bitches, lurking around the venues when he performs. But they get no real time. When Baby Girl is present, no one gets any play. When she's not. He'll pick and choose, if that's his pleasure. And usually, it's not. The dilemma with Kierra however, weighs heavily on his mind, all the time. He loves the little girl. Though he doesn't get to spend any real time with her. He wishes he could just bring her to the house with him, Baby Girl and the boys. And make her a regular part of their family. Then he wouldn't have to deal with Kierra and her threats, at all. But he's not ready to risk the ultimate. His Baby Girl. The 1 he had deflowered. The 1 who has always remained faithful to him, no matter who he showed himself to be. She has been there for him, in every way. He just doesn't believe she'll take him having a child, on her. He feels she would leave him, for sure. Or take his life.

CHAPTER SEVEN
USE WHAT YOU GOT

"BABY GIRL'S VERSION OF TUESDAY MORNING"

Baby Girl has a husband who's living is made by making hits and entertaining people. She is a made woman, who has a mark to hit in the entertainment capital of the world, New York city, in 4 days. She knows how to use what she's got. How to play the hand, she's dealt. It's the way she was raised.

"I need to get him a spotlight in the city," she says aloud, as she sits at her desk.

She's finalizing the details for some hits of her own. Her husband has gone back to sleep, after some very draining sexual episodes, all morning. Young D doing a show in NYC this weekend, would be the perfect cover.

It's 9am, Tuesday morning. 15 hours before the 1st mark is to expire. Young D is sleeping off the Memorial Day events but he has plans of being in the studio, all day. Which is the perfect cover for her noon, *business trip*. The kids are still at Annie's house. Baby Girl thinks over last nights party. She thinks about Kid and Gus' attendance and the bullshit Gus had tried, when he haphazardly handled her packages. That's been bugging her, more than she said or let on too. The inconvenient part of her profession is, not having anyone she can really discuss it with, when something fucked up happens. She would have to be at the manor to talk with senior staff whenever she needs to discuss work. Because discussions over the phone, internet or text messaging or any other form, outside of face to face, is *never* permitted. She'll bring Alfred, Addie Mae and the rest of the senior staff up-to-date on Gus, later.

She also thinks about Kierra Ramsey and how *at home* she acts when she's on their property. Yet, no one in the family actually vibes with her, at their events. She sticks out like a sore thumb and if it wasn't for the friends she brings with her, she wouldn't get any genuine conversation. But still. Baby Girl wonders just what it is that keeps her on the guest list. And how does Kid know her, so fucking well, to be chumming it up with her like old pals at yesterday's event.

"I don't trust that whore," she says aloud, "Let her slip. I just hope she fucks up. I'll be on her ass again, like flies on shit. It's nothing."

She thinks about her brother Kid and how he refuses to come and visit, when her and Young D invites him. But he shows up out of the blue, at the cookout, welcomed but unannounced. Then he stays joined at the hip with that nasty ass trick bitch, most of the day. Except for when he had the audacity to come into her and Young D's home in an attempt to overthrow her and override her authority with; *The Organization.*

"Fuck them both," she says to herself, "I stay trained, aimed and ready."

She allowed her mind to stray, momentarily. Now, it's back to the business at hand. The one that she doesn't get emotional about. Her family business and her daddy's work.

Baby Girl has to get about the business of the day. But she's very thorough and organized. Before going after the 1st mark, she sets up the 2nd and 3rd ones, like any organized cleaner worth their salt, would do.

Hmmm. I wonder what the test tube baby is up too?

She thinks about Chadrella and can't help but giggle to herself. Then she looks through her blackberry for her number. She finds the house phone number.

"Perfect. Folks hardly ever change the digits to their house phones," she says as she picks up her office phone.

She dials the number and a young man answers the phone.

"Hello. Donaldson residence."

"Yes. May I speak with Chadrella, please?"

"Hold on, please."

It figures. With all of the bragging and posturing she had done in college, about how she was going to get out on her own and have a luxurious apartment. This caramel colored snob from a Petri dish, is still living at home.

"Hello. This is Chadrella."

"Hi Chadrella. It's Lovely," she says, "How are you?"

"Lovely, my friend! How are you?" Chadrella asks.

Wow! She still has no friends.

"I'm good. I'm gonna be in your town to scout venues, on Thursday," she says, "Can you show me around?"

"Oh sure. I'd love too," Chadrella purrs, "Who are you seeking venues for? Is this for those brothers of yours or your man or who?"

"Both, really. I never get a break, these days," Baby Girl says, "It's always one or the other. I'm gonna need sponsors too. Is your family interested?"

"Hang on. Let me asked my father," Chadrella says as she lays the phone down.

Good. Let's go on and get his junky ass onboard now. And you can stay the fuck home.

She holds the phone. She can hear Chadrella run off but still within earshot of the phone. She can hear her speaking with Mr. Chadwick *"Crackhead"* Donaldson. He remembers Baby Girl.

167

Oh of course you remember me. You jellied brain hypocrite.

She giggles to herself.
Hurry up, science project and get back to the phone. I have others to kill, before I get to your mush minded father.

To keep his secret, just that. He's more than willing to be a sponsor. Instead of his daughter coming back to the line, he takes the phone. Which is exactly what Baby Girl had expected him to do. He gives her the names of several contacts, with whom he will be certain to have endorse her events.

"As a matter of fact, I'll call one of my cohorts, right now," he says.

She can hear him dialing his cell phone. Then having a conversation with an *Applebee's* owner. The owner says he's willing to sponsor shows for anyone Chadwick Donaldson recommends. And he'll even get the local *Popeye's Chicken* and *Target* to sponsor, as well.

She hears Chadwick say, "Go on and get the venues in line that we usually work with. I'll get back to you with the dates and more information, when it's available."

They hang up and he returns to the phone with Baby Girl.

"Set, Lovely," he says, "What else can I do for you?"

He's hoping she's willing to accommodate him with a sexual favor. She's a pro. So she picks up on that, right away.

"Oh thank you, mister Donaldson. You're the best," she says in a flirtatious voice. "I may need you to help me with a street sponsor too. *This brown sugar* needs some brown sugar. And I know you use to know how and where to cop, all the way in Baton Rouge. So I know you got the connects in Lafayette. I need you to hook me up when I come through. See, I'm all the way grown up now. But I do need this to be on the hush hush. I

168

don't want my sister Chaddy, to know. She's not ready to handle all of that."

He knows exactly what she means. So he thinks. He walks out of the room where his son and daughter are, so he can talk to Baby Girl, in private. That's exactly what she'd counted on. The business she has with him, she wants him to keep secret. She doesn't even want Chadrella to show up. She knew if she brought drugs into the equation. Chadwick would make sure his daughter didn't know Baby Girl would be in town.

Perfect! Leave the little test tube baby out of it.

He then gives her the number to his private line.

He says, "Call this number when you get here. And I'll take care of everything else. I'll hook you up."

"It's got to be top of the line," she says, "I'm talking about *black tar* quality."

"You know your stuff. Don't you?" he asks, with a chuckle that irks the hell out of her.

"It'll be lethal baby. Don't you worry, none. You just bring your lethal side too. I've wanted to see that, for years."

This is more of what she had counted on too. She gives *less* than a damn about heroin. She barely smokes weed. And only with her husband, when she does. She isn't about to shoot heroin, snort it nor chase the dragon. But she knows all the terminology. It helps with her profession, to know a little bit about everything. The Don had taught her that and he'd told her it would be advantageous to her, for her to be able to relate and converse, in any crowd.

"Do you wanna know my hotel room?" she teases.

"Well……,um. Yes I would," he says, sounding like the dirty old man that he is.

"That info would surely help me to do the best job."

169

"Well, you'll have to get a room and I'll meet you there," she says, "I'll call you back on your private line, in the morning. Then you can tell me what room *you're* in. That way, it's discreet until then. Don't disappoint me and I want disappoint you."

He's all in, as they hang up.

She won't call him again until she gets there. She's counting on his heroin dealer, calling that same private line. Sometime that same morning, with information about the sale. And he will have called the dealer, from that same line, at least once. Her not needing an alibi, for later, will depend on it.

Next, she sets up her *real* hotel room at *Fairfield Inn*, for Wednesday evening. With a 5pm check-in time and special instructions. She charges it to Young D's entertainment account. She's not worried about leaving *that* trace. This will be her second hotel stay, in Lafayette. The second room is for when Chadrella is to know that she's there. But she's going to Lafayette, early Wednesday morning, to kill the test tube baby's daddy. He'll be already dead by the time Baby Girl checks into Fairfield Inn, at 5pm. She won't kill him in her room. That's for rookies. Chadwick or Chad, won't be invited to her room. The spot she'll chose for Wednesday morning's stay, for when she hits Chadwick, will be on the other side of town, from where the Fairfield Inn is located.

On that side, there are 3 neighboring hotels. Chadwick will have to acquire his own room for the rendezvous which he thinks he's going to have, with the forbidden fruit. This pedophile of old has been lusting after Baby Girl, since day one. Even when he *knew* she was an underage college student. He has fiend for her since seeing her in his daughters room, over 8 years ago. She had just turned sixteen. Afterwards, every trip Chadwick made back to LSU, he gave her the lustful

170

eye. He wanted her, then. The luscious piece of fruit that was younger than that daughter he couldn't even reproduce without medical intervention. Lord only knows, what the hell he thinks he can do for Baby Girl, *now*.

"Die quick. That's about it," she says to herself and giggles.

Now she needs a set up for Tito Lopez. For this one, in New York, she has to call Derrick's manager, JB. She dials his mobile number.

"Holler at me," Jeff Blackmon says, as he answers his personal cell phone.

"Good morning, JB," she says, "How's it going?"

"It's Tuesday. Beautiful weather. We got a Platinum album and it's selling like crack," he says, sounding very jubilant. He asks, "How are things in the dirty south?"

"Good but needs to be better. Can we get a spotlight for the weekend?" she asks.

"Harvey at Club Upscale has been at me to get Young D back in there, since the album dropped," JB says, "Let me get him confirmed and I'll hit you back."

They hang up.

She knows Young D will like this gig. He loves New York and most notably, Club Upscale. Because it's a huge spot. The stage is 20 x 22. He can get all of his label artist on it, at the same time. Which means, they can do lots of material without a set change. The stage will hold 9 of them. Plus bodyguards and a few dancing ladies too. The club has 3 floors. The 1st floor is where the stage is, for performances. With a huge dance floor or standing room only and countless booths, along the walls. The 2nd floor is a lounge where you can chill at the bar. Which wraps around the entire outer wall. You can watch sports on the wall size plasma TV screens. Or you can shoot pool, on 1 of the 16 tables. Or partake in some legalized gambling, on 1 of the 20 slot machines or Black Jack tables. The 3rd floor is the gentlemen's club. No other explanation is needed.

Within the half hour, JB hits her back. The spotlight show is set, for Friday night. Doors open at 8pm. Young D performs from 10pm to midnight. He tells her, he'll call Young D and tell him, personally. He always does. Rather she does it or not. He's a great manager, with all of their best interest in the forefront.

Club Upscale is the perfect location. Now she can book a hotel room in NYC, with the perfect alibi to cover it. Club Upscale is located in the same block as The W Hotel, which houses Tito Lopez's penthouse apartment. His penthouse covers the entire 30th floor. She books her and Young D a suite, in The W hotel, for the Friday show.

"I would like the twenty eighth floor, please," she tells the desk clerk, on the other end of the phone. "Club upscale will be calling with the rest of the amenities to be added. Thank you."
They hang up.

The 28th floor is great. In case she has to use the fire escape. She doesn't want to have to shimmy down, more than 3 flights of stairs, on the outside of a 30 story building.
Fuck! I hate heights. But it comes with the job.

She has to be on her way to Galveston. So as usual, she leaves her personals on her vanity and a note on Young D's pillow. She plans to hit Dennis Montgomery during lunchtime, before 2pm. He is notorious for his mouth. He's always doing interviews and saying things like, "Organized crime is alive and well. It's responsible for eighty percent of the drug

172

Trafficking, through our American ports."
And other crap like that. Yet, he fails to speak on his part, *in* it. And he also failed to turn down the many campaign contributions he'd received over the years, from these organized families. Her organized family, being 1 of them. He has another interview tonight, with *MSNBC*, to discuss in detail, the families involved. And what plans he's implementing in his final term, to alleviate the docks of this matter. Baby Girl is willing to bet, *all 8 of her homes*, that he wouldn't have even mentioned any of the families that have given him 6 figures per campaign or more. That is, if he was going to be alive to do the interview.

But she won't allow that interview to happen. Not with her family being 1 of the crime families to contribute hush money to his campaign. He won't be doing the interview, so there's no need to worry on that one. He'll be entertaining rigor mortis, long before then. Still, there's a job to do and whether he's going to tell on her family or not. The job is in play.
We'll eliminate you and alleviate the problem of having a damn hypocrite in office. Save that damn cash for my babies.

She grabs her *Get To Work bag*, her overnight *Coach* bag and her *Louis V* briefcase. She has a great plan of action for Dennis' snitchin ass. She leaves home at 10:30am and takes a very relaxing drive to Galveston Beach.

As she reflects again on yesterdays events, outside of Kierra. She can't help but smile when she thinks of all the phases of Hip-Hop music which was represented. West Coast, Midwest, East Coast and definitely, Dirty South. She loves all types of music. But Hip-Hop music is her heart. It's her culture and a part of her upbringing that she learned to love, since

1993. It will always take precedence over any other genre, with her. She listens to it daily, with all types of subject matter. But when she's going after a mark. Picking the correct theme song, as she calls it, is just as important to her as studying and knowing her marks habits.
It's gotta be gangsta!

On her drive to the beach today, she's enjoying; *The Diary* by *Scarface*.
...............so they callin on the government, to try to make somebody quiet.....for the bullshit they done to me......gangster nip......spice one...Tupac....never gave a gun to me!
"I know that shits for real, face," she says as she agrees and listens to more truth speech.

...........bring your ass to where they got me.......so you can feel the hand of the dead body. Nigga don't believe that song.....that niggaz wrong............gangstaz don't live that long!

Scarface is her all time favorite, southern rapper. After Young D, of course. He's from right here in Young D's hometown of Houston Texas and the 5th ward. She knows without a doubt, what wards are now. She loves Scarface's music because he's broad, street and political. He's gangster and at the same time, his lyrics have a message too. The message *Scarface* puts out is basically, "Don't believe the hype."

Baby Girl reaches Galveston with time to spare. She pulls into a local parking garage which is used by office buildings, hotels, restaurants and tourist establishments, as well as guest of these businesses. This is a garage her family has used, several times on visits to the beach. It's linked to local hotels and restaurants. But has no security and very few cameras. Guest of the hotels, park here and often take trolleys and tour buses to the actual tourist attractions and the beach. So the vehicles which are parked here, belong to either tourist, who do very little driving. Or employees, who are on their jobs for 8 to 12 hours, a day. This garage is perfect for her to keep her cover. She can park her Benz here, steal a car for her job and return without alerting anyone. But first, she has to change clothes. She grabs her foldable slim Jim, grabs her overnight Coach bag and checks the garage again, before getting out. There are no witnesses around. She has to go into the hotel public facilities and change into her disguise. Then come out and *"lift a vehicle"*, for her ride over to the ILA offices. She gets out and heads for the elevator that leads to 1 of the larger hotel chains. She's muttering the lyrics from the Scarface song, she was just playing.

"Amer-I-cas always been known for blaming us niggaz for their fuck ups......."

She heads into the Clarion and dips into the large public restroom. She takes the handicap stall. It's large enough to change clothes in. She does so, quickly. Then she whips out her compact mirror and applies her mustache, side burns and man wig. She pulls her brown fitted cap down over her eyebrows. She pretends to be using the bathroom until the last female has left the restroom. Once the coast is clear, she darts out, checking her look in the mirror, quickly.

"Damn! You're a fine ass man, girl," she says to herself, as she giggles and heads out the door.

She zips back to the elevator. This time going to the top floor of the garage. She knows, from her many stays here, that this is where the employees of all the establishments park. The

175

morning shift is here and want be leaving for at least 4 hours. She pops the lock on a Ford Explorer and hops in. Using her vehicle tools, she starts it without busting the column. She's out of the garage, in no time.

Over at the local longshoreman's association building, it's all abuzz with excitement about the *MSNBC* interview team that's due to arrive within a few hours to interview Dennis Montgomery. They have a catering service, setting up tables in their main banquet hall. There's an ice sculpture being carved in the shape of a dolphin which is looking quite exquisite. The maintenance staff are putting together the stage for the live interview. While *"go for's"* and temp agents are working themselves into a sweaty frenzy. Making sure every little detail on each of their list is done, correctly.

Dennis Montgomery has a press conference tonight which will be followed by a question and answer session. His secretary is in charge of getting the question list to him, so he can go over them. He will cross out any and all questions which he refuse to entertain. She's also responsible for going over the speech for the press conference, once it arrives. While Baby Girl is in route, Dennis sits in his office, full of himself.

"Cindy, my speech and questions have arrived by messenger, correct?" Dennis Montgomery asks, over his office intercom.

He's speaking to his main secretary. She tells him, yes.

"Then I need for you to double check them both, thoroughly. And make sure everything is in order, for tonight. Then meet me in the conference room, with both of them, in twenty minutes," he orders.

"Yes sir, Dennis. And mister Wade called to confirm lunch at the Olive Garden, at one thirty," she tells him.

Dennis Montgomery confirms that the lunch date is still on. Then he leans back in his large office chair and lights a cigar. He has a panel of city employees coming to hear him speak tonight, about security on the waterfront. He wants the federal government to oversea security. Baby Girl cannot allow him to make that speech.

Cindy heads to the Conference room to wait for Dennis, who is still in his office entertaining. As soon as Cindy leaves, Baby Girl makes her move. Deepening her voice, so that she sounds like a young man, she heads to the front desk.

"Delivery!" she says, disguised as a male messenger, as she approaches the front desk.

The receptionist has her to sign in, then she instructs her to take the package and deliver it down the hall to Cindy Ball's desk.

Once she passes the receptionist desk, she stays in character until she reaches Cindy's desk. That's when she notices Cindy, isn't present. Quickly, she grabs a large manila envelope from the desk with the return label and postage, already on it. Cindy has a sign on her desk which reads: *In Conference.*

Baby Girl, dressed in her male messenger disguise, has managed to get past the reception area and Dennis' secretary, as a male. There is only 1 door left between her and Dennis Montgomery. She steps to it and knocks.

"Yes, Cindy! What is it!?" Montgomery bellows from behind his office door.

Baby Girl doesn't respond.

"Well, *Cindy*! Come on in, for Christ sake!" he yells, "I told you to meet me in the conference room. But since you're at the door. I assume something is wrong with the speech or the questions," he yells, very obnoxiously.

The door opens and a younger version of Cindy, scurries from his office, adjusting her clothes and checking her lipstick in a compact mirror. She's wiping her hair down while she attempts to fasten her blouse, at the same time.

She says, "Excuse me, sir" to Baby Girl the messenger, as she scoots around her and makes her escape.

Baby Girl goes in with her head bowed. She closes, then locks the door behind her.

"You're not Cindy," Montgomery says, arrogantly.

"I guess she must be in the conference room, son. Lay it on the table, grab a five dollar bill from the tray and leave. Thank you."

He says that while he re-adjust his trousers and tie. Baby Girl puts the package under her arm. Then she pulls her 9mm with the silencer, from the gat pocket of her *Derrick Blake Collection* brown Khakis. She parts his hair, neatly with the 1st shot. He falls into his desk chair with a stunned look on his face. But his lungs are still breathing, momentarily. She approaches him and puts the 2nd shot straight through his heart. Then she checks his pulse and feels that he has expired. She whips out her silver butterfly knife, cuts out his tongue and cuts off his bottom lip too.

"I'll bet you when you woke up this morning. You didn't think by noon, you'd be dead in your office with your tongue and bottom lip cut off. Did you, Dennis?" she whispers to dead mark, number 1.

Then she wraps the tongue and lip in the plastic wrap, she pulls from some other item he had on his desk that he had not too long opened.

"Use what you got, Baby Girl," she mumbles as she wraps them quickly.

She stuffs them into the return address envelope from Cindy's desk. She exits his office, fast. She passes Cindy's desk and the reception area. Luckily, the receptionist is away from her desk now too. Baby Girl grabs the express elevator to the lobby. Then, as she heads out the door, she drops the envelope in the *USPS* blue box, just down the street.

"Special Delivery," she says with a chuckle.

She disappears around the corner of the building and down the street to where she had parked her getaway vehicle. She retraces her steps, back to the garage.

She parks the Explorer, 1 floor lower than it was. Just in case someone knows the SUV and sees her getting out of it. She hurries and this time, she uses a different hotel public bathroom.

She changes out of her browns and back into her girl clothes. Only then, does she feel like she can breathe easy. She goes back and gets into her car and heads out of the garage. She's going to the Olive Garden, for lunch. She had seen on Cindy's desk that Dennis was scheduled to meet a Mr. Wade there at 1:30pm, to go over his speech and high points. She'd only had a light breakfast and by now, she's very hungry. She likes Olive Garden and knows, for sure, they'll have 2 seats opening up, in a few minutes. She arrives at Olive Garden and heads inside.

It's 1:15pm. Mr. Wade is just arriving. She sits at the bar and orders a grilled Chicken Caesar salad.

"I really just come here for the salad, bread and wine," she says to the bartender with a smile. She adds, "I'm usually full after that and have to take my entrée home."

Today is no different. Coincidentally, at the same time she's asking the bartender to box up her pasta dish to go. Mr. Wade is receiving news that Dennis Montgomery will not be joining

179

him, for lunch. Because Dennis Montgomery has been murdered. As the bartender gives her the to-go box, he tells her the breaking news. She plays it to the hilt.

"Oh my God! Who is *he*?" she asks, as she acts like *Alicia Silverspoon* in the movie; *Clueless.*
The bartender fills her in on what she already knows. Then he turns up the sound on the TV. She watches the news for a few minutes, then she acts as if she's afraid to go outside alone. She stands up and excuses herself from the bar, as she looks toward the door with a fearful expression on her face. Seeing a damsel in distress, the bartender steps up.

"Ma'am, do you need me to walk you to your car?" he asks, while flirting, at the same time.

"Will you, please?" she asks, "I hate to be such a baby, about all of this news stuff. But I really am afraid, right now."
He tells the other 2 bartenders to cover for him, for a few minutes. While he walks her out to her car. They say they will. Then he and Baby Girl head out the door.

She unlocks her door remotely, as the 2 of them approach it. She hops in, quickly. Locking it, as it closes with her inside. She starts up her 2007 *CLK63 AMG Cabriolet, Mercedes Benz.* The bartender is waiting for her to put down the window. She cracks it, just a bit, smiles and says,
"Thank you, so much."

"I wanted to give you this," he says, as he slips his business card through the crack in her window.

"Oh. Okay," she says with a smile. She grabs it, looks at it and adds, "Thanks Christopher, so much."

"Call me sometime and maybe I can be your bodyguard, again," he says with a Colgate smile.
She says sure, as she backs out of the parking space and drives away. As soon as she's out of his sight, she drops the top and

Responds to Christopher's suggestion, asking, "Yea and who's gonna protect you from me?"

She giggles as she pops out *The Diary* CD. But she stays with *Scarface* as she replaces it with; *The World is Yours*. She starts her ride home to the song; *Still That Nigga.*

"Cause I am," she says, giggling as she flips the business card from Christopher, into the wind.

She drives home, entertaining herself. She's heading back to Houston to hug her 2 sons, Jordan and her husband. Then, she'll prepare dinner and get set up for her Lafayette trip, tomorrow. She'll leave at 5am, in the morning, going on her *heroin hit.*

She arrives back at her Houston home, before 3pm. Her oldest son, whom they call, *Man*, greets her in the kitchen. She sees no signs of her husband. Not at first.

"Hey, my mommy," her 2 year old and oldest son, Derrick Jr says, with a suspicious smile on his face.

"Hey, man. What are you up too?" she asks, knowing his aptness for getting into mischief.

She is absolutely correct, as she'll soon discover.

"I not do nothing," he says in his cutest baby voice, as he quickly tries to plead his case.

But he's looking guilty. He's covered from head to toe, in flour and chocolate syrup. Amongst other things. Baby Girl goes around the kitchen island to see if she can find the source of the concoction that's pasted to her 1st born. There is a mixture of sugar, *Froot Loops*, flour, raw eggs and chocolate syrup, all over the floor, in front of the refrigerator.

"*Man*? What did you do, son?" she asks in disgust.

She puts the entrée from Olive Garden in the fridge. Young D will eat it, sooner or later. Then she heads to the cleaning closet

181

to get her mop, the bucket and some cleaners. So she could get the mess cleaned up.

"Come on, son," she says with a smile. "You're gonna help mommy clean up this mess, you made. Okay?"

"But I-I *shry* cook da eggs," Lil Man says as he's pleading his case.

"Well, you're not cooking them, baby. Not on mommy's floor," Baby Girl says as she smiles again.

"I cook you da cake, mommy," he tries.

"You're cooking mommy a cake?" she asks, in a voice which says she's impressed with his thoughts.

"Yes ma'am!" he says as he smiles, with chocolate syrup on his cute little nose.

"Oh. Thank you, baby," she says, "And now. Can you help mommy clean up the floor, please? Where's daddy?"

"Him sheeping," Lil Man tries.

"He's sleeping in and you're cooking lunch, ha? Well, we need to be at the manor. So misses Addie Mae can help you with your meal," she says and laughs at her son.

She starts cleaning up the mess. Young D, who was awaken by their laughter, now comes into the kitchen.

"Oh *shit*," he says, after seeing the mess.

"Daddy, you can't go back to bed with a two year old in the house," Baby Girl says to him, as she smiles and kisses him. Young D stretches and tries to awake himself, fully, to take in the mess on the floor.

He laughs and asks, "What was he trying to do, in here?"

"It's not funny, Derrick," Baby Girl says, "Our son was making eggs and a cake, for me."

She can't help but laugh too. They're both laughing while using their hands to try and hide their faces. But now, seeing that his parents are laughing. Derrick Jr takes this as his

182

opportunity to strut his stuff. He's proud of his mess, now.

"I cook cake," he says, over and over, as he struts around the kitchen.

"Well, if his mama wasn't off killing up folks-"

"What?" Baby Girl asks as she instantly fires back at Young D. "Is my place in the home, now? Ha. daddy?"

"I'm just saying, baby," Young D tries, "I didn't know you wasn't around the house, when I brought him from mama's. She wanted me to bring Don too. But then she said, no. I couldn't bring him because you wasn't up there, with me. She didn't even want me to carry him home."

"You should have left man over there, too," she says, "I would have gotten them, when I got back."

"Well, maybe if you let me know that, in advance. Or call me and let me know what your next move is gonna be. Then I would at least know, you're alive," he says, obviously upset with her.

She doesn't say another word. The 3 of them clean up the concoction on the floor, while Lil Man continues to clown. Young D loses the frowns in his forehead. Baby Girl still doesn't speak a word. Not until the mess is completely cleaned up. Then she wipes her son's face and hands and speaks to her husband.

"Do you want something to eat? Now that the kitchen is cleaned, master?" she asks.

"Yes and I'll help," he says.

"Oh no. I'm in the place that I belong in, now," she says sarcastically. "In the kitchen. Let me take my shoes off, so I'll be barefoot too. Does that also mean that I have to get pregnant again?"

"Come here, baby," he says as he hugs and kisses her. "I'm sorry. That was wrong for me to say. I was just worried

183

about you and I said that, out of worry. You know I don't think you belong in the kitchen, barefoot. The bedroom. Maybe. And the pregnant part. That would be okay with me."
"Not with a two year old and a two month old," she says, "No thanks."
They kiss again as the 2 of them prepare to cook dinner together, while Man entertains them and himself.

By the time dinner is almost finished, the guys from H-Town Records plus Soldier, Baby Boy, G-Dog and their crews have all awakened and are descending on the house.
"Happy Tuesday! Now, let's hit the studio, my nigga!" Young Aristocrat yells.
The entire group of over 30 guys, fill the house, instantly. First, Baby Girl has to put Man at the table with his plate. Then she makes her and Young D, a plate. Afterwards, Young D tells the others to grab a plate. Then head upstairs to the studio and he doesn't have to tell them, twice. They take advantage as they gather around the stove.
Young D and Baby Girl's home is split level. The entire top floor is Young D's home studio. He has another studio above his clothing store, downtown. DeJuan, Gat em and High Top, along with Big Daddy, have put together a mixtape. They're letting the others put verses and tracks on it, today. They have other new material to record, as well. They need to get 7 songs completed, today.
"I got lines, on top of fresh lines, for y'all today. My niggaz," Gat em expresses.
He's 18, the youngest of all. He had just made 18, this month.
"I thought you wasn't gonna leave them ho's alone, long enough to write shit," Arafat teases him.
They all laugh, as they finish off their meals.

184

"Alright, let's get these dishes back downstairs," DJ Debo adds, "Then we can get to work."

"Big Daddy and High Top, y'all help me load the two dishwashers," Manolo suggests, "We can't leave this shit in the kitchen, for Baby Girl."

"You damn sho can't," Young D agrees, "I won't get no pussy, for a week, if y'all leave all this shit in here."

They laugh as they head downstairs to the kitchen.

After they've loaded and started the dishwashers, they head back up to the studio to get some work done. They have all put their cell phones on vibrate, which is the rule Young D added, once their got more fame. They have to muffle the mass amount of phone calls that constantly come in, to all of them From *wifey's*, bitches-on-the-side, groupies and all.

"It's five pm," Baby Boy announces, "Let's work."

A studio session can last up the 12 hours or more. Young D wants to get done in enough time to see Baby Girl, before she has to leave for Lafayette. He calls her cell phone from upstairs and makes her aware of his intentions.

"Hey, baby," he says as he listens and hears no anger.

"Hey Derrick. What y'all need, up there?" she asks.

"Nothing, baby. I just wanted to know what time you're leaving out again. That's all," he asks.

"Five a m."

"Okay. I'll see you in bed, before you leave," he says, with a hopeful sound in his voice.

"That's on you," she says and he can hear that she's smiling.

They hang up and he lights a fire under the guys.

"Let's not bullshit, fellows," he yells throughout the studio. "I got a wife that don't like sleeping alone. So I'm gonna need to get out of here, by midnight!"

185

They all laugh as they double time it with their last minute lines, so they can get started recording.

In New Orleans, Kid is up to his old tricks. He's on the phone with Kierra, tonight. He's trying to create drama for Baby Girl and Young D.

"Have you seen that nigga, lately or what?" Kid asks Kierra, referring to Young D.

"At the barbeque, last night. But he hasn't been by here since right after your sister had the new baby," she tells him. "You know, when she couldn't fuck him for six weeks. But I called his mama, this morning."

"You still fucking the nigga?" he asks.

"Every chance I get, Kid. Shit the nigga got good ass dick," she confesses, "I can't front on that part."
She laughs. Kid is furious inside but he conceals it. He needs Kierra to help him to get Young D out of Baby Girl's life. But he secretly wants Kierra, for himself. He has wanted her since first meeting her.

"Are you still helping this nigga keep his secret going, Kierra?" Kid asks.

"Yea. Cause he's breaking me off," she admits, "I ain't fixing to fuck up my income. Just because you've got a hard on for your *own* sister," she says as she laughs.

"She's not related to me, by blood. She's only blood to Six Nine," he spits, "And that's not the reason. I just know that nigga Young D, ain't about shit."

"I've been meaning to asked you, Kid," Kierra says, "What did he ever do to you, by the way?"

"He's fucking over my little sister, wit ho's like you," Kid spits again. "Start wit that."

"Then if he's not fucking with me. Why do you keep

186

pushing me to go after him? I mean. You're contributing to him fucking over her," she tries.

"I'm not making that nigga fuck wit you," he says.

"No but it's like you want him too."

"No I don't want him too. But you're the only one I got connections with and solid proof of," Kid admits, "Just because he's not fucking you. Don't think he's not fucking off with some girl. But I don't have the inside scoop, on them. Like I got with you."

"So you're using me to get information on Young D?"

"No more than you use me to get at *that* nigga and any other nigga, that's making bank," he says, hitting her where it hurts.

"Well, I heard that she's going out of town, tomorrow," Kierra reveals, "Hopefully, he's coming to see Danica while she's gone. Because he don't want me to bring her over there.

"You need to be sure, he comes through," Kid insists. She says she'll call his mother back and make it sound urgent.

She's going to call Annie back and asks her to make sure he visits Danica, this week. Before she goes to Arkansas to visit her great grandmother. Kid is okay with that answer. They hang up, so Kierra can call Annie before the clock strikes 10pm.

No one can call any of Young D's house phones, after 10pm. No one except immediate family. And then, it has to be important. Kierra is not included in that, immediate family.

It's 930, on Tuesday night, when Kierra reaches Annie. She tells her to wait until tomorrow morning and she'll relay the message to her son.

"He's in a studio session, right now and I'm not going to disturb him. Not for this." Annie says and they hang up.

Kierra had started 12 hours ago. On the phone with her

girlfriends, plotting on a way to get Young D to hook up with her. It's Tuesday night. 24 hours since the barbeque and she's still no more sure, if she'll see him then she was before she'd gotten up this morning. She ends the phone calling, the same way she had started it. With her girlfriends.

"If he don't show up tomorrow, then you should just go on over there, Key," Trina suggests. "Roll your bold ass right up to the security booth and tell them you're his baby mama. And you came to drop off his daughter and pick up him and his dick."

She laughs hard. Kierra can't help but laugh too. But she knows that's some shit she's not going to try.

"You're stupid, Trina," she says, "I don't wanna piss his mama off. That could fuck my shit up, permanently. If she gets angry. She's the only link I have to get him over here."

"Yea. I know what you mean, home girl," Trina says, "I don't want you to blow your bank account out the water, like that."

"Kid's stingy ass sure is worried about whether I get some dick from D or not."

"That shit is strange to me, Key," Trina says, "I mean. He's Young D wife's brother and he's helping his mistress cheat on her. Does any of that shit make sense to you?"

"None whatsoever," she answers, "I think it's some crazy shit going on. But I'm gonna ex it out, for now. I need to see D, soon as possible. My shit is aching, for him."

"You got to call his mama back, right?"

"Yes. I'll see what happens in the morning," she says, "Now let's get to the club and make some fuckin money."

Trina is her roommate but she's at another dancers place. They hang up. Later, they meet up at *The Anatomy,* where they all work.

CHAPTER EIGHT
<u>DOWN TO RIDE</u>

"YOUNG D'S <u>OTHER LIFE </u>ON WEDNESDAY MORNING"

After many annoying and unwanted phone calls to Annie's house, Kierra finally gets her time with Young D. Baby Girl leaves for Lafayette, this morning. Young D gets up and tells his labelmates to be ready to get back in the studio, again today. He tells them, he has a meeting to go to and he'll be back. But they know where he's going. He's goes to visit Danica, before coming back to his home studio.

Young D arrives at Kierra's door and rings to bell. She opens the door to greet him.

"Hello, daddy," Kierra tries.

"Don't try that shit, bitch," Young D says, "No way in hell are you gonna call me that.

He has a very heated scold in his voice as he enters her apartment. Kierra is being testy, all of a sudden. She'd heard Baby Girl call Young D, "Daddy" at the Memorial Day celebration and many events, prior that one.

"I heard your son's mama calling you daddy," Kierra tries, as she laughs. She adds, "I just figured that was the name that *all* of your women call you."

"Lovely can call me that and her too," he says, speaking of Baby Girl and pointing to Danica. But to Kierra, he adds, "But you won't."

Kierra leaves it alone, at that point. Her daughter Danica is waiting in the room and she's familiar with Young D. She also knows him as, her father.

Danica loves her daddy. She's a sweet and smart little

girl. Very inquisitive, like most 4 year olds and she asks a lot of questions. Young D tries to answer all of them, as best he can. Today, Danica tells him she's seen him on TV and she likes his videos. To that, Young D says, "Thank you." Then he gives her a kiss. Danica is always asking to come, live with him. Which gives Young D even more reason to feel sadness for Danica. She's an outside child, at best. Even his mother Annie had expressed her doubts about his paternity. Before and after the test was done. But since the test had proven 99.9%, that he was Danica's father. His mother hasn't said much more. Other then, she doesn't see any real resemblance in Danica and him.

Kierra always tells them, Danica looks like *her* real father's side of the family. And Kierra's real father has never been in the picture. Besides, he lives in another state, as well. So Annie nor Young D have had the opportunity to see him and witness if Kierra's claim is true.

Young D spends all of 30 minutes, sexing Kierra. Twenty of those minutes are spent, allowing Kierra to orally please him. Which is her greatest talent, as far as he's concerned. He's certain to strap on a condom too. And he has, since being named as her, *baby's daddy*. He was young, back then. And dumb enough to fuck a stripper, with no hat on. Now, an illegitimate child is the price he has to pay. Kierra is sucking his dick, like the pro she is known to be. While their little girl is in the living room, watching Nickelodeon. Young D thinks of Baby Girl, the entire time and where she is, at this moment. And if she's okay. And also, how unfair this is to Baby Girl. But still, he doesn't have the heart to tell her about this phase of his life. He almost feels like he's Kierra's hostage, to a certain extent. And like she has the power over him, to make him do, *this evil*.

How tangled, a web of lies can get.

Young D sure as hell isn't attracted to Kierra. He never really was. It was just the money she could make for him, back then, when she was selling her body, that attracted him. But since then, Young D has seen her true colors and he truly dislikes what he's seen. He doesn't represent her, on the strip, anymore. He only fucks her, now. To keep her mouth shut about their daughter. Just until he can figure out how to tell his wife and only love, Baby Girl.

Young D's mind wonders back to the early morning hours, following the Memorial Day event, when him and Baby Girl was having another satisfying morning of sex Olympics. Even this mornings quickies, were more satisfying than Kierra is now. Thoughts of Baby Girl, makes Young D's dog as hard as a brick. Kierra gets the benefit of a full hard on, from him, for a change. The first one, in nearly 5 years. Kierra just doesn't do it for him. With the threat of exposing his secret, looming over his head, he finds it difficult to even find Kierra sexually arousing, anymore. She is a gold digger. Period. And Young D is simply embarrassed to have been caught up in her trap. The thoughts of how she has gotten to his pockets, infuriates him. He takes his frustrations out on her genitals, for the final 10 minutes. Yet, Kierra loves it. She's into anal sex, as well. Not a favorite of Young D's but he obliges her, on occasion. Not this one, however. He gets his rocks off, after picturing his wife. Then gets up, takes a shower and gets dressed again. He kisses his daughter Danica goodbye and then he leaves. He wants to get home and to his studio, before his wife finishes with her mark. He knows she doesn't take her cell phone with her, on her jobs. But she'll be calling him, after finishing her work. Like always, he's going to be there and

191

available. He doesn't want Baby Girl to find out about Danica, through him not managing his time wisely. And for certain, not now. Probably, not ever. But he hasn't decided that part yet.

Young D gets back to his house at noon. He meets the rest of his labelmates for today's studio session.

They had churned out 9 tracks, in 8 hours, yesterday. While Soldier, Baby Boy and G-Dog and their crews was still here. Their crews had left, right before Young D had gotten the 2nd call from his mother, last night. Saying that he needed to try to visit Danica, before she goes to Arkansas. Young D figured that was another lie, Kierra had come up with. And he remembers not even wanting to go, at all. But he went. Since his crew was slow to rise. He had told them at 930am, that he would be back before noon to start today's session.

"And y'all niggaz be ready to work again," he had said. He's back home now. Free of Kierra, for awhile and glad to see his labelmates and friends are ready to work. Everybody's in the studio and raring to go. So far, today, they've done 1 track, in the 1 hour since he'd returned from Kierra's apartment.

"Now that's progress," High Top yells.

The studio is a cloudy haze of weed and Newport smoke. These guys smoke, a lot of herb. Young D can't wait to let Baby Girl hear all of the new songs. They're about to start on number 2, when Young D gets a call from his manager Jerry Blackmon or JB, as everyone calls him. He's calling to tell him about a show he has booked in New York city, for Friday night.

"It's at Upscale, man," JB says, "It's a forty K, show."

Young D is unusually suspicious about this show. It came out of the blue, it seems.

"What made them call you, now?" Young D asks JB.

"Actually, I called them," JB says, "They've been trying to get you back in there, since before the album dropped. But after Baby Girl told me, you needed a show up here for the weekend. I called them to see if they could swing it. And they did."

"She told you I needed to go to work, ha?" Young D asks, knowing the makings of an alibi when he hears one.

"Yep," JB laughs, "She's keeping you on the grind, man. You got a family, son."

They laugh and Young D confirms that he'll be there on Friday. They hang up.

"Who is *this* hit on?" he asks himself, not realizing he had said it aloud.

"*Hit*? What are you talking about, man?" DeJuan asks. He was poking his head outside of the booth, about to ask Young D to get him another beer. He overhears Young D, as he's coming back into the hallway, leading to and from 1 of the recording booths. Young D had ducked in there to hear JB, more clearly.

"Oh, nothing," Young D lies, "I was trying to figure out how I can add that part into the next lyrics. That's all."

DeJuan gives him a strange look and goes back into the booth.

Damn! Baby, I don't even know how long it's going to be before I'll be done gave the whole shit away. Just by thinking out loud.

Young D thinks to himself, this time without talking out loud. He makes sure of this, as he goes back into the writing lobby of his home studio, where High Top and the others are. They're writing and waiting for their turn to go into 1 of the booths, to recite their lyrics to the 2nd track.

"BABY GIRL'S <u>VERSION</u> OF WEDNESDAY MORNING"

"How did the session, come out?" Baby Girl asks Young D, as he crawls into their bed, just before 2am and wraps his arms around her.

He's just finished an all day studio session, in his home studio.

"We've got nine tracks done, since five, pee emm," Young D says, proudly. "They're mastered and all."

"Daddy, that's awesome," Baby Girl says, "I know they're hot."

"You're hot," he says with a snicker, "You're staying two days, for this one?"

"I leave today, at five ay emm. I'll do the job. Then check into my hotel, tonight. Or at five, pee emm," she clarifies, "So I can meet with Chadrella, in the morning."

"Where are you staying at?" Young D asks, "Can you tell me that?"

"Yes, daddy," she says as she turns to face him. "I'm staying at the Fairfield Inn, on east Willow street. But not until five, pee emm. It's across from Northgate mall."

"So I can call you there, right?" he asks.

"Yes, you sure can," she says as she gives him a long kiss. Then she says, "You're gonna be in the studio, so I can hear the new stuff?"

Young D says, sadly, "I wanted you to hear them, tonight. But I knew it was late and you have to get up early. So yea. I can do that. Did I make it to bed in time to get some loving?"

"For a real love making session? *No*," Baby Girl says, "But we can get a quickie. If we hurry up. I need to get going, so I can leave, exactly at five."

They spend the next 15 minutes, making love. For them,
194

that's a quickie. Afterwards, Baby Girl gets up to go take a soak in the Jacuzzi. Young D joins her and they extend the sex session, another 15 minutes. They wash each other, then get out of the tub. Young D towel dries her and she returns the favor.

"Daddy, you look so tired," she says.

"I am. But I had to give you what you needed. Before you leave," he offers.

His eyes are barely open. He's still high too. In their studio sessions, with all 4 crews that was there, they could go through a whole pound of weed. Easily. Baby Girl leads him back to bed. She orders him into it and tucks him in.

"Get some sleep, daddy," she orders, "Don't get up until I talk to you. After my job, if you can. I'll take man to mama's, on my way out. Okay?"

"Okay. Thanks, baby," he mutters as he sinks into his pillow.

Little Don had spent the night at Annie's house. Young D falls fast asleep. Baby Girl goes into the vanity to finish her daily. Then, she packs her bags for the Lafayette job. Soon after, she's preparing to leave Houston.

There are 3 motels in the area, where Chadwick had spoke of meeting Baby Girl. And Baby Girl has maid uniforms, for all three motels. She packs all 3 sets of uniforms, then she grabs all of her bags, for the job. She places them in the trunk of her *CLK63. Her work car.* She goes back into the house and into both of her sons rooms. She grabs clothes for each of them. Then packs them into their Louis V suitcases, which read, *Off To Grandma's House.*

"These get a lot of use," she says aloud, "They're always off to grandma's house. It seems."

195

She stays in a constant battle with herself, about not being able to spend a lot of quality time with her husband and children. As she puts her sons bags on the back seat of her car, she thinks about her busy schedule.
I really have to retire, so I can just be mommy.

She goes back inside and back to Derrick Jr's room. She picks him up and wraps him in his favorite blanket. Then, she cuddles him to her chest. She has put everything in the car. Still holding their son, she goes back into her and Young D's bedroom. She has to kiss him, goodbye.
She does. He opens his eyes, slightly.
"Do you wanna kiss your cowboy?" she asks with a smile.
Young D, newly slumbering, wakes up long enough to kiss his oldest son, on the cheek and to lightly pinch it.
"He looks adorable when he's asleep. Doesn't he," Baby Girl whispers to Young D, as she giggles.
"He's adorable, all the time. Just like daddy," Young D says as he smiles, slightly.
They kiss again. Then she whispers, "Do you want a note on my pillow?"
"I'd rather have you, on my pillow," he responds.
"You can have that, tomorrow night," she says, "I promise."
He says, "Okay, baby. I love you. Be careful and come home safe, to my boys and me."
They kiss again and he drifts back off to sleep. She leaves the note. Then she turns off the lamp, leaves the room and locks the house as she heads into the garage. She lays Derrick Jr aka Lil Man, in the front seat and drives up the driveway to Annie's house.

As soon as Baby Girl arrives, Annie meets her at the kitchen door. She was expecting her. She's making breakfast, so she can eat something before she has to leave. Annie seems a bit preoccupied, to Baby Girl. It's very early. But Annie is a woman who gets up before the sun. So it couldn't be that she's out of bed, too early. There's something else bothering her.

"Are you okay, mama?" Baby Girl asks.

"I am," Annie says, "Just got up on the wrong side of that big old empty bed, today. The boys will lift my spirits. Like this little man, right here."

She tries to throw Baby Girl off, into thinking that she needs the comfort of a man. She does. But that isn't what's wrong, today. She takes Derrick Jr, who is still wrapped in his blanket and kisses him on both cheeks. He's still asleep and doesn't even flinch. Annie takes him to his room, in her home and puts him back to bed. Baby Girl follows her. She kisses her son again, after he's laying down. She kisses her youngest son, Don Prince, who is slumbering in the next room. Then she and Annie head to Jordan's room. Baby Girl kisses him too, then they head back to the kitchen.

"Do you want some breakfast before you have to go?" Annie asks.

"I don't have time," Baby Girl says, "But you know I'll take some eggs, bacon and toast, to go."

They giggle as Baby Girl makes her way to the door with her sandwich, still feeling an uneasiness about what has her mother-in-law off of hers, this morning. Annie watches her as she gets into her Benz and pulls away.

I dropped my son at his granny's house. She seems like there's something on her mind, that has pissed her off. Royally! It had better not be, Derrick. But something is not right, today. When I get back, my mission is to find out, exactly what that is.

197

Not knowing it's about the same guest she's been channeling in her mind, Baby Girl files that problem in her mental rolodex. For now. But she will get the bottom of why Kierra, stays on her mind. She hits the road on her way to Lafayette, Louisiana. It's 5am, sharp.

This is the time when she does her best thinking and planning. When she's on the open road. *Alone.* Or when she's on Young D's tour bus, after they've all passed out from partying.

This is the way to see this country.

She sets her cruise control, after five minutes on the interstate. She has never gotten a speeding ticket. Nor has she been pulled over and randomly harassed and searched. Not unless she was on Young D's tour bus. Rappers are always harassed by police. Black men. *Period.* She thinks on that and the fact that she has 2 sons. She thinks of the target that's, automatically placed on their backs because they are young black males. She can't even imagine what she'd do to some red faced, red neck, bigoted ass officer, of the *God damn law.* As Comedian, the late *Robin Harris*, use to say it. If they was to harm *her* black males.

"I would show them who's nicer, with hers," she says and smiles. "That's what the fuck I would do."

She can't stand to imagine harm coming to her children. So she clicks her mind back to the open road.

It's a beautiful morning, already. She can see the sun peeking over the horizon. As she drives east, taking in America, by her own, beautiful self. She has been to many places, in this world, during her lifetime. But southern America is the most beautiful place in America, to her. She may be just a little biased, though. Being that she was born and predominantly raised, in the south.

Musically, she starts her journey, listening to *UGK's* *"Take If Off"*, from *The Corruptor's* soundtrack. She reminisces about the Memorial Day barbeque and how *Bun B* and *Pimp C* tore shit up, for the crowd. She loves it when they have legendary guest, at their home. It's always a blast. Young D and his crew, sure know how to throw a party.

"It's time for some of those *C-town* thugs," she says as she pops in; *Bone Thugs-n-Harmony's, Creepin' On Ah Come Up* and pumps it up, on the hit, *Thuggish Ruggish Bone*.
"We're not against rap….., we're not against rappers. But we are against those thugs!"
"It's the thuggish ruggish bone! It's thuggish ruggish bone…."

She sings along, as she cruises east on interstate 10. Her cruise control is locked on 76 mph.
"Loving your peoples cause we so real…"

Then her mind shifts to the negative side of the barbeque. She thinks about Kierra Ramsey. This is 1 bold bitch, in her opinion. If she is indeed, after her husband.

"I will gouge out your fucking eyes and shove my barrels into your skull. You tramp ass bitch," she says with a lovely smile.
She's seeing herself doing it, *In Living Color*. That's enough to brighten her morning, without the sun. If Kierra is after her man. Then she's going to get to know the real *Lovely*, up close and fucking personal. Baby Girl doesn't just love her husband for his looks and style. She loves his good ass dick too. And she's not in the mood for sharing it with nobody's bitch. She doesn't mind acting a damn fool, either. She raps along to *Thuggish Ruggish Bone*.
"Pull to the curb, smoke with my hustler's. They be lovin' them

199

brain shots. Stay pee oh deeded and tweeted. Gotta get another case from my trunk. Old English, really don't need it. But in case my true's wanna get drunk. They pump bone, so leave 'em alone you don't wanna get shut down. Thugs runnin the nine quad. And best believe we be runnin it thug style….., so what now?"

She has a 4 hour trip to Lafayette, in front of her. She's going to be there, for two days. She figures she'll arrive around 9am, when all of the business offices are open. But she's not going to do any business until tomorrow morning. After she checks into the Fairfield Inn, which she had booked online. The room for tomorrow, is in her real name.

****

Meanwhile, back at the house in Houston, Young D awakes to the sound of the house phone ringing. He looks at the caller idea. It's his mother. He answers it.

"Good morning, ma," he says to Annie.

It's 9am and she's calling him for the second time, in as many days, to inform him that she has talk to Kierra. She has just gotten off of the phone with her.

"She said Danica will be in Arkansas, for a summer stay, after this Friday," Annie says, "She wants you to see her before she leaves. And she said you told her, she can't bring her out here, anymore. Because you don't even want the neighbors to see her here, with a little girl. She wants to know if you can see her, today?"

After a few curse words, from both of them. Most of them aimed at Kierra. Young D tells his mother that he'll go visit the little girl. He'll go visit her, today. They hang up.

Young D sits up in the bed and looks at Lovely's pillow.

200

She has left a note, as usual. **He picks it up and reads it;**
I have to write you these sweet notes, just to remind you that I love you, daddy. I always have and I always will. No matter who or what. You are the best daddy a girl could have and you are all mine. I miss your handsome face, already. I can't wait to meet you right here, on this pillow, tomorrow night. You are my world. Well, after those 2 smaller versions of you, that is. ☺ Keep loving, only me, the same way that I love, only you.
Love always,
Lovely Blake aka, Your Baby Girl
and Wife, for life!

He blushes, openly.
"Nobody does it like Lovely Walker-Blake, baby," Young D says as he peels himself from between their sheets to go take a shower.
He feels extra energized, after reading her note. He isn't planning to go to Kierra's, at all. His plans are to start back with the studio session, early this morning. Because he wants to have 2 mixtapes worth of material finished, by the time he sees his wife again. He hops out of the shower and dresses, quickly. Before he can leave the house, Annie calls the house phone again. He looks at the caller idea. He decides to let it ring and leaves out the door.
He heads to the house his labelmates and crew, sleep in. His cell phone starts to ring before he can make it to the guest house. It's his mother again. He answers it, as he walks.
She's pleading with him to go see Danica, today. Only because she's afraid that Kierra will file a case, at child support enforcement. If she does that, Baby Girl will certainly find out about the little girl. That is not the way Annie wants Baby Girl to find out. And that's the 1 thing that his mother

201

knows, he doesn't want. That's the only reason she's stressing the visit. But deep down, Annie wants Kierra to do, just that.

"I would rather her go to child support, Derrick," Annie says.

"Why would you wish that?" he asks.

"Then we can get to the truth," she says, "The *real* truth."

"Yeah. Whatever that is," he says, "We had a paternity test done."

"I know, son," she says, "I just don't believe it. That child don't look like any of our people. But rather than have her start more shit, today. Or to keep calling my damn phone. Just go and visit the baby and get it over with."

"We'll see," he says, "I gotta go, so I can get these niggaz up."

She says okay and they hang up.

Young D walks into the guest house and locates his labelmates. They're all still laid out from the overnight session. As soon as they hear his voice, they start pleading with him for a little more time to sleep. After all, they was up all night, in the last session, some of them say. They asked him if he'll give them a couple more hours to sleep. Then, they promise him they'll be ready to hit the studio, in a few hours. He reluctantly agrees. Then, he tells them that they had better be up, dressed and already at the studio, when he returns.

"I'll be ready to work, at noon! Straight Up!" Young D yells, "And I ain't gonna be in the mood for no bullshit, whatsoever, when I get back to this muafucka."

He lingers around in the guest house, looking for an alternate way to waste the next few hours. Rather then going to Kierra's. All the while, his labelmates are saying,

"Okay. We'll be ready."

He eventually leaves the guest house. He goes back and locks, he and Baby Girl's house. But he leaves the studio access door unlocked, for the crew. Then he heads off to visit his daughter.

On the drive there, he contemplates how he'll maneuver through this visit. He knows Kierra will want sex, from him. He can feel the queasiness in his stomach, at the thought of her doing a striptease for him. Thinking that will make his nature rise.

"That's only gonna make my breakfast rise," he says aloud.

He drives the 30 minutes or less, out near the 5th ward, to Kierra's apartment. He finds a parking space and parks. He lingers in his car, for a few minutes. He's dreading this visit, so much. It's pass 1030am, as he gets out and walks towards the door.

Kierra must have been looking out of the window when he arrived. Because she opens the door, as soon as he's about to ring the doorbell.

"Hello, daddy," she tries.

"No way in hell are you gonna call me that," Young D says with a look of disgust on his face.

He's all set to scold her and call her a few degrading names too. Whatever it takes, to inflict as much mental pain as he can to this gold digging washed up ass, stripper slut.

Kierra is being testy, anyway. She'd heard Baby Girl call him daddy at the Memorial Day celebration and at many events prior.

"Lovely can call me that. And her, she can call me that," he says, speaking of Baby Girl and pointing to Danica, "But not your trifling ass."

He detests Kierra, like a disease. She always tries to mimic Baby Girl's phases, ways and mannerism. Just trying to impress Young D. But actually, all it does is irritate him. He can't stand it when she tries to imitate his wife, Lovely.

"You can get off that shit, right there. For real," he tells her. "You will never, ever, be anything even close to my wife. So go on and give that shit up."

"I know something I'd like to get on, baby," Kierra says, "Come on in here and give me, my due. Since I can't call you, daddy. Maybe I can make you call me a few names."

"I'm not your baby, either," he says."

Ho, Bitch, hooker, slut, tramp.

He's already thought of a few names, for her. A few that he and his crew, pick from whenever they discuss her.

Initially, during this visit, is when Young D tries to sit down and talk with Danica, for a few minutes. But Kierra is as irritating as a rash, on your ass. Or an itch, in the middle of his damn back.

"Go on in there. Damn!" he says, "I know where it is. You asked me to come see her. Now, let me see her."

Kierra backs off, only briefly. She goes and stands in her bedroom door. Young D knows he isn't going be in this apartment, longer then 30 minutes. Kierra is being impatient and threatening to get loud, on him. So he slowly moves toward her bedroom. As they leave Danica watching, *Nick Time*, with the television as her babysitter. Something she seems very comfortable and familiar, with doing. Young D figures that's most likely where she spends most of her time, while her mama is tricking with, *Jim and John*.

He knew this was never about him visiting, for the little girls sake, anyway. He never gets to play with Danica. Only Kierra. And he absolutely hates her games.

Once he's inside the bedroom, she closes the door. He

leans against it, as he lets his mind wonder off and onto Baby Girl. He's wondering what she's doing at this very moment. And wishing he was having an intimate moment with her. Instead of Kierra.

CHAPTER NINE
GOOD GIRL, GONE BAD
Back to Real Time!!!

LAFAYETTE, LOUISIANA

Baby Girl can't check in. Not under her own name. At least, not this morning. She's not suppose to be in town until, 24 hours later. So what she does at this motel is, she pays cash and uses a random name with her fake ID. She checks into *Motel 6* under the name, *Sharon Jones*.
Chadwick Donaldson is now in play.

As she waits for her key, she surveys the streets. From the lobby, she scans the area around her motel. She notices the 3 other hotel chains, in the immediate area. She can see the maids carts are still out at *Days Inn,* just up the street.
We'll go with Days Inn, today.

"What's good to eat, around here?" she asks the desk clerk.

"Shrimp Etouffee, Jambalaya, Red Beans. Or anything Cajun, seafood or southern. You can get it at, *Chester's.* It's two miles up, this same street, Mrs. Jones," the clerk says, "Just south of the interstate. It's just before the Northgate Mall entrance."
Baby Girl gets her key and her receipt. She thanks the clerk and hops back into her car. She drives around to her room. It's on the back and away from the street, as she had requested. She takes her things into her room. Then she turns on the air conditioner and TV.

I already got my maids gear for Days Inn.

She smiles. First, she leaves in her car, as if she's going to the restaurant the clerk had suggested. She had even mentioned as much, to the clerk.

But just down the street, she pulls into the *Days Inn* parking lot. She gets out and walks around the hotel until she finds the laundry area. There is only 1 attendant in there, at the time and he isn't noticing much of anything. Baby Girl cases the laundry area while standing at the Coke machine. Just outside of it. She spots the extra carts. The attendant is stacking more linens on top of them.

If, and only if, I can get one of those carts. I will leave it in front of the room door. They'll find him quicker, that way.

She checks the area for stairs around the hotel. No camera's outside on the grounds. Nor on the buildings. Not even on the light post, in the parking lot.

I love small towns and small town crime.

She giggles to herself as she walks around on the 2nd floor. She's going to suggest to Chadwick that he stay here. And once she gets his room number, she'll know how to better plan her approach to his room.

After getting the layout, she goes back to her car and back to *Motel 6*.

She's still bumping; *Bone Thugs n Harmony*. This time, she rides to; *Foe The Luv of Money*. *Eazy E* is spitting his verse as she pulls back into the parking lot and around to her room at Motel 6.

"Standing on the corner, straight slanging rocks..., ah shit.., here comes the muthafuckin cops! So I dash, I duck and I hides behind a tree, making sure them muthafuckaz don't see me. My

207

fat sack of rocks, hell yeah I stuffed 'em. Police on my draws, I had to pause and yeah. Its still motherfuck 'em…."

Outside the lobby of her motel, she locates a pay phone. She also has her throw away cell phone, as a back up. She will only make 2 calls, to the mark. She makes her 1st call to Chad's private cell phone from the pay phone, at the Shell station, next door. She lets him know that she has arrived in Lafayette. She can hear the eagerness and anticipation in his voice. It makes her wonder, has he fiend for her, continuously. Since she was 16 years old.
Old, R. Kelly ass, pervert!

"Chadrella doesn't expect me until tomorrow," Baby Girl says, "So don't tell her I'm here. Or our little rendezvous can't happen. Don't tell anybody about this."
He agrees not to tell anyone.
"Check with your dealer and make sure he brings the lethal sugar too," she says, "I ain't no damn virgin, anymore."
She wants to see *what* response she'll get.
"He's got it ready for me, sweetheart," Chadwick Donaldson says, "I've already talk to him. Twice, this morning. He knows I always want the best. He's waiting for me to call him, with where I want him to meet me."
"Okay." she tells him, "That sounds perfect. Get a room at the Days Inn, on Jefferson street. Then call him and give him the information. Don't tell *him* about me, either. I am a married woman, *you know*. If I like his product. Then I'll have you to hook me up, again and again," she add and giggles flirtatiously. Then she adds, "It's nine thirty a.m. I'll call you in a hour, to see where our room is."
"Okay, sweetheart," Chad says, "I want you to bring all

of your emotions with you, when you come to see me too."
She says okay and they hang up.
Emotions, my ass. You're only getting the five A's from me, you pervert.
Accuracy, acuteness, ability and absolute anonymity.

She strips out of her *Donna Karan* travel outfit, quickly. Young D had picked it out. Among many others, while at *Nordstrom*'s, on one of their many trips to New York. She had worn the *Neck Stretch knit dress* over her black leggings. Her bowlegs set off a pair of leggings, like nobody else could. That's what her husband always says. He loves to see her in them. But then, he's usually looking to get her out of them, almost as soon as he spots her curves. She wears slippers on her feet, in this motel room. Because she's not trying to leave with anyone else's cootie's. She takes a hot shower to wash off the road dust. She wants to be comfortable but classy, for her mark, today. She dresses in casual brown khaki shorts and an eggshell wife beater. Both by *jcrew*. For her feet, she chooses her *chocolate mousse Pastry* runners by *the Simmons'* girls, Vanessa and Angela. She loves their line. Although, if her feet grow another half inch, she won't be able to wear pastries, anymore. She grabs the bag she needs for this job. She's only taking her 9mm, as a backup. She stashes it in the bag with her Days Inn maids uniform and other job essentials. She steals a uniform, every time she stays at a hotel. She's already got 1 from Motel 6. Just since checking in. She picks up some take out food and has a quick bite. While she sits in Days Inn's parking lot, waiting for Chadwick to arrive.

It only takes him 40 minutes to get there and get the room key. She knew it wouldn't take him a full hour.
He's a lowlife, child molester, with vanilla pudding for a brain.

209

He's feigning for Young D's wife. That shit would be enough to get him killed, anyway. I knew he would rush to his damn death. It's time to cook pudding, Chaddy.

Suddenly, another car pulls in behind Chadwick's. Before she can re-adjust anything, Chad has already walked around to the drivers' door of the car which pulled in behind him. And Chad is now speaking to the driver, briefly. Next, that guest driver goes into the hotel lobby and returns with the key. Both the unknown driver and Chadwick, drive around to 1 side of the Days Inn hotel and parks. Baby Girl can still see both vehicles. So she waits to see which room they go into.
One eleven. Good. He's on the first floor.

Having the jump on which room he's in, she starts up her Benz and leaves the parking lot. She drives back down to Motel 6. She can still see the door of Chadwick's room at Days Inn, from her motel.
Just the way I wanted it. Yea!

At 1030am, she calls Chad from the throw away phone and ask for the room number. This will be her final call to him. Thus, if they track his last calls, it will show a call from the Shell, just down the street. Then the unknown cell phone number. But there will be at least three calls, from his dealer. She makes the last call and he answers, on the first ring.
"Hello," he says with a tone which says he didn't recognize the number.
She says, "Tell your connect to bring that sugar before I come. I told you I don't wanna meet him."
"It's already here and waiting for you, Miss Lovely," he says, "He got the room, for us too. I didn't want to chance,

using my own name, you know," Chadwick says with a grin. She can tell he's grinning, like a Cheshire cat. She giggles. *Damn. He's gullible.*

"This is my connect, as you say, calling me back. Hold on," he says as he clicks over.
Perfect. Dealer is the last call and 1st suspect.

He clicks back over to her.
    "He wanted to make sure I call him back, if I want more," he says, "So if you plan to chase, all day. Then he'll be ready. Okay, sweetheart?"
    "Okay," she says.
Then she tells him, she will see him in 30 minutes.
It won't even be that long.

She was watching his room door, as they talked. She knows he's in there and waiting, without a doubt. She steps back inside of her room. Quickly, she changes into the Days Inn maids uniform and her *Strawberry Shortcake Pastries.* Then, she hops into her car and changes her CD to a new release. She listens to *Young Buck's, Buss Yo Head,* from the classic CD released 2 months ago; *Buck The World.* Then, she drives back to Days Inn.

    "Alright, rap niggaz. You got 24 hours to live, nigga. Yo times up, right muthafuckin now, nigga. Die Die Die Die Die! Y'all niggaz ain't no killers. Y'all niggaz, some ho's. And y'all act like the realist but you already know…"

She parks on the back side of Days Inn. No one is outside, far as far as she can see. That works in her favor. She gets out,
211

quickly and runs toward room 111. She brings her *Get To Work* and *Louis V* bags, with her. Once in front of his door, she taps lightly. Chad opens it, in a blissful mood.

"Well, hello beautiful," he says, grinning like a nerd who never gets any pussy. He adds, "I was hoping you didn't stand me up. But I see that you're early."

Baby Girl grabs his over aggressive hands and warns him, "You cannot touch the dancer, Chadwick."

He glares in anticipation as he closes the door, locks it and applies the chain.

"You're going to be my captive lover, today," he says.

She doesn't comment. He goes back to the bed and sits down. She sits her bag on the table, next to the window. He comments on the good idea she had, for her to disguise herself as one of the maids.

"You know I'm a politician," he says, "I don't need the scandal."

"I know and you've already told me that," she says, "But no. You don't need *any* scandal. Do you? And neither do I. Which brings me to my question. So who's name is this room in?" she asks.

Another precaution.

"My guy, got it for me," he answers, "James Ross. But it's a fake name. It's not in *either* of our names. That's what's important."

He gives her the, *I-know-that-name-is-awful* expression. She smirks but covers it with a fake smile.

"Can you get that mix going, while I play some music?" she asks, "I've only been waiting, all morning. I had to drive four hours, for this. That's why I wanted top shelf. Oh yes. And I got a little dance that I like to do. Before I get my groove on."

She grabs her portable cd player from her *Louis V* and turns it on. Her *Chopper City* CD is still in the boom box. *Niggaz In Trouble* is the first song to play.
How fitting the title of this CD, is.

He's still smiling, like the cat who swallowed the canary. But Baby Girl isn't. She's giving him attitude. He thinks it's an act. But he'll soon see, that it's very real.
"By all means. Do what you feel like doing," he suggests.
"Make it a speedball," she requests, "Let's not play with it."
"I don't have any-"
"I got some blow," she says as she pulls it out of her bag. She adds, "See, it's just enough to get us right."
He cooks the mixture carefully, on his burner. He looks like a scientist, as he mixes the 2 drugs, together. He has on corrective lenses. Where the bottom halves, look like coke bottles. Baby Girl giggles inside, as she looks at him. He reminds her of *Redd Foxx's* character, Benny from *Harlem Nights*. He's skilled at mixing his drug. But Baby Girl knows she needs to get a little bit more cocaine in this concoction, in order to kill him and kill him, *quick*.
"I like that little burner," she adds, trying to distract him.
He smiles proudly. He's glad to impress her. She's not impressed, at all.
Not! You're just a rich junky.

"I'm gonna put this blindfold on you, once you finish mixing that up," she says.
He looks confused, as he asks, "What about the striptease?"

"That comes after we shoot up," she says, "You have to feel me, with your hands, first. Before you're allowed to see me," she clarifies. "I'll shoot you up, first. Then me. That way, you're already beaming up when I put this ass on you. But first, you have to help me tie you off, baby."

"Shouldn't I undress?" he asks.

"Nah. Don't you want me to do that?" she asks, "I'm gonna do all of that, while we're sailing," she lies.

He holds the elastic tie, tight with his right hand. She holds the other end. She teases him and he falls for it. He feels up her legs. She flinches when he touches her.

"Are you nervous, Lovely?" he asks.

"No. I thought something was crawling on me," she says as she tries to look embarrassed. She adds, "See how bad I need this fix?"

That's what his next guess was, anyway. He's sure, she's jumpy because she needs her fix and he wants to go there with her.

"Okay. Leave it to me and let me put this on," she says as she wraps the blind fold tight, over his eyes.

She fakes like she's going to punch him in the face. He doesn't flinch. She knows he can't see anything.

You're all mine now, Chaddy.

"You are all mine, now," she says to him.

He thinks she means, in a good way. *It is* good, to her. A half a million dollars, good. That's the price for taking out this heroin addict, disguised as a union leader. She grabs his hand.

"Can you see me?" she asks.

He says, "No."

"That's about to change," she says, "I promise I'm going to take you on a long *ride*, boy."

Quietly, she puts her gloves on. Then, even quicker, she adds more powder to the mixture while she continues to talk to him in a sexual tone, about sexual acts. She mixes it, perfectly. She takes her feather boa, out of her Louis V and slides it across his face and down between his legs. She gags. She's not feeling this whole seduction thing, she has going on, with this old ass man. Well, to her, he's old. He's as old as her daddy, Big Dog was.

"Oh, you've got the sweats, daddy. You're ready for it, aren't you?" she asks as she giggles.

He says yes. She grabs the needle and quickly fills it.

"I have to get the bubbles out, baby. Hang on," she says. Syringe and needle in hand, she draws the snowball mixture through the needle and fills up the syringe. He instructs her to shoot him, in his left arm.

He instructs, "But not in the bend of my elbow. Under my arm. That's why I pulled the tie all the way up here. Just give me two cee cee's. Anything more than that, would kill us," he adds as he laughs.

She laughs too. She instructs him to lay down on his back and extend his arm upward to the head board. So she can reach the area he prefers. He does.

Easiest half a mill, I've ever made.

"Here it comes, Chaddy," she says with a devilish grin, as the needle punctures his skin and slides in.

He exhales, in anticipation. Quickly, she empties the entire contents of the poisoned filled syringe, into his underarm. Then she backs off of him. Leaving the needle in place, so it will appear that he over shot himself.

She moves completely off the bed. Anticipating his
215
convulsions. Sure enough, he starts to convulse slightly but the

mixture is so strong, it stops his heart, almost instantly. So fast, his limbs are still flinching and flailing around, for another 30 seconds. Then, he's calm. The room goes, eerily quiet. Even the *B.G.* CD she was playing, stops. Just as she'd programmed it too.

From the time she arrived in the *Days Inn* parking lot, until the time his eyelids stop flinching, was perfect. She checks the clock on the nightstand.
Twenty two minutes, exactly. Damn. I'm good!

She smiles. Then she calls his name. No answer. She picks up his right arm, holds it up in the air. Then, she lets it go. It falls back to the bed. Limp. She checks his pulse. He's dead!
I timed it, perfectly. I'm too good at this.

She changes out of the maids uniform and into her roll up Capri's, with a hot pink wife beater. She's already wearing her *Pastry Strawberry Shortcakes* because they'd matched the maids uniform.
After she's changed, she checks his pulse again.
"I don't want you waking up, after I leave, Chaddy," she says as she laughs.

She removes the blindfold and puts it back in her bag. Still, wearing her gloves, she sweeps the room for traces. Then, she grabs the radio/cd player from the edge of the bed. She checks the clock. It's Noon. She's done.

Keeping on her gloves, she exit's the room. She uses her slim arm chain latch applicator, to put the chain back on the door from the outside. Just as if Chad had chained himself in. She closes the door and checks to see if anyone is around.

216

There is no one in the immediate area. There is a maid cart, 2 doors down. The maid has obviously abandoned it, to go on her break. **Baby Girl** moves 1 of the carts from in front of room 109, to the front of room 111. She sees three van loads of people in the parking lot on the far end, when she's making her way back to her CLK63. She thinks about killing them. But they haven't even looked her way. She hops in her car, removes her work gloves and places them in her bag. She folds her slim arm and places it back in her Louis V bag too. Then, she applies her Cartier frames, starts up her Benz and heads back to Motel 6.

She hit's the street, drops the top and plays, *I ain't fucking with you*, staying with the classic; *Buck The World.*
"I try to take you serious but you think I'm a fool, you think I'm a fool.
I don't know you, niggaz. I ain't fucking with you. I ain't fucking with you!
Niggaz, if I ever caught you up, ain't no telling what I'd do….."

She likes this song with *Snoop Dogg* and *Trick Daddy,* a lot. She likes the whole damn CD. It's the best one she's copped, in a minute. The CD's by his label, have all been satisfying, so far. And she owns, many of them. That is, since *Young Buck* joined the label. She likes Buck's music, out of all the artist on his label. The reason she had purchased *Get Rich or Die Tryin',* is because she found out he was featured on it. *Buck The World* should be another platinum venture for *Young Buck.* If the label promotes it, correctly. She calls him, "Buck Marley" when speaking on him to other entertainers. Not so much, for his love of Marijuana. But because he's brought out the most street revolutionary type lyrics in the Hip Hop game, since *Tupac Shakur.* She even thinks he has eyes, like him. And she

217

said it long before *Vibe magazine* posted them, in there *20 questions* section, some years back. She visions her husband doing similar work, as *Tupac*. Even more so, then Buck has. And she hopes he can collaborate with *Young Buck*, one day soon. Only without the label trash talking bullshit and beefing, that they are known to do. She wants Young D to have a message. Not just glorify material things. She finds that, very elementary.

Her mark is expired now, as she drives straight to Chester's. It's weird how she always feels hungry, after she has put in work.
Two down. One to go."

She sashays into the restaurant and stops at the hostess stand to wait for a table.
"Table for one?" the hostess asks.
"Yes and preferably, on the patio," she answers.
The hostess tells her they can accommodate her, as she seats her, instantly. She places a menu on the table, takes her order for sweet tea and leaves her to ponder over the menu.
As Baby Girl scans the menu, she thinks about Young D. She wonders what he's doing, at this very moment. She wants to call her man and check on him and their sons. But she can't. Not until 5pm. That's still over 4 hours away.
He's probably out of bed and in the studio, by now. Man and Don P got Mama Annie on her toes, fulltime, at the big house. I wonder if the maid has returned and found her cart out of position, yet? I wonder if they are discovering Chaddy, at this very moment?

"Miss?" a voice startles her back into real time.
218
"Yes," she answers, looking up to see her waitress has

placed an extremely large glass of tea in front of her, with a lemon wedge.

"Are you ready to order?"

"Yes. I'll have the small cup of *Gumbo* with rice, as an appetizer. The six large grilled shrimp, Chicken Cordon Bleu entrée. With a loaded baked potato and vegetable medley," she orders.

"Any dessert?" the waitress asks.

"Pecan Pie."

The waitress takes down the order and removes the menu, as she departs to the kitchen window. Baby Girl looks at the fellow diners, on the patio.

At 1 table, there's a middle aged Caucasian man with a cowboy hat and boots on. That's typical Texas but common, in these parts too. He has a *Robert Redford* mustache. Seated, very close to him, is a red headed woman in a barely there, mini skirt and cut off top. She's almost dressed like *Julia Roberts* was, at the beginning of; *Pretty Woman*.

She may not be a hooker but she's definitely a mistress. If Derrick had a mistress, would I even know it?

She thinks about that, for a few minutes. Her Gumbo arrives. She puts the thought of Derrick cheating, out of her mind. She knows he has groupies and industry chicks, at his beck and call. But he loves her, deeply. He's not crazy enough to have a steady bitch, on the side.

"I would turn that bitch into plant food." she says aloud.

Her waitress looks at the obvious prostitute, at the next table. Assuming she's the 1 Baby Girl has directed the comment too, she winks her eye at Baby Girl and whispers,

219

"She comes in with him, once a week. They always sit at the

same table. It's not his wife. His wife's a brunette."

"That figures," Baby Girl says as she smiles.

Her waitress smiles as she leaves the table. No matter how much she tries to revert her thinking, Young D is on her mind heavily, right now. She can't help feeling, something must be wrong. But she knows, she can't call. Not until five pm.

CHAPTER TEN
BAD WEEK FOR POLITICS

It's past noon in Houston too. Young D has made it back from Kierra's apartment and taken a long shower. He heads up the stairs, to the studio.

"Y'all ready to work?" he yells as the rest of his labelmates stroll into the large home studio.

"We're ready!!" they reply, in unison. It's 12:45pm, when they, officially start.

Young Aristocrat says, "We're gonna try to knock out the rest of the second mixtape, today. And add five more tracks to the album. We got nine done, yesterday."

"We doin' the damn thang," Gat Em adds.

"H-Town's Finest Records, *Nigga!*" Big Daddy oozes as he holds in a large amount of smoke, which he has just inhaled from a huge blunt.

He passes the blunt to Young D, while he continues to hold in his smoke. Young D takes it and says, "That Cush, brother. I'm addicted to this shit, main!"

They all agree as laughter scatters throughout the studio. DJ Debo pulls up the first track of the day and instructs DeJuan to hit the booth.

DeJuan is more than ready to get at it. The rest of the guys are seated around the studio, with notebooks and pens. The only sounds are the occasional prompts from DJ Debo to DeJuan and the inhaling and exhaling of weed smoke. As the 5 lit blunts are passed from 1 brother to the other. Not 1 of the 9 guys are talking. They're all composing lyrics for when it's their turn to hit the booth. Young D's thoughts shift to Baby Girl, for a moment.

I can feel you, girl. You made it. I already know you did. I miss your ass and I can't wait to talk to you. Fuck that. I can't wait to hold you. I'm sorry for this morning, baby. She don't mean shit to me. But I don't know how to get rid of her.

He looks around the studio. All of his brothers are hard at work. Writing. Seeing that no one has noticed his momentary lapse in thought, he gets back to his art. DeJuan is done for now. High Top is going in. Next will be, Gat Em and Young D. Big Daddy will finale', this track.
"H-town don't play, we on the block all day!! With green and white shit, protected by AK's!!!"
That's how the hook goes.

They need more drink, in the studio. Young D and Manolo go down to the kitchen. They're restocking the studio refrigerator and bar. As they descend the stairs, Young D can hear breaking news on the kitchen TV.
"Damn! Another *one*?" Manolo says, before he shrugs his shoulders off.
He pulls a case of *Heineken* out of the large walk-in cooler, next to the pantry. He's speaking on the breaking news on TV. It's about a politician from Lafayette being found dead, in a Days Inn motel room, of an apparent drug overdose.
"Yep. That's two," is all Young D can say.
He knows that's his wife's work. But he can't share it with his labelmates.
"Man," Manolo adds, "They found a political dude, dead in Galveston, yesterday. He had his tongue cut out and bottom lip, cut off too."
Manolo continues as he chuckles. He's very impressed by the killings.
"He must've been what's known as a snitch," Arafat says, as he joins

222

them in the kitchen.

He helps them carry boxes of beer and liquor, up to their studio.

"Must've been," Young D adds, while he continues to act unconcerned.

"This is a bad week for politicians, cousin," Manolo says, as he continues to celebrate the Malay.

He adds, "Somebody knocking they crooked asses off, like flies."

"What if the second cat, in Lafayette, was killed too. And they just made it look like he OD'd?" Arafat offers.

"I doubt it," Young D interjects.

He's trying to act unconcerned about the news, all together.

"I ain't even mad at him," Manolo says, "Whoever he is. Them bitches be hypocrites, anyway, man. Don't y'all agree that most politicians be all about they're own gain. And don't give a fuck about those of us who pay their damn salaries?" Manolo says, as he finishes.

"I ain't mad at either one of their deaths," Young D offers, "Not if they was doing some wrong shit. Then they needed to go."

They get a liter of *Patron* Tequila, 3 cases of *Corona's* plus a case of Heineken and head back upstairs. Young D has seen all he wants to see of the news reports. He turns off the television and goes back upstairs, behind Arafat and Manolo.

I'm going to Lafayette, today. To meet my girl, there. And I'm taking our sons with me. Period! Before that nasty ass bitch, Kierra, figure out a way to get to my damn property.

Once Young D is back upstairs, he takes a cold corona and sits back in his seat. He gets back to his writing, at 1pm.

223

Meanwhile, in Lafayette. After devouring her delicious lunch, Baby Girl goes back to her, Motel 6, motel room. Down the street, she can see many police units, an ambulance and spectators around the Days Inn. She stops at the front desk and speaks to the clerk.

"What's going on?" she asks.

"Somebody OD'd in one of the rooms, at the Days Inn," the clerk, who's name tag reads; *Judy* says, "No one can come nor go, from Days Inn. Not until the police have questioned everyone. I got a roommate who works in housekeeping down there. She called and told me. She's mad cause she can't leave, yet. They're saying the guy is a politician. They be the biggest criminals, you know."

"I do know," Baby Girl says, "They say one thing, to get into office. But they do another whole thing, once they get our votes," Baby Girl says as she plays along.

Then she quickly changes the subject.

She says, "Chester's was absolutely wonderful, Judy. Thanks for suggesting it. I'll be leaving really early, tomorrow. I'll leave the key in the room. If that's okay."

Judy tells her that will be fine. Baby Girl exits the lobby, gets into her car and drives around to her room.

She's looking at the scene at the Days Inn. She can see it from the balcony, in front of her room. Other guest of the motel are outside witnessing all the commotion too. Baby Girl notices an ambulance leaving.

What the hell is an ambulance there for? Did the maid pass out? Chaddy don't need no ambulance. He needs a…….."

As the ambulance leaves, Baby Girl is still watching the scene. She can see everything that moves. There's a vehicle which is parked, right in front of room 111. It's a Coroner.

That's more like it. Get in the back o' that hearse.

She recites a line in her head, from *Young Buck's, Buss Yo Head* and laughs. As she goes into her room to get her things together.
It's 3p.m. Baby Girl has no need to check on her reservation at *The Fairfield Inn*, a *Marriot* chain. Her check-in time is 5pm. The Fairfield Inn and Marriott chains, always accommodate them, wonderfully. It's their most used chain, when on the road for H-Town Records tours. She has to wait 2 more hours, though. She removes her Pastries and stretches out across the King Sized bed, for a nap. She sets the clock to wake up at 4:30pm. She has plans to arrive at Fairfield Inn, at 5pm sharp and get checked into her suite.
Then, I can call my babies. All three of them.

****

Young D is well within the insides of the vicinity of Lafayette parish. It's nearly 5pm. He couldn't wait any longer. He and his 2 sons are going to surprise Baby Girl, at her hotel. After his manager JB called him about the New York show, he'd found it impossible to concentrate in the studio. He told the guys to work without him. He had to leave. He would call them later.
DeJuan seemed to understand exactly why Young D couldn't focus on his work.
He'd told him, "Man, you go on and hook up with Baby Girl. We got this. We'll see y'all, later. Go get your girl, brother."
The statement made Young D curious. But he was in a hurry to grab some clothes and put them in an overnight bag. He'd called Annie and had her to pack some clothes for their sons

225

too. If Jordan didn't still have school, he would have brought him, also.

DeJuan has known Young D the longest, of all the guys on the label. They grew up together. He knew if Young D was leaving, without any of his brothers. He had to be hooking up with his girl. At least, that's what Young D felt comfortable with concluding about that statement. He didn't know what DeJuan would've said, had he known what Baby Girl had gone to Lafayette for.

Annie had packed some clothes for Lil Man and Don Prince. Young D had told her and his labelmates, he needed to get out of Houston because Kierra was hounding him to spend more time with her. Since she knew Baby Girl wasn't in town. He and his sons had gotten on the road at 2:30pm. Thirty minutes after hanging up with JB, Young D was on Interstate 10, heading east.

He has averaged 95 mph and covered 218 miles. In just under two and a half hours.

Lovely will be mad to know that I drove this fast, with the boys. But baby, I have to get to you. I really just have too.

****

This is a much nicer spot. Hella better, than Motel 6. The rooms are bigger too.

Baby Girl is pulling in at Fairfield Inn, on East Willow street. The first thing she plans to do, after checking in, is calling her sons and her husband.

I can't wait!

She hops out of her car and heads in, to check-in.

226

Meanwhile, the object of her affection and his 2 juniors on in route to the Fairfield Inn, to see her. She has no idea.

"Mama's gonna be surprised to see us, man," Young D says to his 2 year old son, Derrick Jr or Lil Man .

His less than 3 month old son, Don Prince, is taking advantage of the relaxation of the open road. He's sleeping in his car seat.

"I wan *tiss* my mommy," Lil Man says.

"I wanna kiss your mommy too, man," Young D says, repeating his son's sentence.

They both smile.

"Me too," Lil Man says.

"Me, first," Young D teases as he and his Jr, play sentence tag.

They go back and forth with this, for a few minutes. Until Young D tickles him and makes him giggle.

"I want tom McDonalds," Lil man says, seeing the golden arches, just up ahead of them.

Young D really wants to find Baby Girl, first. Before they do anything close to relaxing.

"Let's go find mama, first," Young D says to Lil Man , "Okay?"

"Okay," Lil Man says, "Din we done dit tom Pren fries. Okay, daddy?"

"Cool, man," Young D says, "After we get with mommy. Then we gonna go get some French fries."

"Cool, daddy!!" Lil Man agrees and giggles.

At Fairfield Inn, Baby Girl goes to the front desk to activate her reservation. The only thing on her mind, right now, is talking to her husband and their sons.

"Reservation for Blake," she says to the clerk.

The clerk starts typing rapidly, on her computer keys. Looking for a reservation, for Blake.

"Yes, ma'am. King sized suite. With Jacuzzi and the best view. And you are our preferred customer. We will supply an amenity, on the house," the clerk says, a few moments later, as the hotel outside line rings.

It's 5:15pm. The second clerk takes the call, while the first clerk continues to assist Baby Girl.

"*Fairfield Inn. East Willow. May I help you?*" the second clerk says.

"Hello," Young D says to the second clerk, "Could you ring my wife? Lovely Blake's room, please?"

"Let me just check to see what room she's in," clerk 2 says, as she mutters, "Lovely Blake is in-n-n-n-n-n *roo-o-o-o-o-m-m-m……*"

"She's standing, right here," clerk 1 says and smiles.

Who is calling me, already? Oh God! Is it Chadrella? Calling my hotel to see if I came in already? She wants to tell me about her father's death.

"Oh!" clerk 2 says, "The phones for you, ma'am."

Baby Girl turns back to clerk 1 and says, "Give me one minute, on that amenity."

Then turning back to clerk 2, Baby Girl puts on her, *I'm-nervous-but-trying-to-act-unconcerned,* face. She takes the receiver from clerk 2.

"Hello. This is Lovely Blake," Baby Girl says.

"It damn sho is," Young D says.

Baby Girl can hear his smile, of relief.

"Hi, Daddy! What's up?" she says.

She's relieved to hear his voice.

Perking up now, she adds suddenly, "I miss you guys, so much.

I was just about to call you, when I got checked in."

"You don't have to miss us," Young D says, "Not for much longer. Look in the parking lot."

Baby Girl puts the phone down and runs to the double doors. She sees Young D's Royal Blue Escalade, sitting on 26 inch shoes. It's parking next to her Benz. She yells back to clerk 1.

"On that amenity for the room. Make it Champagne and strawberry's, please," she says.

Then to clerk 2, she says, "Hang the phone up, for me. My families outside. I'll be right back."

She runs out to the parking lot to greet her sons and her husband.

"Oh daddy!! I am so glad you came," Baby Girl says, kissing him as if she hasn't seen him in a year.

Then, she kisses Lil Man and Don Prince.

"I told you. Me first, Lil Man ," Young D teases their oldest son.

"No, no," Lil Man giggles.

"Let's get settled," Baby Girl says, "I was just checking in. You timed it, perfectly, Daddy. I'm impressed."

"So, can I clean now?" he jokes.

"Not quite," she says as she laughs.

They go back inside the lobby, together. The clerks comment on what a beautiful family, they are.

"Thank you," Baby Girl says, "We're gonna need you to bring a crib and a roll-away bed, to the suite." she ells Clerk 1. She adds, "Can you manage it?"

"We have a pullout queen sofa, in the room and I'm ordering that crib, right now," clerk 1 says.

Both clerks assure her, they will take care of the additions and the amenity, immediately.

The bellman follows the 4 of them, back outside. He

229

brings a trolley and gets their bags from their vehicles. He escorts them to their suite, while the clerks attend to the additions and amenities. Once they have everything set up in their suite, Young D informs Baby Girl that Lil Man wants to eat.

"Are you hungry?" Young D asks her, "Because Lil Man wants mickie Dee's."

"No no, daddy. Man want a Pren fries," Lil Man corrects his father.

Baby Girl and Young D laugh. Then Lil Man laughs too. He loves to clown. He got that honestly, from his father. Just as he did his good looks. Which could be, either parent. They're both gorgeous.

"And what about you? What do you want to eat?" Baby Girl asks Don Prince.

He's just waking up. And a newly awakened Don, doesn't look too happy. He frowns, at first. Then, after recognizing his mother's face, he puts on a huge smile. It's large enough to see, both the top and bottom gums, in his mouth. With no teeth in it. Tears well up in Baby Girl's eyes. Seeing her baby son recognize her face, makes her day. Much more than her marks going out, successfully.

"He's happy to see his mama," Young D comments as he kisses her again. He adds, "And daddy is too."

She's overcome with joy, as the tears flow freely. Lil Man has pulled his favorite toys from his toy bag and is proceeding to strew them, all over the floor.

"He's use to living in hotels, now," Young D says as he turns on the TV.

He's going to play the play station, which was provided by the hotel. He has 2 Playstations, in his SUV.

He runs back out to his Escalade and grabs his Madden

2007. Then he darts back into the lobby and back up the elevator, to their room.

When he comes back into the room, Baby Girl is feeding Don Prince.

"I wanted to feed him, first. Before *we* go eat," she says, "If I don't. He won't allow us eat."

They smile as Young D agrees with her, on that point. His baby son demands attention, when he's hungry or dirty. Like most infants do. But Don Prince gets a bit extra with his demands. He's got his dad's personality too.

****

Back at the Houston home, the labelmates are still recording. Even though Young D isn't there. Things are about to get worse, when unwanted guest show up.

"H-Town Records is in the muthafuckin' house, *Fasho!*" Arafat says.

They had just completed 6 of the 9 tracks, they set out to do, today. It's 10pm.

"D still gotta get on the last four tracks," DJ Debo says, "But y'all are done. Now. On to number seven, gee's!"

Young D had managed to do his verse, on the first song of the day. The 2nd one, he wasn't going to be on. It was during the taping of the second song, that he'd gotten him and his sons packed and bolted to Lafayette. The team knows he'll get his verse's done, on the remaining cuts. Young D spends more time in the studio, than any of them do. With the exception of DJ Debo. DJ Debo is always in the studio, creating beats for his crew to listen too. And then pick the ones they want to turn into another hit. DJ Debo is more at home, in the studio, then in any other room in the house. In the studio, he's in his element. He's pulling up track number seven of the day, when the studio phone's, outside line, lights up.

"Yo. What up?" High Top answers the phone, "What's happenin wit cha, bro?"

"What up, Cuz?" Baby Boy asks, "Y'all still knockin' them tracks out?"

High Top tells him, "Yes and you still got time to hop on the last three. If you're close."

Baby Boy says he and his crew have returned to Houston, from their San Antonio show, last night. Which was the reason they had to leave, yesterday.

"We're about twenty minutes out from you," Baby Boy tells him, "We'll see you, in a short."

"Word," High Top says and they hang up.

High Top relays the message to the rest of his crew. The Studio phone line, rings again. This time it's Young D and Baby Girl.

"Is my home still standing up?" Baby Girl jokes with DeJuan, who answers the line, this time.

"Oh yeah. How you make out?" he asks her.

"I got everything handled, so far. I was so glad daddy showed up, with the boys too," she says, "They made my day."

DeJuan knows Baby Girl loves his best friend, unconditionally. And his best friend loves her, the same. He only longs for the day that Young D gets the stress of his secret with Kierra, out into the open. And hopefully he will see that Baby Girl will forgive him and they can move on with absolutely no secrets.

"Thanks to all of y'all, for letting him come," Baby Girl says, "Here he is. I have to get to the boys. I know you can hear them."

"Oh yeah. Sounds like they're having a ball," DeJuan says as he chuckles.

Young D takes the phone while Lovely pulls Lil Man off of his

232

neck. The 2 of them can wrestle, for hours. If no one steps in and stops them.

Young D takes the phone from her and talks to his labelmates. Baby Boy and his crew arrive while he's still on the phone. They talk briefly, about the San Antonio market. Both labels plan to do the next show there, together.

"We bout to knock the rest of this album and mixtape out," Baby Boy says, "*Shit*. We might start a whole new one. Before y'all fly out, tomorrow, for NYC."
Young D tells him to turn on the speakerphone, so he can talk to all of them, at once. Baby Boy does.

"Hey, niggaz!" Young D shouts.
They all yell back, "Hey D!!!"
Young D carries the conversation through the speakerphone, as his guys pay very close attention. They know he has new information, about the upcoming trip to New York.

"I had to remind y'all that the shuttle will be there to get us, at one P-M, Friday. The flight leaves Hobby Airport at three P-M. Pack y'all shit, tonight. If you didn't, already. When we get back, tomorrow. We can all relax and cookout. Instead of worrying about packing. We can send our luggage to pre check-in and chill out, until Friday."
Gat em and Manolo are the only ones, not completely packed.

"I'm sending them out to do it, now," DeJuan assures Young D, "And they will be ready."
They tell him the progress they've made, since he left. Young D is pleased that the 2 projects are nearly finished.
He says, "We can knock that out tomorrow. And if needed, Saturday too. When we get back from NYC. I'll get my other verses in, Fasho."

"That sounds like a plan!" Gat Em says.
They all talk with Young D and Baby Girl, over the speaker

233

phone, for about 10 minutes. Until Young D orders them back to work.

"Get back to it," Young D says, "I wanna play both cd's for Baby Girl, when we get back from NYC on Saturday. Alright?"
They assure him that all of the songs will be done and waiting on him, to add the finishing touches. They hang up with Young D and get back to recording.

****

Young D takes his family out to dinner, in Lafayette. Baby Girl suggests they go to Chester's. But her oldest son is demanding, *McDonalds.*

"Oh, Lil Man," Baby Girl says and smiles, "Are you ever gonna get tired of McDonalds?"

"Not my Pren fries," he says, again making a case for the delicious French fries at McDonalds, that he absolutely loves.
Baby Girl and Young D laugh. Then they give in to their little man's wishes.
Baby Girl says, "It's after ten, anyway. Chester's is closed. Well. McDonalds, it is."

"*Yay!*"
Lil Man gives a cheer as they turn into the parking lot of McDonalds. They pull up and park the Escalade and he can't wait to get out. They hop out, go in and order their food. Lil Man picks a booth out, in the play land, for them to sit. So he can play, as well. Young D insist, he has to finish his meal first, before he can play. Lil Man makes a *happy plate* of his happy meal. Then, him and his daddy play together and have a blast.

234

"You know I'm buying them a franchise of their own, don't you?" Young D says to Baby Girl, about their sons.
"Did you just decide that?" she asks as she laughs.
"Yep." he answers as he returns the laugh.
"Hmm. How many more secrets do you have, that I don't know about?" she asks.
She's joking with him. But inside, he feels awkward. Only because he does have a secret. And her name is Kierra. Again, he continues to miss these opportunities and chances to reveal that whole fiasco to his wife.
"That was the last one," he lies as he feels a sudden wave of nausea in his gut.
He manages to smile through it, as he continues to play with Lil Man. Baby Girl gets Don Prince in on the action, as she takes him down the slide. They all have a great time at McDonald's, for an hour or so. Before it closes and they have to leave.

****

Meanwhile, back at their home in Houston, things are getting out of hand. Young D's baby mama has taken it upon herself, to visit their house. She has managed to convince security to let her in. They do so, knowing the master and madam are away with the kids. Surely, someone won't have a gig when Young D returns.
Kierra is looking for Young D. Even though she has been told, a thousand times by him and Annie, to never come to the house, uninvited. She knows Baby Girl is out of town. She figures she can monopolize Young D into seeing her, again. Even though he'd been to her apartment, this morning.
"It's late at night. And what I need to know. Is where is

Derrick at?" Kierra asks, as if she has some type of ownership of him.

After going to 3 clubs and not seeing him or any of his crew. She has driven to the home of him and his wife, looking for him. This morning, she'd asks Young D to come back to see her, tonight. Since his wife would still be out of town. He had told her, *"When hell freezes over!"*

She asks him for more time. *Each time* she gets to see him. Young D always says no. But Kierra is never willing to accept rejection. That's no different, tonight. Kierra knows Young D has many; *Sideline Ho's.* Inside and outside of the Houston area. Besides her. So what she's thinking is that he has plans of being entertained by 1 of them, this evening. While Baby Girl is gone. Kierra has plans of running interference. But what actually happened after Young D's visit to Kierra's, was this. He'd left to go to Lafayette because his guilt wouldn't allow him to stay home, tonight.

Still, Kierra shows up at their home and rings the door bell, impatiently. Then she stands there, as if she's agitated because the welcome mat isn't rolled out for her. Gat Em answers the door, first. But he's the doorman from hell, as far as Kierra is concerned.

"He ain't here," Gat Em says and, immediately slams the door in her face.

Gat Em is an 18 year old man now, with very little patience. He is aware of how ill Kierra makes his big boss, Young D. So dogging her out is pleasant, for him. Plus it earns him brownie points with Young D. He goes back up to the studio and takes a seat. He continues his writing, without even announcing her. She continues to ring the doorbell.

The doorbell is set on a red light and a buzzer, for the studio. Inside the producers booth, a large red light illuminates

236

when the door bell is pressed. In the lobby of the studio, there is a mild buzzer. This way, if everyone is upstairs and recording. The buzzer doesn't interfere with the audio recordings in the artist and producers booths. But in the lobby where there is no recording. Everyone can hear it. Someone can answer the door, if they choose too. Gat Em is doing the lyrics, for his last verse of the evening. Alongside him, is Arafat, Big Daddy and DeJuan. Gat Em returns to his couch in the lobby and doesn't announce who's at the door. He just resumes his writing and ignores the continuous buzzing.

Outside at the front door, Kierra lays on the door bell. Finally, DeJuan tells the guys to keep working and he will get the door. He knows it has to be someone whom Gat Em knows, no one wants to deal with or hear from. Just by his lack of excitement after returning. DeJuan heads downstairs.

"She's gonna get fucked, now," Arafat says.
Big Daddy follows DeJuan, down to get the door. DeJuan opens the door and Big Daddy lays into Kierra, immediately.

"What the fuck is your problem?" Big Daddy says, "And how the fuck did you get up in here?"
He is the least patient, of all the crew. And the most direct. He gives her a vacuous stare.
Then he asks, "You need some dick in you or something?"

"Yeah, I do," Kierra answers, "Now where the fuck is Derrick at?"
Again, speaking as if she has some type of privilege when it comes to Derrick "Young D" Blake.

"He told us to take care of you, until he gets back," DeJuan says, as he smiles.
Him and Big Daddy step outside of the door and grab Kierra by her arm. Immediately, they walk her to 1 of the guest houses.

Once they are inside, at 1 of the guest house, they tell her to take off all of her clothes.

"If you wanna get to the boss. You've gotta work your way up," Big Daddy says, unbuckling his dickies belt.

"She knows what time it is," DeJuan says, "This ain't her first time coming here. And it won't be the last. As long as she keeps irritating Young D. She's gonna be fucking us. Because he don't want her and she knows it. Still, that don't stop her from coming on him and his wife's property. Where she can be arrested, if we choose too. And she's always showing up, trying to act like she has some props here. You don't."
DeJuan pulls no punches as he tells Kierra, how it's going to go.

"He brought me some dick, this morning," Kierra says, "For your information."

"Yep and he was so fucking sick from it," Big Daddy says, "He was so sick that he had to be airlifted to another city, to get your fucked up aura, off of him."
She looks at him as if she thinks he's serious. But he's grinning like the Cheshire cat. So she knows he was only bullshitting.

"Get naked, bitch," DeJuan says, impatiently, "And quit stalling."
He's done speaking. He wants to get his rocks off, before the next shift of guys come. Because he knows, there will be more coming from the studio, once they hear that she's back here. And all he wants is some head. Big Daddy, on the other hand, wants some anal action.

Kierra gets naked. She serves them both, at the same time. She gives head to DeJuan while Big Daddy enters her from the back.

It is less then 5 minutes, when Baby Boy and 2 of his crew, join the party. It's now, 5 on 1. Kierra is pretending to be semi drunk. She's done these same guys, before. When she was completely sober, at her apartment. Two at a time, she serves them again, tonight. Just like an assembly line. As soon as she finishes off two and they leave, they're replaced by 2 more. It goes like this, for over 2 hours. Until she has done every guy from the studio that wanted a piece. DJ Debo has a girl in session, with him. He didn't want a turn, tonight. There's Gat Em, who's just not interested in fucking Kierra, anymore. Much like Debo and a few others. He hasn't been excited about fucking her since he was fourteen. Back when he wasn't getting a lot of girls. But since the fame, he has his own share of groupies and top notch girls. And worn out strippers, just doesn't do for him.

"Her pussy is too stretched out," was what Gat Em had said after the last gang bang.
He'll be the 1 who will tell Young D that she came by here. In hopes that he'll kick her ass or have it kicked. He's glad his boss is out of town, though. Because tonight, Kierra could have gotten him busted with Baby Girl. All of the labelmates love Baby Girl, like a sister. She takes great care of them and made sure they all had what they wanted in their contracts. Plus, she made special provisions for their families care. Those who had or have had kids, since signing, had to do allotments to insure their welfare. She is very family oriented and none of them want her to be hurt, by anything. And certainly not something like, her finding out Kierra's secret. They don't even want to see what that would do to her. Needless to say, the label mates don't know what Baby Girl's real profession is. If they did, they'd tell her. Just so she could kill this less than bitch named Kierra.

****

In Lafayette, Young D and Baby Girl are still up with the boys, trying to find some use for themselves in this small town. Young D had brought all of her valuables, when he came in this evening.

"I do miss my wedding rings and my cell phone, when I don't have them," Baby Girl admits, "But rules are rules. I always look at the ring mark around my finger and think of you guys."

As Wednesday night turns into the early Thursday morning, they're riding around Lafayette, trying to tire out Lil Man. So he'll be sleepy when they arrive back at Fairfield Inn. After he finally dozes off, Young D looks at his wife.

"Where is that Days Inn at?" he asks.

Surprised that he has the exact name of the hotel, where she'd hit her last mark, Baby Girl asks, "What Days Inn?"

She makes sure to look as guilty as possible. Because she never lies to her man. Young D gives her a, *don't-you-act-dumb-with-me,* look.

"It was on breaking news, at home," he says as he lets her off the hook, with a smile.

"It's right down this same street, daddy," she admits, "But I don't want to pull into that parking lot and stop. Pull into the shell station, across the street. Next to the Motel six."

Young D pulls the Escalade up to the gas pump, at the Shell's gas station. He's facing the Days Inn. He gets out to top off the tank, for the trip back to Houston, later today. Baby Girl goes inside to grab them all some juices and snacks, for the trip. She glances out at her husband as he's filling up the tank. From where he's standing, he can see yellow police tape, across the door of Room 111. His mind goes back to where he was, while

240

that murder was taking place. Again, he feels nauseated with thoughts of Kierra.

"I gots to get that bitch, out my life," he says, not realizing he's speaking out loud.

"Well that's not exactly what I said, about him. But it's close, daddy," Baby Girl says as she giggles.

She had exited the shell store. She'd walked right up to him, to hand him his pop rouge, Crème soda. His favorite. Which can only be found in the south. Namely; Louisiana, Texas and some parts of Mississippi and Alabama. She gives him a kiss and opens the door of the SUV. She hops in and waits for him to finish up. He laughs, to play off his blunder.

He says, "I'm gonna take your car to the Exxon, next to the hotel and fill it up. Before we go to bed. That way, we can jump right on the highway. Instead of having to gas it up, before we hit the road."

"Sounds good to me," she says, before closing the door.

"Get buck wit me, watch me do the damn thang. Get buck wit me, watch me do the damn thang!"

Baby Girl's cell phone goes off. It's Gus calling her and she finds this, very eerie. He never calls her, at this time of morning. And never, *ever,* when jobs are in play. He knows better. She automatically knows there is some shit in the game.

"Hello," she answers.

"I'm just checking on you, Lovely girl," he says, "This is a busy week. Are you okay?"

"Of course, I'm okay," she says, irritated at him for ignoring the rules.

She asks, "Why are you calling me?"

Gus says it's just to check on her. But she's annoyed. Never in her 8 or so years of professional cleaning. Did he ever call her, while she was in play.

"Gus, this is not procedure," she says, letting her voice rise to show him that she is not pleased.

"Neither is having your cell phone," he says, "How did you get it?"

"You've never called my cell phone, on any other job. There has never been a missed call from you," she says, "Why tonight?"

"I was concerned," Gus lies, "I knew you had a full week. I wanted to make sure you were okay."

"So you call the phone that I'm not suppose to have?" she asks, "That's way too thin."

"How did you get it?" he asks.

"Never mind that, Gus," she says, "We'll talk, later. I'm still on the job. Good bye."

She hangs up as Young D finishes pumping gas and joins her, in the Escalade.

Young D drives back to the hotel. Baby Girls is in deep thought about the call she received from Gus.

Does he know that Derrick has come to meet me? That's not against the rules. Nor is my having my phone, after a job is done. What the fuck is going on and why is Gus really calling me? There's some shit in the game. I know it is. Bastard! I'm going to New Orleans and check the computer. For his sake, he had better be clean.

Then she remembers what her daddy said about Gus Davis. He'd told her, emphatically. To never allow Gus into his office. Never let him have access to his computer, any pass codes or bank accounts. He told her that Gus Davis' only job, was to arrange packages.

Daddy didn't trust him. He had to have a reason for not trusting him. I have to find out what that reason is. Alfred and Addie Mae can tell me. And I will certainly be getting with them, soon.

CHAPTER ELEVEN
<u>DON'T START NONE</u>

In Houston, Kierra has made it home from her gang banging session with the crew's of H-Town and Baby Boy's crew too. She had called Kid as soon as she'd gotten into her car to leave Young D's estate. She had to report back to him about what her and Young D did, earlier today. When he'd come to her place and also, what had just happened at the estate. See, Kid is the one who told Kierra that Baby Girl was going to be gone, tonight. Not Annie. Annie had told her that Baby Girl would be gone, today. But she said nothing about tonight. That was Kid's doing. He knew Baby Girl had packages to do because Gus had handed him some of the work. Which Baby Girl had gotten back from him, immediately. Unopened. But Kid knew the hit he'd once possessed, was for Wednesday and it was out of town. But what Kid didn't know, is where Baby Girl had to go, to do the hit. Kid wouldn't dare tell Kierra what Baby Girl does. But he had to let her know that she was out of town. Because Kid wanted Kierra to go over and try to fuck Young D, at their home. That would've given him more ammunition on Young D. But Kierra didn't find Derrick at home.

So when Kierra checked back in with Kid and told him that neither Young D nor Baby Girl was home, tonight. Kid put her on hold and called Gus, immediately. That was after Kierra tells him that 1 of the guys who was with Baby Boy, had told her that Young D was gone out of town with his wife. Kierra wasn't sure if they had told her the truth. But Kid was grilling her about why she didn't demand to speak with Young D. And now, Kierra wants Kid to verify, if it was indeed true. Or if Young D was just telling his labelmates to tell her that.

Kierra and Kid are using each other, at this point. Kid had called Gus, who in turn, called Baby Girl, just minutes ago. Gus had told Kid that was against procedure, which is a lie. Once the hit to tallied, the pro is off the clock. The 1 who has been breaking procedure is Gus. He had done it when he handed Kid that package and that's not the only time. He's been accepting payments from Kid for information on when Baby Girl leaves town. And her whereabouts, in general. Kid takes this information and uses it at his own discretion. Mostly, passing it on to Kierra so she can call and demand Young D's time. For Kid, he's going through all of this to ultimately, break up Young D and Baby Girl. This morning is no different. But now that Gus has called Baby Girl and sent her radar up. Gus is between a rock and hard place. It will only be a matter of time, before Kid and Kierra will be joining him there.

****

Baby Girl is still pissed. She has put the kids to bed and is pacing the floor, of the hotel room. Young D isn't with her, right now. He has taken her Benz across the street to top off the tank with gas, for the drive home in a few hours. Of course, Baby Girl is waiting up for him. She doesn't do a lot of talking over her cell phone. Not even on a land line. Not when she wants to discuss intimate details of the business, she's in. But she knows she has to get to the bottom of that call from Gus. It just feels wrong, to her. She recalls her daddy Don's words again. Then she remembers how he had a private computer and used it to track Gus. He had a special setup done, so that he could watch any and all of Gus' actions. And at the same time, insure that he was handling the marks demises, correctly.

245

Gus knows nothing of that computer. But he's always bitching about not having access to my daddy's office. I'm going to have to get with him and watch his demeanor, while he's around me. I'll do it after we come from the east coast.

As soon as Baby Girl returns from New York City, on Saturday. She plans to have a long talk with Gus Davis. Something is out of order and she wants it fixed, immediately. Or he will have to go. And the only way out of the killer-for-hire position that he's in, is to die out. They're not even afforded a release or a retirement option. Because they don't have to physically deal with marks.

While thinking, Baby Girl gets out towels for her and Young D. As soon as he returns, they're going to shower together and go to bed. But their not going to sleep. At least, not right away. She's trying to get very emotional, this morning. She's got to have her stress reliever too.

****

In Houston, the guys are still in the studio. They're about to wrap the session, when a discussion about Kierra is started.

"Man, that ho is gonna always be a ho," DeJuan says to High Top. "That bitch showed up looking for Young D. Which she knows can get her killed. But then, D's not here. So she fucks his whole crew."

"And she acted like she didn't know why he would never claim her ass," High Top says.

"She's a used up ass, ho," Gat Em offers, "Her pussy is sloppy as fuck. I don't see how y'all even hit that bitch."
They all laugh.

246

"Out of the mouth of babes," Baby Boy says as he chuckles.

"Shit. She was here," Arafat says with a yawn.

"Grown men don't turn down no free pussy, son," Big Daddy adds.

"Nigga, you wasn't even hitting the pussy," DeJuan says, "You went in that ho's ass."

"It was tighter," Big Daddy responds and there is roar of laughter.

Then Debo says, "It's time for all us to shower and get some shut eye, man. Make sure all of your shit is packed. Before you lay down. Or be prepared to stay your ass in Houston."

They all file out of the studio and head to the guest houses. DeJuan, DJ Debo, Baby Boy and 2 of his crew are staying in Young D's house, tonight. While him and Baby Girl are out of town. They all shower and hit the sack. It's nearly 3am.

****

In Lafayette, Baby Girl and Young D are still up. He has returned from filling her Benz up and they have taken their shower too. They're finally in bed and both of their sons are still asleep.

"Daddy, I need some loving," Baby Girl says as they spoon with each other, under the covers.

They have just finished a hot shower, the boys are both sleeping and they had shared a blunt on the balcony, before getting into bed.

"So was you glad we came to see you? Or was you mad?" Young D asks.

"I was *so* happy to hear you on that phone, Derrick," Baby Girl says, "And then, to see you in the parking lot. You had been on my mind since I left home. I just felt like something was wrong at home, today. So when I saw the three of you. I was thrilled, daddy."

"I got another thrill for you too, baby," he says, pulling her chin up to his until their lips meet.

They kiss hard as he lets his hands roam her body. She moans and pulls him to her.

"I need it, daddy," she whispers, "I need to taste you."

She journeys downward to his penis. He knows without a doubt, she loves to pleasure him. He seems to enjoy her oral skills to the maximum, when she's upset about some facet of their lives. This morning, she's upset with Gus Davis, for the phone call. She gives Young D the benefit of helping her to relieve her mind of it. She takes his dick into her cool mouth and Young D moans. Baby Girl gets the head of his dick, good and moist. She makes slurping sounds as if she's devouring her favorite flavor of a snowball. She balances herself between his legs and takes his large dick to the back of her throat.

"Oh, yes," Young D moans.

She continues to suck his dick into her mouth and out. And up and down, until she can feel his body tightening. As a test, she moves her tongue to his balls. He moans. Then she licks his asshole. His dick begins to soften, instantly.

"That ain't me and you know it," he says, "Get back to the good."

She grins, devilishly and comes back around to his balls. She suckles them, while she pumps his large dick.

I knew my man's ass was exit only. But every now and then, I have to try it. Just so I can see this dick go limp. That tells me everything I need to know. I'll get it back to hard as calculus. No problem.

248

She puts his dick, back into her mouth. She going for broke now. As she fondles his balls too. He's loving this action. She gets the precursor to his nut and acts as if it's the first nourishment she's had, this year. He dick is rock hard, again. His breathing patterns are choppy. She knows he's about to shoot off his load of liquid love juice. He cums as if he's been saving it up for months. She sucks him off, in just under 6 minutes. Young D is in paradise as he pulls her up to him and kisses her nose.

She smiles and whispers, "You lost focus?"

She asks that question since he kissed her nose, instead of her lips.

He can't speak, just yet. He uses his reserve strength to pull her on top of him. He grabs her at the hip area and pulls her bottom, all the way up to his face. Placing her legs to either side of his head. She sits with her pussy in his face. Exactly where he wants it.

He does his duty. She rolls her hips to the music of his lips and he gives her, hers. It takes no time at all because she was ready for it.

"Oh daddy, yes!" she screams as she lets go of some love juices of her own.

He sops it up, like honey. Ecstasy is such a familiar place, for both of them.

"Get it on out of you, baby," he coaches, "Wet this pussy for yo daddy, Baby Girl."

She goes wild. She loves his sex talk.

Suddenly, he flips her over onto her back and enters her, swiftly. She lets out a yelp upon penetration of his large and extra hard penis.

"I want this baby," he says as he goes right to his work.

"Oh daddy it's so good. I love you, daddy. I love you."

249

"I love you too, baby girl," he says as he plunges his dick into her flesh, hard and regular.

Within minutes, she's in ecstasy again. And he's right there to coach her through her second trip of the session.

"Show me I'm the man, baby," he whispers as he watches her sex faces.

He loves them. They turn him on and motivate him to keep doing what he's doing, to please his wife. That's his 1st priority. Making sure she enjoys every lovemaking session, they have. He hasn't missed his mark, this morning either. She's on her 3rd orgasm by the time he throws his head back and joins her in orgasmic bliss. They convulse against each other, for the next minute or so. Neither 1 of them can stop their bodies from jerking and gyrating. Nor do they try too.

After a few minutes, they slow down to slight shivers. He holds her tight and places tender kisses all over her face and neck.

"That was the shit, Lovely," he whispers, after catching up to his breath. "Damn, I love fucking you."

She's thoroughly satisfied and ready to sleep in his arms. He obliges her.

While she was upset over events of today. All it took was her sweet dick from her husband, to help her slumber. She goes fast asleep. Young D lays there thinking of today, at Kierra's apartment. He loathes that woman to the point of physical sickness. He didn't think twice about hopping on the highway and meeting the love of his life. He wasn't willing to hang around Houston and be stalked by his baby mama.

****

In Houston, Kierra isn't pleased that Young D hadn't

hung around Houston. Kid had gotten impatient with her, during their call and hung up. So now, Kierra and her roommate Trina are at the apartment catching up on each others night. Since Kierra had been off from the strip club, Trina wanted to know what she had gotten into.

"How the fuck did you let that nigga get away?" Trina asks.

She had just come in from a night at the Anatomy and found Kierra, half asleep on the couch. That made it apparent that Young D hadn't come back to spend the night. As if he would.

"I told his ass to come back but he didn't," Kierra mutters, "I went out looking for him. I knew he wasn't at Anatomy-"

"Nah and he wouldn't be. Because he be ducking you, Kierra," Trina says, interrupting her and laughing. She adds, "You're like a worsen ass mosquito to Young D."

Trina laughs. Kierra doesn't. She continues her thoughts.

"When I didn't see him at any of the clubs," Kierra says, "I went to his house."

"You got in?!" Trina asks in surprise.

"Yea. I did."

"How?" Trina asks.

"I blew the guard," Kierra says, "He let me suck him off. Knowing Young D wasn't even at home. That bastard."

"His crew probably hipped them to that," Trina says, "So he wasn't there? How do you know that, for sure?"

"Kid told me about it, later," Kierra says, "I hit him up, after I got back here. He said he knew for sure that Young D is wherever Baby Girl is. But he didn't tell me how he knew. Or where they was. I know he was right, though. Because I just know."

"Oh. And you know this, how?" Trina presses.

251

"When I went to the estate, last night," Kierra says, "All of his boys was there. With Baby Boy and his crew."

"You went inside?" Trina pries.

"Not in his main house. No," Kierra answers, "But they joined me, in one of the guest houses. If you know what I mean."

"Damn girl. Why you didn't call me?" Trina asks, feeling left out of the action.

"I really didn't have time too. Plus you was working," Kierra says, "DeJuan told me to get naked. And you know he never fucks with me. Not if Young Derrick is anywhere around. *Only* when he's not available."

"Damn! So you handled all of them niggaz, yo self?" Trina asks in disbelief.

"Yea, I did," she says proudly, as she does the *Jay-Z* motion of brushing the dirt of her shoulders. She adds, "And I know why they call that nigga, Big Daddy too. He's got a big ass dick."

"Ugh. Bigger than Young D?" Trina asks, because she has to know.

"Oh, hell no!" Kierra says as she stretches her hands to demonstrate the size. She says, "That nigga Young D is Guinness Book of world records, type of big."

Then she presses Trina. She asks, "How the fuck do you know that Young Derrick is big?"

Trina gives her that, *now-you-know-I-done-had-some*, look.

"I told you, back then. To leave my man, *alone*," Kierra says.

"It was just that one time, girlfriend," Trina admits, quickly. "And from the looks of it. I'd say he is Baby Girl's man. That's how it looks to me."

Kierra shoots her the bird and the evil eye. She doesn't

252

like to admit that part. She lays back down on the couch and covers herself up. It's nearing light outside, as Trina retreats to her room. She calls back to Kierra and asks, "Kee, where's the baby?"

"She's sleep, in her room," Kierra says.

Trina goes on into her room to undress for bed. She knows that her roommate had possibly left her 4 year old daughter, at home alone. Because it wouldn't be the first time, if she had. It was common for Kierra to leave Danica at home alone.

It is nearing 6am and daylight. They are just going to sleep.

****

Woke up screaming, fuck the world today I've, had it up to here, ex girlfriend got custody today cause, they say she feels……..
Woke up screaming fuck the world today I've, had it up to here……..

Baby Girl is awakened by her cell phone ringing. Groggy and wrapped tightly in Young D's arms, she reaches for it. She grabs it, flips it open and answers without fully opening her eyes.

"Yes, hello," she whispers.

"Hey, Lovely. It's Chadrella's cousin, Gina ."

Hearing this voice startles Baby Girl and she sits up, immediately. Young D is roused from his sleep, by her moving suddenly. But he lies there, trying to train his eyes to see her, in the dark room.

"Oh. Gina is it?" Baby Girl asks, "Is Chadrella alright? I thought I was suppose to call her at eight?"

Why is she calling me now? Does she know what I did to her daddy, Chaddy?

"You was suppose to call her at eight," Gina says, "But she asks me to call you and tell you that she can't meet with you, today. Her father has passed away."

"Oh my God. No! What happened? How is she doing?" Baby Girl says, as she puts on an Oscar winning performance.

"She's not good. She's had to see a doctor, overnight," Gina says, "We're at the hospital now. The whole family is taking it, very hard."

"I won't ask you what happened. But I will send some flowers, from our entire family. Tell her I said I'm sorry about her dad. And I do know what she's going through. I lost all three of my parents. Two of them while we was at LSU. She was a huge part of me, getting through that," Baby Girl says, testing her ability to lie on cue. "It's going to be okay. But it will take time. Tell her, I'll call MJ and Tony and let them know too."

"She wants me to asked you for a favor," Gina says.

"Okay. What's the favor?" Baby Girl asks as she holds her breath.

"She asks me to asked you, if you will attend the funeral. As her friend. She doesn't have any. Other than the ones from college," Gina says, "You and MJ."
Baby Girl thinks of how pitiful that just sounded. But she knows it's true. Chadrella never had any friends. But Baby Girl has to give Gina an answer.

"I'm not too good with funeral's, Gina," she says, "I haven't been to one, since my mom's. Tell her I will do my best. If my husband Derrick, MJ and her husband comes with me. Then I might can get through it. Without upsetting her family, too much. I don't want to do that. I don't want to be a distraction, for them to have to deal with too. I hope you understand."

"I do," Gina says, "Try to come, if you can. She asked for you, personally."

"And you said, you're her cousin?"

"Yes," Gina says.

"You're handling it, really well, Gina," Baby Girl says.

"I am her cousin, on her mother's side," Gina says, "I didn't really know mister Chadwick, that well. He didn't allow me and Chadrella to play together. Not really. Not as kids. We had to sneak to see each other, after we got grown."

"Wow. I'm sorry to hear that," Baby Girl says, "But tell her I will send flowers. And I will do my best to be there, for her."

"Okay. Thanks. Bye-Bye."

"Goodbye." Baby Girl says as she hangs up and snuggles back close to Young D.

He was waiting for her to come back to his arms.

"She wants you to come to the damn funeral now, ha?" Young D asks.

"Yes, she does," Baby Girl says.

"You're not going. I know you're not gonna go, right?"

"I don't think I can," she says.

Not because she'd killed him. But because the last three funerals she'd attended was her real father, her daddy Don and her mother.

"I got you. Regardless of what you decide to do," he says, "Okay, baby?"

"Okay," she says.

They have their morning lovemaking session but have to stop midway.

"Oh, he's hating," Young D says as they both laugh.

Don Prince is waking and demanding to be fed, immediately.

"Time to get to your real job," Young D says, "I think

I'd better handle my part. I'll go grab some breakfast for us and man."

He kisses her. Then he goes into the bathroom for his daily, while she attends to their 3 month old son.

After breakfast, Baby Girl and her family check out of the hotel and head back to Houston. Shortly after 9am. Young D is in the Escalade. He's in front of her. He's traveling at a high rate of speed. She's nervous. He's driving fast, with the kids in there with him. They ride with him because all of their amenities are in the Escalade. Lil Man has his Playstation with games and Don Prince has his DVD player with his favorite movies. Still, Baby Girl doesn't want him to drive so fast, with their most prized possessions onboard. She accelerates her Benz and passes him. She takes the lead as she grabs her phone and calls her man.

"Hey, there," Young D answers in his jubilant tone.

"Hey, daddy. What's up?" she asks.

"Trailing you. With a couple of little men, who look like me. Riding with me," he says with baited breath.

He's thinking she may react negatively to him driving, so fast. Before she'd taken the lead.

"You was gunning it, daddy," she says.

She didn't like it. He agrees to slow down. They cruise at eighty and eighty five, for the remainder of the trip.

In three and a half hours, they arrive safely back at their Houston estate. They have approximately 24 hours before they have to fly to New York City. It's thirty hours before Tito Lopez goes into play.

CHAPTER TWELVE
ROCK STAR VIBES

For Baby Girl, the remainder of Thursday is spent tidying up her homes, in preparation for their road trip. She cleans the boys rooms, the guest rooms, the kitchen, bathrooms and even, the guest houses. Her head is filled with warm thoughts of the previous evening she'd spent with her husband and sons in Lafayette, Louisiana. She's happy they decided to surprise her. She's also happy that Chadwick Donaldson went down easy, too. But she's not happy about the call from Gus. Still, she doesn't allow it to interrupt her planning of Tito's demise. As she cleans, she's making mental notes on how Tito will expire. Not only how he'll expire. But she's going over the tools she need, as well as what all she needs to mail ahead, to NYC. She always takes her time with the mental preparation. That's the reason she's taking on extra cleaning. To give herself more time to plan his execution. Their guest houses will give her the extra cleaning time, she needs. The guest homes are usually done by the cleaning services. But Baby Girl has the time and needs to plan her *"daddy's work."* So she cleans them. The studio, on the other hand, is not her responsibility and Young D made that clear to his mates, from the beginning. "My wife is not your mama and she ain't no fucking maid," he had said to them. "Clean up your own shit and we'll be alright to record here. Leave it fucked up. And we'll be driving downtown to record."
The guys took that advice to heart. They have done well picking up behind themselves. Even after the sessions that Young D missed, when he'd left them to go to Lafayette and meet his wife. They left the studio, perfectly clean. Although, Baby Girl feels like DJ Debo and DeJuan, most likely did the

majority of the work. She has no complaints. As long as the work is done and everyone is satisfied. They do their own laundry, as well. She only washes clothes for her immediate family. That is, when she's around long enough to do chores. She's around long enough today and today, she even has time for laundry. Not to mention, her and Young D had purchased 2 washer and dryer sets for their utility room. This way, she can be sure and get all of their laundry done, in only a few hours. The labelmates use the utility room to do their laundry, as well. So it made sense to have 2 sets. And Young D is still considering adding washer/dryer sets to the guest houses, so that Baby Girl has their 2, all to herself.

She hums a tune as she gathers laundry. She brings the hampers from the closets, of both their sons rooms. Then her and Young D's room. Don Prince and Lil Man's laundry is done, first. Once their sons clothes are started, she begins to separate her and Young D's laundry, into piles. As she's preparing to do their white clothes, she catches a whiff of some knockoff perfume, mixed with a females odor. It's on 1 of Young D's white T-shirts. Baby Girl is familiar with this order because she has smelled this scent before.

"This shit is dreadful," she says, "When did he wear this t-shirt?"
She searches the house for Young D. She finds him in her office, using the computer.

"Hey, daddy," she says, "When did you wear this t-shirt?"

"I don't know. I don't even know if I *did* wear it," he answers, knowing to automatically cover. Just in case. He asks, "Why?"

"It smells like a mixture of cheap perfume and sex," she says as she giggles a bit.

But without completely laughing it off, she says, "Was one of your fans playing with her coochie before she hugged you?"

"It ain't no telling," he tries.

"Well, this t-shirt is telling plenty," she says, "Have you been with one of your ho's, this week?"

"Baby. I've been with you. This week, last week and the next week," he says, "Why do you do this?"

"This is not my smell, daddy," she says, "You do agree with that, right?"

"Oh, for sho. It don't smell like you," he says, "But it don't mean I was fucking nobody, either."

"When did you wear it?" she asks again.

He doesn't even have to think for very long. He knows he wore it, yesterday morning. When he'd gone to Kierra's apartment. But instead, he lies.

"Probably, Memorial day. Had to be Memorial day. That's the only time I've been out. Other then meeting you in Lafayette, yesterday," he says with conviction.

"This isn't an item I picked out, for that night," she says, "I didn't see you with this on, either. Try again."

She doesn't wait for his response. She's leaves the office and heads back to the laundry room.

As soon as she's out of sight, Young D calls DeJuan.

"Come to Lovely's office, for a second, man," he says, "I need a hot one."

DeJuan comes from the studio, immediately. Young D tells him about the conversation he has just had with Baby Girl.

"I wore it," DeJuan says, "I'll let her know, right now."

He leaves Young D in the office and finds Baby Girl in the laundry room. He has to let her believe that he has worn Young D's shirt. Just to cool things down. He goes for it.

"Hey, sis n law?" he says with a grin.

"What now, brother?" she asks, knowing he wants something, just by the wide grin on his face.

"Young D just got all over my case, in your office," he says.

"For what?"

"For going into his shit again," DeJuan says, "Without asking him."

"Going though his shit?" she asks, "I don't understand."

"I'll put it like this, "he says, "I think I owe you an apology and an explanation."

"Oh yeah? For what?" she asks, figuring her husbands best friend is going to come through, trying to keep him out of the dog house.

He's done this, many times. For 1 reason or another. But usually, it was for them being out late.

"For wearing your husbands clothes," he says, "Without asking."

"Oh, is that so? So it was you?"

"Yeah. I needed a clean white Tee to wear. Because I was being lazy and hadn't done my laundry," he says, "He was gone to meet you. So I just went in his closet and grabbed one. He's got about a hundred of 'em, hanging up in there. And he gets pissed at me, for wearing one. Like he ain't wore my shit before, without asking me. I wasn't trying to create more work for you and I'll wash it, if you want me too."

"No, DeJuan. I'll wash it," she says, "So when did you wear it?"

"Last night," he says.

"Do you do this, a lot, DeJuan?" she asks.

"Nah. Not a lot. But it's not my first time, either. I just never had sex, the other times I was wearing his clothes. And if

260

it has to be. Then it'll be the last time," he says, "Because I can see that it has upset both of y'all."

"Who did you have sex with, while you was wearing it?" she asks.

"Whoa. Baby Girl you've never went there with me."

"You never left a bitch's scent on my husbands clothes and I had to smell it, either," she says, "Who?"

"Just some tramp, who showed up while we was in session," he says, "But I didn't do no nasty, in this house. I swear, on everything I love. I took her to the guest house."

"Daddy knows this tramp too," she tells him.

Just as he's starting to feel like his lie is iron clad.

"Nah. He don't. I doubt it."

"Well. I don't doubt it," she says.

"Baby Girl. For real, he don't know her," he tries, "It's a tramp I met, this week and he wasn't with me when I met her. I just got lonely and decided I wanted some comfort. Without the hassles of a relationship. She's a specialist in that department and the only reason I buzzed her through, last night, is because y'all wasn't here."

"Really. Well, let me put you up on something, family," she starts, "Maybe you don't *know* it. But he knows her."

"Why do you think he knows this tramp?" he asks.

"Because this scent is in my laundry, *every fucking time* I go out of town and come back," she reveals with that *nigga please* look on her face. "And you already said you hadn't worn his clothes *and had sex in them,* before last night."

He has no comment. At least not right away.

Baby Girl asks again, "So, who is she?"

"I don't even know her name, Baby Girl," he tries.

"Then maybe Derrick can tell me," she says.

DeJuan isn't sure what to say, next. But he reaches.

261

"Well, maybe now I should go back and scream on him," he says, "But I should also tell you what I just told him. I'm not the only one in our crew, who's had her or that's been wearing your husbands clothes."

"Thanks, DeJuan. I know you love me and Derrick, together. Thank you," she says, not willing to hear him dig himself any deeper.

She excuses him and goes back to her household chores, with a smile.

It smells like that cheap ass bitch, Kierra, to me. Just give me the muthafucking reason.

She has errands to run before the trip, tomorrow. She figures, now is as good of a time as any.

She leaves and goes to the post office. She has to overnight their packages to New York. She's sending them to The W Hotel, addressed to H-Town Records and herself. The hotel will accept the boxes and packages for them and have them there, waiting when they arrive. Her work gear is included, as well as the labels.

Then she heads to her favorite florist and makes arrangements for flowers to be sent to the Donaldson's in Lafayette, from H-Town Records. She sends her condolences and an apology.

I will not be attending Chadwick Donaldson's funeral.

She calls MJ, on her way back to the estate. She has to tell her about Chadrella's lose, as well as her request.

Upon hearing of the death, MJ and Tony send flowers but opt out of attending, as well.

"We wasn't close to her, Baby Girl," MJ says.

"*I know* we wasn't," she says, "That's why I was so

shocked when her cousin asked me to attend, as a friend. She paid us to hang out with her. It's not like we was around her because we enjoyed it or anything."

They laugh as her and MJ talk in depth, about their college days with Chadrella. MJ barely remembers her father but she does remember Chadrella wanting Tony Ray.

"That bitch would've got the brakes beat off her ass," MJ says, "That is, if her pockets wouldn't have been so damn fat."

They both laugh again.

"I know that's right," Baby Girl says.

She has reached the main house at the Estate. Annie's house. She's going to stop in and talk with her, before going on home.

Before going in, she sits on the driveway and continues her conversation with her best female friend, MJ. She touches on the t-shirt incident and tells MJ how Young D and DeJuan handled it. She tells her, she feels they're trying to hide something but she can't be 100% positive.

"You think he's lying for him, don't you?" MJ asks.

"No. I *know* he is. Because that's what they do," she says, "Derrick is fucking someone, other than me. I don't know what their relationship is. But there *is* a relationship."

"Baby Girl, you are his wife. Of course, if you think you smell something different. You're gonna say he's fucking around," MJ says, "But you have no proof. And besides. Young D ain't a cheating bastard, like Tony."

"That funky ass t-shirt was proof that he's a cheating bastard," she says.

"Where is the shirt at now?" MJ asks.

"I burnt that shit. I don't ever want him to wear it again. I would know it, if he did."

"The scent is really familiar to you?" she asks.

263

"Hell yeah, it's familiar," Baby Girl says, "I just can't place where I've smelled it before. But it's familiar."
Baby Girl doesn't want to tell MJ her suspicions about Kierra. Just in case she has to kill her. She wants to be certain of it, first. But she has smelled that bitch, on occasion. And she's almost positive, it's her. Her and MJ hang up and she gets out to visit her mother-in-law.
One more event and I'll know, for sure. Even if I have to invite her ass, personally.

She goes inside to visit with Annie. Young D has already called and told his mother about the t-shirt conversation. So Annie brings it up before Baby Girl can even introduce the topic to her. That assures Baby Girl that either, she's on the right track. Or there is cover up going on and everyone knows about it and is a part of the cover up. Annie starts right in, as soon as she gets inside of her home.

"I heard about the funky ass t-shirt, you found in the laundry," Annie says.

"Oh Lord. He called and told you?" Baby Girl asks, making sure disbelief is in her voice.

"Yes. I think you had just made him aware of it," she says, "Then he called me. Stressing out about it."

"There was no reason to call you," she says, "I mean, he got DeJuan and the guys down there, to give him a ready made lie, whenever he needs one."

"Oh boy," Annie says, "I don't know about all that. But I do know that you and Derrick need to talk this out. Amongst yourselves. That's what I told him and leave everyone else out of it."

"That may be true," she says, "But I don't even wanna talk about it, any time soon. I don't know what I would say,

264

right now. I need some time to think about it."

Annie tells her to take all the time she needs. But to be sure and get to the bottom of it and not let it slide. She promises her mother-in-law that she will.

"I have to get back down there and pack our suitcases," she says, "We'll be back to kiss the boys, goodnight, I'm sure."

"On that, you *both* better be sure and do," Annie says, "No matter what else you two, talk on. My grandkids need both of you. Okay?"

"Okay, mama. We'll be back," she says and with that, she heads home to finish the packing.

Back at her and D's home, Baby Girl packs her and Young D's suitcases for the New York trip. Then she sits them by the front door.

"Everything is ready for NYC, you guys!" she yells.

But she finds out that no one is in the immediate area. Automatically, she knows she has struck a nerve, that neither of them know how to calm. This is why they're all out of reach and keeping their distance from her.

Upstairs in the studio, DJ Debo, Young D and DeJuan work on finishing up Young D's verses. Once his final verses are laid, DJ Debo does the mastering of the 2 CD's. The CD's are complete and ready for the promotion and distribution stages by 7pm.

"Hey, we got these knocked out, in time to take them with us, tomorrow. If y'all wanna perform some of it, we can," DJ Debo says.

"We'll hold them for San Antonio," Young D tells him, "We break new music, in the south, first. Just to get a vibe on how the dirty, feels about it. Before we branch out with it."

"Yea. Because NYC may hate it and it could actually be a damn good song. You know what I'm saying," DeJuan adds as they all chuckle.

They decide to bring the new music for their listening pleasure and just perform the 3 hour set, DJ Debo originally prepared.

"I gotta let wifey hear these," Young D says.

"She said anything else to you about the t-shirt?" DeJuan asks.

"She ain't said nothing else to me, at all," he says.

"She's smart, D," DeJuan warns, "She said she's smelled the scent before. Every time she comes back home, from a trip."

"That's cause that bitch stinks," he says.

"I know you strapping up, right?"

Young D looks at him with a face that says, *I can't even believe you had to ask me that.*

"Just checking, D," DeJuan says with a chuckle, "So the smell is from *the apartment*. I guess."

"That's her stank ass, DeJuan," he says, agitated. "Her whole vibe, stinks. I'm not shocked that there's an odor. I be sick, just thinking about having to be near her. The shit is sickening. *Literally*."

"We need to make that shit go away, homeboy," DeJuan advises.

"Tell me about it," Young D says.

They sit out the session with DJ Debo as he tweaks the 2 mixtapes and finalize the recordings. During this entire time, Young D stresses over the t-shirt talk. He knows he won't be able to keep up the charades with Kierra, much longer. He doesn't want too. But he doesn't want his wife to find out about his situation with Kierra, by smelling her scent on his clothes, either. That leaves him no wiggle room, whatsoever.

266

Baby Girl has been around the 2 of them, at the same time, at their family events. So she would knows that at no time, have him and Kierra ever acted chummy enough to be hugging each other.

So why else would my clothes have her scent on them? She's going to kill me. I would rather be dead, if I can't have my Baby Girl.

Young D can't get over the fact that he's between a rock and a hard place. Over a bitch that he wishes he had never met. At least, if he's going to have to argue with his wife, it needs to be over a female that he's willing and wanting to fuck with. Not some washed up ass, stripper slash prostitute. Who uses his desire to stay with his wife, as a means of getting to his dick.

This shit needs to go away, is right! I need to put a hit on her ass and let Baby Girl take her out. But she'll notice when that kind of money comes out of our budget. Fuck!

At 9pm, Young D and Baby Girl go up to Annie's house to get their sons ready for bed. Baby Girl takes Don Prince into their bathroom, for his bath. While Young D runs the bath water for Lil Man's bath. He wrestles with Lil Man for a few minutes, before helping him to take off his clothes. Then, Lil Man gets into the tub, under the watchful eye of Baby Girl. She's bathing Don Prince, in the same tub with his brother. They both love to splash, so she gives them time to play in the water. Before actually bathing them.

      Annie sees this time, as opportunity. This will allow her the time she needs to confront and advise her son, about this new situation. She's still concerned about Kierra, Danica, the t-shirt and the negative affect this could all have on her son's marriage. That is, if Baby Girl finds out about his secret.

Annie loves to see her son with Baby Girl and a mother knows what's good for her son. Baby Girl is good for him. She has seen her son go from a street hoodlum, not caring if he lived or died. To a family man, father, husband and a provider, for his entire family. So, while Baby Girl is busy with the boys in the bathroom. Annie steals a few minutes of Young D's time to discuss it.

"So have you two had a chance to talk?" Annie asks.

"No. Not yet. She's not talking to me, right now," Young D says.

"Over the t-shirt?"

"Yeah. Well, the smell on it," he clarifies.

"A wife knows her scent, on her husband. Just like a mother knows her sons scent too."

"She told DeJuan, she's smelled it before."

"DeJuan? Why?" Annie asks.

"He tried to cover for me but she didn't believe him."

"She told me that, already," Annie says, "And she didn't sound like she believed him. I don't like this, son."

"I don't either."

"When are you gonna tell her about Danica and be done with it?" Annie asks.

"I don't know how too."

"Just tell Baby Girl."

".... Just tell me what?" Baby Girl asks as she's holding a slippery wet Don Prince, while chasing a wet Lil Man. Who'd jumped out of the tub and started running around the house naked.

"I want a baby," Young D says suddenly, as an answer to her question.

"Well, here," Baby Girl says with a smile as she hands Don Prince to Young D and takes off after Lil Man again.

Annie can't help but snicker as Lil Man runs and slides around the corners of her house, trying to escape his mother. Young D looks at his mother and gives a sigh of relief.

"Tell her, son. The sooner the better. Mark my words," Annie warns.

Once the baths are done and boys are sound asleep. Young D and Baby Girl go home and get ready for bed, themselves. They don't discuss the t-shirt issue before going to sleep. They don't discuss anything else either.

****

The airport shuttle arrives and they all load up for the drive to *Hobby airport*. They take flight and after, just under five hours, they land at *LaGuardia airport* in neighboring Queens, New York. Their car service is there and waiting. The lead driver Carlos, lets them know they're ready to take them to their hotel.

"Upscale got it going on," High Top says as he gives props to the club which had invited them to the city.
He likes the plush accommodations they've provided and lavish way they're being handled. Starting with the car service.

"This is like the Morales fleet and shit," Arafat adds, "With the Hummers and Benz trucks and shit."

"And their, on time," Big Daddy says.
They hate to wait for a ride. Which happens sometimes, when they're on the road. They love it when the car service is there at the airport and waiting when they arrive. Now they're in route to The W Hotel, where they'll stay for tonight.

They arrive at the hotel within minutes and unload. At the front desk, Baby Girl gets them checked in and to their separate suites and all of their bags, sent up to their specific rooms. Then she goes to the concierge to inquire about the packages she had sent, overnight.

"Yes, ma'am. We have them for you," he says.

"Good. I'll sign for them now," she says, "And I'll need a bellman to deliver them to the room numbers, that I apply to them."

"Yes, ma'am."

She signs for the packages. They are then rushed upstairs with the rest of their belongings. It's just after 5pm, in New York City. Traffic is crazy and the hustle and bustle of working people leaving work on a Friday evening, has the streets gridlocked. The only way to get anywhere in this city, during the decent hours, is mass transit or walking.

That's why I wanted the same hotel that my mark lives in. Instant access. And a delay for the emergency assistance and the police too. Because it's a Friday night, in Manhattan. Perfect.

Young D's show doesn't start until 10pm. That's one hour after Tito Lopez goes into play. She checks the itinerary. Club Upscale has arranged a buffet style dinner for H-Town records, in 1 of the hotel's largest ballrooms.

"It smells wonderful," Baby Girl says to JB.

He had arrived at the hotel, shortly after they had. The dinner buffet, set up for them, has the entire lobby of the W Hotel smelling of prime rib and chicken cordon bleu.

"Let's get everybody in here to eat, first," JB says, "And then, we might have time for sound check."

The crew head into the ballroom to partake of the food they've been smelling since they arrived. After having their fill of the grub, they have time to do a quick sound check, at 7pm.

Later, in their suite, before time to head to the venue.

270

Young D tries to have a conversation with Baby Girl.

"You got work, tonight?" he asks.

"I'm not discussing that and you know it," she says, "Yet you still insist on asking me, every time."

"Are you ready to talk about what I'm suppose to tell you?"

"No, I'm not!" she says, "We have 2 small sons, already. One less than three years old and one, three months old. So why would you even go there, right now?"

"So if I wanted to talk to you about having a girl. I can't do that?" he asks.

"No. Not unless you're having her," she answers, without so much as even making eye contact.

This is the way he knows when she's conflicted about something. He feels it's most likely, about the t-shirt situation. But she won't be forthcoming with it. Not on her own. She's the type that will make him expose it. Or pull it out of her. He doesn't want to do either, right now. He just wants to know if she believes him wanting a baby, is *really* what his mother was advising him to tell her about. And now, he knows for sure, that she doesn't.

She doesn't believe that's what we was talking about. I can tell.

Baby Girl goes into the bathroom to start a hot, relaxing bath. Young D yells to her, from the desk in the room.

"Are you going to the venue with us!?" he yells.

"Yes!" she yells back.

So much for that conversation.

Young D will have to try again later. Tonight, Baby Girl is preoccupied with her hit. And his show, being a hit.

"Can I get some pre-show?" he asks.

271

She doesn't answer. She thinking he had better figure out the right move to make, right now. Or shit is going to get a lot more stressful for him.

What a foolish question? I have a right to that dick, Derrick. Your job is to bring it to me, automatically. Not asks me, if you can have the pussy you're married too.

He decides to go for it. Never going to be denied his wife, he comes into bathroom and joins her in the sunken tub. They indulge, as usual. Just without the conversation. She isn't ever going to be denied, her husband either.

CHAPTER THIRTEEN
<u>SHOW TIME</u>

The car service picks them up at *The W* and takes them to Club Upscale, for 9:45pm, sharp. Even though, the club is only 2 buildings away. This is the Upscale way of treating it's most valuable guest. Young D released an album that went platinum, in 1 week. And it is over 2 times platinum, in less then 3 months. Young D has catapulted H-Town records to an elite status. No one expects the labels premiere artist to walk. Not even, 2 doors down. Besides, with all of the fans who have Upscale packed and the hundreds that pack the sidewalks, because they couldn't get in, Young D would've been mobbed on the sidewalk.

The club is filled, to maximum capacity, in anticipation of MC Young D, The Kilo Clique, Big Daddy and The PA. The guys are led to their separate dressing rooms. JB handles the particulars for the show. While Baby Girl secures the payment. After the payments are secured, Baby Girl goes into Young D's dressing room and lays out his show outfit. DeJuan and DJ Debo gets everyone else in order. No other female travels with H-Town records. At least, not on H-Town records tab. If the other guys want a female assistant, like Young D has. Then they'll have to pay her out of their salaries. Same as Young D does with his wife, Baby Girl.

Young D is smoking his show blunt and relaxing, while Baby Girl is laying out his show gear. He tries to talk to her again.

"Do you wanna talk now, Baby Girl?" he asks.

"I'm good, daddy," she says, "Concentrate on your show. I'm good."

She takes this opportunity to call Annie's cell phone. So she can check in and talk to the boys. Annie has some good news, for her.

"Bruce and Jordan wanna move to Houston, with us," Annie says.

"Oh that's the bomb, mama A," she says, very excited, "I wanted them to do that, all along."

Bruce has just finished his junior year of high school. Jordan has past to the 8th grade. Both of them are playing football and basketball.

"We can get them registered and moved now," Baby Girl suggests, "While school is out."

"Sounds good to me." Annie says as she agrees.

She tells Baby Girl, she'll get the ball rolling by getting their records transferred and checking with the school board, in Houston. She wants to see how the credits toward graduation will stack up. And how it will affect their eligibility for playing sports.

Next, Baby Girl talks to her sons. So does Young D. Then they hang up. The room is eerily quiet as Baby Girl and Young D, still haven't found the words to say to 1 another.

"It's Showtime!" JB yells as he sticks his head inside the door of Young D's dressing room and tells him to hit the stage.

"That means it's hit time!" Young D yells back, as JB is moving further down the hall.

He looks at Baby Girl to get her expression. She has none. He knows why. She's in play.

****

Baby Girl had cased *The W Hotel* when the guys left to do their sound check. She mapped out her course, for Tito's expiration. Their suite is on the 28th floor. The Presidential

274

Suite. The best suite, at most hotels and the 1, Baby Girl and her husband usually occupy when their on the road. But not at The W, New York. At the this hotel, the best suite is the Penthouse. They could never get the penthouse because it has a permanent tenant. A big balling ass, drug kingpin named Tito Lopez. He'd had the luxurious suite completely renovated and designed, to his specifications. He had trap doors and safes installed too. The most important reason why Baby Girl booked the presidential suite for her and Young D is because of the hit she has. There is a fire escape off of the terrace, which leads up to the 30th floor. *The Penthouse*. Which belongs to Tito Lopez. Tonight, Lopes is having a huge costume party. It's an annual party which is called, *The Lopez Masquerade*. He ordered top of the line strippers and hookers. Amongst other things, for the party. Baby Girl has her French maids outfit, specifically for this reason. Her research told her, he would have hookers and strippers. They'll be part of her camouflage.

H-Town records set starts at 10pm. Baby Girl watches the first 10 minutes of the show. Then, at 10:10pm, she darts backstage and into Young D's dressing room. Quickly, she changes into her French maid outfit. Complete with a full length cape and a wig. Plus a masquerade mask for more disguise and hooker makeup. She attaches her Ipod to her skirt and puts her earplugs in.
Music check. Let me bump that, Straight Outta Ca$hville, for this hit.

Baby Girl leaves her personals in her satchel, next to her husband's bags. She checks the hall for stragglers and sees none. She makes a run for it and darts out the rear door. The W is 2 buildings down from Club Upscale. Making a hasty

275

approach, Baby Girl reaches a mass of people, who are going into the Masquerade party. They're all wearing costumes. She's able to blend in perfectly, with these guest. These are people going into the lobby of the hotel for Tito's party. She goes up on the elevators, which is carrying the entertainment and the girls. The main reason she chose to ride up with them, is because her research said they are being handled separately and differently, then the regular guest. For one, they aren't being searched. She'd counted on that. When they get to the Penthouse, they separate the girls from the music entertainers.

"I need all of the strippers to come this way. You'll need to sign this list, over here," 1 of Tito's goons says, "This is so we'll know who all was here. We don't want some whore, filing a charge from this party, who wasn't even at this party. You know what I mean?"

He and the other goons laugh at his corny ass attempt to be humorous. Baby Girl knows some of these very girls, she's in this side room with will be assaulted tonight. She only hopes she can kill Tito, in time to spare the worst of it. She scribbles the name; Constance Nix. Then slithers on into the party, undetected.

Once she's inside the penthouse, she surveys the main room for other pro's. She doesn't see any recognizable faces. Rookies don't count. She moves through, quickly. Shunning advances by many male patrons, who are attending the party. Finally, she spots Tito. He's near the rear of the room, by 1 of the back hallways. He has 1 call girl with him, already. Baby Girl remembers her from the sign-in line. She wants to be the 2nd girl. Her research had revealed Tito likes to start off his parties with the 2 hottest call girls, in his bedroom. Then work his way through them. Until he's seen them all or doesn't care to see anymore. She's determined to get in that room, first. So she can spare the other girls of the plight they'll face, if this party continues for too long. Baby Girl starts doing things to get noticed. It works. Tito spots her, immediately. Because she's, so tall. Tito notices her bowlegs and that clinches it. Still, she gives him very suggestive eyes and body language. She can tell he's interested. Suddenly, he sends 1 of his goons over to her to proposition her for a night with him.

"Mr. Tito Lopez requests your presence for a dance, in his private suite," the bodyguard says.

He tells her they have to go to a more secluded area, for the dance. She looks in the direction that he points. She can see Tito Lopez going in the same direction. She bites.

"Let's go," she says, keeping her masquerade mask on.

She's careful not to make eye contact with Tito's guard. She follows him up the long hallway which leads to several private suites. He escorts her to the very back suite. The biggest and best one. The guard stays at the door while she goes in. Tito has to see her face, first. If he likes her, she will remain in the room. If he doesn't. He'll send her back out and replace her with another girl.

She's inside of the door now. She sees Tito and the call girl. Immediately, Tito turns up the lights and demands she remove her mask. She does. Apparently, he likes what he sees. He tells her to come on over, as he dims the lights again. The hooker is already engaging in oral sex, with Tito. She hasn't seen Baby Girl's face. Tito has 1 hand on a satchel. Next to the couch. His other hand is on top of the hookers head. Baby Girl looks at the satchel. She's not worried that it could be a weapon. Even if it is, he want have time to get to it because she's already got the jump on him. While he's getting head from the hooker. They'll never even know what hit them. She's got them covered. Now, she's thinking of how she can get the guard to come back in. He has to die too. He's seen her and can describe her. Except for her face. But she knows, 1 sweep of the hotel for 6 foot women and she'd be in a line up. One look at her legs and she'd be headed to Riker's Island. On a 1st degree murder charge. Not to mention, if they went back and compared unsolved murders in areas where she has been with her husband's tour. She would make history. Like a Gotti or Capone.

I would never see my sons again. Because I would never allow them to visit me in nobody's prison. I would no longer be a role model to them or anything I wanted them to see and get use too. I need to get that goon in here.

"Can I bring your bodyguard in here too?" she asks Tito, "I think I'm enough for two guys and a girl. I like tag team action."

Tito bites instantly. He's so jacked up on cocaine, Oxycotin and God only knows what else. That he's ready to be a regular ole freak, tonight.

"As long as you fuck me, first, bitch. *Sure*," Tito says as he laughs in his obnoxious way.

"Okay. Well let's do that now, then. Let me fuck you first," she says, boldly.

She has his attention. The call girl seems a little jealous. That is, until Baby Girl gets in her ear.

"Lets both of us do him, together and my pimp will pay you, five Kay," Baby Girl adds.

The call girl bites. She asks, "Do you do girls?"

"No, not usually," Baby Girl says, "But for you. I'll make an exception. Only you can't watch. Here. Put this on."

Baby Girl puts the blindfold on the call girl. Then, she starts her Ipod.

It's playing, *Bonafide Hustler* from *Young Buck*. Then, she lets the call girl kiss on her neck. Tito is loving this girl on girl action, so much, he doesn't pay any attention to Baby Girl's hands. She pulls her 9mm with the silencer, from her garter snap and puts 2 rounds into Tito's chest. She can hear him gurgling for air over the music. While the call girl is back to giving him head. She gets more intense with it. Thinking the gurgling noise he's making is because he's about to cum. He gurgles. Finally, Baby Girl cuts of his air supply, by pinching together his Esophagus and his Trachea. He's dead by the time *50 cent's* verse is saying,
"That Haitian nigga wit the guitar, that say gone to November."
Then Baby Girl has to close his eyes as she kisses his forehead.
Bye-bye, baby!

She turns her attention to the stripper or call girl or whomever. It doesn't matter what she prefers to be called. She's dying, next. They can get the preferred name correct, on her tombstone.
    The call girl is clueless as to what has happened to her *John*. Baby Girl kisses her chest as the stripper pushes her tongue against Baby Girl's denying lips.
Not the tongue. You just gave this fool head, bitch!

Baby Girl plants a bullet in her left ear. She slumps over. Baby Girl puts her head, back on the top of Tito's dick. As if she's still giving him head. She pulls a throw over Tito, to hide the 2 holes in his shirt. She pulls his *Kangol* down over his head. She puts his hand back on top of the dead hookers head.
    Now she has to get the guard in this room. She turns to the door, as Young Buck's verse starts.
"I been out here for too long, I deserve to get a bird. The fiend's
279

know my name now, from standing on this curb. I got blood on my shirt,…….."
She turns to face the door. Then she walks toward it and cracks it open. As she's opening the door, she puts her 9mm behind her back. She talks to the guard, from around the door. She can see up the hallway. The penthouse is filled to capacity, by now and extremely noisy.
Perfect cover!

"You niggas know me, from fillin' up ya heroine needles, We ain't scared of the road, you already know, I don't trust no hoes,"
　　　　"I asked if I could fuck you too and Tito said yes," Baby Girl oozes to the guard. "So come on in."
He comes inside and locks the door back.
"that's how T got pop'd, she told it to the cops."
He spots Tito, who appears to be getting some head.
　　　　"Oh, baby," The guard says, "You must have been feeling left out. She got him covered, over here. Well you can suck my dick. Since he's too busy, for you."
"Me and Preist had the streets on lock,.."

As the guard gets closer, he can now see that the hooker is dead.
"I'd open up shop, around the clock..,"

He turns to Baby Girl and at the same time, he's reaching for his gun. Baby Girl puts 4 quick shots in him. He falls into the large glass window, shattering it. But it doesn't break. He's leaning against it. He's still breathing and trying to recover. And he's trying not fall to his death. The large picture window with the great view of the New York skyline has shattered and is barely staying up. The guard is trying to raise his weight off
280

of it. Baby Girl isn't going to let that happen. She takes a drop step and kicks him hard, in the chest. He falls out of the window. Flipping and flailing. Like Gruber, who died at the end of the 1st *Diehard* movie. The guard falls 30 story's, to his certain death.

"A*nd I ain't gon stop, we at it again, we getting em for 10.*"

She kills her IPod. It's time for the getaway. She never needs time for a Yayo verse. *Ever.* She grabs the satchel from the side of the couch. It may be full of money. Tito kept 1 hand on the handle of it, the entire time he was being entertained. It has to be something valuable.
Collateral.

She peeps in it and sees stacks. She doesn't have time to search it fully, as she checks her watch.
"Eleven pm."
    She hit's the fire escape and rapidly descends it, for 2 floors to her suite's balcony. She enters through the suites bedroom terrace. She closes the patio door quickly and locks it. Now that her job is done. She dips into the bathroom and changes her clothes. She puts the French maid outfit and disguise, in a plastic bag. She unfolds the box she'd brought with her, to send the outfit back home in. Quietly, she packs the plastic bag and Tito's satchel into it. She tapes it up and addresses it to their Estate, in Houston. She will mail it before their mid-morning flight. Now, she's dressed in her nice, form fitting couture outfit. It fits her, perfectly. With her matching sandals and her coordinated handbag, it's time to get back to her husband's show. She's going back to Club Upscale for the remainder of the set. But there's something waiting in the suite that she hadn't counted on seeing. Nor had she allowed for.

Not at this moment. When she comes out of the bathroom and into the living area of the suite, she gets a shock.

Annie and Angela have flown in, with her 2 sons, plus Jordan and Bruce.

"Baby Girl? I didn't know you was back there," Annie says.

"Yes. I came back to change clothes," Baby Girl says quickly, "I had a little accident. I didn't even hear y'all come in. Mama Annie, you didn't say you was coming out here, when I talked to you. But I'm so glad you did."

She plays with her sons, after hugging Annie, Angela, Bruce and Jordan. At the same time, she's trying to shield the awkward feeling she has.

"I was already here," Annie says, "We was at the airport. Right before D was suppose to go on. We only been in here, about fifteen minutes."

"I had to come back and change, twenty minutes ago," Baby Girl says, "I didn't even hear y'all come in."

She smiles.

Angela adds, "You was so quiet. I didn't know you was back there."

"So who's going back to Upscale, with me?" Baby Girl asks, knowing she needs to get back soon.

"I am," Angela and Bruce say in unison.

Mama Annie agrees to stay with the babies, so they can all go.

"We got us a good movie on, anyway," Annie says, "Y'all go on and have fun."

The 3 of them leave the suite, hop on the elevator and descend to the lobby.

Once they're off the elevator, they see the whole lobby, in a buzz. There are many people screaming and talking loud.

"A man just jumped to his death!" She heard someone exclaim.

"He was shot up." Another bystander proclaims. Baby Girl says to her family, "Come on, y'all. Let's get over to Upscale. This crazy New York night life, is not for me."

They get back to the club by 11:30 and catch the rest of Young D's set. When he's done, they all go backstage while he changes clothes. He looks at Baby Girl.

"I like *that* outfit," he says as he holds the bag which has her 1st outfit and her personals in it.

"Thank you, daddy. I wore it for you," she says.

Young D is being facetious. He knows she's wearing a different outfit then she had on, earlier.

"Mama and the kids came up. Did you know they was coming?" Baby Girl asks.

"Not until after sound check," he says, "My bad. I forgot to tell you. But then, you didn't want to talk."

"Oh, okay. Well, our boys are here and Jordan too."

"I saw Bruce, out there," he says, "I'm glad they're out of school. Now they can travel with us, sometimes."

She agrees with him.

"That's a good idea," she says, "They can travel with us. Between football and summer camps. Mama Annie is going to get them registered for school, in Houston. I'm really happy they wanna live with us."

"That's cool with me, baby," Young D says, "And we've got plenty of room."

It's settled. Two of her brothers are coming to live with her. She's very excited about that.

As they make their way to the limo, she's thinking about Six Nine. She's going to do her part, to make sure he sees Jordan. She wants Jordan to know his real dad and have a father/son relationship, with him.

"We'll call him when we get back to Houston," Young D says, "And tell him, Jordan is staying with us. And now, when he makes a trip to Houston. He can see his son too."
Baby Girl agrees as they get into the transport cars and pull back up the street to the hotel.

There is even more commotion, outside The W. The concierge comes out to greet their cars. He ushers them past the police presence, paramedics and reporters. Baby Girl tells him, she has a package to mail out.

"Can you handle it, for me?" she asks.

"It would be my pleasure, ma'am," the concierge says, "I'll get it shipped out, tonight."

"Thanks."

The labelmates are watching, all of the commotion outside of their hotel.

"What the hell happened, round here?" Gat em asks.

"Some man jumped from a window," Angela says, "Somebody said that when we was leaving for the club."

"Then another person said he got shot up," Bruce adds.

"Might've been a bit of both," Arafat says as he laughs.

"He wasn't a politician, was he?" Manolo asks, "You know they've been offing them, one a day, lately."
He and the labelmates laugh, at their own wit. They don't have a clue that the single hand which has brought them the material for their comedic outburst, lately. Is no one other, than their bosses wife, Baby Girl. And she shows no signs of guilt or breaking. She's cool. Young D looks at her. She looks at him. The labelmates decide to stand around downstairs, for a while to get the story. Not Young D and Baby Girl. They want to get on to their suite and see their sons. Or at least, that's the excuse they give.

Led by the concierge, they make their way through the lobby and onto the elevator. The concierge is coming up with them, to pick up Baby Girl's packages. On the elevator, Young D is still staring at his wife. He's in awe, at how cool, calm and collected, she is.

As if she had nothing to do with this circus of events, that's taking place. It's really a turn on, though.

He says, "We're gonna talk, in the suite."

"We've got company, in the suite," she says, "We can talk in bed."

"I plan to do more than talk in the bed, baby," he says, while the concierge is there to insure that she won't go off on him, if she so desires.

But she doesn't. She's much more clever, than that.

"Hmm. Well, it's always good to have a plan," she says, with a slight smile.

They get off the elevator and head to the suite. Making cute conversation, on the way. She dips into the bedroom and grabs the packages for the concierge, who's name is Gregory. Gregory takes the large box which contains her *killer* French maid outfit, accessories and the satchel.

Concierge Gregory says, "I'll get this out, tonight. I have a total of seven, to mail out. Do you need a receipt back?"

"No, Gregory," Baby Girl says, "You don't have to do that. Your word is plenty. I'm sure it will arrive, just fine. Just bill it to the room. That receipt will suffice."

She gives him his tip and a, "Thank you, so much."

He thanks her back and leaves.

Young D speaks to and hugs his mother. He grabs his 3 month old son from her hands and pretends to toss him up in the air. Don Prince chuckles. Lil Man wants to be tossed up, for real. Annie takes Don Prince while Young D obliges Lil Man with a toss up. So high, he nearly scrapes the ceiling. Young D catches him and tosses him back up again. Lil Man giggles uncontrollably, as Young D tosses him up over, over and over again.

"Did you rock the house?" his mother asks.

He gives her a look of disdainfulness as him and Lil Man wrestles on the living room floor.

Mama Annie giggles and says, "Well, I was just asking."

"Of course I did. I killed it. You already know," he says. She smiles proudly. She loves that her son is making a living, doing exactly what he loves to do. Hip-Hop music. He takes a break from wrestling with his son and goes into the kitchen. His mother has arranged the food which was delivered for him and his labelmates.

"I'm about to grub, sho nuff," Young D says.

He grabs a few chicken fingers. He gives 1 to Lil Man, in each of his hands. He eats 1, himself. Baby Girl is making the three of them and Jordan, a plate. She sets the table and they all sit down to eat a late night snack. Annie joins them in the kitchen. She's feeding Don Prince mashed potatoes. He's loving them.

"Mama's baby wanna eat this food too," she says as she coo's at him.

"He tearing that food up," Jordan adds.

They all giggle as Lil Man agrees with Jordan.

The labelmates, Angela and Bruce come in, from downstairs. They've got the story on the commotion, at The W. Or at least, what is being speculated.

"Hey, y'all. It was three people killed in this hotel, tonight!" Gat em says, "While we was doing our show."

"What!?" Annie exclaims, "Please tell me you are kidding!"

286

Young Aristocrat adds, "He's not kidding. It was a kingpin and a hooker killed in the penthouse."

"And the dude that was found on the street, was shot up, up there too," High Top adds, "Then, he fell or was pushed, out of the window."

"Yeah," Gat Em says as he laughs, "They had a big drug and sex party, up there."

"Oh my lord," Annie says. She can't believe what she's hearing. "Did they catch the guy who did it?"

"I don't think so," Arafat says, "Hotel security told me, the cops ain't even lift no prints. Cause there was over 350 guest in and out of that penthouse. But they're still holding everybody, who was at that party."

"And they're going over the surveillance footage, from the hotel," DJ Debo says, "But security says, they don't see shit on it, that they can use."

"I know the front desk came up here and checked the patio, to be sure it was locked," Annie says, "They said there may be a guest, a loose on the fire escape. They didn't want him barging into other guest rooms. They didn't tell me, people had been murdered."

"They lied to you, mama," Young D says, "They wanted to make sure the killer didn't come through here. Because they know I'll sue the hell out of them. After I kill the fool who came running up in here and harmed *mines*."

"Oh, son," Annie says as she laughs, "You wouldn't have known nothing. Until he was in here. Doing what he do."

"I might know more than you think," he says as he laughs. "I know how to handle killers, the way they need to be handled," he says, looking at Baby Girl with sultry eyes.

"Mmmm. Then maybe you should be on *NYPD*," Baby Girl adds, "Sounds like they need you."

"Shit. That's where the criminals at," Annie adds, "You know they killed that boy, on the morning of his wedding."

"*Sean Bell*," Baby Girl clarifies.

"Yes. That's his name," Annie continues, "And they probably won't do, a *day*."

"Not until we tear something up," DeJuan says.

The others cosign him. He hasn't commented on any of the hotel, murder talk. He's just listening to all of his labelmates, speak on it. He's always quiet. DeJuan is loyal to his best friend Young D. Thus, to his labelmates too. He just doesn't talk much. Baby Girl notices the look on his face.

"Could've been a training opt, for real," she says.

DeJuan snaps his neck and looks at her. She doesn't make eye contact with him.

She just smiles shyly. DeJuan says nothing, still.

"You need to opt to train me, in that room, back there," Young D says.

He's pointing towards their bedroom. She continues to smile. Then she says, "Okay. Just don't put on a white t-shirt and we'll be good to go."

Young D had managed to forget about that t-shirt and Kierra's ass, for hours. He knows he's gonna have to discuss it soon. Maybe even, tonight.

"Are we going to the afterparty?" Angela asks.

"*We?*" Annie questions.

"Yes. I wanna go too," Angela says, "I'm gonna be with all of these famous labelmates."

"I'll go for awhile too, mama," Young D says, "She can go."

Angela comes over and hugs her brother. He spoils her too. Not quite as much as he does, his sons and his wife. But he does. Their half brother Corleone, spoils her as well. If he wasn't in Houston, right now, running the store. He'd be here. And Angela would be asking them both for money. Young D gives her a 100 dollar bill.

"And that's all you're getting until fourth of July," He declares.

Angela laughs a doubtful laugh. Father's day is still 2 weeks and a day away. No way will she have to stretch a hundred dollars for that long.

"Not when my brother and my sister-in-law are rich," Angela says with confidence.

Baby Girl and Young D look at her and smile.

Baby Girl adds, "Amen."

CHAPTER FOURTEEN
A FAMILY THING

"I love these new tracks, daddy," Baby Girl says.
She's in their suite with him, listening to the 2 new mixtapes the labelmates completed before flying to New York. The 2 of them had gone to the after party with his labelmates. But only for a short time. Young D wanted to get a feel for the crowd, before allowing his young sister and Baby Girl's young brother to attend the party, without them. The crowd was energetic but security was more than ample to keep them safe. Young D and Baby Girl didn't want to stay at the party. Angela and Bruce did. Young D felt it would be okay for them to stay. Besides, he wanted to have some private time with Baby Girl. Not only did he want to calm her nerves, over the t-shirt situation. But he also wanted the real details of the hit at, *The W*. She wanted to leave because she's still in play until 10pm, tomorrow night. Young D had gotten his mother settled in the suite, across the hall from theirs, before they left for the party.
Annie had told them both, "I'm keeping my grandbabies."
She wants her son and his wife to talk about their problems and make it right.

They're now laying on the couch, in the suite's living room, listening to his labels newest music tracks.
"So you're really feeling them?" he asks.
"Oh yes. They're tight. Y'all did the *damn* thing."
"So did you," he says.
She looks at him and smiles. Knowing what's coming next. "How did you do this one? Did you get hung up and had to do all three?" he asks, "Or was they all on the list?"
She tells him to settle down and get ready for bed. Then they can talk.

"I told you earlier, '*We could talk in bed*'. You thought I was kidding?" she asks.

She looks at him, with sensuous eyes. He's all in as he heads for the bedroom. She puts on a negligee' and joins him. His eyes dance as he smiles.

"Oh that's fly, baby," he says of her night wear. "Why don't you come here and get close to me."

She does as she's asked.

They start off with lighter conversation. She reminds him, they have to leave a copy of his summer tour dates with JB. He tells her, he'd given it to him before they left for the show. She smiles, kisses him on the nose and they both giggle as they snuggle up together.

"The lips don't get any?" he asks playfully.

She kisses him on the lips. He slips her the tongue and she accepts it. They kiss with fervor, for a long time. She can tell he wants to be closer to her. But she's got to make him sweat. Just a little bit longer. She pulls away from his kiss.

"I just want to know, one thing. Are you having an affair?" she asks.

"You kill people, baby," he says, "Do you think I wanna fuck with that?"

He doesn't lie, exactly. But he's not forthcoming with the truth, either. Basically, he tap dances.

"I love you, Lovely. There is *no* doubt in my *mind* that I chose the right woman to spend the rest of my life with. And raise a family with. I couldn't do any of this without you. Please tell me, you know this."

She tells him she believes he loves her and wants to be with her. But she also knows that he's reluctant with some truth too.

"Lots of men love their wives or significant other. But they still cheat," she says.

"I'm not cheating and I don't wanna do that," he tries. She wants to believe him. But she knows, her nose doesn't lie. She wants to make love to him. More than she wants to learn of some whore, he may or may not be fucking. So she changes the subject, before he can.

She says, "You know we're going to Philly, on the tour?"

"Yeah. That's cool, right?" he asks.

He booked it with her in mind and he can tell there's a big reason for her mentioning it.

He adds, "But you know something more. What's up?"

She tells him when she was doing the schedule and added Philadelphia. She had called her oldest brother, Six Nine. In hopes that he knew how to contact their other siblings. He had told her, he was close to getting a cell phone number for 1 of their brothers. The oldest 1, who's 2 years younger than he is.

"So he's eight years older than you?" Young D asks.

"Yes. And the other four are one year behind each other," she says.

They do the math. Her 5 brothers in Philadelphia, ages range from 29 to 33.

"Big Dog was busy, wasn't he?" Young D asks and they both laugh.

"Yes he was. He had to be. To get nine kids. Spread across the United States," she says, "In fifteen years."

"Are you sure it's only nine?" he asks.

"God, I hope so," she says, "That's all he told us about. I believe him. May he rest in peace."

He tells her, he hopes she's able to locate her siblings. He really thinks it'll be good for her. Surely, some of these siblings have wives and kids. She'll absolutely love to have lots of family to invite down to Houston and New Orleans, for visits. He's going to do everything in his power to help her locate them.

"Now," he says, "Tell me about the hit."

He glows. She looks at him and shakes her head.

"Daddy, you are way to infatuated with my profession," she says as she laughs.

"I can't get you to stop," he says, "So you have to tell me the scoop. Every time."

Then he asks, "Baby you pushed the dude out of the window?"

"Sort of," she says, "He was already off balance. I just gave him a swift kick in the chest and he went sailing."

"That's gangsta," he says with a chuckle.

"That's business," she corrects him.

He asks her to tell him how it all went down and she does. He gives her, his full attention as she gives him the sorted details.

"After I was done, I needed an escape," she says, "And you know I couldn't risk going back through the party. So I went out on the Penthouse terrace. That shit was scary. I just went for it and came in through the patio," she starts.

"That's why you went out there, after our bath?" he asks.

She says, "Yes. I was leaving it unlocked. So I could get in. Just in case I had to use the fire escape. Which I did. There are no camera's out there. But I feel like they'll put some out there. After the triple murder."

"I thought you went out there because you didn't feel like talking to me," he says.

"That was the other part," she says as she giggles.

"Baby, you're off the chain," he says, "So where's the loot? Wait. Let me guess. The dude who came and got the packages?"

"Yes," she says as she smiles, "I've already sent the outfit, tools and the loot to Houston."

"He's accessory, after the fact. He don't even know."

293

"Well. I gave him a huge tip," she says.

They laugh again. Then he puts his hand in her hair and pulls her face to his.

"I'm in love with a professional killer," he says as he kisses her.

"You're in love with a Morales heir," she corrects him, as he kisses her again. Then she says, "*T-Pain* is in love with a stripper. So it could be worse."

He becomes tensed. He doesn't know which way she's headed with that last statement. He waits for her to elaborate.

"I strip for you," she says with a chuckle.

"I'm in love with the Don's daughter," he says, "And she's the best killer-for-hire, in the world."

"Oh, daddy. Now that's what you call, *dangerously in love*," she says with a grin.

"It's time for us to lay down," he says with very suggestive eyes.

He escorts her down on the pillow. Then he strips her of her negligee' and moves in for the kill.

The rest of the labelmates and family party until the event ends. The cars bring them back to the hotel. Annie had moved the majority of the foods to their rooms. Knowing they'd be hungry when they came in. They was all grateful to her for looking out for them. Angela and Bruce grub with the labelmates until they have their fill. Then they go to their suites and go to sleep. Their flight leaves at 10:45am.

****

Father's day weekend brings forth another reason to celebrate at the Houston estate. Six Nine comes through and spends a lot of time with Jordan. He'd also brought Sandra and Roger III. Roger III and Jordan are closer now, as brothers. They text and talk on their cell phones everyday, since Jordan moved to Houston. This makes Baby Girl, very happy. She wants these siblings to stay in touch and connected. She still longs to meet her other brothers. Jordan is almost thirteen. For him to have closeness with his only blood brother, who is 16, is a wonderful thing. The 2 of them are inseparable at the event. Along with Brad Jr, Kid's son, who's twelve.

Noticeably absent at this event, is Kierra. Kid isn't at the event either. Unbeknownst to Baby Girl, Kid *is* in Houston. The word she'll get later, is that he was staying at a hotel. But the truth is, he's actually at Kierra's apartment. And most likely, they're scheming on something else to try to do to Young D.

Annie has finally stepped up to the plate, as far as Kierra is concerned. After the t-shirt situation, she knew something had to give. And if she wanted to help secure her only son's marriage, then she had to lay out the unwelcome mat, for the thorn in his side. She uninvited Kierra, last week. When they returned from New York. Kierra had called, like usual, as soon as they got back home. But Annie wasn't entertaining her bullshit anymore. She told her emphatically, that she wasn't going to allow her on her property, anymore. She told her that her son had no interest in her sexually. And she'd found out that, *that* was ultimately what she was calling for. It was never really about Danica. Annie revealed to Kierra that she still doesn't believe Danica is her grandchild, either. She even told her, she'd advised Young D to have another paternity test done. Kierra didn't like that idea, of course. But she didn't dare burn her only bridge. Which is Annie. She told Annie, she understood and she wouldn't show up on her property anymore, uninvited.

295

After Kierra hung up with Annie, her and Trina was discussing the call. Kierra remembered how much Kid was, for her being with Derrick. So she called him. She told him what Annie had said and that she wasn't allowed over there, anymore. Kid had told her, he wouldn't be going over there again either. He was more pissed off, than Kierra was about her not being able to have access to Young D's property. Trina had even made a comment about it as she listened on the speakerphone. Kid told Kierra that he would be in Houston, for father's day weekend, with Six Nine. But he wasn't going to go to Baby Girl's house.

"Not since she's being so stupid and allowing that nigga to fuck all over her," Kid had said.

****

The week following Father's day, is when the H-Town records tour stops in Philadelphia. While Six Nine was in Houston, staying at the Estate for Father's day, he had a much anticipated surprise for Baby Girl. He had a phone number for 1 of their siblings, in Philadelphia. Baby Girl had gotten the number of their youngest Philly sibling. His name is Sammy Wells. He's 29 years old.

Young D and H-Town Records are on the 1st half of their summer tour. Today, the tour bus is 20 minutes outside of Philadelphia. That's when Baby Girl decides to try and call Sammy's number. After only 1½ rings, a male answers.

"What up?" a male voice says, on the other end of the phone.

"Hello," Baby Girl says, "May I speak with Sammy Wells, please?"

"Who this?"

"This is Lovely Walker-Blake. I'm his sister, from New Orleans."

"What up, though!!!" Sammy says and she can hear that he's smiling. He goes on, "Hey, Lil sis! I've heard about *you*, for years! But I didn't think I would *ever* hear from you."

"Oh me *too*," she exclaims, "I've been hearing about all of you guys. For all of my life too, Sammy! I'm with my label. We're on tour-"

"Tour? What do you do? Do you sing....rap?" Sammy asks.

"My husband does," she says, "He's MC Young D? You heard of him?"

"Oh snap! Hell yeah!!! We all got tickets to his show!" Sammy says and he laughs loud.
He's very excited to hear that he has a family connection to MC Young D and the H-Town records crew.
"Y'all got a hotel or what?" he asks.

"We're on our way in, now," she says, "We're staying at the Marriott. Off Roosevelt Expressway. The show is at St. Joe's. But you know that, already."

"Oh yeah. Me and wifey got tickets. Roger, David and Frankie got tickets too."

"Oh *wow*! So there's a Roger in your family too? Named after daddy?" she asks, again smiling.
Sammy says yes and she will meet all the family, as soon as they can get to the hotel to meet her.

Within 20 minutes, the tour bus arrives at the Marriott. They pull in and are received by a crowd of people. Mostly Baby Girl's brothers, their mother, their significant others and their kids. Plus a few others who they told they was going to meet MC Young D and H-Town records. Even more fans had followed their tour bus in, from the highway. Young D and the labelmates unload the bus quickly and head into the lobby to get room keys and sign for perks and amenities. The fans follow them inside the lobby which becomes, instantly crowded and chaotic. The staff alert security while, at the same time, accommodating Young D and his family. The fans try to follow them up the elevators but security arrived and was able to contain the majority of them in the lobby. Young D and his labelmates get settled into their suites and bring all the family upstairs to get acquainted.

Baby Girl meets 4 of her brothers. Roger Wells is 39. He has a wife named Bianca and they have 3 sons: Roger Jr, who is 13, Ricky, who's 10 and Ryan is six. Frankie is the third oldest of her Wells' brothers. He's thirty one. He doesn't have any children. He's openly gay and has a life partner named Charles Moore, Sr. Charles has a 10 year old son. His name is Charles Jr and he lives with his mother, in Prospect Park. The 4th oldest is David, who is thirty. David has a live in girlfriend and her name is Renita. They have a 3 year old daughter named Kimberly and she's a showstopper. She loves to imitate, whatever is on television and radio. Sammy is the youngest, at 29. He and his wife Kenyetta have a 5 year old daughter named Ciara. All of the brothers have the last name; Wells. Their mothers name is Cassandra Wells.

"I have five brothers who live here, right?" Baby Girl asks.

"That's right," Sammy assures her. "Teddy is locked up. But yea. You've got five of us."
She finds out Teddy has served 5 years, on a 25 to life sentence, for murder. He has a daughter named Tunisia. She's here today. She's 8 years old.
Sammy says, "I live here during the off season-"

"You're with the Colts, ain't you, man?" DeJuan asks.

"Yea. I'm a cornerback for the Colts," Sammy says, "Me and Kenya live out in Lafayette Hill. Golf country."
Baby Girl is so overjoyed. She has a huge family now and another city to visit family in. This is a great day, in her life. One she has thought about, for years. She only wishes her parents, all 3 of them, was still alive for this.

"Wow! Well I'm twenty four," Baby Girl says, "This is my husband, Derrick. Better known as MC Young D. We have two sons. Derrick Jr is two years old and we all call him, Lil Man. Then we have a three month old named Donovan Prince. We call him, Don P."

"Like the rapper from the A-T-L, ha?" Frankie asks.

"More like my big daddy, Don Morales," she says as she smiles.

"He was the boss man, down there," Miss Cassandra Wells says, "That was Big Dog's boss."

"That's true," Baby Girl says, "He married my mother. Daddy was suppose to get her number for him from the start. But we *all* know the player type that he was. He kept the number for himself."

"Don Morales was rich!" Miss Wells says.

"Yes. He was *extremely* wealthy and powerful too," Baby Girl confirms. "I miss, all three of them."

"He could have married me," Miss Wells says as she giggles.

"He had a thing for my mother," Baby Girl says, "And once I was born. He was determined to be my father. So he courted my mother and kept Big Roger away from her. Until she fell for him."

"That wasn't hard to do," Young D adds, "If you knew the Don. He sat it out for misses Wanda Morales and for my

wife Lovely here, too. That was his only demand, from me. Give her what she's use too. Or leave my mansion, now."
They all laugh. Then Young D gives the whole run down of the family and label. Everyone is hitting it off and getting along great. Before long, Young D and Sammy have made a deal. There will be tickets for the family when the Colts come to Houston. And tickets for the Wells family when H-Town records come to Philadelphia.

"Family is good, ain't it?" Young D asks.
They all laugh again as they enjoy each others company.

Later, the Philly crew join them for the pre-show buffet dinner, in the banquet room. Baby Girl and her brothers catch up on years of each others lives, in a matter of hours. They blend together, so well. She wonders why it took so long for them to finally meet.

Cassandra pulls out the photo albums, she'd brought. Baby Girl is determined to see each photo and know what was going on in it, at the time. She sees lots of pictures of her father, Big Dog. Album after album, she goes through with Cassandra and her brothers. They do this, right up until Showtime.

The huge show is electric. Every single 1 of Young D and Baby Girl's guest, have a splendid time. They party for a little while in the hotel bar. But the tour bus has to get on the road. They have to travel to the next city. The next show is in Harrisburg. Tomorrow night. Sammy, Kenya, David and Renita have decided they haven't had enough of the H-Town records show. They're going to follow the tour bus, on into Harrisburg, for the next show.

"I'm not done meeting my baby and *only* sister, for the first time," David says as he smiles big.

Sammy agrees and so does, Baby Girl. She's happy they're going to come along, for the next show. Roger and Frankie would come too but each of them have to work, in less than 8 hours. Still, they grab a quick bite to eat with them. Then Frankie and Roger say goodbye and head home. The tour bus and it's followers, hit the road at around 3am.

They reach Harrisburg, by 5am. Baby Girl gets them all settled in the Courtyard by Marriott, Harrisburg Hershey hotel, on Eisenhower boulevard. Her new family gets rooms, adjacent to theirs. She gives the itinerary to the front desk and checks for messages. While the guys and guest head upstairs to get some much needed shut eye. Baby Girl is pleased to see that *Philadelphia Steaks and Hoagies,* over on fourth street and *Tj Homestyle restaurant* off of Bridge street in New Cumberland, are both providing the food spreads, all day tomorrow.
That should be good.

She heads upstairs to join Young D in their suite. He's waiting up for her.

"I thought you was tired?" she says.

"I am. But I can't sleep without you," he says smoothly.

"Uh huh. Well we need to keep it like that," she says with a smile.

"I plan too."

She slides into bed and right up under him. She's hardly thought about the t-shirt situation since leaving New York. 1 thing is for sure. He hasn't smelled like that stinking bitch, since. As a matter of fact, she hasn't smelled that funky ass perfume anywhere. Not in his clothes, the laundry nor at Annie's house. She knows that scent belongs to Kierra. But she wants to get something solid, before bringing it back to her husband. And she will. But this morning, she doesn't want to

301

discuss anything mute or negative. At this point, she just wants him to ravish her body. He looked so good on stage, earlier in Philly. Seeing him perform in front of a packed arena was 1 of their biggest dreams, since meeting. He longed to perform alongside of Kid and Baby Boy, Soldier, G-Dog and Geezy. And have Mark D do a track, just for him. Baby Girl and Young D both looked forward this. The day that Young D was the main attraction. The headliner. Together, they've gotten him to his shining moment. She watched the show from stage left and imagined what she would do to him, when they went to bed. At the same time, his female fans were trying to get on the stage and do it to him, then. She thought it was hilarious, watching her man, bob and weave, trying to keep from having his clothes ripped off. But now, he isn't wearing any clothes. And that's just the way she likes him.

She grabs his dick in her hand and begins to kiss him. He responds in kind by playing with her nipples, as she goes down on him. Taking him to the back of her throat, she moans. He trembles. Again, she takes him in. Then back out as she lets her tongue tantalize the tip of his dick. He can only tremble and moan as he lays back. Willing to be her captive. Something the groupies can only dream about.

"Oh, baby," he whispers.

She knows he loving it and she loves giving it to him. 3 minutes later, he makes his deposit and she receives it. Swallowing was something she had to grow into and she handles it like a pro, this morning.

"Let me taste this sweet pussy," he says after catching up to his breath. "Before I tear it out of the frame."

He goes down on her as she closes her eyes and for the next hour and a half, they reconfirm their love for 1 another. He fucks her like he has to perform excellent. Or she's going to leave him. He fucks like his life depends on it. Because to him, it does. The courtesy call for breakfast, comes just as they're both catching up to their breath, for the third time.

"I think we should grab something and bring it back to the room," he suggests.

They get up and dress comfortably. They go downstairs to the breakfast buffet and get biscuits, eggs, sausage and grits with gravy. She gets Apple Juice, Milk and Orange Slices, for both of them. They head back upstairs to their suite. They call and talk to their sons, while they eat and finally, fall asleep after 7am.

Three hours later, Baby Girl, Angela, Kenya and Renita go shopping together. They hit up *Macy's* at Harrisburg mall, first. Baby Girl shops for her entire family. Plus her new nieces and nephews, at a record pace. Then they have the driver take them out to *Colonial park* mall. They all do major damage, at this one. Renita had brought their daughter Kim, to Harrisburg too. But she'd let her stay at the hotel with her daddy David and the guys. She buys her lots of cute outfits, as trade off. Baby Girl looks at the little girl clothes and smiles at how cute they are. Seeing the little pinks and pastel outfits, she thinks about the night Young D said he wanted another baby.

"Derrick wants a girl," she says suddenly, "Girls clothes are always so cute. Let me stop looking at them. Before I become to vulnerable."

They all giggle. At that moment, she notices they've picked up a few followers, as they continue from store to store.

"Kim will have you *really* wanting to take her home, with you," Renita says, "She has already asks your husband if she can ride the bus with y'all."

They all laugh. Kenya calls Sammy, back at the hotel. To check in. The guys are having a ball, being entertained by Kim. She takes an instant liking to Young D. While Sammy is talking to Kenya, he tells her, Kim is following D, all around the suite.

"She's been on his heels since you guys left to go to the mall," Sammy tells Kenya, who can hear David talking to Kim.

"Daddy's baby girl? Do you like him?" David asks his daughter.

"Yes," she says as she giggles.

She reaches her arms upward, for Young D to pick her up. He does.

"I want a little girl," Young D says, "You wanna come to Houston and stay with me and your Auntie Lovely? You'll have two brother's, already."

"Yes," Kim says with the cutest smile.

All the guys laugh. It's cute to them, to see her crush on Young D. Instantly, his mind starts to wander. He has thought a lot about having a little girl with Baby Girl, lately. When he'd said it at his mother's house, a couple of weeks ago, it wasn't totally false. But he does want to have a little girl, with his wife. At the same time, he still agonizes over the little girl he's made with Kierra. Sure enough, that sickening feeling returns to his gut.

Meanwhile, Baby Girl and the ladies have completed their shopping. Renita tells them she needs to get a hair and nail touch up. The others say they can use the same. Kenya comes though with the ideal hook up. They start to leave the mall. Not noticing they still have followers. All except Baby Girl. She hasn't lost sight of the 3 guys since they initially started following them. Outside of *Gap Kids*. Angela, Renita and Kenya are following the driver, towards the car. Baby Girl intentionally walks way ahead of them. That way, she stays between the guys and their car. That's when Guy 1 approaches Angela and stops her, dead in her tracks.

"What's your name, baby?" Guy 1 asks.

He tries to put his palm on her chest and enforce that she stop and talk to him. But Baby Girl tells Angela to walk around him and come on. She does. Then guy 2, from the group of 3, steps to Baby Girl. The 3rd guy stops in his tracks in front of Kenya.

"Where you bitches going too?" the 3rd guys ask.

The driver suggests they move on. Guy 2 threatens him.

"Hey, old man. Don't catch a fuckin' sunroof. Out here in this muafucka, son," Guy 2 says as he walks toward their hotel chauffeur, like he intends to do him harm.

Baby Girl walks up behind guy 2. Keeping her hand in her shoulder bag. She doesn't have a gun in it. But she has her boa knife and she knows how to use it.

"Larry. Go on and open the car doors for us, please," Baby Girl says calmly.

That's when Guy 3 leaves Kenya and approaches her. Guy 2 turns toward her, as well.

This is exactly what Baby Girl wanted. All 3 of their attention. Come at her and allow the others to get to the car. And they're cocky ass attitudes have forced them to do, just that.

It's easy to kill 3 people with 1 knife, when they're situated close together. And no. She isn't subscribing to that OJ Simpson theory either. There is no way his old washed up, dumb arthritic ass could've pulled that shit off, in Los Angeles. Not alone. She could have, though. *Easily.*

"You tryin' to overlook my fuckin program, you sexy bitch?!" guy 3 asks, in a loud and very disrespectful tone.

Baby Girl can tell that he's trying to convince himself that he means it. However, she's not convinced. His gestures say, he wants to strike her. And she wishes a nigga would. Just give her the motherfuckin' reason to gut his ass. Real quick.

Larry gets the doors open and pops the trunk. Before the ladies can store their bags in it, guy 2 and 3 reach into the

305

trunk and grab 2 of Baby Girl's bags from the first mall. She reacts naturally. Taking her boa knife and quickly slicing the rope string. She grabs both bags as they release. Leaving guys 2 and 3 holding, only the rope string and a deer-in-headlights look on their faces. The other ladies and Larry, have that same look.

"That could've easily been your dicks," Baby Girl says with a gorgeous smile, while eyeballing half tough ass, guy 3.
As the ladies and their chauffeur take in the heroic efforts of Baby Girl. The 3 would-be strong arm guys, take a minute to regroup and figure out what they should do next. If anything. It takes less than 2 minutes and Baby Girl has all of their bags in the trunk. Plus 1 tool out of it, before she closes the trunk again.

Now she has her *Get To Work* bag, on her arm and her weapon hand inserted. In other words, she has her 9mm in hand and she's ready to conduct an orchestra. If the need arises. She knows these would-be robbers are paralyzed in confusion, at the moment. So she tells the others to get on in the car. All but Kenya, get in. The 3 guys are still looking dumbfounded as a crowd starts to gather. They're going to need to save face and Baby Girl figures this is where they will start to shout obscenities and female bash them. But Baby Girl has the jump on them. Guy 2 keeps his eyes trained on her. While guys 1 and 3 are pulling on the door handles and requesting Larry unlock them. Baby Girl insists that he don't. He takes her advice. They stay put. Leaving the 2 guys on the outside, looking in. Guy 2 still stares at her. This is when she goes on the offensive. Because she needs this scene to end now. It doesn't matter to her, if it's peaceful or not. At this point, she's going to do whatever it takes to make it home. In the same shape, she left home in.

"Is there something else you want?" Baby Girl asks the 3 guys. "And be careful. Because you just *might* get it."

"Is you some kind of ninja or some shit?" Guy 2 asks with a dumb looking grin on his face. "I need to be getting yo digits, baby."

He's actually checking her out as if he has plans of asking to see her later.

The other 2 guys rejoin him. Te 3 of them go from wanting to rob them. To wanting to hook up with them. In just a 5 minute swing. Baby Girl finds this hilarious.

These muthafuckin idiots was just trying to jack me. Now he wants to get my number? Get the fuck out of here, before I enact the self defense option that the criminal justice system will surely give me the benefit of. For marking y'all young black male asses.

Baby Girl doesn't even want to answer guy 1, 2 or 3. But Kenya, who feels a bit bolder now, takes the liberty.

"We are women, who are not in the mood to be messed with," she says, "Today or any other day. Not like this."

"Oh well. My bad, baby," Guy 3 says, as if that fixes the entire assault.

"It sure is *your* bad," Baby Girl says, "Now how do y'all want to end this? That's the only conversation I'm interested in, at this point."

I went from being bitch to baby, in five minutes. ☺

Seeing that she's standing in an offensive position, with her hand in her bag, the 3 guys start to slowly back away. She tells Kenya to get in the car, again. This time, she does. Baby Girl keeps her eyes trained on the 3 guys as they retreat to their vehicle. They're trotting away. Holding up their oversized jeans, which have to be *at least* 6 sizes to big, with their pinky fingers and wide legged. They're trotting toward a shiny old school, Chevrolet Caprice Classic. Baby Girl watches them as they hop in but they don't leave. Figuring they're loading weapons, Baby Girl gets into the front passenger seat. Just as she would if, Charles was driving.

Get a seat with a view.

She's watching the Caprice Classic, which is still sitting in the same parking space with the engine running. When Larry pulls out, the Caprice Classic pulls out and follows them.

They're on their way to get they're hair and nail touch ups. Baby Girl asks Larry to open the front sunroof. He does. She's watching the Caprice to see if they pull up, on either side. She's going through the sunroof and take them out, if they do. But they stay a healthy distance behind them and never pull up to either side.

They must really be trying to get with us now. After all of that dumb shit, at the mall. These boys aren't bright, at all. Is this the way guys come on to girls now? Damn! I'm glad I missed out on the courting phase. If this is the shit they expect us to deal with.

While Kenya, Renita and Angela discuss the incident and Larry joins in. Baby Girl watches the Caprice Classic. She doesn't even bother to alert Larry that they're being followed. She's itching for this scratch. There is 1 rule that is definitely universal. Never, *ever*, for any reason, fuck with a woman's shopping bags. If she hasn't asked you to carry them. Don't even offer too. Not only did the 3 attempted jackers, not take heed to the rule. But they was trying to take the bags. After they was already paid for and in the car.

That's just cause, to kill a motherfucker!

They finally arrive at the salon, which is a little drive to the outside of Harrisburg. The Caprice Classic follows them there. They get out and go in. What do you know? The 3 unwanted guest, get out of their car and follow them inside the salon.

"Good afternoon, ladies," a nail techs yells, "And gentlemen. Come on in. How may we help you?"

In the meantime, Baby Girl's unwanted guest are telling the stylist and nail techs, to give these 4 ladies anything they want and it's on them. Baby Girl tells them, thanks but no thanks. They aren't interested in anything they're offering. Including their money. The 3 guys each get pedicures while the ladies are getting hair, nails and pedicures. Still, the guys try to get the ladies to be interested in them. Still, the ladies tell them, they aren't interested. These 3 guys are very persistent. Still.

CHAPTER FIFTEEN
STALKED UPON A JOB

The ladies finish up their do's and nails. Then they head back to the hotel. The Caprice Classic is still on their tail. At this point, Baby Girl could care less if they know where they're staying. Because she now knows that they're only a danger to themselves. As soon as they pull into the parking lot and while Larry gets the concierge to help with the packages, Baby Girl approaches the Caprice Classic. The driver, guy 1, lets down his power window. He smiles at her as she leans in. She's the 1st to speak.

She says, "Okay. Since you guys have followed us around, all day. We need to get some names. Driver, who are you?"

"My name is Roderick," Guy 1 says, "What's yours?"

"Later for that," she answers. She asks guy 2, "What's your name?"

"My name is Ricky," he says.

Then she looks at guy 3 and asks, "And you are?"

"Mike, is my name."

"My name is Lovely," she says, "And no it's not some code name or street name. That is my government name. But those who love me, call me Baby Girl. Now what is it that you want, that has you following us, all over town?"

"I want your phone number," Ricky says.

"Well, you're still not going to get that," she says, "Now. What is it gonna take for y'all to stop following us?"

"I wanted to ask that girl out. Over there. When I first approached her," Roderick says, "That's before Mike started with the gangster shit."

Baby Girl calls Angela, over to the car. She comes over, while Kenya and Renita go inside to tell their men what had happened with the 3 guys. Angela stands next to Baby Girl, as she introduce the 3 guys, by name.

"This is Mike, Ricky and Roderick," she says, "Guys, this is Angela. She's my sister-in-law. Angela, Roderick wanted to ask you out. Are you interested?"

"I don't think so," Angela says as she laughs, "You just tried to jack me, nigga."

"These two started with that shit," Roderick says, "I was about to ask you for your number. Before they started wilding out."

"It's true, that Mike and Ricky started with the ignorance, first," Baby Girl says, "But you went along with it."

"Cause that's my boys. That's all," Roderick says, "We wasn't gonna to do anything to y'all."

"I know that. Because y'all are too damn slow," Baby Girl says as she laughs, "But Ricky and Mike. Y'all were the ones who grabbed my bags, out of the trunk. So Roderick might be on to something. I got something for you, Roderick."

"What's that," Roderick asks.

"A ticket to the H-Town records show, tonight," she says.

Ricky and Mike start to protest. They're telling her how bad all of them wanted to go to the show.

"These two had money to go but I didn't," Ricky says, "I don't do the trap thing. I work a real job and I didn't have enough left to get a ticket. After I helped out at home."

"And since we're boys," Mike says, "We can't go without our dude. You know?"

"Why didn't y'all just buy him a ticket?" Angela asks Roderick.

"Because he's a man and he didn't want us too," Roderick answers, as Ricky shakes his head.

311

"I don't agree with drug money," Ricky says, "My mama would never allow that kind of money, in her home. That's why you got kicked out, Rod."

Roderick and Ricky are brothers and fraternal twins. Mike is their 1st cousin. Together, they're a rap group, who are seeking to sign a deal. The reason they had gone to the mall, in the first place, was to pick up some blank CD's. Then they was going to burn their material on a few hundred of them. At the show tonight, they was planning to attend it and give them out. But since Ricky couldn't get a ticket, they're new goal was to hang around outside and pass out Demo's. They was just hoping to get 1 in the hands of anyone, connected with H-Town records. Not even realizing that they was about to die, at the hands of the wife of the leader of that pack.

"How are y'all going to call yourselves a rap group?" Baby Girl asks, "And you're not going to check out H-Town records, when they're in your town?"

Then the 3 guys confess their love and respect. Plus pour their hearts out for the guys on H-Town records label. They tell Baby Girl and Angela, how much they've dreamed of signing with them. It's easy for Baby Girl and Angela to see that they're being truthful.

"So you know we want to go to the show," Roderick says, "Young D is my favorite rapper."

"And Young Aristocrat is mine and my idol," Ricky adds, "He's a soldier. Like *Tupac* was."

Angela and Baby Girl smile cunningly, at each other. Just then, Renita and Kenya appear at the Courtyard front door. They come out, walking toward the Caprice. Behind them are Sammy, David, Kim and the entire H-Town records crew. Baby Girl and Angela catch a glance of them, right before the 3 guys do. They smile as they see how large the 3 guys eyes are.

312

"Damn! There go Young D, right there!" Roderick says.

"I call him, daddy," Baby Girl says as she smiles.

"And I call him, brother," Angela says as she giggles.

"Ah, man!" Roderick says as all 3 of the guys faces start to show disappointment.

Not with seeing the H-Town artist. But with the way they're actually coming to meet them. By first, trying to bully their family into giving them some attention.

"That equals no game, right?" Baby Girl asks Ricky, as she smiles and says, "But since you're such a positive person. I'm going to let y'all make it. And introduce y'all to my family. Do y'all have a demo?"

"Hell yes!" Ricky answers with major excitement.

By now, Young D has made it to his wife's side. He isn't in a good mood, at first.

"What the fuck is going on?" he asks Baby Girl, while mean mugging the 3 guys, who are still in the car.

"Get the fuck out the car, nigga," Big Daddy orders as he pulls open the passenger door.

Baby Girl calms them down, quickly. Saying, "They aren't any harm, family. They're actually huge fans. They was just being what our young black males *today*, seem to think makes them hard. But they're ultimately, trying to get a date."

"Well you're not available," Young D says quickly, while mean mugging them, even harder.

"Oh they know that now," she says, as she smiles at him and gives him a kiss.

"We want to come to the show, man," Ricky says, "We didn't mean no harm. We just saw four beautiful women and was just trying to get our swag on."

"And y'all didn't see this huge rock on her finger?" Young D asks, still not willing to back down.

313

"*She* got a huge one too," Sammy adds, as he holds up Kenya's left hand, for them to see her wedding rings.

"That was our bad, man" Roderick says, "We just played it wrong. They're beautiful. And I really wanted to holler at Angela, from jump."

"He did. He wasn't wilding, in the beginning," Baby Girl says, "Ricky and Mike are the ones who grabbed for my bags." She giggles as she points to them.

"Yeah. But you cut the strings, so quickly," Mike says, "I thought I was cut. That shit was so smooth."

"You really don't know how lucky you are, that my wife knows what is and what's not, a real threat. Do you?" Young D asks him.

"We thought she was a ninja type or something," Mike says.

"I asked her if she was," Ricky adds.

"I'm more dangerous than a ninja," Baby Girl says with a smile. "I'm a female, who had just bought a lot of clothes and wasn't willing to part with them."
They all laugh. As finally Young D and Sammy invite the guys to get out and formally meet all of them. Roderick gets out and so does Mike. Big Daddy had already pulled Ricky out. They all head inside and back to their suites. Three guys heavier.

"You play for the Colts, don't you?" Ricky asks Sammy, as they get on the elevator.

"Yes. I do," Sammy says.

"Cornerback," Ricky says, "You're bad as hell, man. Damn. Is *all* of your family famous?" he asks Baby Girl.

"All of them. Except me," she says, as they get off the elevators and head to their suites.

They go inside Young D's suite. The ladies have to show off what they had gotten from the mall. They have fresh outfits for the show tonight. They had gotten their hair and nails done, at a salon in Penbrook. Just outside of Harrisburg. The salon belongs to Kenya's college roommate, Tasha. Tasha Bolds and her employees had hooked up their hair and nails. Plus they're coming by the hotel later, to do their makeup.

"I told them I was going to get them backstage. If they come through, for us," Baby Girl says, "And they came through. They came through."

She struts around as if she's modeling on a runway. The other women mimic her. They cackle as they strut their stuff, around the suite.

"They do look good," David remarks.

Young D and Sammy agree, with a smile. They receive a quick kiss from their significant others.

"Just tell her, not to overdo the makeup. Okay?" Young D asks.

Baby Girl says okay. She's not much for makeup, anyway. She likes to highlight her skin. Not cover it up.

Next, Young D gets the entire story of what happened, from the mall up until now.

Then he says, "Y'all lucky y'all didn't get shot. She comes from a city where it's legal to shoot a person, who's trying to jack you."

"I thought she was going too," Roderick says, "She kept her hand in her bag, the whole time."

"Until she cut those bags out of our hand," Ricky adds.

"I would've cut *y'all*," Big Daddy says as they all laugh.

"I still might," Young D says with a chuckle, before he asks, "So y'all a rap trio?"

"Yes indeed, man," Roderick says, "I want you to hear some of our stuff. We can play it for you, in the car. If you got time."

"Nah, man. Let's go on the tour bus," Young D says.

"Yea. If y'all sound like something. We can hook up a little collab," Young Aristocrat offers as Big Daddy cosigns.

"And set this shit off, right," High Top adds.

"I can work with that," Arafat agrees.

"That would be the bomb shit!" Mike says.

At this point. All the men head out to the tour bus. While the ladies relax.

Baby Girl rings the concierge to check messages. And to let him know what time to have the sponsors set up the pre and after show meals. The show starts at 11pm. It's 4pm now and everything is set, so far. She has her and Young D's gear laid out. She gets a glass of blush wine and relaxes for awhile too.

An hour later, out on the tour bus, the men have developed a good rapport. Ricky, Roderick and Mike have apologized, so many times, that the H-Town records guys have started to make jokes about it. That's the best compliment the 3 guys could have hoped for. During their 4 hour session, they manage to, not only hear some good tracks from these Harrisburg natives. But they also record 2 songs, together. Young D and DeJuan guarantee them a spot at the show.

"We're gonna let y'all go in, with us," Young D says, "Maybe even open up, for us."

The Harrisburg trio choose their group name, right there on the tour bus. They're going to call themselves; *The 717 Boys*. This is the area code of Harrisburg.

The chances of them signing a deal with H-Town records, is looking better by show time. They stay and have dinner with the H-Town label. And even have their family members to bring over clothes for them, to wear to the show.

Young D has decided, he'll let them do a song, as an opening act for tonight's show. They don't know it yet. But

316

when he comes out, he's going to see if the Harrisburg fans think he should sign them. If they erupt in cheers. Young D's going give the trio an opportunity to get a deal with his label.

By 10pm, they're all at the *Pennsylvania Convention Center*, getting loaded and preparing for the show. The 717 Boys are going to perform their hit single, which is already getting a little radio and a lot of club, play.

They do the opening act and the crowd receives them, well. Then H-Town records tears it down. When Young D propositions the crowd, on The 717 Boys behalf. The convention center rocks with approval chants and screams.

"Alright!" Young D says, *"I'm gonna take y'all word, on them! We're gonna give them a shot! Y'all cool with that?!"*
They nearly tear up the place. And just like that, the H-Town family is 3 guys larger. The 717 Boys are going to travel on the bus with them. The H-Town family get a quick introduction to the Flowers family. That is The 717 Boys, last name. They come from a big family. Their mothers pack bags for them and Ricky's mother takes the responsibility of letting his job know that he'll be on the road and may not be returning. But he will call them on Monday night. Baby Girl can't help but notice that Ricky and Roderick's mother seems a little uncomfortable with them leaving. Baby Girl just thinks it's a natural mothers reaction, to seeing her sons off. But she'll learn later that it's much more than that. Still, the 717 Boys are going to Houston, when this leg of the tour ends.

Tonight was another great show for H-Town Records. After the concert, everyone says their goodbyes to the Flowers family. Baby Girl's family follows them again. Sammy, David and their family are going to catch 1 more show. Before they head back to Philadelphia. The tour bus, 3 guys heavier, heads on to Trenton, NJ.

CHAPTER SIXTEEN
OLD *MARK'S*………..

The week of the 4th of July holiday, begins with everyone back in Houston. The 3 week tour is done. With more shows scheduled, for later. The 717 Boys are still with them and they're still loving the life. Roderick and Angela have talked a lot, by now. They've become closer. Young D and Baby Girl keep a watchful eye on them. Angela has confessed to Baby Girl that she likes Roderick, a lot. So Baby Girl encourages her to get to know him. At the same time, she tries to get Young D to give Angela room to find her independence.

This week, H-Town records have shows lined up from Lafayette to El Paso. Today starts off, like any other typical Monday. Young D is slow to rise and so are his labelmates. They still have to pack the tour bus for an afternoon show, in Lafayette. Then, they have to come back to Galveston for a show, later tonight. Baby Girl isn't going to make this trip. She's staying behind for a meeting with Gus Davis, on his request. He's coming to town, this evening. She really wants this face to face meeting. Just so she can get a real feel of how his attitude is, these days. The Lafayette hit or him calling her while she was in play. Left a worst taste in her mouth, then him trying to give Kid her packages. It's a bitter taste that she's determined to sweeten. As soon as possible. But as always, she's going to be smart about it. And further, she has no idea that her *not* making the short tour, has already been broadcast.

She has just returned from *Subway* with the 6 party platters, for the tour bus. Angela and Annie assists her in getting the bus stocked for the guys. Annie has made 3 cakes, 5 dozen cookies and 6 dozen brownies, for their desserts. After stocking the food on the bus, Baby Girl goes to her bedroom to help Young D get his gear together for the short trip. She packs his suitcase, zips it and tells him it's ready to load.

"We'll be back before sunlight, baby," Young D tells her, "We got Lafayette, at three. Galveston, at nine. Then I get *Lovely* before the sun comes up."

He smiles as he holds her from behind and kisses her on the back of her neck. She lets him. Their relationship has been strained, a bit lately, with the whole t-shirt situation, *still* not being resolved. But their love life hasn't suffered, in the least. They're 2 hot people who love sex with 1 another. Something's are not to be forfeited. No matter how perturbed, 1 may be.

After putting his suitcase on the bus and getting his labelmates in motion, Young D comes back to find Baby Girl.

"We need to talk, baby," he says as he grabs her hand and leads her to their master suite.

He has just put his suitcase on the bus. It contains his show gear and a change of clothes for after each show.

"We need to take a vacation, *alone*," he says after they take a seat on their huge bed.

"Our Anniversary is coming up, in fifteen days," she says with a smile, "do you know how long we've been mar-"

"Six, *sweet* ass, years," he answers, before she can finish her sentence.

Then he tells her, he's got something already set up for their anniversary. And he promise her. This is going to be the best anniversary, yet.

"I've been wondering, if we could work on a little girl for our six year anniversary?" he asks with a smile.

"Don P isn't even four months, yet," she says with a shy grin. "Lil Man had a chance to be the baby, for almost two years."

"I know, he did. But it'll take nine months for the new

319

baby to get here. He'll be a year old, at least. Depending on how long it takes for us too. You know. Fertilize the egg."

She giggles but says nothing. She knows he's going to want an answer. And she's not ready to give him one. Not yet. Not until they iron out that other situation, first. Still, he looks at her with longing eyes. He loves his wife. He really does. And he has to find a way to get that monkey, known as Kierra, off of his back. Before she costs him everything in his life, that has made it worth living.

"We can talk about it, some more later, daddy. You know we can," she says, "But I have to have closure on that affair topic. Before we can think of bringing another child into this world. We have to come to a head. You know. An understanding about that funky ass t-shirt."

He says, "I agree and we will. Just as soon as I get back for this trip. It's been bugging me, that it's *bugging* you. So we're gonna get it out in the open and done with. Okay?"

She smiles, "You're really serious about this new baby, ha?"

"As serious as a mark, in play," he says as they laugh. They take a half an hour to themselves, in the room, for Young D's pre-show. He tries to never do a show, without making love to his wife, first. It's become a ritual, of sorts. In their relationship and it's 1 that they both love to the fullest.

The tour bus pulls out at noon. On time, as usual. Lovely gets back to her household chores. She's getting things cleaned and set for their 4th of July celebration event. This holiday, she'll have her brothers here. From New Orleans, Atlanta and Philadelphia. All of her brothers will be here. Except for Teddy, who's serving a life sentence in the mountainous part of the country. But his daughter Tunisia is coming to meet her new aunt. Her mother hadn't been able to get her to the Pennsylvania shows. Kenya had told Baby Girl, there was some baby mama drama, going on with Tunisia's mother. So Baby Girl had taken the initiative to call her and personally, invite them both. Tunisia is coming. Only Tunisia. Her mother isn't ready to relive those years with Teddy. Not just yet.

Six Nine and the brothers from Philly have only talked on the phone, so far. But in less than 2 days, they will meet face to face. On the fourth of July, right here at Lovely's home. She has butterflies in her stomach, already. She had grown up, an only child. And had longed to have siblings in the Don's house. She had all the brothers from the third ward. But not until after she'd turned 11 years old. Later, Don and Wanda adopted Jordan. But the size of the family she has now. Is more like what she had always dreamed of and longed for. She's already singing as she works around the house. Her mood is very jubilant, today. And no one is even due to arrive until early tomorrow. The New Orleans crew are coming in, by 9am. Then, Six Nine and Kid are going to the airport to rent vehicles. They're going to meet and then bring back, all the family members who are flying in from Philadelphia. All of their brothers, the brothers significant others, their kids and their mother, Cassandra Wells will be here. But Baby Girl has to get through her meeting with Gus Davis, before any of that will take place.

Gus arrives at 5:30pm, sharp. Him and Baby Girl go to her office and get down to business.
"What's so urgent and who is it from?" she asks.
She figures there must be a professional hit on her life. To warrant a sit down meeting with Gus Davis, at his request.
"Genolli's, is what's so important," Gus says.
He tells her of a new hit on her, from the Genolli family. He

321

also says the hit at the supermarket wasn't from Genolli. It was from Pantango. The mark had worn misleading family signature gear, intentionally. He was trying to provoke war.

"He isn't the pro, for the Genolli family. Mark is," Gus says.

"He wasn't a pro, anyway," she says, "He was a recluse. It was obvious he was a loner. And Mark's losing streak, isn't going to improve, anytime soon. If he's coming at me. He's gonna have to shit or get off the pot."

"Miss Lovely. I don't want you to get *too* damn cocky. Be careful," he warns.

"First of all. The name is *misses* Lovely and *only* to my husband. I'm not damn cocky. I'm damn *good*," she says, "I'm just stating a fact. Mark has never beat me at anything. And this one *here*, I can't afford to lose."

Then she asks, "What side are you on, Gus?"

"Yours, of course. I'm looking out for you. Like I'm paid to do," he tries.

"I'd like to see it show. *Just* a little," she says.

He leaves well enough alone. For now. He gives her the particulars on Mark Genolli. And Mark becomes a mark, tonight. Baby Girl has to take him out. Before he can get her.

With pro's, the process is different than it is with a regular mark. The pro's meet each other, first. The meeting is set up through the family's agents. Usually they meet over dinner or at a bar for drinks. One tries to convince the other to concede. The meeting's always in a public area. And as history has shown with the face-offs. The 1 who initiates the meeting is not the aggressor. No mark can be done at the meeting. If a pro ends up dead, at the meeting. That pro's family is denounced and every member of the family is automatically marked. No families go against the code. There's too much to lose.

"You will not be calling him for any meeting, Gus," she orders, "Don't even get your palm pilot out, for that one. Let him call me if he wants a date. I *clean* marks. I don't date them."

"Okay, Lovely.--"

"Call me, Baby Girl," she says, "My fathers are dead. Only Derrick can call me by my government name."

"Okay, Baby Girl. You have his information. Do what you do. Just be careful."

She's agitated with Gus. His behavior in the past months has been suspect. She isn't going to jump to any conclusions in sight of him. But she's a smart young lady. She knows the business, too well. Something isn't right about her agent. She's going to assess the business in the very near future. Gus could be up for *replacement*. Which means termination. *Literally*. There's no retirement plan for an agent. It's a lifetime gig. Permanent. Until you expire or get terminated. The only way to leave is death. Natural causes or otherwise. But an agent doesn't simply leave. *Ever*. In any way, other than not breathing. Gus is on a very thin line. Baby Girl can hear Don Morales' voice in her head. She reflects on the things Cherry and Addie Mae said. Gus is suspect. That's not allowed.

She bids Gus farewell, just before 7pm. Annie calls and tells her that her, Angela and the boys want to ride to Galveston for the show, tonight. Baby Girl says it's a bet and they can leave in an hour.

"It'll be a surprise," Annie says.

"Yeah but for who?" Baby Girl asks.

Annie laughs and brushes it off. She has prepped everything, in preparation for the 4th event. She'll do more, tomorrow. But for tonight, she wants to get out of the house, just for a bit.

Baby Girl had gone through the satchel which belonged

323

to Tito Lopez, before the summer tour started. In it there was 2 kilograms of powder cocaine. Young D and his labelmates took charge of that. They sold the powder in bulk and split the profits, amongst the label. The cash belong to Baby Girl, though. It was $250,000. She'd made another $250k, for the hit. In 1 night, she'd pulled down a half million dollars. She had taken the cash to the safe, at her office, in Morale's manor. It would be safe there, for sure. No one ever goes into Don's office. *Her office.* They always keep valuables and large amounts of cash, in 1 of the many safes at the manor. She can count the times she'd been in the office, before it had become hers. She'd been in it 4 times, in her life, to be exact.

The 1st time, she was almost five. The Don was teaching her, her weapons. She had a purchase book with photo's and she had to be able to tell him each weapon, it's capabilities and it's place in weapons history. He had given her 1 week to learn them. Then she had to come into the office, sit down at his desk and recite the entire book. The 2nd time was when she was introducing Derrick or Young D to her parents and asking for their blessings in allowing them to date. The 3rd time she had shown up at her high school, high off weed and smelling of alcohol. She was on the verge of expulsion. But the Principal called Donnie Morales as soon as he found out she was in trouble. Don had picked her up and took her straight to the manor and his office. He kept her in there, until she had sobered up. He never told Wanda, a word about it. But Baby Girl had extra chores to do, for a month. The 4th and last time, was when Don had been diagnosed with Kidney failure and he knew he was going to expire. After he found out about his illness and resolved that he wouldn't inform anyone. He had taken her into his office to go over the business. At that time, he informed her that she would be the new Boss. If anything were to ever happen to him. She was barely out of adolescence. Now, she's 24 years old and the boss. The Don had made it clear to her when he'd said, *"This office is for Daddy's work. Don't ever come in here, unless I invite you or it becomes yours."* She never questioned, disrespected, disobeyed or forgot that order.

Baby Girl, Annie, Angela and the boys left for Galveston in less than 1 hour after she dismissed Gus. They arrive, park and quickly rush to the backstage door. Several of H-Town's security, escort them in. Before they can even get to Young D's dressing room, she spots Kierra. A security guy tells her that Young D had a meeting with her. Like that was okay. Or as if he, the security guy, thought Kierra was some business person. Baby Girl is in work mode, just 5 minutes after she arrives at her husband's show.
What the fuck is she doing, down here?

She approaches the area where Kierra is standing. Or more like, leaning against the wall. She can smells that cheap ass, knock off perfume scent from that white t-shirt, clear across the hall. She looses it, automatically.
"What the fuck do you want?" she yells to Kierra.
"I'm here for the show."
"Why are you back *here*?" Baby Girl asks.
Kierra tells her, she has a backstage pass.
"I don't give a fuck. A backstage pass, doesn't give you permission to come to the dressing rooms. Did you know that? Who brought you back here?"
"Security," Kierra answers.
She looks intimidated, as she answers Baby Girl. But Baby Girl doesn't give a damn if she is or not. She demands to know

325

which security brought her backstage. And what was his reason for bringing her?

"On who's authority?" Baby Girl asks.

Kierra doesn't have an answer for that question. Baby Girl hasn't stop moving since the time she hit the back hallway and spotted Kierra. Quickly, she finds the culprit.

Coincidentally, it's the same security who'd just told her about the so called meeting Kierra had with Young D. As the security guy is giving her, his excuse for allowing Kierra to come back. Young D and DeJuan are coming from the tour bus with their preshow weed and drink. Young D sees Baby Girl before she sees him. He freezes, momentarily. Then DeJuan tells him to let him handle it. They approach Baby Girl, Kierra and the others. Young D grabs his sons. Lil Man is happy to see his daddy. Don P grins from ear to ear. But Baby Girl is obsessed with finding out, 1 thing. And 1 thing only.

"Just exactly who is this bitch, here to visit?" she asks as she points to Kierra.

By now, the rest of the labelmates and The 717 Boys are coming in from the bus. Everyone is stunned to see Baby Girl talking to Kierra. They don't know what's been said. Nor do they want to be asked any questions about her. The 717 Boys are just learning about the situation with Kierra. They know not to breathe a word of it, already. They lag behind the other guys. Then quickly, they duck into their dressing rooms, leaving DeJuan and Young D in the hall, to explain Kierra's presence. DeJuan walks directly up to Kierra.

"Oh, so you made it in, ha?" he asks.

She plays it off too. But Baby Girl isn't believing it. Security has already admitted Kierra met with Young D. Young D approaches Baby Girl gives her a kiss. He can tell she's pissed. He asks her to come on and bring the boys and his family, into his dressing room. She reluctantly follows him but her eyes never leave Kierra. Kierra is noticeably nervous. DeJuan tells her to come with him, down the hall and she does.

Inside Young D's dressing room, Baby Girl is telling him, she doesn't believe DeJuan is seeing Kierra.

"I know he's not and that's all I'm gonna say," she says, "That bitch smells just like that funky ass t-shirt."

Young D asks her to refrain from using bad language in front of their sons. Then Annie takes the boys, Angela, Bruce and Jordan. They go out to the tour bus. She's hoping Young D and Baby Girl will talk things over. She passes Kierra and DeJuan by the back door. She gives them a look of displeasure and discomfort too. Neither of them speak a word to each other. They're just standing there. DeJuan is actually trying to convince Kierra to leave.

Meanwhile in Young D's dressing room, Baby Girl is furious. Young D continues to try and calm her down. Suddenly, she storms out of the dressing room and down the hall. She's heading straight for Kierra.

"You're here for my husband. Ain't you bitch? Admit it!" she yells.

"Well. Alright. Yes. I am," Kierra admits.

Baby Girl lights into her. She beats her about the head and face. Quickly and brutally. Kierra fights back but Baby Girl is too much for her. She's wiping the back hallway with Kierra. This makes Kierra's friends Trina and Venetta, who had come with her, think of tag teaming Baby Girl. They're about to join in when Baby Girl pulls back and draws her 9mm. They don't advance any further. Instead, they grab Kierra and retreat, hastily. Young D, who'd run out after her, reasons with Baby Girl to put the gun away. She doesn't until Kierra and her 2 friends are out of sight. Young D, with help from DeJuan, manages to get her to put the weapon away. Eventually she does and they go back into his dressing room. He has a show to do. She lays out his gear while he pitches his denials to her. She doesn't believe him. She tells him so, emphatically.

"I don't believe your lying ass!" she screams, "You must want me to kill that whore!"

"I wouldn't even give a damn," Young D says with conviction.

She looks at him, shakes her head and storms out the door. She's heading to the tour bus. She doesn't even want to be around him, at the moment. Plus, she's still looking for Kierra and her posse. She wants to finish that bitch, once and for all. She hasn't even thought about Mark Genolli, since leaving Houston.

Once outside, she notices there's no sign of Kierra or her friends, anywhere around the venue. Baby Girl should know because she covered the entire area, within 20 minutes. She'll find out later, security made them leave the premises. She'll also find out that the same guy in security, who had allowed Kierra and her friends backstage. Had already fucked her too. That's why he gave her access. Because she gave him the pussy and the ass, prior to her admittance. But she's long gone now.

"Good," Baby Girl says, "She's lucky she got the chance to walk out. She could've been carried out."

"Calm down, baby," Young D says, "Don't say something you might regret, later."

Young D had eased out to the tour bus to make up, immediately. No way is he going to allow his wife to be upset with him, over a baby mama by default, turned fatal attraction.

"I regret even coming down for this show, Derrick,"

Baby Girl says, "I knew I was gonna be the one surprised."

It must the be the ice or the money that I make. They talk behind my back but they won't say it to my face. Bitch! Say it to my face, say it to my face. They talk behind my back but they won't say it too my face.

Baby Girl cell phone rings! That's her default ring tone. Not someone who has an assigned ring tone. It's just the break she needs. The excuse to walk away from Young D, at the moment. She looks at her caller ID and recognizes the number. It's Mark Genolli!
What the fuck does he want? Oh, he's trying to mark me? Is it him? I'm going to enjoy this.

She's going to milk this phone call from a strange number, for every drop it's worth. And make Young D feel insecure, for a change. She knows Mark is calling to ask her for the initial meeting. She answers with a flirtatious ring in her voice.
"*Hello*," she says, intentionally trying to sound seductive.
Young D is instantly irritated as he listens to his wife's end of the conversation.
"Hi, Mark" she smiles and bats her eyes.
"How are you, dear?" Mark asks and Baby Girl moves another foot away from her husband.
"Oh, okay. I knew you'd be calling." she says and giggles. "Dinner?" she asks, as she covers 1 ear, as if to be drowning out background noise. Then she asks, "Where?"
Young D steps to her. He stands directly in front of her. She continues smiling.
Young D asks, "Who are you talking too?"

329

"It's about work, Derrick," she tells him, intentionally sounding impatient.

"Derrick? Oh, I'm not daddy, now?" Young D asks, rather perturbed.

She puts up a, *"please hush so I can hear"* hand, which only infuriates Young D more. But he isn't about to leave the bus. Not until he knows who is on the other end of her phone.

"Okay, look here. This is not a good time," Baby Girl says to Mark.

Mark is definitely flirting with her. He always has. She's only playing with him now, to make her husband jealous. And it's working.

"Tomorrow morning, sounds great. Send me the details," she says with a smile.

Young D grabs her phone.

"Who the fuck is this?!!" he yells but Mark Genolli has already hung up.

Young D is indignant. They both are. Baby Girl likes seeing him worry about her, for a change. She'll calm him down, later. But for now, he can be mad as hell. She most certainly is.

Young D goes inside the venue and they do the show. Baby Girl and the family watch and enjoy. Even though, Young D got no *"preshow"* sex, his set is still spectacular. The Galveston crowd are very rowdy. Five fights break out, during the show and by the time the show finally ends, it's midnight. Young D puts Bruce, Angela, Jordan and his mother on the tour bus. He drives the 2007 Chevy Tahoe, back to Houston. Carrying his wife and their sons. She may be angry. But he's going to talk to her and she's going to listen. Whether she wants to or not.

CHAPTER SEVENTEEN
..............*AND NEW SHOES*

First, Young D tells Baby Girl to look in the bags, he'd stuffed on the 2nd seat with their sons. He had filled the back seat and the hatch, also.

"Look in the bags," he tells her.

"Why?" she asks.

"Because I asked you too," he says, "It's something for you."

She grabs the 1st bag and looks in it. She has to smile. In the bag, there are 3 shoe boxes. She searches the other 2 bags. Young D had bought her the entire collection of pastry shoes. The ones she didn't have and another pair of the ones, she did have.

"That way, you keep a fresh pair," he says.

"Thank you, daddy," she says, "This is very sweet. You know how much l love these sneakers."

"I would do anything for you, Lovely," he says solemnly.

"Will you stop seeing that tramp?" she asks.

"Okay. Yes. If that's what you believe. Then yes," he says, "But it ain't like that, baby."

"How about we just don't discuss her. Until after my family leaves, on the weekend," she suggests, "I don't want to ruin my family reunion. And needless to say, she ain't invited."

"Works for me. I don't wanna discuss her ass, after they leave either."

She rolls her eyes at him. Then she says, "Yes. I am mad at you, daddy. But the shoes. The shoes are a nice touch."

"I'm always thinking about you, Lovely. And my sons. Always."

Lil Man takes over the conversation, for the next 5 to 10 minutes. He pulls a bag from the 3rd seat and starts inspecting it. He can see that there's clothes in it, for him. They have his name on them. They're from the Derrick Blake, little boys collection. Baby Girl is pleasantly surprised. She immediately straps Lil Man back into his car seat and instructs him not to unlock it, ever again.

Then to Young D, she asks, "They launched the line?"

"Not yet. In those bags are the first pieces. I had JB to bring them to Lafayette, today. I wanted to bring them home and surprise you," he says, "Surprise."

They both laugh. She climbs to the back and pulls out the other items. There are, at least 8 outfits each, for their sons. Complete with matching sneakers, casual shoes or boots. There are 8 outfits for her, with accessories and lingerie too. Of course, he has 8 outfits for himself too. The newest items from his line.

"I got gear for everybody," he says, "I left the stuff for Mama and the rest of them, on the bus. They should be seeing it, right about now."

She tells him, thank you. He asks her, if he can have a little kiss. She obliges him. Even though she's still angry with him. She's willing to let it go, for right now. For the sake of their sons. He promises her they can finish the subject later.

"Now, who was the dude that called your phone?" he asks.

He tells her that she was a bit too friendly, for it to be work. She tells him it was another pro. And that's why she wanted to sound extra carefree.

"Work, daddy. Just work. It was Mark Genolli."

"What does he want?" he asks.

"Just my life," she says, "There's a price on *me*, now."

Young D swerves the vehicle but gains control, immediately.

332

"How do you say that shit, so calm?" he asks.

"Don't use that language in front of our sons. *Remember*?" she asks.

"Baby, why are you so calm?" he asks.

"Because I'm not worried about it," she says.

"I'll kill that muthafucka, if he even thinks about coming near you," he says.

"How do know he's *not* near me?" she asks.

"Is he? Was he at my show?" he asks.

"No. But you would've never known it, if he was," she says, "There are rules to this professional game. Follow them or you're a rogue. Any killer, worth her salt, wants to be able to kill within the rules. Or it's pointless. You're going to die. If it takes the Pentagon, to do you. The rules are the only thing that keeps the order and the honor, in this game."

"Do you know where he is?" he asks.

"Uh huh," she says.

"Let me guess. You can't tell me," he says deflated.

She smiles and shakes her head. No.

"What was the call about? Can you tell me that?"

"The count off," she says, "And that's all you're going to get, Derrick."

"I'm not letting you out of my sight, until I kill his ass," he says.

She leans into him and puts her mouth near his ear.

"Nonsense. You're going to work, just like normal," she says, "When the time is right. I'm gonna kill him," she whispers in his ear, then she kisses it.

She follows the kiss with a little nibble. This only diverts his attention, for a few seconds but not for long.

"I'm worried," he says, referring to the hit on her. "And you're turning me on too, baby. Do you mean too?"

333

"I always wanna to turn you on," she says, "You should never ask me that. No matter what issues we have. Just know it will never change that. And don't worry. He can't beat me, daddy. He never has and he never will."

"What does he want? Did he send details? I heard you saying something about details," he says, "What details? About how he plans to do it?"

" I can't tell you-"

"Bullshit! You're gonna tell me, baby. What does he want?" he asks, very impatiently.

She gives him an impatient look. He knows the rules of her profession. But it doesn't mean he'll ever like them. Still, she doesn't waste time explaining them as she sighs and looks ahead.

"What does he want?" he persists.

She doesn't answer, as she watches the road, through the side window. He reaches over, grabs her chin and turns her head toward him.

"I'm waiting," he says.

"Then you'll just have to wait a little bit longer, daddy," she says as she places his hand back on the steering wheel.

She turns her attention back to the window and the side view mirror. He drives on but he's not done with her. She's going to have to tell him a little something to tied him over. Before either of them sleep.

Baby Girl knows her husband's persistence. She's had over 10 years to get familiar with his ways. In his mind, heart and in actuality, he is her protector and the protector of their sons and land. He's the King of their castles. The ruler of his domains. He's the provider for his immediate and extended family. He *is* the man. He's her man. And he wants an answer. An answer to what Mark Genolli, the man who has come to kill

334

his wife, wants. Young D isn't going to accept a non informative answer from her. Not when her life is involved. Never in a situation about her safety. What *real* man would? So there's no need for her to even waste time with some made up explanation, as far as he's concerned. He's too familiar with how things are typically laid out, in her profession. He already knows there has to be some kind of a true response to Mark. Young D wants to know what Mark has asked for. He wants to know now. But Baby Girl is stubborn too. So she's going to try to play him off, anyway. She thinks to herself.

Come on. I just beat a tramp bitch down, over him. Not even six hours ago. He needs to be treading, carefully. Not trying to demand anything from me. Not until he comes clean about that nasty trick. And that funky ass shirt. Let's see…., what else can I talk about?"

She tries changing the subject first, to see if that works.

"I love all the new gear, daddy. It's beautiful and very thoughtful," she says, "Thank you, so much. We're all gonna look, *so fresh and so clean*, for the fourth of July."

She looks over at him. His lips are pursed and his face is still impatient. He has the same look their oldest son exhibits, when he wants his way. He's angry, for sure. He has that impatient look. He doesn't even respond.

"Great," she sighs and continues looking out the side mirror.

She focuses on car lights that have been behind them, for a distance. At the same time, she's watching for vehicles getting on the road, just after they pass an intersection or service station. No one says anything. They drive the rest of the way to their Estate, is in silence.

****

335

The day before the 4th July is filled with more preparation. It's also the day, Mark Genolli is suppose to *"send the details"* about whatever meeting, he's trying to arrange for him and Baby Girl.

Meanwhile, Young D has been watching her phone, blackberry and palm pilot since the drive in from Galveston. If she goes into her office, he goes in there with her. She goes to the bathroom. He's there. The kitchen. He's her assistant. Even bathing their sons, he's the helper. He's everywhere she is and she can't shake him, today. She's becoming more and more frustrated with him. Simply because she can't get any privacy. Thing is, he knows he's frustrating her. But he doesn't care. Her life is in danger. He's not going away.

"Daddy, give me a break, please. I have to work," she tries.

"Go head on and work," he says, "I ain't stopping you."

"I *can't* work," she says, "Not if I can't get any breathing room."

She looks at him, very impatiently.

"Well Baby Girl, it's like this," he says, "I can't breathe if you don't make it back to our room. Can you understand that?"

Just then, her text messenger goes off. He grabs her phone.

"Are you trying to get me killed!?" she asks.

"Just the opposite," he says.

He goes further, telling her he's trying to make sure she doesn't get killed.

"Well, if that's true," she says, "Let me handle this, the way I have too. I'll fill you in, if that's what you want. But rules are rules. I have to do this according to code. Or I'll be violating order."

He holds onto her phone and refuses to hand it to her.

336

"Ah man," she says, "Okay. Whatever, daddy. You say you want to protect me. Yet, you're putting me in grave danger, right now. If I didn't love you. You'd be dead, already."

"Are you emotional," he asks, intentionally toying with her as he holds her phone, still.

He looks deep into her eyes. She can see his pain. His worry. His insecurities. This isn't just about her being killed. It's also about her knowing that Kierra was backstage. And her feeling as though, she *had* to beat her ass. She knows something is up between them and he knows, she does. So now he's worried about her having correspondence with a man, she has known longer than she's known him. He's worried that he may get lucky.

What if this Mark Genolli gets the upper hand and renders her unconscious. He will rape her, for sure. He wants her and I know he does. She's told me that a million times, since we met.

He knows Mark has had a crush on her since she was 8 and he was 14. Shit doesn't change, that much. He may be pretending to want dinner, to set up a hit spot. When all the time, he just wants to get close to her. Young D isn't willing to risk, any of the above. He holds onto her phone and gives her a despairing look. Until finally, she gives in. Something she would do, only for him. Because she knows he would never demand she did. Unless it was tearing at his sanity. She never could stand to see him in pain. Nor does she ever want him to worry about her fidelity. She explains to her husband, what her next move has to be.

"Mark has to receive a response to his text message," she says, "He won't know who sent it. Okay. So, here it is."

She decides to let Young D in on this part of the set up. And hopefully, he'll back off enough that she can handle her

337

business the usual way. She tells him to check the text message and see what Mark has sent. He does. Young D opens her LG 515, her throw away phone and summons up the text message center. They read the message, together.

"He wants to meet for lunch, here in Houston, And he wants you to pick the spot," he reads.

"That's normal," she says.

What's normal?" he asks.

"For the aggressor to want the target to pick the spot," she says.

"Why is that?" he asks, "If he wants to kill you. Wouldn't he *tell you* where to meet?"

"If he was ready to kill me, yes," she says, "I suppose so."

"But you're picking the place. So you *could* set him up and kill him," Young D suggests.

"That would make me a rogue," she says, "A recluse. Going against the organization, is a death sentence. He knows how much pride I take in being the best at this, daddy. He'll have a team staked out, for just that sort of thing. Sure, he may die there and they may not be able to get me, there. But they can report it. Then, well you already know the rest."

"Okay baby. You want me to answer his text message?" he asks.

"Yes. I need to tell him where to meet me for dinner," she says.

"Get some soul food," he says, "Fill him up and weigh him down."

They chuckle.

"So should I go with, *This is it*?" she asks him, "Because our restaurant could be too much of an advantage, for me. In his eyes. He'll come loaded."

She's trying to make him feel included because he's not going to leave her side. Not after finding out there is a hit out on her life. Plus this man, who is meeting her from a meal, is the man who is suppose to do it. At this point, Young D doesn't give a damn if the code says a pro can't be terminated, at the first meeting. He's not a pro, from the organization. He's a street professional and he knows a street nigga don't go by any real codes, when it's termination time. So he isn't giving Mark Genolli that benefit either. He'd better be on his best fucking behavior, in all areas, when he meets, *his* Lovely. She is the best and she may not be worried about Mark getting lucky, for the first time. But Young D is. And he's not letting her out of his site. Period!

"No. Not *This is it*. Invite him to the fourth of July event," he suggests.

"But daddy. That's not until tomorrow," she tries, "And that's our estate. He may not accept."

"Well that's when you're available and I can watch him," he says, "That's the best for me. You never told me of a time limit, before. Why can't it be here, at the event?" he asks.

"Because this is my home. This is where my loved ones live."

"But you said you ain't worried about him beating you," he says, "So what? Is he gonna pass on the hit to someone else, when he looses?" he asks.

"No," she says, "He can't do that. The hit info does have to be logged in. But not until after the hit is carried out. He won't be doing it."

"No, you'll be the one entering the information. Not him," he says, "He probably already knows where we live, anyway. He's a pro and all that. But our security is pretty damn good. You trained them. Remember that."

She has to admit. He's made a very good point. The event *would* be the most secure place to meet. After thinking about it, she has to ask herself.

"Okay, Derrick," she says, as she concedes just a little bit, "You make a good point, baby. I mean. How do I know Mark hasn't gone rabbit? There's no solid proof he won't break code. Their family have done it, in the past. So have the Pantango's. So you make a valid point."

After hearing that, he isn't willing to waiver any. On where the meeting place will be.

"Then hell yea. He needs to come here, baby," he says, "That way, if he fucks up. He dies here. I'm not under the fucking code. If he rub me the wrong way. I'm poppin' his ass. Tell him to meet you here. Unless you want me following you until he's dead."

She concedes, for the first time. Something feels right about what he's saying. She listens to her man.

"The event, it is," she says with a smile.

She tells him exactly what to text. He does and they send it. They also tell him to,

"Bring a date or one can be provided, if you would like. Just let me know, today."

Mark texts back, immediately and confirms that he'll be at the 4th of July event by 2p.m. He also texts that he was hoping Baby Girl would be his date. Young D wants to kill him, today. But he remains in code and classy. For Baby Girl's sake, as he types him a reply.

"We'll arrange a date, for you."

Young D doesn't let up. Not even a little bit. He is her Siamese twin, today.

She has to go to the supermarket to get some last minute items for Annie. He accompanies her. Not only on that errand but everywhere she goes. And when she goes up to Annie's house, he follows her.

"Derrick I thought for sure, you would be in the studio," Angela says.

"You thought wrong," Young D says to his only sister. Baby Girl is there, in the kitchen with the ladies. Young D is right there. Helping her, Angela and Annie do prep work for tomorrow's huge event.

"Okay. Can someone tell me, who are all entertaining us tomorrow?" Annie asks.

Angela wants to know too. They know the family's labels are going to perform. Because they're always on the list. But they want to know who the additional performers will be.

"We've got the *Grand Hustle family*, coming through," Young D says with a smile.

Angela is thrilled. She loves *T.I.* and *Young Dro*. *P.S.C.* known as the *Pimp Squad Clique* and *Alfamega* are coming, as well.

"I know Dro is gonna do, *Shoulder Lean*," Angela says as she imitates the dance.

Baby Girl joins her and they clown, for a bit. Hearing the laughter brings Lil Man scurrying into the kitchen to see what all the fuss is about.

"*T.I. vs TIP* dropped today," Baby Girl says, "We just picked up a few copies of it, this morning. Derrick has been tagging along with me, all day."

"We bought every copy, *Best Buy* had," Young D adds, before turning to Baby Girl and adding, "And that's daddy, to you."

She rolls her eyes and giggles as Angela runs to grab a copy of the new CD. Then she pops it in the house sound system.

In minutes, *T.I.'s*, *Big Shit Poppin* is bellowing throughout the large home.

"It's the King, *homie*," Lil Man yells as everyone cracks up laughing at him.

He loves it. He's riding his H2 through the house, while his baby brother Don Prince rides shotgun, strapped into his car seat. Young D chuckles at his junior.

"That young man is too grown," Baby Girl says of her oldest son.

They all laugh but admit that she's right.

"But he's very intelligent," Annie says.

"Yep. He's very smart and he's only two," Angela adds as Young D and Baby Girl smile, proudly.

Lil Man can say his alphabets. He can count past 500. He knows his address. He knows his parents and his grandma Annie's cell numbers. And he can also spell his entire name. Baby Girl feels the latter wasn't a hard accomplishment. After all, his name is on his clothing, daily. Thanks to his father's clothing line. That's what she used to help him learn to spell his name.

"We just have to stop him from trying to make the little Don, spell it. Like it's *his* name too," Annie says as she laughs.

"It's a great name," Young D says with a chuckle.

"True. But so is Don Prince Morales-Blake," Baby Girl chimes in.

"True that," Young D agrees.

"We'll just call him, little Don, when he gets older," Young D says.

They get the inside prep work done. While DeJuan and the labelmates make sure the outside set ups or ready to go. They oversee the grills and smokers and have them ready to go. They also get the stage set and ready for the speaker system to be set up tomorrow.

By 1pm, everything is ready. Now the family can finally

relax and enjoy their evening. All of their guest will start piling in, the next morning.

Young D brings Baby Girl with him and the labelmates to H-Town's Finest Clothing. Corleone had called to say the new items have arrived and they're selling fast. Before he can even get them on the shelves and racks, some items have already sold out, straight from the boxes. The Houston fans can't wait to get their hands on the new items from the Derrick Blake collection.

Young D and his labelmates arrive at the store by 130pm. He's going to sign autographs while he's there, in his store. The females scream and go crazy as soon as they see him exit the Escalade. The fellows are slapping dap and no doubt, exchanging stories about how real they know Young D and H-Town records. Meanwhile, Young D and the labelmates make their way in through the back door. They locate Young D's half brother Corleone, who is happy to see him arrive.

"This place has been packed all day. The new stuff got here yesterday morning. And it's selling like crack, up in here," Corleone says as he laughs.

He has done very well with the store. Profits are up over 88%. That is just since Father's day weekend. A little over 2 weeks ago. He expects this week's sales to tower over that week, by a long shot. In the meantime, Young D greets his followers.

"Welcome to H-Town's Finest Clothing, everybody!" Young D says, over the intercom. "I want to sign some stuff for all of y'all. I really appreciate the support. So let's get it on."

His fans love the gratitude as they line up to get an autograph. Some opt to have an item they just purchased, signed. Others have their receipts autographed. Some get him to sign their sneakers while others have him to sign their body parts. Overall, the afternoon is great and very prosperous.

4TH Of July 2007

All of Young D's businesses are closed today. His grandparents, who also run his restaurant, are here. It's 6am, around the Estate. Annie and her mother Patricia or grandma Pat, are in the kitchen. Already cooking the fixings and sides. The chef, Young D's grandpa Rudy has the grill's going. Corleone and the staff from the restaurant and store are all here to help with the cooking and serving, for this event.

Young D and Baby Girl are yet to rise. They stayed up late last night, getting the homes ready for all of their guest. They'd also had a few sessions with each other and didn't go to sleep until after 3am.

DeJuan had taken pleasure in telling Kierra, she would not be attending this or any other events, in the future. She was bothered and at the same time, she's planning her revenge. DeJuan warned her not to do anything stupid.
He told her, "Or it will back fire, in your face."
But it doesn't mean she won't do something stupid, anyway. She always does. But she has been warned. All bets are fair, after the warning.

Baby Girl and Young D are up by 7 and dressed in regular gear by 730am. They join the rest of the family and get the last minute jobs done.

"Okay. It's all ready to go," Annie announces, "We can all go and get sharp as a tack now."
Young D and Baby Girl grab their sons and head back home to dress them. Six Nine phones her, while she's dressing Don P.

"We're at the gate, sis," Six Nine says.
She phones the guards at the main entrance and inform them to let the 3 SUV's through the gate.

Within minutes, they're entering the gates of the Estate.

344

Six Nine has brought his oldest son Roger III, back again. He brought Sandra back with them too. She has come, along with 2 of her sisters and 1 brother. Kid has brought his 4 children too. All of his kids names have variations of his name. And they range in age from 12, down to 4 years old. He didn't bring a female acquaintance. Baby Girl finds this, odd. Geezy is in the 3rd SUV with his daughter Fallon, who's 7 years old. He also brought his flavors of the month. He's brought 3 dates, with him. Baby Girl feel there's no need for remembering the names of the females, who attend with Geezy. They'll never return. However this time, he has brought 3 girls. 1 is a beautiful Italian girl. Her name is Rosetta. Baby Girl and Young D are planning to seat her next to Mark Genolli.

The New Orleans family pile out of their vehicles, speak to everyone and make themselves comfortable. They either sit outside, under a Gazebo. Or in 1 of the homes, in the air conditioning. After all, it is the 4th of July in Houston, Texas. The temp is already a balmy 80 degrees and is just before 8am. Six Nine, Kid and Geezy leave for the airport, right away. They're going to pick up the 16 family members, coming in from Philadelphia.

"Instead of renting vehicles, we can take our V's, man," Geezy says, "We can get them back here with three SUV's."

"How are they gonna get around while they're here?" Six Nine asks.

"I've got plenty of cars, brother-in-law," Young D says, "They'll be cool."

With that, the New Orleans trio leave for the airport. Their guest and children mingle with the Houston family and have a good time.

DeJuan has left specific orders with the gatekeepers, not to let Kierra through the gates. Kid didn't get that memo. As he's heading to the airport, he detours to go pick Kierra, Trina and Venetta up in his SUV. Then he heads on to the airport.

When they all return from the airport and pile out of the vehicles, Baby Girl, Young D and DeJuan are not outside to see them. Annie is though and she takes charge, right away.

"Ah, Kierra come here. You and your friends. Kid, you too," Annie says and they come to her, immediately.

Annie says, "These three girls are not permitted on this property."

Kid says, "I don't understand, why not? They always come."

Annie tells him, not anymore. Not since the fight, 2 days ago. They're to refrain from coming within 100 yards of this Estate.

"I signed a restraining order. So get them off my land, *this* instant," Annie orders.

Her mother Pat, father Rudy and Corleone are there to enforce the order, as well.

Suddenly, Young D exits his home. He sees the 3 uninvited guest. DeJuan and Baby Girl come out behind him. Baby Girl sees Kierra. Young D can see the mood change in her face, instantly.

"What the *hell*?!" Baby Girl shouts.

Young D grabs her and yells, "DeJuan. Get those bitches from around here, man. I got Lovely."

Baby Girl is struggling to get free. Young D pulls her back inside their house and holds her there. He doesn't allow her to get out of his grasp. She's livid. Young D does allow her to see through the door window. She can see the 3 girls, get into Kid's vehicle. Just before DeJuan can get up there to them. Kid starts up and leaves. Even though he sees DeJuan is still approaching. When DeJuan gets to Annie, she tells him they've already sent them on their way.

"If Kid don't like it," grandma Pat adds, as she has

never liked him. "He don't have to come back here, either." DeJuan questions what Kid said about the girls having to leave. They tell him.

"Okay. We'll have to let him know too," DeJuan says, "I'm glad y'all got it handled. Now, who is this?" He spots a 2008 *Maybach*, being escorts and chauffeured towards the Estate. No one knows who this guest is. Ground security stops them before they can advance past the property gate. Leon from security, radio's to DeJuan.

He says, "This is Mark Genolli. He says he's a guest of misses Lovely."

DeJuan calls Baby Girl. Her and Young D confirms Mark Genolli's invitation.

"And there's a package here for you," Baby Girl says to DeJuan, "It's from Addie Mae, from the New Orleans manor."

"Okay. That's my homemade cookies," DeJuan says jubilantly, "I'll get them, in just a second."

Then he goes up to the gate and personally, escorts Mark down to the grounds.

CHAPTER EIGHTEEN
THE KILLING FLOOR

Young D gets Baby Girl calmed down enough to join their guest. She comes out to greet her brothers and all of their guest. Kid hasn't returned. But when he does, she's going to have a word with him. For now, she greets Mark Genolli.

"Hello, second place," she says.

"That was a long time ago," Mark says.

"Yes it was. And things get better, with time. Even first place," she says, "But you wouldn't know that's even possible." They greet each other with a slight hug. Young D watches and nods. But he doesn't shake Mark's hand when he extends it. Mark takes his seat next Rosetta and they begin with some light conversation. But each time Baby Girl is within earshot, Mark says something charming to her. Even though, Young D is within earshot too. And Young D is the 1 who answers each of Mark's flirts.

"Yes. My wife is very beautiful," Young D says, "Thank you, Mark."

Baby Girl adds a coy remark. To let Mark know she doesn't appreciate nor accept, any of his compliments or out of place innuendo's.

"Thank you, daddy. For setting him straight," she says to Young D, as she adds, "Mark! What a fitting name."

She can be just a facetious as Mark Genolli can. She giggles and continues mingling with her family. Wisely, Mark backs down. For now.

Soldier, Baby Boy, G-Dog and their families show up, just as it's getting closer to the time to start eating.

"We've got some damn good timing," G-Dog says as he laughs.

They all get a plate and settle in. Before long, they get the card playing and game tables going. The music is going. The kids have the rides and attractions to keep them content. And Lil Man has his pony rides again. But he's still insisting on having a real pony. Young D tells him, he'll get 1, this year. Young D takes a business card from the caretaker of the pony rides. He's going to find a black Shetland pony, for his son to own. After hearing Young D confirm it, Lil Man is content.

DeJuan catches up with Baby Girl, after he picks up his package. There was something in the package, for her as well.

"This box has your name on it," DeJuan says.

"Oh this is from Alfred and Addie Mae," she says, "Secret herbs and spices. *Colonel Sanders* and *KFC* ain't got nothing on Morales manor, brother."

She laughs as she heads over to the food prep people. Then she's going to get the last few numbers, from her Philadelphia family. Plus make time to deal with Mark Genolli.

Over near the food gazebo's, Baby Girl can see that Mark and Rosetta are still chatting. She's ready to get this initial meeting over with. So she can just kill him. Baby Girl has met all of her new, extended family. She has updated her blackberry with all of their addresses and phone numbers. After seeing to it that all of her guest or taking care of. She's now ready to get on with the business at hand. She walks over to Mark Genolli and gets his attention.

"We need to meet, soon," she says to Mark, "So you can get on with your day."

"Actually. I'm having a great time at Blake's Estate," Mark says, "It feels just like home."

"Oh it is home," she says, "*My* home. Where I'm gonna grow old and gray. With my sexy and very satisfying daddy, right here."

She gloats as she wraps her arms around Young D.

"We'll see," Mark says.

"You're motherfucking right, we will," Young D spits, "Now get on with the goddamn meeting."

DeJuan is there too. Him nor Young D are going to leave Baby Girl's side. Not as long as Mark is living. So finally, the 4 of them move to a secluded table, to discuss business.

Baby Girl reminds Mark about all of the marksmanship competitions, he's lost to her. He can only agree. He did lose them all.

"But what happened to the English accent?" he asks, "It added to your sexy."

"I'm not English and it was out of place, in the hood," she spits back, "So I got rid of it. Just like I was taught to do, with anything else that tries to hinder me."

She is sharp.

"I use to love hearing you say my name, when we was young," Mark says. He's trying to antagonize her. "You use to say it like, Mock. Instead of Mark. It was *so* sexy."

"Don't make fun of me. I'll get you, for that," she says.

"I would let you have me too," Mark continues, "If you talk like that again. It was the accent that threw those competitions. I was mesmerized by your sexy voice."

"Bitch ass, nigga. I will buss yo fuckin head, right now. If you don't pull up," Young D interjects, "You ain't gonna sit here and flirt with my wife. And for damn sho. *Not* in front of me *and* at my home too."

Mark quickly apologizes. Then he gets on to the point of the meeting.

"The reason for this meeting is. Well, one is the obvious. And two. We're going to be up for the same target in a few weeks."

"Which goes right back to one," Baby Girl adds.
They both know Mark cannot give the targets info. Even if they both had it. Which neither of them do.
Baby Girl says, "Okay. I look forward to collecting my reward."
She's so over this meeting and Mark Genolli. And she's ready for it to end. She's having visions of sugar bullets, dancing into his head. She smiles. Mark frowns as he looks into her eyes. He knows, for certain, he's in play. He wouldn't dare try to underestimate the female, who has whooped his ass for years. He knows it is time for him to excuse himself from this event and end this meeting. She adds, "Get on with your day."
Mark thinks about how Baby Girl put it. He agrees with her. It's time for him to get on with his day and his game plan.
　　"Do you mind if I take a plate, to go?" Mark asks.
　　"Not at all. I'll get it for you," DeJuan quickly offers as he looks at Baby Girl.
She points him to the lady who's in charge of making, plates to go. DeJuan goes directly to that server.
　　DeJuan makes the server aware that he needs 2 plates to go, for Baby Girl's guest and his driver. The server makes the plates and hands them to DeJuan. He grabs the 2 hefty plates. He covers them with foil paper and gives them to the driver. Along with 2 ice cold Cokes. The driver is pleased that he was given a plate, as well.
　　"Thank you, so much, sir," the driver says, cordially.
　　"No problem. But man. I know y'all not about to eat Barbeque, in that Maybach," DeJuan says.
The driver gets into the Maybach and starts it up. He puts the air condition on blast, to cool the inside. Before Mr. Mark Genolli is permitted to get inside. The driver puts both their plates and cokes, inside the small refrigerator in the back.

"We'll eat, when we get back to mister Genolli's condo," the driver says, as he thanks DeJuan again.

DeJuan nods. He's feeling like, back at the condo is where they need to be. Because that is where and when, Mark will plan his strategy for Baby Girl and the new marks demise.

The driver escorts Mark to the car and opens his door. Mark gets in.

"It's time for Mock to go," Mark says smugly to Baby Girl, as he smiles.

"I couldn't have said it better," Baby Girl replies.

The Maybach leaves, immediately.

Mark and his chauffeur have a stop to make, before they go back to the condo.

"I need to get some silver tip rounds for that bitch," Mark says, "She's like a *fucking* cat. She has nine lives or something."

"A cat, ha?" Billy the driver says, "That means she got pussy. She's a sexy ass broad, Mark. You never fucked her?"

"Not yet," he says, "I will, before she dies, though."

"How about we don't shoot her, first," Billy suggests, "Let's fuck her. Then kill her."

"That sounds like a plan," Mark says, "We can deviate. Just a little bit."

They chuckle it up, as they head into the gun and ammo shop.

Back at Blake's Estate, Baby Girl has still not been successful at shaking Young D. Now, DeJuan is glued to her too. They're determined to be at her side until they see a report that Mark Genolli is dead. She excepts that both will get a training opt, today. Baby Girl checks her watch.

"It's twelve thirty, Baby Girl," DeJuan tells her.

He noticed her checking her watch, for the time.

"I need to be out, for an hour or so-"

"Let's go," Young D interrupts.

DeJuan agrees. She doesn't even waste time, trying to make her case for them to stay behind. They are going to get a crash course, in the killer for hire craft, today. Young D already knows what she does. His best friend DeJuan, is about to learn too. Though, he acts *strangely* familiar with what's going on, already.

I know Derrick didn't tell DeJuan what I do. He wouldn't do that. But he probably knows Mark Genolli wants to kill me. Yes. That's got to be what it is.

She heads into her home and the 2 of them follow her. She gets her *Get To Work* bag and leaves, all of her personals. Young D is by her side. DeJuan is just outside of their master bathroom. Young D sends him to get the vehicle.

"Leave your personals, daddy. And don't get prints on anything you're bringing with us. Bring your gloves."

Young D leaves all of his personals. DeJuan brings the 2007 Avalanche and they leave, immediately. Before she can even say it to him, Baby Girl notices DeJuan has already left all his personal items behind.

"Training opt?" she asks him, as she smiles.

DeJuan looks puzzled. He doesn't respond.

"Just making conversation. I don't usually get to do that, when I'm going to work," she says as a cover.

The remainder of the ride is in silence. Young D has a rush. For a long while, he's wanted to be on the inside of his wife's profession. He has wanted to ride shotgun with her, when she's going to assassinate a mark. He's here now and his adrenaline is pumping, like a 1st time base jumper. He has his 45 caliber

353

pistol, in his waist. Baby Girl is seeing something in DeJuan, that she'd noticed before. At times, he seems to know the business without being told. He never participates in the guessing sessions, with the labelmates. Not when they're discussing someone she's murdered. Not when they're trying to figure out, how that person bought it. DeJuan seems to be on the same page she is, during those times. But she figured it was just pure conjecture. But just in case, him or Young D have any illusions about who's in charge. She makes it clear now.

"I do the killing. *Understand?*" She says to both of them.
DeJuan says, "Understood."
Young D is slow to answer. He's pissed off with Mark Genolli, for disrespecting him and his wife at their Estate. That's what Baby Girl has always told him. He's too emotional. The number 1 no-no, of the profession.

"Daddy?" she says and waits for him to answer.

"Understood. But baby. You'd better get the jump on him," Young D says.

"She will," DeJuan interjects.
They look at DeJuan. Young D shakes his head. Baby Girl smiles.
He knows the profession.

Young D chuckles as he questions DeJuan, "How do you know? How did you come? This is my first time coming?"
DeJuan shrugs his shoulders and says, "Right place at the right time. I guess."

They drive into the parking lot of the condo's. They notice the Maybach pulling in. Mark Genolli and his driver Billy, are just arriving.

"I want to get at them, while they're eating," Baby Girl says, "Or just chilling out. I'm gonna call him before we go in."

"But baby," Young D exclaims, "There they go, right there!"

"Daddy, this ain't a drive by," she says.

DeJuan giggles. Baby Girl tells Young D to calm down. She assures him, she will get the jump on Mark. It's at this time, she reveals to them that his driver Billy, is a pro too.

"He's really a bodyguard, for Mark. Not just a driver," she says.

"Then he's got to go too," Young D and DeJuan say, in unison.

"I do the killing, guys," she reminds them.

Mark and his bodyguard have stopped to chat with 4 bikini clad debutantes. Near the entrance to his condo. The females look as if they have just left the pool area. They're toweling their hair and bodies dry. They speak, for a few minutes. Then the females move on to a condo, 4 doors down from where Mark and Billy enter. Baby Girl gives them 5 minutes inside the condo, before she calls.

"They probably arranged for those girls to come back, later. That gives me, roughly thirty minutes to take them."

"We're here too, sweetheart," Young D reminds her.

"Oh I know this, daddy," she says as they laugh.

They watch as Mark and Billy stir around inside. They haven't closed the door yet.

"They didn't take the plates in," DeJuan says solemnly.

"They're not done with the car," Baby Girl says, "Hang on."

Just then, the bodyguard runs back outside to the Maybach. He retrieves the 2 plates and cokes, then he hurries back inside. DeJuan smiles as if he feels like they had heard him. Baby Girl calls Mark and puts him on the speaker phone. Not necessarily for Young D and DeJuan to hear the conversation.

It's so it sounds like she's still outside, at her family event. At the same time, she's bidding her time. Her offense had started, before she dialed. Mark sees her number on his caller ID. He answers on the 2nd ring.

"My English speaking, beautiful black Barbie doll," Mark says, "To what do I owe the pleasure of this phone call? Tired of slumming with that gang banger husband of yours, *already*? It only took seeing me, as a grown man, to make you start calling me?"

Mark is an obnoxious prick. Baby Girl shakes her head and smiles. The hardest job for her, right now. Is keeping Young D from saying anything. She answers Mark.

"Well, something like that," she says.

Young D looks at her and frowns. She smiles at him, gestures her hands to tell him, to be calm. Not emotional. She continues her conversation.

"What can I do for you, Lovely? And that name has always fit you, so perfectly," Mark says, "What can I do for my future, Lovely?"

"Call me Baby Girl," she says, knowing he won't submit. She adds, "Commit suicide and save me the count."

"Ah sweetie," Mark says, "I'll be in first place and I know how much that'll disappoint you. How about I kill you, first? Then do me and let them call it a crime of passion?"

Mark loves the fact that he's arrogant. This is going to make killing him, so much sweeter for Baby Girl.

"Did you cook this amazing food?" Mark asks, "It smells divine, Lovely. Are you fatting me up, for the kill?"

"Of course, I am," she says as she laughs, "I don't want you to go dying of starvation. Before I can murk your ass."

"You know you never gave me the opportunity to be your friend," he says, "I think we could be great together."

"With you dead and me living," she says, "We will be. I'll make sure your name goes up in special letters. But in red, though. Red is for, second place. Now let me know when you're done eating. So I can invite you to the killing floor, mister second place."

"Really, Lovely. The food is good. That's probably the only thing that's good about you," Mark taunts, "Your aim was only good, back then. Because they moved the targets closer, for the little girl."

Young D has grown tired of his coyness. He wants to do him and do him, now. Baby Girl has something working that he knows nothing about. She just needs for her husband to be patient. Mark is eating his meal, right now. He's being callous toward her and so impolite. He's smacking in her ear and snorting when he laughs at her. Mark has always been good at, *put downs*. That was the 1 thing about him that Baby Girl always disliked. But what he says next, sends Young D into fit of anger.

"Billy says, not only would he like to fuck you, before I kill you. But he's gonna make you cook him a meal, first. I told him, he can have a turn after me."

They can hear the bodyguard laughing, in the background, as he's cramming his mouth full with their delicious food. Mark is on a roll.

"The chicken is scrumptious. And this potato salad is-" Mark stops talking. They can hear Billy calling his name but Mark doesn't answer. Then Billy doesn't call him again. It's quiet on the other end. Young D's curious about what's happening. He thinks they've escaped. Baby Girl looks up to see if anyone is exiting the condo. They're not. And she knows they haven't gone out the back door either. Young D looks to either end. Wondering if they've gone out the back way.

357

Baby Girl says, "Let's get out and go in."
DeJuan hops out of the truck, in record time. Young D hops out behind him. Baby Girl grabs her work bag.

They move in quickly and bolt through the still opened door. She closes it behind them and locks it.

Once inside, they see Billy and Mark. Both are still seated at the table. Both are still living. But they're no longer eating. They're slouched down in their chairs, with no control over their body's functions. Baby Girl giggles.

"These motherfuckers look like they're frozen in place," Young D offers.

"I don't think they can move," DeJuan offers but he doesn't look shocked.

Baby Girl advances toward them and checks their pulse. They both look at her, in dismay. They can't move anything but their eyeballs.

"They're extra paralyzed. I know the server hooked them up. But someone else had to have slipped these guys, another dose. Or a *mickie*, of sorts," she says as she laughs.

She looks at DeJuan. He has control of his facial expressions. He's not showing guilt. But someone had to have doubled up the doses, on her marks.

He's in training. I think Albert and Addie Mae are training him. But I can't give that up. He has too. Oh God! Derrick is really going to worry the hell out of me, about hitting. Especially, if his best friend is.

"They have had an unhealthy dose of Pancuronium," Baby Girl tells them.

Pancuronium is a drug which, along with another potent drug, is used in lethal injections. But by itself, Pancuronium causes the muscular skeletal to relax. In the right amounts, it takes affect within 2 minutes of congestion. The paralysis last for 1½ hours. So, 2 minutes into their meals and all of the bullshit talking had come to a halt. It takes up to 4 hours before 1 is rendered able to move again. One and half hours, is 80 minutes longer than Baby Girl will need.

"Talk that shit now, Mark," Young D taunts, "Y'all bitches wanna fuck my wife, ha? Your dicks ain't big enough." Baby Girl laughs as she lets her husband have his say. He was patient, long enough. Now he can tell them how he feels. She doesn't like anyone to get on his bad side. And they had better not disrespect him. Mark and Billy have done both. Not only have they come into his life, wanting to kill his precious wife. But they talked of fucking her, before they did. Baby Girl can hear The Don's voice, echoing in her head;

The Pantango's and the Genolli's will never be our friends, Baby Girl. Never accept an offer, from either family.

She gets close to Mark's ear. It's her turn to be facetious, obnoxious and down right, rude.

"Fucking you is an offer, I have to refuse, mister Genolli," she says, "Or is it, Mark? You're Mark. You are *a mark*, Mark. *My* mark. My daddy told me, at age seven, that I would most likely end up killing you, one day. In order to live, in peace. Isn't it amazing how I got the drop on you? You always did underestimate me. Mister, second place. What a fool."

She giggles as she pulls her gloves tighter. Young D and DeJuan step back and watch her work. She's in the zone now. She does a little of her English accent for him. As a dying man's request.

"Oh, Mock. What a dreadful dilemma, I find you two in. It's a bloody shame, I can't aide you farther," she says.

359

Then she shoots Billy between the eyes and advances to catch his head before it bangs on the table. She kisses her forehead. Then drops it.

"Sweet dreams, Billy."

Young D is impressed as she turns her attention back to Mark Genolli.

"The thought of me, always beating you, must have aggravated you, so much," she says, still with the accent. "But I did kill your bodyguard, first. This way, you still maintain your second place ranking. Wasn't that thoughtful of me?" She bends down to his ear. She whispers, "Does the accent still do it, for you, Mock?"

She can see his pants become wet. He has urinated himself. There's a puddle of piss, forming under his chair. Young D smiles. Baby Girl raises up from her whispering position. She puts a bullet in that same ear. He's dead. She turns to the guys.

"Full sweep and no prints, guys," she says, "Double time it."

Her, Young D and DeJuan, fully raid the condo. Taking all valuables. They exit the condo and head back to the truck. They hop in and look around.

"No one saw us. Let's go," she says.

They remove their gloves. They casually pull away and head back to the Estate. And back to their family and friends.

"She's still the best, muthafuckaz!" Young D screams in excitement.

She smiles, then slips him the tongue.

"Oh hell yeah! I'm already ready," Young D says, referring to his nature, while DeJuan is cracking up, while driving.

"Damn a training opt," Baby Girl says to him, "I think we're ready now."

DeJuan knows exactly what she means. He says nothing. Young D can't stop kissing her. He wants to *clean*. That's a fact. But the joy he feels, right now. He can't even explain. He has faced down a professional killer, who wanted to kill his wife. And he watched his wife, take two killers down. There is no greater feeling in the world for him, then just knowing she's safe.

"Now, baby. You're safe now, right?" he asks.

"Until they get another pro," she tells him.

Mark and Billy was the best professionals the Genolli family had. Both were trained from childhood, as she was. They were in the top 5, with her. Before she killed them. She is number 1, of course. Mark was number 2. Big Dog is dead now but he was number 3. Billy was number 4. There is only 1 other person alive with the skills to come Baby Girl's way. And that person is, Emilio Pantango. He is ranked number 5. Which is actually, number 2, as soon as the last 2 deaths get recorded. The Pantango's aren't going to take up the Genolli's war. So, unless Emilio is hired to kill Baby Girl. Then she's pretty much, in the clear. For any other hand, hired to kill her, is no match. She'll snuff them, before they can get close enough. 1 things for sure. She is forever on the Genolli's hit list, for taking out their top 2 pro's and their blood family. But this is nothing new. This has been an ongoing war, for 4 decades. But as for right now, she has demobilized the Genolli family. They have to train someone and get them to her level. Before they can even attempt to come at her again. That's just not going to happen.

As they get back amongst their family and guest, at the event, Baby Girl notices Kid still hasn't come back. She'll get the chance to speak with him, later. That is the 2nd thing on her list. 1st thing on her immediate agenda, is to find out who had placed a hit on her, in the first place. Who had hired Mark Genolli and Billy Campanili to kill her? This would have to be someone who really wants her dead. And a part of her wonders, if her 1st and 2nd priorities are 1 in the same. But then, she quickly dismisses the thought. She's clear on who assisted her, today. How well he had done, before they got to the condo. She had the jump, for sure.

There is another thing on her brain. That other thing she will ponder. Is rather or not she will try to train her husband to clean.

I don't know. He might be okay at it. DeJuan too.

That white t-shirt situation is still to be discussed and it shall be. Now that her husband has had experience, in her work world. Surely, he has to know that *honesty is the only way*. And Kierra, will have to be nullified and soon. Young D will only have 1 choice, on that issue.

Then she clears her mind completely. She's going to enjoy this wonderful 4th of July, with her extended family. She has changed her clothes. Now she heads out to the basketball courts. It's time for her and her 2 true teammates, to take on any and all competitors.

Young D and DeJuan have changed clothes too. They start the basketball games, calmly. As if they hadn't just murdered 2 people, less than an hour ago.

THE END OF PART ONE

THE ORGANIZATION- PART ONE, ALL BY MY LONELY

THE ORGANIZATION SERIES:
All By My Lonely-part one [New Year's 2014]
Still By My Lonely-part two [Fall 2014]
The Real Family Unit-part three

Find website and social network with Author Black Coffee below:
http://blackcoffee.homestead.com/WHATSNEXTFROMBLACKCOFFEE.html
----

THE TIME WILL REVEAL SHORT STORIES
#1 MORE THAN 4 ADMIRERS-RELOADED
"The Threat to a Legacy."
#2 MR. WRONG AND THE RATS-RELOADED
"Sweet Ray, Sonya, Shuntay & Tina"
#3 THE CREW'S PRIORITY-RELOADED [2014]
"The Females of the Crew"
ALL WORKS AND ORDER FULL SERIES AT:
www.truesrelatepublishing.com
www.blackdollone.com

The Time Will Reveal-Novel series
TIME TO LEARN-RELOADED part 1
TIME TO GROW-RELOADED part 2
TIME TO LOVE-RELOADED part 3
TIME TO KNOW-RELOADED part 4
TIME TO FEEL-RELOADED part 5
The Making of AJAY- Every Man-RELOADED
TIME TO SHOW-RELOADED part 6 [2014]
AJAY AND EBONY 1- Time To Give part 7 [2015]
AJAY AND EBONY 2- Time To Live part 8 [2015]

Amazon.com/Author's page: http://www.amazon.com/-/e/B008S1WOZ2
Fan Page on Facebook:
https://www.facebook.com/TimeWillRevealFanPage
THE ORGANIZATION group:
https://www.facebook.com/groups/TheOrganizationByBlackCoffee/
THE TIME WILL REVEAL group:
https://www.facebook.com/groups/BlackCoffeeCrewNation/
Twitter:
http://www.twitter.com/AuthorBlkCoffee

363

MORE PLACES TO FIND: Black Coffee
Instagram:
AuthorBlkCoffee
Tumblr:
Lovely T. Brown
LinkedIn:
Lovely T. Brown

Black Coffee's info page:
http://blackcoffee.homestead.com/BLACK-COFFEE.html